QUICK-TRIGGER COUNTRY AND G STANDS FOR GUN

A WESTERN DOUBLE

NELSON C. NYE

Quick-Trigger Country and G Stands for Gun
Paperback Edition
Copyright © 2022 (As Revised) Nelson C. Nye

Wolfpack Publishing
5130 S. Fort Apache Rd. 215-380
Las Vegas, NV 89148

wolfpackpublishing.com

This book is a work of fiction. Any references to historical events, real people or real places are used fictitiously. Other names, characters, places and events are products of the author's imagination, and any resemblance to actual events, places or persons, living or dead, is entirely coincidental.

All rights reserved. No part of this book may be reproduced by any means without the prior written consent of the publisher, other than brief quotes for reviews.

Paperback ISBN 978-1-63977-953-6
eBook ISBN 978-1-63977-952-9

QUICK-TRIGGER COUNTRY AND G STANDS FOR GUN

QUICK-TRIGGER COUNTRY

ONE

OLD "I PERSONALLY" Ruebusch, resident manager of the biggest cattle outfit in the Tombstone end of the Territory, packed his lower lip with snuff and, creaking comfortably back in his swivel, ran a disparaging stare over this latest addition to the Roman 4 crew. The youngster, in part because of the color of his hair but mostly because of his chip-on-shoulder attitude, was known by the sobriquet of Turkey Red and was down by that name on the timesheet.

The manager, who had never been caught in a generous impulse, gave him plenty of time to get rid of his assurance. For a wagon train stray who couldn't remember his own folks, the kid figured to be doing pretty well for himself since spreading his blankets on a Roman 4 bunk. He'd been accorded a certain brusque deference because of his demonstrated speed with a pistol and this had naturally led him mistakenly to assume himself a man among men, a concept he appeared to value and an illusion which had upon occasion caused him to act a whopping fool. All of which Ruebusch was pleasantly aware of. "Like it here, do you?"

The kid, rolling down the off corner of his mouth, allowed that it would do. He hooked both thumbs in his cartridge belt and scrunched his eyes with a hint of impatience.

"You look almighty young," Ruebusch said.

The kid's chin came up with an affronted glare. a regular ape, Ruebusch scornfully thought, reminded of the man the kid took for his model. He hooked out a drawer with the ease of long practice and hoisted the bottle-glass shine of his boots. "We spend half our profits building up a tough crew and every time a job comes up needing half a gram of savvy every qualified hand on the place is off somewhere."

While he gave this a chance to get properly sunk in, Ruebusch hiked his cold stare from the kid's scuffed boots to the cocky slant of his sweat darkened stetson. A prize sap, Ruebusch thought, letting it show through his expression. A brand for the burning if he had ever clapped eyes on one. Wouldn't top the scales at 120 with his boots on—including those special built-up heels by which he hoped to appear taller than his actual five foot five.

"How old are you, Turkey?"

Resentful color crept above the open top of the kid's shirt collar. "Old enough to earn what you're payin' me."

Ruebusch said, "You ever been shot at?"

He watched the kid's blue eyes narrow. Red understood where the talk was being hazed, but like he wanted it out in the open he said, "If it's Fanshaw that's bothering you I can have him off that crick before another sun gits up."

Ruebusch worked his jaws around and spat. "Don't see what you could do that Strehl and Buck ain't tried already."

Buck Linderstrom was the Roman 4 ramrod and, like Ruebusch himself, had stock in the company. Strehl was a boot licking straw boss who'd already shown signs of having it in for the new hand.

Ruebusch, still eyeing him disparagingly, said: "I personally couldn't afford to send a boy on a chore grown men is scared to tackle. I'll ride in tomorrow and hash it over with Wyatt Earp."

He waved Red toward the door, smugly pleased when the kid proved his estimate right by stubbornly refusing to move from his tracks. "What you need for this chore," Turkey Red growled, "is guts. And I've got 'em."

Ruebusch snorted. "I never measure guts by the size of a fellow's lip. You stay away from that place. Instead of ramming around like a two-bit copy of that damned Curly Bill, if you want folks to think you're big as you figure you better go scrape that fuzz off your mug!"

* * *

SHE WAS Ruebusch's wife and Red had kept that in mind for the whole two months he had been with this outfit. Holly was her name and even when, increasingly, he'd been singled out to ride with her he hadn't allowed this intimacy to suck him into any open disregard of the trust implied by the privilege. This was a big unsettled country and there were a lot of tough hombres riding through these hills; his skill with a pistol was what had earned this preference. Red had never doubted it. And yet, sometimes he'd got some awful queer notions and it had taken a deal of will power to remind himself that she was a married woman, just impulsive and uncommon friendly. She didn't mean nothing by it. Just her way—a little skittish, maybe, but that was understandable in a girl scarce turned eighteen.

Buck Linderstrom had told him off to reset a number of posts that had got loosened during the bronc stomper's work in the breaking pen recently. The morning was half shot by the time he had got finished and Linderstrom had told him to ride over to Willow Springs and see what all was needed to put the line shack there into shape for winter use. It was a good seven miles from headquarters and he hadn't covered two when Holly came riding up and allowed she would go along with him.

"Mister Ruebusch know about this?" Red said.

She gave him one of those long slow stares and let him see the quick flash of her teeth. With that honey colored hair she sure made a picture. "He doesn't know I'm around half the time," she answered, scornful. "Always up to his ears in those accounts. Come on, I'll beat you to that catclaw thicket!"

She was off like the dust sifting out of a twister but he got there ahead of her without half trying. High Sailin Brown—that was his own private horse—was one of the fastest hides to ever come out of Texas, a Billy he'd got off a saddleblanket gambler who had waited too long after laying down his character. The horse looked pudding-footed but could run like a Neuches steer.

She came up out of breath, eyes bright and hair flying. He watched her tucking the strands back in place and caught himself wondering what she'd do if he grabbed and kissed her. It got him pretty steamed up and downright shamed and riled besides. "You better be gettin' on back," he growled. "I'm like to be gone the best part of the day and Mister Ruebusch—"

"Fiddlesticks!" Her eyes came up at him through the shine of her lashes. "What's the matter with you, Turk?"

"Ain't nothin' the matter with *me*," he scowled, recalling that scene with the manager last evening and thinking thoughts that were best put plumb out of his mind.

She was watching him curiously with head tipped back and her eyes getting darker and her chin more pronounced like it almost always seemed to when things didn't shape to her liking. "If I didn't know you better I would think you didn't want me."

He didn't try to figure that out. He said gruffly: "I got work to do."

"You're not expecting to work all the way down and back are you?"

He scowled at High Sailin's ears. "It don't look right," he said, "you traipsin' off with me every time I—" and let the rest of it go with his ears getting red.

Her cheeks turned a little stiff, and then her lips pulled back. "You thinking of Ruebusch?" She laughed. "He thinks you're part of the scenery."

His teeth grated together and she leaned nearer, putting a hand on his arm. "I wasn't trying to demean you, Turk. It's just that what you said was so...so *ridiculous*." Then her eyes showed rebellion. "It's true enough though—about Ruebusch, I mean. All he thinks about is figures—"

"He sure knows how to pick 'em!"

Red shouldn't have spoken like that and he knew it; it had kind of slipped out in the bitterness of his resentment. And he wouldn't have been surprised if she had really torn into him.

She looked more astonished than anything, astonished and halfway pleased, he thought, startled. She dragged a deep breath away down into the inside of her and the bulges of her shirtwaist shaped more provocative than ever. It didn't seem to Red that she had very much on under it.

The way she twisted her face around, looking up at him, had something different about it, something strange, almost...exciting. "Do you really think so, Turk?"

She was watching him with her bright eyes half shut. His heart got to banging. Her horse fetched her nearer. He tore his stare away from her. He didn't want to do anything foolish.

He said in a kind of half strangled way, "It's time I was gettin' over there," and ribbed his horse with a heel. She ribbed hers, too. He didn't say any more about not wanting her with him.

They rode perhaps three miles without either of them breaking the country's deep silence. Red kept his stare on the gullied slopes ahead of them but he could feel the looks she kept turning in his direction. They came up onto a bench and he could see the green tops of the trees at Willow Springs and an edge of the shack showing gray through the branches.

"Turk—" She reined her horse closer. He saw her hand reached out and felt the grip of fingers, felt it tighten on his arm. "You don't know what it's like being married to a man old enough to be your father."

Red kept his eyes on the shack.

After a moment she took her hand away. Her walking horse sidled nearer and their knees came together and rubbed to the rhythmic motion. He felt sweat crack through the pores of his skin and it was all he could do to keep his mind on his business.

She said, "I've got the whole of my life still ahead of me, Turk. I want to live it, not be shut up in a monastery!"

Red's thoughts plunged around like a bronc with the hobbles on.

"I know. I married him. I thought we'd travel," she said bitterly. "I didn't know I was going to be buried in this godforsaken place. He treats the furniture better— at least he uses it! I don't see what I ever—"

Her voice choked up. She reined her horse away from him.

"You won't ever have to go hungry," he said.

She did pretty near fly into him then. "There are hungers more cruel than going without eating."

They'd come up to the springs. "You better try it sometime," he said, swinging down. He could have told her plenty about going without eating.

He led High Sailin off into the trees. He found a place where there was some lush looking grass, loosened the cinch and took off the bridle. Told Holly she'd better let her pony feed too and took a look at his shadow. Going on for twelve o'clock. He went up to the shack.

It could stand some going over. Didn't look like it had even been slept in since the outfit had wangled this range off Tadpole. He'd been riding for old man Glover then, combing brush-splitters out of the San Pedro for him.

He pushed open the door. Rats had got at what grub had been left here. A big sack of beans was scattered all over and the left wall bunk could do with new slats. A lid was gone off the stove and water stains showed where the roof had been leaking. Probably take a full day to get the place fixed up. Have to fetch out some boards and...

But his mind wasn't on it. He kept remembering the way she had looked at him and the scent of her nearness, and Ruebusch thinking he was part of the scenery.

Calling up Ruebusch didn't help him much now. He could hear her moving around outside, humming a little, tapping the leg of a boot with her crop. And a fluttery trembling crept up through his stomach as he recalled the feel of her leg brushing his. He looked around the shack wildly. The thing to do, he knew, was get the hell out of here. He was heading for the door when he heard her scream.

He dived out of that shack like hot grease from a skillet. She wasn't in sight. Both horses had their heads up, ears pricked forward, staring in a direction where the willow screen bulked heaviest. He ran toward it, not forgetting he was riding for a tough and brutal outfit. He didn't know what he expected to see—Apaches, maybe, or some of the fellows this spread had done dirt to. He had his gun up and ready when he plunged through the trees.

He saw the springs and the stock trampled mud around the edges of them and for a couple of heartbeats that was all he did see. No Indians, no outlaws, no dispossessed ranchers. Just the springs and the willows and the sun beating through them throwing up little flashes off the leaves and the water. Then he gave a sudden start and slipped his gun back into leather.

She was face down in the weeds about six feet to the left of the water. Motionless and crumpled.

He stared with the breath piled up in his throat. He had to swallow three times before he could get enough air to breathe with.

His eyes raked the clearing without finding anything to explain what had happened. His ears couldn't catch any sound of departure. He moved nearer studying the ground all about her. No loose rock. No sign of a struggle. She lay with one arm doubled under her, one leg drawn up and her disarrayed skirt hiked over the knee of the other.

He got her turned over. There was an earth stained place on her forehead where her face had been in the dirt. She didn't look too pale but there wasn't much breath going in and out of her.

Picking her up with great care, and bad worried, he moved through the trees. The scent of her hair, the clean woman smell of her, did nothing to calm the jumbled whirl of his thoughts. He put her down on the grass in a patch of blue shadow and felt uncommonly helpless.

With this sense of inadequacy heavily riding him he was turning to go dip up a hatful of water when a groan came out of her. He wheeled back to peer down at her. Her lips faintly trembled.

She moaned again as he bent over her, abruptly flexing an arm. Her eyes came open. Wild as a stallion bronc's they looked. She snatched her legs up under her and came half onto an elbow before she saw him and sank back, shaking.

"Sho," he said, dropping down beside her, "you'll be all right now. What happened?"

"That awful snake! Oh, Turk—" she moaned. She flung both arms around his neck and clung to him sobbing like a frightened child. "There, there," he soothed, "you're all right now."

"But it hurts so, Turk—"

"My God! Did the damn thing strike you?" He pulled loose and reared back, getting hold of his gotching knife. "Quick! I better...where'd it git you?"

She blinked tear streaked lashes, swallowed a couple of times hard and shuddered. "It...it was my ankle, I think."

"Well, get off it," he said, "and let's have a look at it. Which ankle is it?"

"The right one." Her fingers kept nervously picking at her skirt but she pushed out the foot with a little whimper of pain. "Do...do you suppose I—is it swollen much?"

"I can't tell with your skirt over it that way."

She looked flustered, cheeks coloring, but pulled it up a short inch. "Can't you...sort of tell by feeling?"

"I can't feel nothin' through that boot!"

She lay back on her elbows. "I guess you'll have to pull it off."

He was careful as he could be but it didn't come

easy. He was tempted to slit the leather with his knife but she shook her head. "Just pull a little harder."

Sweat rolled off his chin. He kept tugging. Her eyes were closed tight. She never let out a peep. Not even when her skirt fell back. He reckoned she'd passed out but she hadn't. "That stockin'," he said, looking dubious. With her eyes still shut she reached up under her.

"You can pull it down now."

He looked the ankle all over, and it was something to look at, but he couldn't find any punctures. "You sure this is the one?"

"Oh, yes!" she cried, wincing. "It feels just as though it was *broken*."

It wasn't broken. It didn't look to him like it was much swollen either. He felt it over carefully. "Must of wrenched it," he muttered, "when you jumped clear of that snake. Here, see if you can stand."

She smoothed down her skirt and gathered the hurt leg under her. He gave her a hand and she came up but sagged into him. "Oh-h!" she cried, trembling. She got her free hand hooked around his belt and breathed deeply. "Are you sure it's not broken?"

"Try wigglin' it," he said.

She took the hand away from his belt and put the arm around his shoulder, letting him feel the softness of her. And that was when, glancing down, he saw more than either of them had figured on. Someway, getting up, the neck of her waist had come unfastened.

There was a fluttering in his knee joints. His ears felt hot. She said, "I can't—I know I can't. If you will help me get to the cabin, Turk...Do you suppose you could carry me? My head's just whirling around something awful."

There was sweat on Turk's face and a cyclone inside him as he picked her up and started for the shack. Her head came against his shoulder, the soft mass of her hair pushed against his cheek. His grip suddenly tightened.

He kicked the door shut with his heel.

TWO

HE FELT like a treacherous dog when he got the door wrenched open and they came out of the shack into the yard's bright glare. He looked at the willows with their green leaves hot and still and at the patches of brassy sky showing through them and at the horses off yonder still cropping at the grass, and was surprised in his shame to find the world had not collapsed. He would have pulled away from her in a nausea of revulsion but she was too wise to let him. She clung to him tightly. "You mustn't blame yourself, Turk—we couldn't help it. You know we couldn't. Don't worry. No one will ever guess." Over and over she kept reassuring him softly, pressing herself against him, until his chin came up a little and his arm finally tightened around her slim waist.

She settled more heavily against him then. She even managed a wavery smile. "After all," she said with an attempt at lightness, "the sky hasn't fallen."

"But Ruebusch ..." Turk scowled.

She pushed back against his arm. "You can't think I'd be fool enough to tell!"

"It ain't that." He frowned at her bare foot, trying to pull his thoughts together. "I'll get a job someplace—"

"You're not thinking of leaving!"

"We'll both leave," he said. "You can't go back to him now. First place, I wouldn't let you—"

"Let me! Are you crazy?"

He stared at her blankly. In the jumbled whirl of his own emotions he found it difficult to concentrate, impossible to achieve any real degree of coherency, and naturally assumed her own condition no less chaotic. "We'll make out all right. Quick as I can git a little money put by we'll start a herd of our own. Have ..."

He caught the look of her then, the glassy brightness of her regard. He saw the edge of one lip crawling off her white teeth. "You think I'd run off and live with you in a shack on a shoestring?"

"It won't be that bad. I've got a rep. I'll git work—"

"You *are* a greenie!" Scorn flashed through her glance and she twisted out of his arm and stood away from him, angry. She pushed the yellow hair back out of her eyes. "Things are bad enough now without—sometimes I think you're impossible!"

He tromped hard on his temper. He made allowances for her. "We got to look at this sensible. When two people's in love—"

She laughed then, threw back her head and laughed like a loony. "Love!" She wiped her eyes on her shirtwaist, still shaking with a kind of hysteria. Her voice railed out at him. "You think I'd throw over all I've got as his wife to run off with a kid that isn't dry behind the ears? There are a lot of things I *haven't* got but give me credit, anyway, for more intelligence than that!"

Turk gaped at her dumbly. There was a roaring in his ears and he could feel the leak of sweat between his shoulders and he was recollecting now how it had been around here before Roman 4 had offered him twenty more on the month than he'd been getting from old man Glover. She'd been doing her riding with Linderstrom then and it seemed to him abruptly he'd been as big a chump as Ruebusch.

A swirling haze blotted out the mocking curl of her lips and he moved a step or two toward her blindly, the fingers of his hands becoming stiff as flexing talons. Then the haze thinned away and he could see her again.

The scorn was gone from her now, dissolved and washed away in fright. Her eyes looked like they would burst from their moorings and she was pale as he'd ever seen her. She stood as though frozen with a hand up in front of her, but he had hold of himself now and blackly turned away from her, spurs jangling harshly as he strode to High Sailin.

He snatched the bridle off the horn and rammed the bit in the gelding's mouth and, bending, yanked the slack from the cinch and got bitterly into the saddle. He stopped then, turning for another black look at her.

She wasn't paying him any mind now and the color was back in her cheeks again, her mouth almost ugly in the clamp of her lips. He watched her pull on her stocking, stamp into her boot and go off through the willows in the direction of the springs. Pretty soon she came back, slamming into her saddle. She had left the horse bridled but she had to get down again to tighten the cinches, and he let her. Let her lead off too, silently swinging in behind her.

* * *

THEY GOT PRACTICALLY in sight of the ranch without speaking. Turk, during those miles, rode prey to his tumultuous emotions. Shame and the flare of resentment and, behind these, the heat of the steadily building fury shook him by turns and left him incapable of an approach to calm reasoning.

At first his thoughts had shrunk away from the magnitude of what had transpired in that shack at the line camp, but finally he had looked at his guilt and accepted it. What was done was done and it seemed to him now that all along he must have sensed in their growing intimacy that these continuing contacts must result in what had happened. Right there, without realizing, he glimpsed a part of the pattern, but his mind was too full of other things either to follow it further or track it back to its obvious source.

Holly's jibs still rankled, still cut at him like whips, and the scorn of Ruebusch yesterday came back to feed his resentment and fan even brighter the sorrel flames of his mounting fury. And yet, by some grim alchemy of associations beyond his grasp to fathom, the girl had got into his blood. In spite of everything he still wanted her. He could not see her as she was but only as she had seemed to him, and the ecstasy of that moment returned again and again to fan the sparks of his anger.

He left her two miles short of headquarters, turning aside without a word, sending High Sailin obliquely off through the brush. He would show her, by God! He would show Ruebusch, too! If it was the last thing he did!

He reined the big brown toward the Whetstones. He could see their slopes blue and purple in the distance above the tawny shimmer of the surrounding sunbaked range. Fanshaw's place lay over against those slopes and, though he didn't expect to run into any Apaches, he didn't aim to be caught napping. This was gun-packing country with the law mostly served from a cutaway holster and the one that got it bellering first was generally given the verdict.

It was a violent land, yet even so lead poisoning, as Turk saw it, was something a fellow usually had to contract. And the ones that got down with it mostly had it coming—like that crazy damned Fanshaw with his jaw stuck out around that buffalo gun.

He had settled five-six years before with a piddling jag of longhorned cattle on a spring that came out of the south flank of the Whetstones. He never owned one inch of land; Roman 4 held title to some of it.

Roundtank Springs fed an all-year creek that watered twenty miles of Ruebusch's best grazing, the only drink his stock could conveniently get without they browsed clear east to the San Pedro. Willow Springs was good enough but the range had been overgrazed and there was stock along the San Pedro that belonged to hostile outfits. Since Fanshaw had been in the country first Ruebusch had tried to put up with it, taking his sass and breeding his cows for him.

They figured now it was a mistake.

Roman 4, owned by Eastern capital, was a big operation. Too big, Turk thought, to be getting stewed up over one old mossback and a jag of crossbred cattle. But it looked like bigness could get to be a kind of a disease, and Ruebusch and Linderstrom had halfway got to viewing themselves as a second Murphy-Dolan when Fanshaw damned the creek up. He hadn't opened his mouth. Just put in a charge where the water spilled through the notch below his place and closed off the whole stream. It would spill over some time but Ruebusch needed it now.

A couple of weeks had gone past before he got wind of it. He lit into Linderstrom. Linderstrom got onto his horse and rode over to throw the fear into Fanshaw. This, at any rate, was how Turk had got it, but Fanshaw's old Sharps spoke louder than Linderstrom. He'd gone back three nights later and got run off again. Next time he'd sent Strehl with half the Roman 4 crew and the creek was still dry where the Roman 4 grazed it. There was Roman 4 cattle piled up all along Fanshaw's fenceline.

Turk reckoned this was a job cut to order.

* * *

THE FIRST GRAY light of approaching dawn was thrusting timid fingers up into the eastern blackness by the time Turk got back to the place where he'd parted with Holly. There was a wind scooting down off the higher bluffs, larruping his face with its lifted grit. It was raw enough to hunch a man's shoulders and Turk had his wipe pulled up across his nose, chin settled deep into the threadbare collar of the brush jacket he'd had lashed on behind his saddle.

He wasn't really paying much attention to the weather, his mind being occupied with things more satisfactory. Off ahead a couple of miles at Roman 4 headquarters the lamps would be pushing yellow shafts through the thinning gloom; and the crew, breakfasts downed with scalding cups of black Arbuckle, would be catching up their mounts to get about the long day's riding.

He dragged the wipe off his face as he rode up toward the gate and brought his chin up out of the collar of his jacket. He wasn't expecting there'd be many hands around this late but what there were he figured to have known there was one fellow on this Roman 4 payroll that, by God, could get the job done.

Old Pablo was in the corral with his milk pails, Emilio helping him. Turk saw Pablo twist his head and stare a long moment before settling back to his work. Emilio cursed and blew on his fingers, regained his hold on the horns and hunched bony shoulders.

Turk didn't care whether they spoke to him or not. They'd chum up all right when the news got around. He felt seven foot tall riding through the gate hugging the prospect these next minutes would unfold. The prospect of him being accorded a man's due.

The fragrance of wood smoke was a strong homey smell in the rawness of the morning. The cavvy—the band of saddle stock—in the horse trap stood and watched him solemnly, and he looked at the animals a second time with the first faint stirring of unease. There hadn't ought to be near so many. He saw Parins with folded arms in the open door of the cook shack and wind pulled a waterfall sound from the tossing branches of the cottonwoods.

Turk looked at Parins. "Be over in a minute," he called with a wave.

The cook didn't move. He didn't say anything either. Turk latched onto something else then, the reason for the trap full of horses. The crew hadn't left! Four or five of the outfit hunkered on their boot heels by the side of the bunkhouse. Another still shape was back of a window in the harness shed and three other men were watching from a corner of the barn.

The winkless stares of that silent crew at a time when those men would not normally have been here was unexpectedly something Turk had not counted on, but he shrugged it aside and swung down before the house. The day was too far advanced for the need of a lamp though one still spread its pale effulgence against the window of Ruebusch's office.

Turk had lived with this moment all the way back from Fanshaw's and would not be put off stride by such trifles. He couldn't still the pounding thump of his heart but he went up the steps with a display of nonchalance that would not have shamed the god of his deportment, Curly Bill, himself. He was reaching for the door to the manager's office when it opened. "Come in," Linderstrom said, stepping aside to give him room.

Ruebusch was back of his desk. "Sit down, Turkey."

It was the first time the manager had ever made such a courteous gesture. Something clicked far back on the edge of Turk's emotions and his glance, sweeping around, picked up the shape against the left wall. It had a face like a nutcracker —all nose and chin. This was Strehl, the pet gun hand. And behind Turk was Linderstrom. Ignoring the chair Turk moved a little to the right, watching the manager pack snuff against the front of his lower denture.

In a way Turk felt a little sorry for the bastard.

"Where you been?" Ruebusch said.

"Over to Fanshaw's lookin' out for your interests. Doin' what the rest of these yaps hadn't the guts to."

There was a growl from the left and Strehl's hand started hipward. "Go ahead," Turk sneered. "Go ahead and drag it."

A kind of wheeze racked Strehl's breathing but he let the hand fall away.

Linderstrom grinned.

The old man was furious. "Am I to understand you went over there after I personally told you to keep away from Fanshaw?"

"You been tryin' to git him—"

"Just a minute, Turk." That was Linderstrom. "Suppose you tell us what happened."

Strehl said with a snarl, "What the hell you think happened! He got run off same as—"

Turk was starting for Strehl when Linderstrom grabbed him. Ruebusch yelled, "You're fired! Get off my ranch!"

Turk stared at him, thunderstruck. He couldn't believe he had heard the man right. His ears got hot and a quiver got into his knee joints and a kind of red fog rolled up out of the corners until all he could see was the old man's apoplectic face.

Ruebusch was shrunk so far back in his swivel another inch would have turned the chair over when Turk became aware of Linderstrom's fingers. They were sunk into his left shoulder like the fangs of a wolf and there was a gun dug into the middle of Turk's back. "Take it easy, kid," the ramrod said, easing him carefully back away from the desk. "I've got ten men outside just bustin' to take a crack at you. You better keep that in mind if you aim to come out of this all in one piece."

He relaxed his grip and stepped back but kept his gun up. "Now suppose you tell us what went on over there."

Bootsteps banged across the boards of the porch. The door flew open. A dust covered rider stuck his face in. "Boss, there's water in..." He saw Linderstrom's gun and his jaw sagged.

Linderstrom shook Turk's shoulder. "You blow that dam?"

"Sure," Turk said. "I told you I'd took care of..."

"What about Fanshaw? Where was he when you were—"

"The little son of a bitch has killed him!" Ruebusch pounded the desk with his fists. "I won't be responsible —I call you boys to witness! You heard me tell this wheyfaced pup to stay away from there!"

Strehl's nutcracker face came apart in a grin.

Linderstrom prodded Turk with his pistol. "Outside," he said and, when they hit the porch, "I'm afraid you're up against it, Turkey. By rights we ought to turn you over to Wyatt Earp but damn if I can sell a man that's et my grub down the river." He gave Turk a push. "Get aboard that bronc and punch a hole through the breeze."

THREE

IT TOOK him two weeks to get to Tucson and he was still plenty riled when he got there. He guessed, in a way, he'd had it coming but that didn't make it any easier to take. He'd been put on and took off like a sheepherder's coat, first by Holly and then I Personally and he wasn't far from convinced the two were all of a piece.

One thing he was sure of. They'd had to get Fanshaw off that creek and, thanks to him, they had got him off—got his range and his buildings and his damned wall-eyed cattle! And the Roman 4 was a big enough outfit that when Wyatt Earp (who packed the tin in that country) got to sniffing around, all he'd ever catch wind of was a gent called Turkey Red. He'd been whipsawed like a greenie—like the very kid she'd named him!

Turk writhed every time he thought of it, clenching fists in a bitter fury each time his mind called up the steps by which, cold-bloodedly, the Roman 4 bosses had set out to make a catspaw of him...the snide remarks and grins, the skeptical laughter. They had played him like a fish on a line.

But they couldn't have gotten away with it so cute if he hadn't inadvertently done most of the ground work, trying so desperately to impress them with an importance he'd no right to lay claim to.

He saw plain enough now that he'd been shoved on the dodge by his own tomfoolery, reaping the harvest his own duplicity had planted; for the hell of it was he hadn't killed that damned squatter. The obstreperous old stinker had tripped over his own rifle and just about blown the whole bottom of his face off—but try and get Earp to believe that now!

* * *

HE PUT up at Levin's which faced west on Main between Pennington and Ott, because it was handy to the stages and therefore to the news. He didn't hear anything though about Fanshaw's killing and after a couple of nights, having run out of cash, he headed for Silver Lake.

This was a body of water on the Santa Cruz River roughly two miles south of town. It furnished, among other things, power for a flour mill; the main other thing being a two-floor hotel which was gathering a reputation for some pretty wild goings-on.

He got a job as the barkeep's third assistant—two bucks a night plus grub and stable privileges. From ten till along about three in the morning that place was a gold mine. Tucson was doing a lot of bragging about its "culture" but when the nabobs came to Silver Lake with their women Turk didn't see much difference between them and the customers of Bob Hatch's dive back in Tombstone.

The tavern faced east across the lake with the Tucson Mountains back of it and a gallery across the front with great tall posts that ran clean up to the eaves. There was a railed-in balcony anchored to these posts where the girls the place furnished could take the air on sultry evenings. It could only be got onto from those little second floor rooms, which was where the girls did business. A flossy bunch with little signs on their doors like *France, Portugal, China, Argentina, Peru* and others too queer sounding for Turk to remember. These females cost the management three bucks a night to help kid the customers they were enjoying the life of Reilly.

The first floor was mostly given over to the bar and gambling rigs though there was another brace of cubicles at the back which were rented to sports who had brought their own fun. The sixth night after Turk got his job the boss called him into his office.

"You look like you got a head on your shoulders. Flack's been too sick. Think you could handle this job for the evening?"

Flack was one of the bouncers though at Silver Lake he had a more refined title. "All you've got to do," the boss said, "is perambulate around and keep your eyes skinned."

"Skinned for what?"

"Ha, ha," the boss grinned. He rolled the cigar across his gold inlay. "Ever worked in a place like this before?"

Turk shook his head. "I been punchin' cattle."

The boss nodded. "Guy that can handle cattle

won't have no trouble with the kind of trade I get." He put a pair of brass knuckles and a sock on his desk. "Busted heads is cheaper than a bunch of broke-up furniture. There'll be a fiver in it for you. Anyone starts to raise hell you take care of him. Quick."

Turk put the stuff in his pocket. "I'm stony," he said. "How about a little dough?"

The boss glanced in the book and shoved across his five nights' wages. "You can't wear those duds. See Arch —he'll fix you up."

Arch did. Like a man in a dream Turk caught the string tie and white shirt, the black cutaway and trousers and, when he got into them, felt like a monkey. Arch had to fix the tie for him. He was some surprised when he met himself in the mirror. He didn't look near as foolish as he'd imagined. He'd have passed in Tombstone for a regular high roller. "Your color's a little rugged," Arch said critically, "but considering your size, that might be an asset."

"What the devil's this sock for?" Turk asked, holding it out.

Arch looked at him and grunted. He took the sock and, going to a bucket, thrust a handful of sand into it, smacked it on his leg a couple of times and handed it back. "One of them clowns gets rough you wrap it around his noggin. Now get rolling and keep your eye peeled."

It was early yet. Things didn't generally get into full swing until the hands of the clock got to crowding midnight. The bar when Turk stepped into it was practically deserted. There were a couple of dudes shooting the breeze in a corner and one of the girls from upstairs held down a table with a glass of pale tea. Turk thought she was the one from Timbuktu, though if he'd seen her anywhere else he would have taken her for a Yaqui.

A well-dressed gent who looked about half crocked hung against the bar with a watch on one fist shooting the breeze with one of the barkeeps. And one other fellow, a big guy rigged like a rancher, had a foot on the rail. Turk eyed this one morosely with his thoughts irrevocably prowling back to the Roman 4.

He went outside and rolled a smoke. It didn't give him much satisfaction. Despite all the figuring he had done, and all the pent-up wrath and bitterness, he still knew deep inside him there'd never be another to fill the place he'd given Holly. He called himself a fool but it don't change anything really. She'd got into his blood and that was all there was to it; no amount of soul searching or barbed prods from his pride could drive away the things she stirred in him.

He pitched his smoke into the night and went back.

The man in rancher's garb still had his foot on the rail. There was something about him that kept dragging Turk's glance around. Big enough, he looked, to hunt bears with a switch. Turk kept thinking he might catch a look at his face but the way the man was standing the glass didn't show it. His hair was black beneath the white ten-gallon stet-hat and he had broad shoulders—almost broad as Curly Bill, Turk, thought, his eyes abruptly narrowing. Behind the fancy shirt and pinto vest and the black-and-white checks that hugged his legs like skin, the man's shape was enough like Bill's to...

Turk sucked in his breath. The man had turned his face to say something to the barkeep, and that profile—by God, it *was* Curly Bill! Curly Bill at Silver Lake!

Turk, astounded, moved across to an empty table

where a deck of cards lay open and, dropping into a chair, began to lay out a start in Klondike the way he'd watched the house men do when they were waiting around. Over the cards he watched the big man at the bar.

Curly Bill around Tombstone was a name to conjure with. He was dark and ruggedly handsome and Turk saw the Yaqui setting out bait and thought to himself she might as well cut stick. This was too big a gent to waste his time on the likes of her. He must have felt the pull of Turk's stare for his head tipped up and his black eyes rummaged Turk's face in the gleam and shine of the back bar mirror.

Turk, flushing a little, dropped the stare to his cards, putting the jack of spades on top of the king of hearts. A voice at his shoulder pointed out the mistake, and Turk's swiveled glance found the Yaqui from Timbuktu leering down at him. "Oo is these man?" she asked in a husky whisper.

Turk swept the cards in a heap and got out of his chair, nettled as much by her interest as by the cheap perfume with which her presence enveloped him. He brushed past her brusquely heading for the door.

The midnight sky was filled with white fluffy clouds. A breeze off the lake brought a rank smell of shore and yonder, across the dappled blue and silver of the intervening range, the lamps of Tucson gleamed like cats' eyes. He was not surprised at the big man's lack of recognition; always he had worshipped Curly Bill from afar, his attempted emulation the sincerest form of flattery. A mouse tiptoeing after an elephant.

But even a mouse might aspire to be large, Turk reflected morosely. It was hard to put into words how he felt about Bill. The man cast a whale of a shadow. Everything he did was bold, assured and confident. The country spoke of him in whispers and there were two schools of thought: one considering him a godsend, the champion of the ranch crowd; the other whispering behind his back that he was one of the ringleaders of the wildest gang of cutthroats the border had ever known. Turk had never heard of anyone saying such things to Bill's face.

He meandered the length of the gallery, wondering what had fetched Bill to a place like Silver Lake. He slapped at a persistent mosquito and water lapped the bottoms of the boats beyond the tamarisks. Roman 4 came into his thinking again and he tried to imagine what Bill would have done and a woman's laugh, coming off the lake, called up tantalizing visions of the taffy haired Holly. He growled. "You goddamn fool!" and went back inside.

The games were packed three deep in the card room and blue layers of smoke swirled and drifted under the green shades of the lamps. Clack of chips and clink of glasses. Talk curled around him like the voice of a thousand locusts.

No trouble here. He pushed on through and stepped into the bar as a burst of applause hammered the walls with its din. This was for the establishment's latest sensation, Rosarita, a Zincali dancer according to the billing; but Turk had overheard Arch telling Flack she was an alley cat the boss had picked up with a bottle of pulque in the *barrio libre*. Turk had watched her before. He stayed to see her again.

She was dark as a wood cutter. Golden eyes and black hair. A tawny panther of a girl in scarlet rags, sombrero and naked feet. Possibly a gypsy, Turk thought, but no Zincali. Her bones were too fine for an Indian; she had a different shape of face.

She'd been coming down the stairs. Now she paused to flash white teeth at the assemblage. She was insolence personified. The applause became deafening. She pulled off her hat and set it sailing over their heads. It was slanting toward Turk when a dozen hands flashed up, all hungrily reaching. Two pulled it down within three feet of his own outstretched arm. A man swore in angry protest. Turk saw a fist lash out, heard it strike against flesh. The red sombrero disappeared, was thrust aloft and shaken vigorously.

Curly Bill had it.

Turk pushed the sock back into his pocket. The girl made a face and Bill's laugh rang out and he called something to her that was lost in the uproarious cheering. "Rosarita! Come on, Sweetness, dance for us!"

You might have guessed she was the toast of Tucson the way that bunch of hombres yelled. She accepted the acclaim with scornful eyes and came onto the room's tiny stage as though it belonged to her, untwining the tattered scarf from her hair. The bull fiddle, the guitars and the five string banjo cut into the din with a quick beat of chords. The shouts died away. The roll of a drum began to build up excitement.

She jingled the coins on her wrists, tapped a foot. Suddenly the wild whipped-up music caught her, caught her up the way wind catches up dust and papers, spinning her across the boards of the stage in a pulse thumping blur of scarlet cloth and bare legs. She came out of it stamping her feet and head bobbing, the black mop of her hair flung straight up and then down to the clack of the castanets in her fingers. The music's weird rhythm was immeasurably quickened and she went spinning away like a leaf in a gale, skirt and jacket vibrating and twirling like a pair of red ropes against which her willowy body flashed naked.

It caught Turk's breath as it had before. It caught the rest of them, too. Applause struck the walls in solid crashes of sound. Gold and silver coins bounced and rolled about her feet while she refastened the jacket and eyed the crowd insolently through the tumbled mass of her midnight hair.

She flung it back off her face completely ignoring them, down on her haunches gathering up the bright plunder.

Curly Bill started toward her through the crowd, the chinstrapped hat a blob of color where it dangled from his arm, shoving men off his brawny elbows uncaringly.

Then Turk saw something that turned his eyes sharply narrow. The man Bill had used his fist on was moving, gliding after him silent as a stalking cat. Sensing trouble Turk plunged after them.

Someone got in his way and by the time he'd ducked around Bill had reached the platform. He had one hand on it, bending forward, and the girl turned her face to peer up at him.

The second man, a Mexican dressed like a *charro*, was almost up to him. Turk saw the flash of steel and, ripping the sock from his pocket, plunged forward, striking blindly.

The blow missed the man's head and struck his hunched shoulder. The knife clattered from his hand. Then Turk was into him, slugging and taking his fists in return. The man's eyes flashed with hatred; he was wild to get loose. The blast of a gun ripped through the uproar, in those narrow confines the sound becoming enormous. The Mexican staggered back against a crush of other Mexicans, the frozen strain of their faces etched upon skin that was like pounded putty in the smoky flare of the lamps. The whites of the wounded man's eyes rolled up into his head and he half twisted, crumpling, spilling into Turk's legs.

Turk staggered back. There was a long-barreled pistol in Curly Bill's fist. The gray stench of powdersmoke swirled from its snout and the slitted stare back of it was like polished jet. The girl sprang erect, snatching her hat and whirling stairward. The room was a blur of shocked white faces. Turk put his hand against Bill's chest. "Quick man—move! Git up them stairs!"

Bill was going to argue. Turk gave him a shove. The planes of Bill's cheeks showed a dark rush of anger. He tipped up his gun. Its bore looked big as a cannon's.

"You want to git us *both* killed?"

Curly Bill snarled, furious. "You think I'd run from a greaser!"

A growl came out of the crowd. Someone shouted. Back of the bar Arch yelled: "Tie into him!"

Turk saw the flash of a bottle sail past their heads, saw it burst in a shower of glass on the stair rail. The second bouncer, Grigsby, shoved a popeyed face through the cardroom door. Turk saw his hand drive hipward. Flame roared in Turk's face and he thought for a second his eardrums were broken. Grigsby grabbed at his middle and folded into the wall.

"Get outa my way, Red!"

That was Arch again. His voice streaked like a gate hinge. Turk saw the sawed-off coming over the bar. Bill saw it too and leaped stairward. Turk almost stepped on his heels in his hurry.

Maybe Arch was afraid of hitting Turk; he didn't fire. Other men weren't so squeamish. Five slugs knocked holes in the plaster of the stairwell before Turk made the landing and scuttled upward out of sight.

He saw the dancer's bare feet flying down the hall. "Never mind the girl—" he panted. "Take the first unbarred door you git hold of!"

Bill did. It was China's. There was a man by the bed trying to get into his pants. Bill cracked him over the head with his gun barrel. The man toppled backwards. China cursed in several languages.

"Out of the window," Turk gasped. "We'll have to go down those posts."

Bill was halfway over the rail when Turk got through the window. Turk did not do any lingering either. Half the barroom was coming by the sound from the stairs. He swung over the rail and let go. He thought the ground must have driven his knees through his shoulders. He heard Bill running.

Bill swung back. "Which way's the stables?"

Turk got onto his feet. "No time for—that. Got to git through them trees." Bill was off like a shot. Turk, quartering after him, heard the bunch from the bar spilling out across the balcony. A cloud passed across the light from the moon. There were shouts from the balcony. A shotgun's racket filled the air with shrill whining. Something whipped at Turk's coat skirts; then he was diving into the tamarisks.

Curly Bill came out of the shadows. "There ain't nothin' out here—what I want is a horse!"

"Yeah," Turk panted. "Like to have one myself. Come on. There's some boats around here someplace."

Curly Bill stopped short. "Boats!" Turk saw his face twist around. "I ain't gittin' in no boat—"

"Then stay here," Turk growled, too worried to stop and argue. He was a little riled, too, considering the changes he was taking. In the gloom of the windy shoreline he found three boats pulled up with their bottoms half out of the water. He grabbed the oars out of two and caught hold of the other one. "If you're comin' jump in."

"They'll pick us off like settin' ducks!"

Turk got his pistol out of his boot and tucked it inside the waistband of his black gambler's trousers. He put the extra oars in the boat. He was sliding the boat into the water when Bill, snarling under his breath, got it.

Turk could hear those fellows dropping off the balcony, could hear them shouting and cursing as they ran circling and panting through the roundabout shadows. Because of the trees and the clouds which covered the moon about all he could make out was the black slant of the tavern's roof, but at least a part of the racket seemed to be coming straight toward them. He jumped aboard with a final shove and caught up an oar.

Bill was still muttering. Turk glanced at the sky. In what looked to be seconds the moon would be free. He told Bill: "Git that white hat off and keep out of sight." He didn't wait to see if Bill minded; he put his knees on the leaky bottom and used an oar like a pole. When he couldn't touch bottom he used the oar for a paddle.

They had more oars than he knew what to do with. He was scared to try rowing.

"I don't think they'll look for us out here," he whispered, staring up at the clouds again, "but if they spot us don't throw any lead at them. If they ever make sure who we are they'll git horses."

They made another thirty feet. "Here they come," Bill growled.

They were fifty yards off shore by then. The bunch were beating the tamarisks and jabbering in Spanish. The boat drifted on for another ten feet and then a yell sailed up and the whole push came boiling out to the shoreline. Turk pulled in his oar and shouted, "What the hell ails you?" not reckoning they could see any better than he could.

They didn't fire anyway. They asked in Spanish if he'd seen two gringos in big hats. Turk replied in their lingo that he was trying to catch fish. He heard them do some more muttering. The moon came out and Turk sank back as the bunch on the shore cut off through the trees still arguing.

In the back of the boat Bill got up on a seat trying to squeeze some of the water out of his soaked pantlegs. "I'd as like be shot as drowned!"

"You got a hat," Turk said. "Start bailin' if you're worried."

Bill took the remark seriously. He got to work on the water. He kept right on working until they reached the other side. Turk poled the boat into the reeds and got out, Bill following clumsily. Brush came down to within a few feet of the shore. When they got through it they emptied their boots out. "Road to town," Turk said, "will be over that way," pointing.

"We might stay a lot more healthy if we keep plumb away from it."

Bill, snorting, struck off toward it, Turk reluctantly following.

Before long he wished his boots were several sizes larger. The wet leather bound on his ankles had made his feet burn. He moved quiet as he could and kept his ears peeled. Curly Bill said finally and rather testily Turk thought, "You hadn't no call to take chips in this deal—Why'd you do it?"

Turk shrugged.

"Women!" Bill said, and shook his head disgustedly. He didn't speak again till they came limping into town. After they'd gone half a block he said grudgingly, "Worked with cattle, ain't you?"

"I've chased a few," Turk nodded.

"What do they call you?"

"Turkey Red."

Bill pulled up, astonished. "Well, by gawd!" he said, and chuckled. "You're the guy that kilt that squatter!"

He didn't say any more until Levin's hotel was in front of them, dark and silent except for a lamp's pallid gleam above the abandoned desk by the stairwell. He swung around then and faced Turk. "You ever git in a tight, boy, you call on Curly Bill."

* * *

TURK HAD FIGURED to put up at Levin's himself but he couldn't very well after Bill had turned in there. Someway it didn't seem fitting. He didn't want Bill to think he was sucking around.

He clumped on down the street. There was a

stage pulled up before the front of the Palace and he waited in the shadows until it rolled off, heading for Prescott. If Bill had heard about Fanshaw, Turk reckoned he was a marked man and he saw no use in taking needless chances. If the word got back to Wyatt Earp the marshal might decide to come over here.

He thought of finding a saloon. The streets were deserted and, after tramping a few blocks, he swung back. To hell with Earp! Turk's feet were killing him. He saw the shine of lamps coming out of the stage depot. It was too late to get into a hotel now and, looking like he did, he didn't think a hotel would take him. He tugged his hat brim down and went into the depot's waiting room.

There was a drunk spraddled out on one of the benches. A couple of drummers swapping jokes were holding down another. The agent looked up from his desk behind the counter and put his face back into his papers when Turk limped past without speaking.

Turk dropped onto a bench. He wished the hell he dared take his boots off but was scared if he did he'd never get them back on. Tomorrow, he reckoned, he'd have to go out to the lake again, or send someone else, to pick up High Sailin. He sure didn't aim to get rooked out of his horse.

He took a squint at the clock. It had "Butterfield" wrote across it and showed later than he thought. He guessed maybe after he got High Sailin he would take a ride over around Skull Valley and get another ranch job if he could find a place needing help.

He went over the events of the evening. Curly Bill, by grab! Made a fellow feel pretty important. Kind of conspicuous, too. Wasn't many guys could boast helping out a gent of his caliber.

He shot a look at the drummers. They didn't even know he existed. Gave him a queer feeling, kind of. He reckoned their eyes would bug out if they was to know he had just been hobnobbing with Curly Bill Graham.

In this Arizona country Bill was by way of being about as talked about a jasper as Billy the Kid was over in New Mexico. All across these borders miles wild tales of Curly's daring furnished the exciting raw materials for supper yarning around the campfires of the cow camps. He was fast becoming a legend. Depending on where and to whom you listened you could hear pretty well nigh anything. He was champion of the small spreads. He was called a 'scourge' of the ranges. He was the Robin Hood of the wastelands. Syndicates and politics were doing their best to ruin the country, buying the courts and sheriffs. Everybody seemed to be out to *get* theirs. Curly Bill was the solitary rock in this time of transition; he stood foursquare for the cowboys. He didn't kowtow to anybody and the moguls walked in fear of his vengeance ...

Turk must have drowsed. He was wakened by the racket of a just arrived stage. He could see people getting out of it, and one bunch of hostlers leading off the teams while another using plenty of "language" was hitching fresh broncs in their places.

The whip and guard came in with the mail pouch and the drummers got up and grabbed their bags and stomped out. There was enough damn noise for a herd of bull buffalos and plumb in the midst of it Turk's heart got to pounding like a battery of stamp mills.

He had to look twice before he could believe it, but

there she was all right, dressed to kill and headed straight for him. Solomon in all his glory had never got up any carefuller to catch the eye.

She had a lavender cloth hat with feathers on top of her gleaming high piled hair and a lavender dress with a smudge of black ribbon and lace around the collar, and a yellow cloth bag on a loop around her waist. A yellow parasol edged with lavender was clutched in her hand and there was four million pleats in the skirt she held up to keep from falling over it. Every guy in the place turned his face around to gawk and she sailed past them all, coming straight up to Turk.

His ears got hot and in a way he kind of wished that he was back at Silver Lake but, like most of his wishing, it didn't go him any good. She came up with her hand out—the one with the bag on it—and her face all lit up with surprise and excitement. "Turkey!" she exclaimed in that deep throaty voice that always chased tingles up and down his back gone. "But this is marvelous of you —I didn't expect you to *meet* me."

Turk muttered something, gulping, but might as well have saved his breath. She had hold of his arm now, smiling, looking up at him til you'd have thought they were honeymooners—leastways, he made no doubt everyone else had latched onto that notion.

"Well!" she said, pouting. "Aren't you even going to kiss me?"

Turk glared around at the grinning watchers. Holly, following his look, made a face and said, "Silly!" Then reached up a gloved hand and patted his cheek.

Turk guessed his mug looked like a fire had been built under it. He got hold of her elbow and started hustling her toward the door, making out not to hear or see a thing till they got through it.

"Where's your case?" he grunted, eyeing the heap of luggage the driver had set down beside the stage's back wheel.

"Right there—that one," she smiled, pointing.

He reached down and got a hand on it. She stood back, trim and neat as a basket of chips, and he could feel the old adam start to push and pummel and pound again. He had figured to be plumb done with her but, watching that tongue crawl across her red lips, was willing to admit he might have made a snap judgment.

She gave him one of her twisted smiles. "Where are you staying, Turk?"

He mighty near dropped her case on his foot. A dozen crazy notions got to larruping through his head, but the shining one that got him was that actually he *had* misjudged her. Either that or she'd changed her mind, and he was in no condition to find fault with miracles. It never occurred to him to wonder how she had known he would be in Tucson.

He had trouble with his breathing.

Her eyes got big and sparkly. She slipped a hand through his arm and hugged the arm against her. "They'd remember me at the Levin—couldn't you find us something out on the side streets? It doesn't really matter except that we're together, does it?"

It surely didn't to Turk. He couldn't get his thoughts untangled or the scent of her out of his thinking long enough to give any real thought to it. He hoped this meant she'd decided to team with him permanent; it didn't seem like the moment to jaw about it though and any suspicions he may have had he choked down as being unworthy, wanting desperately to believe her sweet surrender was complete.

With her squeezing his arm against her like that he couldn't hardly tell up from down. Any place would do for the balance of the night—it was pretty near light already, he thought anxiously, wondering if they could find a place now. In the morning—later, he reckoned, they had better hit out for the border; Ruebusch wasn't likely to take this lying down. Turk could speak enough Mex to get by. He would get him a job with some big hacendado. When they'd got enough dough he'd get some stock of his own...

He found them a room at a place on South Meyer.

It wasn't right, he knew that; knew that nothing was like to ever make it right either, but few things in this world were the way a man would want them.

He had most of the answers. Still it wasn't like he had figured it would be. Time they got to the room most of his lift had worn off and his thoughts weren't tracking the way he would have had them. A queer unease had gotten into him and it made him irascible and clumsy. She was willing all right; she was at him no sooner than he had got the door fastened.

"Plenty of time for that," he said scowling. "What about Fanshaw? What did Ruebusch do?"

She gave him a kind of odd look and tossed her hair back. "He rode into Tombstone and told Fred White you'd had a quarrel with Fanshaw and killed him."

White was town marshal, not a Deputy U.S. Marshal like Earp was.

"Why White?" Turk asked.

"He told Johnny Behan too." Behan was a deputy sheriff. "Said you were always getting into fights with people, that he'd finally had to fire you. White said it was *uncommon funny* that right after you'd shot him Fanshaw's dam got broke open so conveniently. Ruebusch said the old man blew up the dam himself after they'd settled their differences with five thousand dollars. He said he imagined you and Fanshaw had been in cahoots and that you'd probably killed him in an argument over the money."

Turk scowled in silent fury but when Holly came snuggling up again he took hold of her like he meant it. Her eyes went shut. He could feel her tremble. Her hands came up and pulled down his head. He felt her mouth spread and it was just like kicking the roof off the world.

They were both breathing hard when she let go of him. She reached for her fastenings. "Tomorrow," Turk said, "we'll light a shuck for the border ..."

Her eyes looked like two pieces of glass. "Have we got to go through all that again?"

"Through all what?"

"That stuff about me going off with you."

Turk said tight and careful, "What about it?"

"I'm not going, that's what about it. Tomorrow or any other time."

Turk was staring but he wasn't really seeing her. He got back into his coat and picked up his hat.

Her lips curled. "Always running!" She pushed back her hair. "Where are you off to now?"

"I'm goin' to join Curly Bill."

She looked at his set face and laughed. Then the jeer fell out of her eyes. "You crazy damn fool—"

Turk pulled the door shut behind him.

FOUR

THIS WAS Arizona in the time of the locusts, a hair-triggered realm in the throes of transition. A great unrest was setting in all across the American nation. The East was paving the way for the spectacular rise of Boss Tweed and a motley host of imitators and, across the line in New Mexico, the great trading monopoly of Murphy-Dolan had its back to the wall in that fight for survival which historians have recorded as the Lincoln County War; Billy the Kid was running wild and thumbing his nose at Lew Wallace; and that great cattle thief, John Chisum, was nearing the end of his string.

The country's morals had done a flipflop and all over the vast and sparsely settled Southwest armed banditry was paying enormous dividends. Tombstone was in its heyday and honkytonk row set the pace men lived and all too frequently died by. It was the day of the cattle kings, of great combines. Ruthlessness was rampant. Millions of longhorned cattle roved the great ranges of Chihuahua and Sonora and many a respectable American was engaged in hazing this beef across the line—so many, in fact, that it had become an established business. And there was no one more expert at promoting this industry than rollicking, burly Curly Bill Graham.

He was rightly dubbed the "scourge of the ranges." He frequently shanghaied a thousand head at one swoop and was not averse to selling gringo cattle to the dons. The Mexican steers he disposed of to contractors supplying the San Carlos and other Indian agencies. He sold them to frontier slaughterhouses and to unscrupulous ranchers who shipped them East to Cincinnati, Kansas City, Chicago and St. Louis. New cattlemen bought from him to augment their herds which he frequently depleted for his sales below the line. He was well on his way to becoming the "international menace" and had already been the subject of several debates in Congress.

It was a mark of the times and a commentary on law enforcement that he went freely about his nefarious business at will. He was a familiar and jovial customer in the gambling houses and saloons of booming Tombstone. A reputation for wildness, even for downright banditry in other places, was openly winked at by denizens of this silver camp; they were much too busy acquiring wealth of their own to be overly concerned with the didos of the cow crowd.

Sometimes Bill rode with forty men at his back; he was seldom to be seen without a half dozen and was no guy to yell boo at. For all his robust good looks, his uproarious pranks and dimples he was always, grimly under these, strictly a man with his eye on the main chance. And deadly as a timber wolf. Practically every outlaw in the southeastern end of the Territory owed some form of allegiance to him; he was tied in also with the vested interests, the political setup which was making Arizona such a paradise for wanted men. Johnny Behan, the Tucson sheriff's deputy for the Tombstone end of Pima County, was openly friendly as were many of the country's ranchers. It was not too greatly to be wondered at that a youngster of Turkey Red's antecedents and naive impressionability, seeing only this fellow's outward self and the general esteem and standing accorded him, should seek to make himself over in Bill's image.

* * *

TURK LOST no time in making for Curly Bill's stamping grounds. There was a strong streak of rashness woven through his nature which, given focus by his need of belonging and fired by rankling memories of Holly's scornful refusal to take him seriously, sent him across the wasteland miles with no care or thought for the consequences. He would show her, by God—he would show them all! A full moon looked down from the blue-black skies as he reined High Sailin up out of the mesquite brush and greasewood of the desert and followed the stage road on to the mesa to see the lamps of the silver camp gleaming like drops of soapy water through the night.

Away from the town the darkness didn't look so black. Off to the north by a little east the Dragoon Mountains raised silvered escarpments looking lost and lonesome in that immense spread of distance which beyond was called Sulphur Springs Valley. Northwest the humpbacked shoulders of the Rincons thrust up out of the San Pedro gloom. West, and much closer, were the peaks of the Whetstones looking like steeples whacked out of black paper. Farther, southwest, the lines of the Huachuca's made dim blue tracery, and dead south stood the Mules between this mesa and the border, a scant thirty miles by horseback. Due east were the Cherrycows, brooding like a sleepy hen above the San Bernardino and true pale Pedregosas.

A wind was rolling up off the flatlands, not truly cold but strongly hinting of cold weather to come, puffing and snorting like a bronc with the wheezes. Turk pulled his gambler's coat a bit more snugly about his shoulders and turned up the scanty collar to protect a throat not yet used to being without its neck rag.

He stared morosely at the lights of Tombstone, not so easy now that he was here about his actual chances of hooking on with Graham. A lobo wolf's howl coming off some ridgetop uncomfortably reminded him of Deputy Marshal Wyatt Earp who was so rapidly building a rep in this town. But the place was teeming, everyone said so, and among the six thousand people headquartering in the town he guessed, with reasonable caution, he shouldn't have too much trouble keeping out of Earp's sight. Fred White wouldn't know him or Earp either, probably. Earp and his brothers had plenty to do keeping peace in the place and he was over here primarily to collect back taxes which should be a big enough chore to keep any agent occupied.

Turk cuffed his flat topped felt a little lower over his eyes and dug High Sailin a poke in the ribs to let him know he still had a man aboard of him. Maybe Bill wouldn't choose to remember their meeting. But he was said to be a man which kept his word no matter what; and after all, by grab, Turk *had* done him a favor.

He wondered again what it would really be like to be riding in the company of Curly Bill. A pretty breathtaking business, he reckoned. He was a pretty fair hand with cattle; maybe Bill would use him on some of his forays below the line ...

His unease grew almost to the proportions of premonition while he strove unsuccessfully to convince himself that Earp would not deem him worth bothering about. Hadn't Frank Leslie—him they called "Buckskin" on account of his preference for that sort of clothing—dropped Mike Killeen in a gun fight right on the steps of the Commercial Hotel? Hadn't another guy called "King" shot and killed young Johnnie Wilson in the very middle of Allen Street with people thicker than flies all around him? And both of them turned loose! Both of them tough eggs that cared no more about upping the death rate than they would about weevils getting baked in their biscuits. Still and all Turk couldn't feel comfortable. Wyatt Earp was a very persevering kind of man, and he was friendly with Ruebusch. Which might make all the difference.

Just in these few weeks he had been gone Turk noticed the signs of change and growth. The town had spread all over hell's kitchen. And racket— Cripes! He shook his head in astonished wonder.

Fabulous fortunes were associated with Tombstone and fabulous violence in the eyes of the East. The town was being featured in the big eastern dailies. Boston, New York and Philadelphia papers had their own correspondents living right on the ground. Gamblers—"high rollers"—were considered the equal of anyone. Harlots and purse snatchers tramped cheek by jowl along the streets with respectable citizens and sometimes, he thought, you couldn't tell them apart. He had heard that White favored restricting the women to particular sides of certain designated streets. He was honest, Turk reckoned, as the country would let him be, though some folks figured he listened too much to Earp.

These Tombstone people were great ones for bragging. They took a heap of pride in their iniquities and boisterousness and, according to their tell, things held smart in New York and San Francisco were hauled by the freighters or by relays of fast riders to be admired or served up with gusto in the tonier establishments of this roaring camp. You could get the best coffin varnish, the finest squabs and oysters, the flossiest women—almost anything imaginable, so long as you had the price or the connections.

It was the most celebrated town in the Territory. One mile high and a place where the roofs could be took off for anything.

* * *

THE WIND DIDN'T SEEM to be blowing near as gusty by the time Turk got to where the sounds of the place enveloped him. Where the stage road became the main street, which was called Allen, a crew of carpenters working in the light of flaring lanterns were rushing a new clapboarded building to completion. Wagons of all kinds and descriptions appeared to be everywhere and cursing mule skinners and ranch hands, and even a sprinkling of horse soldiers in blue coats and yellow neckerchiefs, were shouting, swearing, howling and laughing till the din was like nothing Turk had ever heard in his life.

On his left as he'd entered town he'd seen the clutter of shacks and mud boxes of the Mexican quarter. The Chinese quarter came next, north on Second and back off a piece to the right. Traffic got heavier and he found it harder to wedge High Sailin through. By the time he reached the Can Can, a hash house at the northwest corner of Allen and Fourth just beyond the stage barns and O.K. Corral, the signs of growth were everywhere apparent. And deadfalls. Violins, banjos, guitars and tinpanny pianos were whooping things up to a fine noisy frenzy and there was plenty of light along both sides of the way. Plenty of people, too—the boardwalks were jammed with them, talking their jaws off and tramping every whichway.

He put the big gelding across Fourth and passed the Occidental Hotel on the right, the Cosmopolitan on the left with the Occidental Saloon alongside of it and, over again on his right, the blazing-windowed front of the Grand Hotel. The snarl of traffic was getting so bad his progress was almost at a standstill when Turk squeezed High Sailin over against a line of racked horses and stopped, blinded and half strangled in a lemon fog of dust whipped up by the rumbling passage of a train of heavy ore wagons.

He was wedged there for ten minutes before he found a chance to get moving again, and then only at a snail's pace. A boisterous bunch of what looked like cowpunchers pushed through the green batwings of Bob Hatch's saloon which was next to the Alhambra;

and a couple of doors along he saw the Crystal Palace's sign.

They had a little more room after they got across Fifth. Sixth, as Turk knew, was where most of the cribs were, the hangouts of Rowdy Kate and Dutch Annie, Blonde Mary and Crazy Horse Lil, Madame Moustache and a whole flock of others. He was able to wedge High Sailin up to a tie rail before he got quite as far as Sixth, about seven doors beyond the Arcade Saloon and on Allen's south side just ahead of some empty lots.

Waiting for a break in the traffic he crossed to get onto Allen's north walk, thinking he might find Bill in the Arcade. It didn't seem to him very likely that in any such seething crush of humanity he was going to be recognized as the fellow being hunted for the killing of Fanshaw. Two-thirds of these people had probably never heard of Fanshaw.

Some of Turk's caution, along with his uneasiness, began to wear off. When he reached the Arcade Saloon he pushed into it. The bar was packed six deep already and as soon as he was able to get turned around he headed for the street, letting the walk's crowd jostle him back down along to Fifth.

Where in the world, he wondered, did all these folks put up at? The buildings were mostly of frame and adobe, a few of them actually having second floors instead of the foolish false fronts so much in vogue throughout the West's cowtowns. Wooden awnings projected out over the board walks which flanked the front of each establishment, and the walks were flanked by horse crammed hitch rails along both sides of Allen's sixty-foot width.

As he came to where Fifth made its slash square

across it a string of wagons groaning beneath high piles of lumber fresh cut and hauled from the Cherrycows appeared; a careening stage jolted in from the left and the dust got so thick you could taste it. All around Turk folks were swearing and shouting, declaring wagons ought to be kept off of Allen.

When he was able to clear his streaming eyes the crowd he'd got locked into was half across the intersection. A bunch of skallyhootin' horse-backers came out of the wagons' fog, tearing into Fifth and sending everyone jumping to keep from being run down. Turk swore at them with the rest and barreled on into the lights of the Crystal Palace. He couldn't have got into that place if he had wanted to.

He gave up the hunt, thinking maybe tomorrow he would have better luck. Of course Bill might not even be around, might be off on one of his cattle gathering trips or holed up with some woman—he was quite a hand with the ladies by repute.

Bob Hatch's bar wasn't quite so crowded and Turk was able to get in although not to wet his whistle. He pushed on through to the rear and shoved open the door into Bob's back room. There was a game going on, draw poker by the looks, and Curly Bill was in it with the dollars stacked high in front of him. One stack was gold —double eagles.

Turk closed the door and stood back against the wall, uneasy again now he'd run Bill to earth. After sweating the game for about twenty minutes Turk saw one of the players pitch down his cards in disgust. "I'm strapped!" he growled, and got up and went out, viciously slamming the door shut behind him. A couple of the players laughed. They spread out a little and went on with the deal. Somebody opened, a couple of gents raised and Bill raised them; the two others dropped out. The opener took one. Both the raisers took three. Bill stood pat. The opener showed a pair of jacks and got out. The first raiser bet fifty dollars, the second man hiking it another thirty. Bill saw these and kicked in another hundred. Both men quit and Bill raked in the chips with a laugh. "Pair of sixes," he said, but nobody asked to see them.

"About time we were breakin' this up," someone said and Bill, lifting his stare, saw Turk. "Well, look what's here," he said, and all their heads turned. "That's the kid Wyatt Earp's been huntin' for—feller that downed Fanshaw."

Turk could feel the riled blood burning into his cheeks and he knew deep inside him with a cold desperate sinking that he'd been a fool to come here, and a bigger fool to have taken Bill's gratitude for granted. Probably Bill didn't even figure that Turk had helped him getting away from that bunch at Silver Lake that night. The words strung. Gratitude or not, Bill hadn't needed to tell the rest of these yaps that Wyatt Earp was after him!

With the blood still roaring through him Turk saw Bill wave a careless hand, heard him say in that same half hoorahing tone, "Don't let them duds or that starved look throw you—feller's apt to gaunt up some ridin' fer Ruebusch. Boys, meet Turkey Red."

Several of them nodded, a shade more interest in their stares; and Turk, with temper cooling, understood Bill had been trying to help him, trying to make him appear more acceptable to those tough hands around the table. "With the right kind of chance," Bill said, "I figure he'll pull his weight with our bunch." He grinned at Turk. "Guy behind all them whiskers is Jim Hughes," he said. "Next gent's Tom McLowery—big rancher over towards Animas. That rusty-haired hellion is known as Tex Willbrandt. Squatty one's Jake Gauze."

Only Tom McLowery bothered to stick his hand out. He had a lean capable looking face and a quick strong grip that impressed Turk favorably. Gauze looked distinctly hostile. The other pair just looked at him without any feeling one way or the other.

Bill said, "We got a little business to git off our chests. Tex, you and Turk sift along to Frank Stilwell's; we'll pick you up there soon's we git away. Where'd you leave your horse, Turk?"

"Over by them empty lots across from the Arcade."

"All right. You boys shove along then."

Tex ducked his head and Turk followed him out. As they pushed along through the thinning crowds that were still afoot on the walk outside Turk covertly eyed Tex Willbrandt more carefully. He had quite a reputation as a rough and tumble fighter and was no slouch with a six-shooter. Lath thin he was, a steel spring kind of man with a reputed penchant for peppermint lozenges, of which he had several in his mouth at the moment judging by the whiff Turk had caught of his breath. His clothes sagged loosely from the bony shoulders. He had a rust colored mustache, streaked and wild above his mouth, and roan bristles sprouting thickly from the jut of his short broad chin. A faded blue wipe was knotted loosely about his neck and alkali grit was ground into the whole look of him.

Halfway down the block he said something Turk didn't catch, there was so much gab around him. Willbrandt leaned closer. "I said you sure you know what you're doin'?"

Turk looked at him blankly.

"Gettin' mixed up with Curly Bill," Willbrandt said. "Hardcase outfit. No place for a feller with his whole life ahead of him."

Turk's ears got hot and resentment welled up in him. Willbrandt's pale Texas eyes read the signs and he said dryly, "Understand, it's no skin off my nose what you do. But now's the time to get goin' if you aim to pull out."

Turk said thickly: "I know what I'm doin'. When I need a wet nurse—"

"Don't call on me," Willbrandt said. He nodded darkly. "I left my bronc back of the feed store. I'll meet you where you left yours." He didn't wait for an answer but ducked away through the crowd.

Turk, scowling after him a moment, moved on. It wasn't easy to put into words the things he felt about Bill; he was all the things Turk wanted to be but knew, deep inside him, he likely never would. He didn't have the size of assurance. He didn't have the ready grin, the jovial laugh or the reputation—though that last, he reckoned darkly, was something he sure could latch onto. And traveling in Bill's wake would be the quickest way to get started. Bill wasn't only big in himself; the way he did things was big, attention catching, important. Bill might be a thief but he was no two-bit thief.

And then, abruptly, the whole bottom dropped out of Turk's world. He stopped, frozen motionless, incapable even of swallowing.

Less than six strides away and coming straight for him was old I Personally Ruebusch, flanked by Strehl and Linderstrom. Strehl grinned nastily. Linderstrom kept his thoughts to himself.

All three of them pulled up about an arm's reach away with Strehl's fist dropping against the butt of his gun.

FIVE

ALL ABOUT THEM people had stopped and now were frantically striving to get themselves out of the way. Ruebusch looked wild enough to burst his surcingle, too nearly berserk for that business of Fanshaw wholly to account for it; and Turk's mind leaped to Holly.

He licked dry lips.

In spite of everything though, the Roman 4 boss was making a rolling-eyed effort to hang onto his passions. "You were warned to stay out of this country," he said harshly, and then his fury got away with him. Thrusting his jaw within a half a foot of Turk's he snarled, "You sawed-off little whey-faced whelp! What have you done with my—"

Turk, pushed beyond caution, slammed a knee in his crotch and, when the man doubled over, hit him so hard he went back into Lindstrom all spraddled out and before Strehl could get his gun clear of leather Turk had his own dug into Strehl's belly.

Turk's face had gone white as a wagon sheet.

Strehl was scared, too. He understood that one

grunt could put him under a box lid. "Go on and draw," Turk rasped, "you white-livered polecat!"

Strehl's eyes looked ready to pop from their sockets and Linderstrom's jaws were clamped together so hard gray ridges of muscle stood out from them like ropes.

Ruebusch was still gagging and there was no telling what might have been the outcome of it if Johnny Behan and a couple of his sidekicks had not come running up just then. All the rest of the crowd that wasn't wedged into doorways had ducked plumb into the jammed traffic of the street; but Behan had hopes of being sheriff come next election and likely figured this a chance for catching a few votes from Roman 4.

"What's the matter here—what's goin' on?" he called, shoving up.

Strehl knew better than to open his mouth and Ruebusch, still moaning, hadn't yet caught up with his breath. Turk said, "This hogleg is set on a hair trigger. It's like to splatter this skunk hell west and crooked if you make any move to put your nose into it."

The under sheriff's eyes raked a fruitless look about him and apparently decided he'd got into the wrong stall. He backed down with a parched grin and took off, his companions following.

Turk, cooler now, pushed Strehl off his gun and moved far enough back to catch all three within its focus. "All right, you sinkers," he said gruffly, "git goin'."

It did his soul good to see the blotched look of Linderstrom's mug. Ruebusch got himself up off the walk's dusty boards with his face like green cheese and pawed around for his dentures, but mostly Turk watched Linderstrom. "If this looks to you like a good night for dyin' don't let me stand in the way of your doin' it."

Ruebusch lurched off with Strehl right on his heels. Turk could hear the hard grating of Linderstrom's teeth but the man wheeled away without opening his mouth.

Turk's knees got so weak he nearly had to sit down.

He dropped the pistol back in his pocket and tried to pull himself together. That was coming too almighty close for comfort. He looked around for Willbrandt but didn't see anything of him. Traffic was starting to pull out of its tangle and people were fanning out onto the walk again when it crossed his mind Ruebusch might go to Earp. He'd heard someone saying earlier Earp had recently resigned his tax job with the sheriff to support Bob Paul in the coming elections, but he was still deputy marshal and probably still friends with the Roman 4. It looked a mighty good time for Turk to make himself scarce.

He cast a glance over his shoulder and saw Bill and some other gents coming out of Hatch's Saloon. Watching his chance, Turk cut across the street and made a bee line for the hitch rail where his horse was. He hadn't covered half the distance when a man cut in ahead of him bound in the same direction.

The light was poorer over here because the fronts of a lot of these buildings were dark, but something in the way that yonder man moved narrowed Turk's stare. He could feel his muscles begin to pull tight. The man's head swung around and Turk went flat against a store front.

The man was Fred White, the Tombstone town marshal!

* * *

TURK SCARCELY DARED BREATHE.

He didn't know what to do. He didn't imagine White had spotted him but if the lawman wasn't on the prowl for him what was he doing over here and heading so pat in the direction of Turk's horse?

Turk wished he had never come back to this country. He felt a powerful urge to grab the nearest racked bronc and tear out of this. But an unwillingness to abandon High Sailin stopped him. He reckoned a man was a plain damn fool to let himself get so worked up about a horse.

White had moved on again. Turk moved too, sticking close to the buildings. The star packer was stepping out faster now, striding past High Sailin like he wasn't even there.

Turk shook his head. That White was a sharp one. He watched him cut into the vacant lots and vanish, fading into the shadows.

He was cute, all right. On account of the buildings cutting off Turk's view he couldn't make out if White had stopped or not, or which way he'd been headed. He might even have swung back, be waiting right now behind that last building.

Turk was mad and scared but not yet plumb foolish. He wasn't anxious to get his neck stretched—not even for High Sailin. But he didn't want to give the brown up unless he had to. He cautiously edged nearer to the corner of that last building, belatedly aware of a deal of caterwauling back of him.

Curly Bill's bunch, he saw, twisting his head. Noisier than hell emigrating on cart wheels. He noticed that a couple of them were flourishing pistols. Shouting and shooting and howling like Apaches, they came tromping along through the heavy dust, singing and bellering and calling ribald remarks. They weren't using the north walk and no one else was either, not with them throwing all that lead so promiscuous. Glass was breaking all over and Turk could hear Bill's hearty guffaws riding high above everything. There wasn't any real harm in it. Clowning, that's all it was.

The vacant lots were just ahead of Turk. This last building had a narrow railed porch tacked onto the front of it and was set back a stride or two to accommodate this appendage—a rooming house by the look of it. Yes, there was a sign on the door. Turk's glance swiveled streetward. High Sailin with pricked ears was watching the yonder commotion and blowing softly through his nose like he couldn't make up his mind if he should snort or send out a challenge.

Turk was about two jumps from the hitch rack when he caught the slam of a door. Seemed to have come from the shadows of the empty lots and now, away back, he saw the bulk of a shack and a man running from it, coming this way and coming fast, Fred White! Three other shapes back of him were cutting west around the rooming house to hit the street behind Turk.

There was no time for thinking. He could dive for High Sailin and give White a target or he could try to get back down the street.

He did neither. He fastened a hand on the railing of the rooming house porch and pulled himself over, desperately hoping in this gloom they wouldn't see him.

He hadn't hardly got settled before White reached

the street. He ran right out into it. Curly Bill's racket stopped. Turk glimpsed the men who'd been with Bill taking off like scared rabbits. He saw Bill swing a look around and then, still brandishing his pistol, break into a run toward the lots.

White cut him off. "Give me that gun!" he said.

"I wasn't doin' none o' that shootin'—"

"You give me that gun!" White cried, furious.

The two weren't a dozen steps away from Turk's concealment. Bill, grumbling, held out the pistol, butt forward. That much Turk saw plain. And White reaching for it. Then something blurred at the corners of his eyes and he saw the other three—the ones who had left White to swing around the building—flit past the end of the porch, sprinting streetward.

"Watch out!" Turk yelled, never stopping to think.

Everything happened at once then. With the yell still pouring out of him Turk saw Wyatt Earp throw his arms around Bill. He couldn't understand how White had got hold of Bill's gun barrel but he saw flame gout out of it. White, screaming, doubled over, both hands clutched to the front of him. Bill's hat fell off and Earp bent his own gun over the top of Bill's head and Bill went down sprawling.

Turk saw Earp drop beside them, squatting on his boot heels. Muzzle lights bloomed and Turk guessed that was Bill's crowd firing out of the dark, trying to cut Earp down. He could see the dust jumping up all around Earp. The two men who had dashed out there with Earp crouched nearby firing back at them. Turk heard Earp shout through the uproar. "Put that fire in Fred's coat out," and saw the nearest man—it looked like one of Earp's brothers—squirming forward and bend over him, slapping.

The racket of guns dimmed away and quit. Morgan Earp, looking up, said, "He ain't goin' to make it."

Wyatt Earp got to his feet. "Take him over to the shack. Keep your gun on Bill, Virg. I'll get them others."

"One done the hollerin' was on that porch," Morgan threw after him.

And that jarred Turk into some awareness of his own fix. His stomach muscles knotted and chills clawed his back as he watched Earp wheel toward him with that long-barreled six-shooter tipped up in front of his chest.

No one had to tell Turk about the prowess of that gent. Wyatt Earp was hell on wheels. The toughest tin-badge on the border.

Sweat cracked through the pores of Turk's hide. If he fought he'd be cut down in his tracks and if he gave himself up he'd swing for Fanshaw's killing, damned by the talk right out of his own mouth!

SIX

"PSST—IN HERE!"

Turk guessed he must have died a thousand deaths before he caught that guarded whisper. There wasn't anything wrong with his legs though. He was through the crack of that rooming house door before the oncoming marshal had taken three steps. He got a faint whiff of fragrance and guessed it was a girl who was easing the door shut. The tiny clink of the bolt sounded monstrously loud.

He couldn't see a thing but felt her hand touch his arm. He felt her breath against his cheek. "Pull off your boots."

With a sense of shock he knew her then—the Zincali dancer from Silver Lake. A dozen questions pummeled his mind while he got out of his boots and then her hand was in his, gently tugging him forward. "Stairs," she whispered, and he crept up them after her, holding close to the wall to keep the treads from creaking. He stumbled on the landing and half fell into her, feeling the willowy slenderness, smelling the clean sweet fragrance of her hair. They must have turned down a hall; she pulled him into a room, softly closing the door. Turk found a chair and jammed it under the knob.

The darkness was less opaque here, partially dispersed by reflected light from the street. He could see her standing near him, as intently listening as he was. He crossed to the window and, raising it a crack, put an ear to it. He didn't hear anything but ordinary street sounds. He didn't relax either. He wheeled toward her again, remembering her golden eyes and black hair, knowing he couldn't stay here, his mind still whirling with the clamor of questions prodded up by that business of Bill and Fred White and Wyatt Earp and his brothers. He was worried about Bill and about himself too, and knowing Earp's rep as he did he had a right to be.

"I don't think," she said, "we'd better chance a light."

Turk stared through the shadows. He said, "I've got to get out."

"I know. They're bound to search. Would it help if I took your horse around back?"

Turk said, "It sure would. I think a heap of that horse." He thought of something else, the danger she might run in helping the escape of a man who had Wyatt Earp on his trail; and he shook his head at her. "No," he said gruffly, "you've risked plenty as it is."

She must have sensed his confusion. She came nearer, saying softly, "I'd be glad to get him for you."

He took a turn about the room, made vaguely uneasy by her tone. He swung back. "If you're really bustin' to do somethin'," he said, "you might take care of him for me till I can send somebody after him."

"I think you can trust me. There are box elder trees just outside the back door. You could wait here while I ride your horse around."

Turk wanted the horse and she made it sound easy. "All right," he said finally, "if—"

"You'd better count on giving me five or ten minutes. As soon as the way is clear I'll bring him in from behind. Do you know where you'll be going?"

Turk, about to blurt Charleston, said instead, "I'll find a place. How'd you know I was out there?"

"I'd better get your horse. We can talk about that later."

After she had gone he sank down in the chair she'd taken away from the door and pulled on his boots, removing his spurs and thrusting them into a pocket. But almost at once he was buckling them on again. If he needed them at all the need would be urgent and he'd better chance their racket than be caught with bare heels if he got into a jackpot.

He hoped Curly wasn't bad hurt. He was still disturbed over that business of the pistol. He felt positive he had seen Bill hold it out butt forward. How then had Fred White come to have hold of its barrel? It didn't make sense and yet how else, if White hadn't, could that bullet have crashed into him?

Turk got up and prowled the room, more bothered than he was admitting. And it wasn't just White or his own fix—that girl bothered him too. She had saved his life. No getting around that part —but how had she known he was out there? Or in this town? And what was *she* doing here? He had an uncomfortable feeling she might have followed him, and that didn't make any sense to him either. Up till tonight he hadn't spoken ten words to her.

And there was the startled surprise he'd felt hearing her talk just now. At Silver Lake she'd spoken a kind of back alley English, regular foreigner lingo. And she was no Zincali—he'd have bet his boots on that!

He went to the door, quietly pulling it open. He listened a moment, hearing nothing to alarm him, and carefully felt his way to the pitch black head of the stairs. He was about to start down them when the creak of a board came up out of the darkness.

Turk's knees started shaking. His eyes stared wildly through the gloom, picturing it filled with gun-drawn possemen. But when after several moments nothing further had broken the quiet he attempted to convince himself it had been a timber settling.

He drew a long breath, feeling a fool to be getting so goosy over nothing. Bill wouldn't be standing here shaking like a ninny; he wouldn't be letting Turk trail with him if he thought Turk hadn't no more guts than this.

The thudding pound of Turk's heart slacked off a little. He wiped his hands on his pants and again took hold of the banister; and that was when he heard the stealthy whisper of moving feet. Frozen motionless he heard the feet pace the lower hall and then the sound of a bolt carefully drawn from its socket. A low mutter of voices came up to him then and he waited no longer.

Back in the girl's room he went at once to the window, easing it up and raking the street with bitter eyes. He didn't see anyone watching. He didn't see any way of getting down from here either.

He pulled sheets off the bed and grabbed the blanket off the foot of it. They'd search the ground floor first. He left the girl's room, thinking there was bound to be a window at the hall's far end.

There was. He saw the dim square of it just as a thunderous knock shook a door down below. "Open up!" Earp's voice came to him, and then a jabber of protests under cover of which Turk got to the window. He pushed up the sash and saw the empty lots below him darkly shadowed by this building and the bulking shapes of a pair of tamarisk trees. He swiftly knotted together the untorn sheets and the blanket, only then discovering there was nothing to tie the top end to. Booted feet pulled groans from the treads of the stairway.

Turk stared desperately at the ground twelve feet below him, but there was nothing else for it. Letting go of the sheets he threw a leg over the sill, squirmed around and pulled his other leg out. He let himself down to the length of his arms, then let go of the sill and dropped.

Twelve feet was no great height and hanging by his fingers he didn't drop that far, but he dropped far enough to hit off balance and be thrown. And when he scrambled up his left ankle drove pain through him. He had to grit his teeth to put weight on it but he dared not stay where he was and he didn't dare go round to the back now, either—Earp would be sure to have somebody watching the back. Probably the front, too, but at least out front they'd not be watching so careful.

He limped into the deep shadows of the tamarisks, coming out on the side of them away from the building. Then he moved toward the street wanting to whistle but unable even to achieve that dubious cover. His throat was like cotton, his heart pounding madly.

He didn't see anyone in front of the rooming house, didn't see High Sailin either. But there were three horses tied at a rack across the street and he crossed diagonally toward these, ignoring those racked closer at hand. They'd be looking for him to grab the nearest horse he could get his legs around.

Pain from his hurt ankle pushed a cold sweat through the pores of his skin and he could see obliquely ahead of him the corner where Charlie Storms last year had gasped out his life with an unfired pistol still in his hand. The light was dimmer out here in the street than it had been when he'd got trapped on that porch but it still lacked a lot of being as poor as he could have wished for. He had almost reached the north walk, with hope at last beginning to swell through him, when he saw a man with a rifle watching from the corner of a building two doors this side of the Arcade's entrance. Then he saw the other one. This second man was stepping into the street on an angle that would put him between Turk and the horses.

The shock of it almost choked off Turk's breathing. His face turned stiff and his legs were like lead and it was all he could do to keep his hand from his holster. But the man wasn't sure or he'd have brought up the rifle; he had both hands on it holding it squared across his thighs, chin a little forward as he waited for Turk to come up to him.

By a tremendous effort of will Turk kept to his course, fighting down the pull of his outraged nerves that would turn him aside, spook him into a run. He wouldn't get ten feet that way and he knew it; but it was hard—bitter hard, to limp up to that fellow, knowing what would happen if he got stopped now.

He was three feet away when the man with the rifle swung it around in grim focus. "Just a minute."

In the frozen calm of desperation everything else fell away from Turk but the black still shape of that man against lamplight. The man was not to be fooled with. It showed in the tone with which he said, "Where you off to?"

"Pick up my horse."

Although he could not make out the man's face against those lights Turk could feel the man's stare raking over him suspiciously.

"What's happened to your gun?"

Turk checked the impulse to look down at his holster. It took more will to keep his hand away from it. Some kind of trick, he thought; yet there'd been something in the way the man had asked that question that was a plain indication he was standing without a weapon. The gun had probably jounced loose coming out of that window. He said, "Over at Con Quilton's. Damn thing was gettin' too hair-triggered for safety."

For the space of three heartbeats they stared at each other. "Where's your horse?" the man said.

Crossing over Turk had noticed that one of the three at this rack, its companions, had not been tied. It stood a little apart with the reins over its neck. Having brought off one gamble, Turk now tried another. "Right behind you," he said, and knew before the words had half got out of his mouth that, this time, it wasn't going to work.

He didn't wait for the man to call him a liar. All he got was an impression of movement in the man's right shoulder but it was enough to send him into headlong action. Flame tearing out of the rifle's barrel almost blinded him. But he was into the man then, regardless of the pain, right fist driving straight and hard to the man's belly. The man staggered backward, doubled over, gasping. Turk's next blow almost unhinged the man's jaw.

Turk lunged for the pitching horses. He tripped and stretched his length with horses and lamplit buildings all scrambled together wheeling crazily around him. Waves of nausea rolled with him through a roaring sea of light streaked blackness and his left shoulder burned with all the agony of fire. He heard boots pounding toward him and someway clawed up out of the dust in time to see the frantic horses tear away with the ripped-loose tie rail. But the one with the reins up stood like a rock.

Big he was, a roan with the promise of plenty of bottom. He was trembling with excitement, one hoof pawing the ground. The whites of his eyes showed when Turk reached for him and his ears went back, his head twisting snakily. Turk's hand missed the reins and the horse reared, whirling, when Turk tried for the horn. Turk almost sobbed in frustration, but just when he figured he was caught afoot in this jackpot a man crashed out of the shadows behind him and the frightened horse spun and came plunging straight at Turk.

Swaying back, Turk grabbed and his hand hooked the horn. The horse was going like a twister when the seat of Turk's pants slicked into saddle leather.

SEVEN

HER FATHER often declared with a little shake of the head that Rosarita cared nothing for the old Spanish customs and even less for traditions which she personally considered insufferable. "Traditions," he would remark with a long face put on for the benefit of shocked listeners, "frequently affect the Little Sister with a great deal of the same emotion which causes the brave bull to go after a red flannel cape."

Rosarita sometimes smiled when she heard but she had never denied the veracity of it. Born out of her time in a land shackled by custom she believed in the inalienable right of a woman to work out her own problems—and this in a day when the women of the Americans north of the border had not as yet dared even to dream of emancipation. She was a forthright young person with more than a little of the Moor about her look and sufficient courage and intelligence to live her life in accordance with her own set of values.

She knew where to find Turk's horse, for she had discovered it while returning just now from another of her unfruitful attempts to contact the elusive Jake. Which was how she had happened so providentially to be at hand when the Curly Bill – Fred White business had gotten Turk trapped on the porch by Wyatt Earp. After seeing his horse, which she had remembered from Silver Lake, it was the most natural thing in the world for her to bide there a while, just inside the ajar door, on the chance of again catching sight of the young gringo.

There was an earnestness, a wholesome lack of sophistication, about this Turkey Red which set him apart from most of these Americans so variously going about their life's work of piling up gringo dollars. He was perhaps as uncouth and rough as the others yet she had sensed in him a difference which inexplicably attracted her.

She looked covertly about her while speaking quietly to his horse and not seeing anything which alarmed her, swung lightly up into the saddle, totally unmindful of the amount of bare leg this displayed. She was at home in the saddle as most of her nationality, having practically lived in one all of her life. She had no difficulty with High Sailin. Reining him away from the rack she directed him uptown, taking in the sights and smells of this place as any Gypsy miss might.

Opposite the Can Can she wheeled him left with her knee, turning him south on Fourth, looking over the dwindling throngs of noisy people still abroad on the splintery planks of the walks. Why were the Americans, she wondered, always so loud? This boisterousness amounted almost to a national trait like their unquenchable lust for dollars. Even their songs—at least the ones you heard most in their cities—seemed to depend for popularity on catchiness and gusto. In her own land the peons preferred more leisurely airs and their ballads most frequently told of death and unrequited love. She thought that love was perhaps her people's main preoccupation. Possibly because they generally had so little else.

She swung left again on Tough Nut Street, going past the deserted shine of lamps seeping out of the front of the Arcade Hotel. Traffic was greatly reduced in this section. Only a few rumbling ore wagons churned up the dust and most of the buildings were dark, although here and there dim flickers of light still feebly showed from the cabins of miners scattered along the right slope.

She quickened High Sailin's pace with her knees, aware that women were not expected to be abroad here at this time and that any encounters she might chance to have would be with men whom liquor had put in an unruly frame of mind. She put a hand on her leg to make sure she had her knife. Naked steel worked a salutary effect on drunken gringos.

She turned north on Fifth, sending the brown into a dark and cluttered alley they would shortly bring her quietly to the trees she had asked Turk to wait in. Before she'd gone ten yards rifle sound slammed against the walls of the buildings and she bent forward, stopping the horse, listening with caught breath to the uproar beyond them. Was the redhead out there?

Boots, ahead of her, swept into a lifting run going streetward, and that seemed answer enough. The "star packers", as Jake called them, must have surrounded the rooming house and someway flushed him into the open. With a mounting sense of insecurity she heard a further racket of rifles and panic drove her heels against the brown gelding's ribs as her twist of the reins sent him through the black murk between buildings.

Before he came out of it a rushing thunder of hoof beats tore through the shouts and the swearing, building into a wild drumming which fled south and went dim in a fading flutter of beaten pulsations. She stopped the brown horse in the alley's mouth, watching the sprinting shapes of men jerk loose knotted reins and pile into their saddles. There was still a tight constriction in her throat yet she breathed easier now, confident that Turk would elude them.

In any event it was in God's hands and she would go and light a candle beneath the Virgin's picture. Later, some time before morning, she would set out for Charleston and the corral of Frank Stilwell. Sooner or later that maddening Jake would turn up there; and who could say, since he had taken up with Bill, that this impetuous gringo of the flaming red hair might not also be found there?

* * *

CHARLESTON WAS a collection of mud and frame shacks squatted down in a crotch of the San Pedro River some ten miles from Tombstone. The "town" was kept alive by a stamp mill and by the money Curly Bill's bunch squandered in its deadfalls. The place numbered at the most perhaps five hundred persons. The muddy river crawled half around it and ancient cottonwoods gave welcome shade. There was a deal of promiscuous shooting and someone got killed nearly every night but it was more noisy than wild when you stripped the brags away from it.

Jim Burnett was the big wheel at Charleston. "Justice of the Peace" he called himself but the only peace he had ever really valued was the piece of change he could shove in his pocket. He made up his own laws and enforced them at the business end of a double-barreled shotgun. He was a "card," to use Curly Bill's own word for him.

The place was trying its enthusiastic best to be more cussed then Tombstone. There wasn't a church within ten miles of its racket. There were dancehalls and gambling dives, one hotel, a schoolhouse and a vociferous pack of mangy dogs. And that was about the size of it.

Turk assimilated most of this listening to the loafers jawing and whittling around Frank Stilwell's. It seemed to him that his wounded shoulder took unconscionably long to mend but this was probably mostly due to all the blood he had lost on that wild ride from Tombstone. Nearly two weeks had passed before he was up and around. Stilwell told him he'd come in dead beat, out of his head and "talking a blue streak." Frank said half the town had turned out to get a whack at them Earps and had stood on their guns for two solid hours before going back to their whisky and women. According to Frank, that was considerable of a tribute. Turk guessed he meant to the Earps.

Frank had bedded Turk down in the hay of his loft and by the time Turk was able to be up and around quite a few things had happened in that part of the country. Curly Bill had been tried and turned loose of White's killing and was someplace off in the hills gathering cattle. The county elections had been held and the law's tin stars had been reshuffled and, according to local tell, were apt to get reshuffled again by the look of it.

Charlie Shibell, over at Tucson, had been reelected sheriff by 47 votes. But there'd been some talk of fraud and the Earps had got the 104 votes from the San Simon district thrown out, which gave the sheriff's star to Earp's friend Bob Paul, who wasn't liked around Charleston. Curly Bill, it was hinted, had stuffed the San Simon ballot boxes; one of the names put down as a qualified voter being Hiram J. Gander which, upon investigation, was found to belong to a rooster owned by a Galeyville boarding house proprietor. Several cows, it was contended, had also voted. But Shibell had gone to the courts with his case and Wyatt Earp had stood off a mob of five hundred who had aimed to hang a gambler known as Johnny-Behind-the-Deuce. In spite of the thrown-out votes, however, popular Johnny Behan had kept his deputy's job, which suited the folks at Charleston right down to the cracked earth's grass roots.

Turk, not much interested in politics, let the most of this talk go in one ear and out the other. But Wyatt Earp, he learned, was still packing *his* badge and, being Federal, it was good all over the country. Another thing he heard was that rustlers had raided the Roman 4 and got off with 300 head of prime beef. He wished that he could have helped them.

But the old sap was stirring. The hole in his shoulder was pretty well scabbed over and he was anxious to earn his keep. He thought this morning that he would eat uptown and grinned at the tough look of himself thrown back by the water in the horse trough where he'd sluiced off his face and slicked back his shaggy mane. He guessed he'd ought to stake himself to a shave.

The broncs in the pen were all eating their heads off. He saw Frank with some other gents hunkered out front, passing gab and interminably whittling. Billy Clanton was one of them and Tom McLowery was there and old Jim Hughes with his jaw full of brown tobacco and a black browed hombre he reckoned was Jake Gauze. It was this black browed one that seemed to be doing the bulk of the talking. He broke off when Turk came up.

Frank Stilwell rasped his round cheeks and said, "Turkey, I guess you know Jake—he just rode in from Pine Mesa. Curly's over in Galeyville. Jake's fetched the word we're to all go over there day after tomorrer."

Jake Gauze, a sour lumpy toad of a man, threw Stilwell a riled look. "You don't have to tell the whole country about it."

"Hell, Turk's all right. He's with us," McLowery said— "you heard Bill take him on yourself."

Gauze backed around to his horse and got onto him. "The only stranger I'd trust is a dead one," he snarled and, raking his bronc with the steel, rode off.

"Crazy as a gopher," Hughes grunted, shaking his head.

McLowery stared after Gauze disgusted. "He'll give us trouble one of these days. All he thinks about is killin'."

Billy Clanton grinned. "He's got plenty of company. Curly's shore some riled over the way Wyatt buffaloed him that night of White's passin'."

"This place is too handy to Tombstone," Hughes said.

McLowery's lip curled. "Bill ain't forgetting that and I ain't either. Them goddam Earps is ridin' for a fall." He twisted his head around to scowl at Billy Clanton. "Got them fellers located?"

"Most of 'em," Clanton chuckled. "Give us another couple months and we'll have every waterhole from Mexico to the Muggyones. We kin ride from hell to breakfast an' never sight a hostile rifle."

He noticed Hughes looked at Turk and quit talking. Turk felt suddenly uncomfortable and couldn't think why he should. It was no skin off his nose if they wanted to grab all the waterholes. Far as he'd ever heard the Clantons and McLowerys were up-and-coming ranchers. Sure they probably drifted off a few loose cows when opportunity offered, but everyone did that. It was the way you got a brand built up. Nothing but common practice.

Turk's glance went beyond young Clanton just then and through the bars of the corral he saw the horse that had brought him from Tombstone that night and idly wondered what the animal was doing here. Frank Stilwell had told him he'd taken care of that horse, which he'd supposed to have meant the man had got rid of him. It kind of gave him a shock to see the horse still around. He was about to take it up with Frank when Jim Hughes allowed he'd better be getting himself an outfit. "And nothin' fancy," he said as Turk reluctantly got up. "Man could see that white shirt you're wearin' forty foot away at night." And Stilwell said, "I'll stake you to a bronc. Git yourself a rifle an' cartridges."

Frank pitched away his stick and got up and closing his knife dropped it into his pocket. After rummaging awhile he finally fetched out his purse. "If you're short I might lend you a couple of bucks, though Bunny won't like it."

He was always dragging "Bunny" into any talk that touched on finances. "I'll make out," Turk said. "This Bunny you're always bringin' up... Who is she—your wife?"

"No," Frank said while some of the others showed grins, "though I don't much misdoubt but what the thought has occurred to her." He brushed the shavings off his pantlegs and looked up at Turk kind of sly like. "Speakin' of women, what you figurin' to do about yourn?"

"Mine!" Turk gasped. He stared in confusion and his face felt as though it must be twice as red as fire. "I don't know what you're talkin' about!"

"Might be you don't at that," Frank conceded—"she only come round while you was outen your head. Dang good thing Bunny wasn't here, by gollies—heavin' my bottle of horse medicine right through that new winder light! Said she'd brew up her own stuff, an' never left your side fer two whole days an' nights. Hell, I s'posed you knowed all about her."

"If he don't," Clanton chuckled, "he can find out quick enough. She's got her a job over at Jawbone Clark's." And McLowery said, "You better ease up on her careful. She give Milt Hicks a whole quart of forty-rod in the puss—bottle an' all. Said she didn't care for the way Milt was eyein' her!"

Hughes' head went back in a belly shaking guffaw as Turk wheeled away with burning ears. Frank called after him but Turk kept going; and Billy Clanton chortled, "Watch out fer that left leg, boy—she's got a knife up her garter."

Turk kicked a horse apple hell west and crooked. He felt wild enough to halfway consider whirling around and taking the whole works on. He knew well enough now what girl they were talking about and, while he was relieved in a way to know it hadn't been Holly, the thought of that dancer following him here sure graveled him. It made him more embarrassed than ever to think of her up there pawing him over and him not even knowing a damn thing about it.

For perhaps a dozen strides he heard their whoops and guffaws and then he caught the squeak of a gate hinge and the lifting thud of hoof sound, but was too riled by then to look around and see what was happening. Like a door had been shut, all sound abruptly ceased.

In spite of himself, Turk slowed. These were Curly Bill's friends, and maybe he *was* acting the part of a chump to be showing resentment of their rough banter. Perhaps he was inclined to set too great a store on dignity; this hoorahing could be a first if rather boisterous indication of that which he prized most—acceptance, an acknowledgment that he was one of them. All his life he had wanted to belong, to be an accepted part of something; maybe it hadn't been his youth so much as temper which had barred him. At least their laughter wasn't hostile, as the look of that cross-grained Jake Gauze had been.

Turk stopped on this thought, and it came over him then with cold chills running through him that the silence around him had become too intense. He suddenly wanted to turn and was afraid to.

"Get off my horse!" the angry voice said flatly.

"Get out of the way or I'll run you down!"

That was Clanton. Not fooling, either. Something was winding up to happen back there, something coldly wicked, something ugly... Turk's head twisted.

Jim Hughes with all his whiskers, round-faced Frank and Tom McLowery made still and brittle shapes against the bars of the corral. Billy Clanton, about six lengths from the enclosure, was mounted on the horse that Turk had ridden here from Tombstone. Square in his way sat Wyatt Earp on another. He had a hand clapped to gun butt and his eyes gleamed like blue agate. "Get off," he said again, "and get that saddle off."

Clanton's look was black with anger but he got down and pulled his gear off. Earp's boots struck the ground and he walked up and put a rope around the blue roan's neck. He spun abruptly, yanking Clanton's pistols from their leathers. "You won't be needing these for a while. I'll be leaving them in the road for you on the other side of the bridge."

They stood glaring at each other through the frozen breath-locked quiet. "If I thought," Earp said at last, "you were the one that stole this horse from me I'd settle your hash right now."

Those were fighting words and the lash of his stare left no doubt in Turk's mind that he meant them to be so, yet nobody moved or even batted an eyelash.

With a grimace of contempt Earp swung into his saddle. He sat shortening the rope he had put on the roan and was turning the one he was on around when Billy Clanton snarled on an outrush of breath. "Next time it won't be that bronc we'll git but *you!*"

Earp gave him a long hard look. "Any time," he said thinly. "Make your play whenever it suits you and fetch all the friends you've a mind to."

He lifted his reins and cantered off up the trail.

* * *

FOR A COUPLE of moments no one said anything.

Turk felt mortified for them, almost ashamed to have seen the man face these boys down. All his thoughts were in turmoil, his sense of fitness shaken, his scale of values threatening to crumble before his eyes. Were these Bill's friends that suddenly looked so much like coyotes?

He heard whiskered Jim Hughes let his breath out and watched him slump emptily down on his boot heels. McLowery wiped a hand against his pants and looked at Stilwell. Clanton slammed around and loosed a spate of rough talk. Frank said, "Mebbe Bill was right to shift headquarters over to Galeyville."

Clanton raked Frank with the edge of mean eyes. "Just because—"

But Turk had heard all he cared to. He felt too letdown and smothery-miserable to want to listen to any more of these fellows' jawing. He turned away like a man on his first trip with stilts and headed blindly uptown, bitter-squirming with the knowledge of what one kill-crazy badge toter could do to four of Bill's friends without even raising his voice.

EIGHT

IT SURE GAVE him something to chew on.

By the time he'd got up to where he could see Cruikshank's barber pole his thoughts had swung around to viewing things considerably closer, like the almighty narrow margin with which he had come out of that deal himself. Only for walking off like he had, with the boisterous racket of their ragging hooting after him, he'd probably now—like that horse—be on his way back to Tombstone! It had been God's own mercy Wyatt Earp hadn't noticed him.

He thought maybe he'd be wise to change his mind about that shave. This red fuzz along his cheeks and the bend of his jaws wasn't near as hard to take as the prospect of feeling a rope around his neck. He had just been plain lucky and that was all there was to it. He thought now he might have been a shade harsh in his judgment of Clanton and McLowery and of Frank and old Jim. Maybe there was more to living than things seen bold in blacks and whites. Maybe there was gray shades, too, that tended to get lost most times in issues more apparent.

Turk was a little astonished to find the way his mind could slip around to other views. Before he'd come to Jawbone Clark's the most of the gimp had worked out of his legs and the turn of his thoughts had taken on sharper focus. Maybe Curly Bill's friends had damn good reason for letting Wyatt Earp tongue lash them like he had; it was possible Bill's own orders had stood in the way of their natural reactions. There might be wheels within wheels he didn't know anything about.

He was willing to leave it at that for the moment. He wasn't even riled now at the thought of Rosarita taking so much on herself and brazenly following him down here. But on one thing he stood firm: If Bill had moved his headquarters like that talk back there had hinted, it hadn't been on account of he was scairt of that damned marshal. Turk knew this man too well for that. Curly Bill wasn't scairt of anything!

Turk had been aiming to go and have a talk with that dancer but decided to put it off. He bent his steps toward the Mercantile and, still with his thoughts whirling around pretty free like, was passing the Eagle Hotel when a man said so close he caught a whiff of his breath, "Jumpin' crawfishes, boy—git hold of the bit an' pull up here a moment!"

Turk sent a hand toward his holster, then dropped it, looking sheepish. It was Tex Willbrandt talking, and he'd been doing his share of drinking by the wavery way he stood there.

"Hi, Tex," Turk said, and the rusty-haired man grinned, beckoning him over beside the porch where he had managed to anchor bony shoulders against the rail.

"Been lookin' fer you," he grumbled, peering around and lowering gruff voice to a conspiratorial whisper. "Bill's got a job fer you," he said, loudly belching. He got a handful of Turk's gambler's shirt in his fist and wobbly-legged led him around the side of the building. He was sucking on one of those everlasting peppermints but the reek of cheap whisky was so all-fired potent the lozenge smell had hard work getting through. He loosed a couple of hiccups and tugged Turk, stooping, under the alamosas' branches. "Wantcha t' meet two of my buddies," he wheezed and, at a table set back in the sundappled shadows, Turk saw the riled faces of two men looking at him.

Tex introduced them as Charlie Thomas and John Ringo. They were dressed like most of Bill's bunch in puncher garb, and both had guns strapped around their middles and wore big hats and had bright spurs on their expensive looking boots. Thomas would have looked right at home with Linderstrom's outfit, having the earmarks of a gun hand; but the other fellow, Ringo, was something else again.

Turk was plenty impressed, having heard more than a little about John Ringo. He had the face of a discouraged preacher and about as large a reputation as the Earps' friend Doc Holliday. He was an educated man, Turk had heard, and one of the real he-catawampuses of Curly Bill's outfit. It was said he drank to drown a secret sorrow and was related to the Youngers.

Turk gave them the kind of nod Curly favored. Ringo grunted. Charlie Thomas just stared. Tex said, "Turkey, Bill wants you to come a-runnin'—wants you over there to Galeyville quick as you kin git there. Ain't that right, gents? Didn't—"

"Another of his grandstand plays," Ringo snorted, "like plugging Fred White right under Earp's nose."

Turk would have had to been green as Sulphur Valley grass not to have caught the biting sarcasm of that; and he looked at Ringo, surprised and half minded to put the man straight, only Tex, with a fleeting glance at Turk's face and looking suddenly almost sober, said too quick for him, "Aw, you know Bill never meant nothin' like that, John. You heard what Earp said. That gun went off accidental. White had holt of the barrel—"

"And you never thought that was funny?" Contempt twisted Ringo's handsome face. "You've watched him practice that roll by the hour, same as I have. I say he handed that gun to White butt first."

"You're just sore," Tex said, "account of—"

"You bet I'm sore," Ringo growled, and went back to his drinking. "No curly-haired bastard is going to short-change me!"

Tex caught hold of Turk's arm and pulled him away from them. "C'mon boy," he said, "I got somethin' out here t' show you." He led Turk around to the back of the hotel and there was High Sailin, standing on his reins and with a new saddle on him looking chipper as forty jay birds. The horse let out a little whicker and came up and nuzzled Turk's shoulder.

Willbrandt grinned. "Cripes, you *are* tickled, ain'tcha! Bill allowed you would be. You'll prob'ly find him at Babcock's bar. You better git right over there. I got the idea this deal is important."

* * *

GALEYVILLE WAS a boom silver camp strewn along the damp rim of a dark stony mesa thrust out of an ash and sycamore tangle that was Turkey Creek Canyon on the San Simon side of the Cherrycow Mountains. The place had been named for John H. Galey who'd struck oil in the East and was still taking ore from the discovery mine. Since no usable wagon roads were available and transportation was reduced to what a fellow could pack out on burros, he had put in a smelter. The main section of the community flanked the rim of this sawed-flat hill, with the dives and the stores all facing the bottoms across the broad width of what passed for the street. All, that is, but Nick Babcock's bar which was the biggest of the lot and had the whole other side of the town to itself with its back side squatted right above the gurgling creek.

There was a live oak growing out in front of Nick's place and under its shade Bill was comfortably ensconced in an old fashioned rocker. He had a bottle of beer in one big fist and his six-shooter barking from each jump of the other.

He was picking off a line of empty whisky containers set up on their necks in the middle of the road. Quite a crowd had collected and Turk could see the glass fly every time Bill squeezed trigger—he was sure suspending business in that dive across the way. While he was poking fresh loads in the cylinder, one of those gents standing nearest cried, "Yippee—watch this!" and, grabbing out his own iron, drove a .45 slug right through his own left leg. He yelled like a stuck pig while all the rest of the hyenas laughed fit to kill themselves—all but Curly.

He reared out of his chair with a disgusted grunt.

"This yere roadagent's spin ain't fer clowns an' damn fools! Takes a sharp sense of timin' an' you got to know how to do it. Put your finger in the guard," he growled, "with the gun held upside down, butt forward." He proceeded to demonstrate, pinwheeling the heavy Colt's around the hub of his finger and banging away every time the barrel leveled. When he got done there wasn't a whole bottle out there.

Turk watched him punching out the spent ones, replacing them with live shells thumbed from his belt. Bill's glance, coming up and around, crossed Turk's face and he put the big pistol away with a nod. Turk took this to mean that their talk was to be private.

He rode on, picking his way through the still-grabbing tatters of the dispersing crowd and sliding down from his horse in front of Nick's batwings. He let go of the reins and pushed through the weather-grayed half-leaf doors, backing up against a wall while his eyes, narrowed now, compensated for the dimness after all that outside glare. The place was practically empty. A drowsy looking gent with his shirt off back of the bar was trying to entice a botfly to light enough to hit him.

Curly Bill came in and Turk followed him to the bar—the longest one he had ever seen, painted black as a coffin and crisscrossed and splintered with the tracks of old battles. Bill twisted his head and gave him a grin. "You name it, kid."

"Whatever you want'll be good enough for me."

Bill reared back and slapped the bar. "Hear that, Kelly?" he whooped, laughing. "We're goin' to make a real hand outa this 'un!"

The apron tried a grin for size. If flapped a little around the edges but Turk didn't care and reckoned Bill never noticed. It felt like coming home to be around him; good to hear the boom of that rollicking laughter. As he had in the past, he again stored up in his mind how Bill stood, how he carried himself, that bold and confident roll of his eyes. Turk would have given five years of his life to be like him; and Bill told the barkeep, "A bottle of your best and a pair of clean glasses, for my friend Turkey Red has rode a long way to git here." And he flashed Turk a wink.

Kelly set them on the bar. "Fetch 'em along," Bill said, and Turk packed them in the back room after him, trying to give to his walk the same roll Bill's had. He put the stuff on a table while Bill was shutting the door.

Pulling up a chair Bill sat down across from Turk. He knocked the neck off the bottle and filled both their glasses. "Here's mud in your eye!" Bill tossed his off and, putting down the glass, settled both elbows on the table with a confidential nod. "How well do you know that old goat at Roman 4?"

Bill was like that, one minute talking like a grubline rider and the next using words that had you fighting your hat to get a line on their meaning. "You mean Ruebusch?" Turk said, stalling.

Bill filled up their glasses again, and still with that half smile quirking his mouth corners, nodded.

Turk tried to hold his voice level and speak as casual as Bill had, but the craving to get back at that bunch for setting the law on him was too strong for containment. "We could snatch that old coot blind!" he cried.

Bill pushed his glass around, edging its bottom into the rings on the table. He didn't seem to have heard Turk. "How much store does he put on that fluff he's got? Would he put up hard cash to git her back, do you reckon?"

Turk stared like he couldn't believe his own ears. "You mean...Holly?" he gulped.

Bill looked right back at him and his eyes, of a sudden, did not seem quite so twinkly. Then he was nodding again, big and sure; the Bill Turk remembered. "You been around there some, ain't you? How'd that pair strike you? Reckon he'd go fer five thousand?"

Turk couldn't think in that first stunned surprise; he could only sit there, jaw hanging, like he didn't have all his buttons.

"It wouldn't be so tough," Bill grinned. "But would he go for it? Would he go to five g's to git her back in his bed?"

Turk could feel the sweat cracking out against his collar. He couldn't get the tongue down off the roof of his mouth.

The upper lids of Bill's eyes kind of tightened a little, the creases deepening at their corners. "You ain't sick, kid, are you?"

"Gosh, Bill...I dunno," Turk said.

"You don't know what—if you're sick or if he'd go fer it?"

Turk tried to pull himself together. He reckoned Bill was figuring to work this deal for him, to square Turk's account with Roman 4 and at the same time to pick up a few bucks for his brother. Turk tried to put the uglier side of it out of his mind. It hadn't occurred to Bill, of course, how Turk might feel about Holly; and it wasn't anything that he could talk to Bill about. Loose one breath of suspicion and a girl's good name was gone.

Turk squirmed in his chair, hardly knowing what to say but all too keenly aware that he had got to say something. And then some other things crossed his mind and he saw he'd got to convince Bill that there were less risky ways. He shook his head. "Too much chance of somethin' goin' haywire. Town like this ..." He shook his head more emphatically. "I don't expect in the first place we could ever git hold of her—"

"You needn't fret about that."

"And besides," Turk said, desperate, "while I don't mind runnin' off a few steers or horses, it would sure go plumb again' my grain to get mixed up with—"

"You won't git mixed up with it," Bill pushed Turk's glass at him. "She's already grabbed."

The place got so still you could hear the birds in those trees beyond the window and the scuff of boots going past outside. "Hell," Curly laughed, "you don't need to look so damn solemn. Drink up—time's awasting," he said, shoving back in his chair and thrusting his legs out. He stretched burly arms, yawning. "A well setup piece...I guess he'll kick in, all right."

Turk wasn't half hearing him. He had to lick his lips twice to get the words out. "When'd you grab her?"

"Couple or three weeks ago. You don't need to worry, she ain't damaged none—yet. Most of the boys don't even know she's here, and"

Turk was back in Tucson at that place on South Meyer, seeing Holly's face again, hearing her say, "You crazy damn fool—" when he'd bragged he'd join Bill. The vision blurred and then cleared with him frozen to that walk on Allen Street in Tombstone, staring at Ruebusch's mottled features, seeing the wild shine of his half-crazy eyes. Turk knew what the end of that question was now; and there was a kind of gale whirling around the inside of him and his thoughts wouldn't track, but he understood now what had pushed Ruebusch at him. The goddamn chump thought his wife had run off with Turk!

Bill was looking at him, curious. Turk pushed a hand across his damp cheeks. A sick emptiness was inside him and he caught up the refilled glass and drained it, gagging on the stuff and having to fight to get his breath but someway wishing he'd had to fight longer.

He wanted mightily to tell Bill Ruebusch wouldn't pay. But he knew he couldn't do that, scared of what might happen. Pretty near anything could happen in a place like this. He couldn't even tell Bill how he felt himself about Holly—or could he? Was there some way he could enlighten Bill without revealing all?

If there was, Turk couldn't find it. Nor dared he ask where they were holding her.

Bill pushed to his feet, stood considering him a moment. "You better git some rest, kid. Got a heap of ridin' to do in the mornin.' We'll talk of this again."

But Turk couldn't leave it there. Confused, uncertain, horribly afraid for her, he got out of his chair, catching Bill's arm as Bill turned toward the door. "What if he won't pay?"

Bill's head came around, eyes quartering over Turk's face like steel fingers. "You got any reason to think he won't?"

Turk's glance fell away with the hopelessness of it; and he stood there knowing his mouth was open and not finding any words with Bill seeming so still and terribly strange of a sudden. It was like he wasn't the same person.

Then the frozen rigidity was gone and Bill grinned. "You better hit the hay, kid. Way you look now you couldn't ride nothin' wilder than a wheelchair. What's happened to your gun?"

Turk's hand went like a sleepwalker to his waist, then he remembered. "Lost it," he muttered, "gettin' out of a window."

"And ain't got the price of another, eh?" Bill sloshed a hand in his pocket, flipped a gold piece at Turk and said, "Go over to Harbaker's an' git yourself heeled. Kelly'll fix you up with a bed. I'll see you later."

NINE

TURK FELT PLAIN SICK.

How long he stood eyeing the closed door after Bill left he never knew. Time had no meaning. Nothing had meaning but the fact of Holly's capture; that she was somewhere in this town and had been here, Bill's prisoner, for more than two weeks. At first it hadn't seemed possible, but now that his shocked mind had had more chance to grasp it he was able to see how it tied in with other things, like Ruebusch jumping him and that rustler's raid that had taken 300 head of cattle from Ruebusch's ranch—that was when they'd grabbed her, probably.

He picked up the double eagle that had rolled beneath the table and thrust it absently in his pocket. He could imagine her feelings, the awful strain she must have been under, the desperation of knowing she was finished with Roman 4. Ruebusch, feeling as he did, would never take her back now—or would he?

The man had obviously seen or been told something which had caused him to distrust Turk's relations with the girl. Else, when she'd disappeared, he would not have been so quick to believe she'd gone to Turk, as the man plainly did. No, Turk thought morosely, Ruebusch would have washed his hands of her by now.

In the present confused state of his emotions Turk entirely overlooked the man's most likely reaction, the natural desire for revenge which he would almost certainly be nursing, a desire bound to have been whetted by their recent clash in Tombstone. All Turk could think of in this moment was that he'd got to find Holly and someway get her out of Bill's hands and away from here. Bill would shortly—if indeed he hadn't already—be dispatching a demand for her ransom.

Turk could understand Bill's place in this. It was obvious. Bill couldn't help himself. He'd been trapped in this deal just as surely as Turk was. Some of his bunch—guys like Thomas and Gauze—had grabbed the girl with an eye to what her husband would give to get her back safe and sound, and had probably told Bill he'd better ask for five thousand. It was as simple as that —and what could Bill do? His control of this bunch must be a delicate business; they'd never stand for him turning her loose without a payoff ...

This brought other considerations to Turk's mind. Like what the bunch would do if Turk himself succeeded in freeing her—the spot it would put Bill in, and himself.

He went out the back door and walked around to High Sailin and got his shell belt and holster and headed across the road, looking for Harbaker's, which he reckoned would be either a gun shop or mercantile.

It turned out to be a general store with a case and gun rack off at the left rear behind the leather goods and horse furniture. Turk counted it lucky he still had a few bucks of his own and bought, first of all, a dark blue shield-fronted shirt and a black neckerchief to go with it. He also paused to look at some hats but finally decided to make the one he had do till he was in greater funds.

Picking his way through the saddles and stacked blankets and the head stalls and harness hanging from pegs, he went over to the gun case. There he purchased a single action Colt's .45 after trying out several for heft and balance. He slipped it into his scuffed holster and got a box of cartridges although he still had a few in the loops of his belt. Made him feel kind of mean, in a way, arming himself with Bill's money for a project which, if he could bring it off, would practically amount to double-crossing Bill.

Back at Babcock's bar, after he'd put up his horse, he braced Kelly about the chances for a bed. There was a balcony built out around two sides of the room and there were doors opening off it which he reckoned most likely was where the beds would be. Kelly, twisting his neck, took a look up the stairs and Turk, turning also, saw Bill coming down them.

"Fix him up," Bill said and, coming over, stopped beside Turk, giving him a poke in the ribs with his elbow. "See you got your pistol," he grinned, "an' what's this—a new shirt? Good idea," he nodded, approving Turk's choice of colors. He tossed the barkeep a key. "I sent a man off with the news to our friend. Mebbe he won't be feelin' so high an' mighty now. We'll show him, by God, who's runnin' this country! Outside of right around here, who ever heard of old man Ruebusch? But they've all heard of me, kid—clean up to Washin'ton!"

His laugh rang around the walls of the room and came back to give him a kind of pat on the shoulder. It was the truth, though, Turk thought; and then his eyes narrowed down as the batwings flapped and Jake Gauze came into the place. The same perpetual beard stubble darkened his cheeks and the high flat face, as he came to a stop, showed a sullen resentment as his glance locked with Turk's. And then his look jumped at Bill. "What's he doin' here?"

Bill showed his gold tooth. "You got the deal all lined up?"

"I ain't talkin' in front of no blabbermouth kid!"

Turk, flushing, started forward. Bill's arm hauled him back; and Bill's elbow, digging Turk's ribs, fetched a grunt that was lost in Bill's laugh as Bill said, "Ever see a more roundabout guy in your life, kid? Jake's so damn careful he has to git a drink from the dipper! Haw haw haw!"

Jake glared, swung around and went stomping out.

"Hell," Bill said, "now he's mad again, dammit. You go on an' ketch that shut-eye—Kelly'll give you a shout when we're ready to ride." He slapped Turk's shoulder and wheeled off after Gauze.

* * *

"BAD ACTOR, THAT FELLER," Kelly said, shaking his head. "Killed the Brayton boys here in a flare-up last week—meaner than a centipede with chilblains."

"Speakin' of centipedes," Turk said, "You got anythin' I can chew on?"

"You can hev a couple of these," Kelly grunted, setting a plate of picked-over sandwiches on the bar.

They didn't look very fresh but Turk bit into one anyway, reckoning they'd stay his hunger till he found time for something better. He put five of them away and then got a beer to slosh them down with. "You don't seem to have much business," he remarked.

"Little early yet," Kelly said with a sniff. "When that smelter bunch knocks off we'll hev three aprons busy." He waved a hand at the stairs. "Better kitch that sleep now if you aim to; goin' to get a mite noisy come lamp lightin' time."

When Turk still stood there, the barkeep said, again waving at the stairs, "Just take any of them rooms that's empty," and went back to polishing glasses.

Turk climbed the stairs and pushed open the first door he came to, tossing the paper-sacked shirt on the rumpled blanket-covered bed that left just enough space to bypass it to the window, which Turk went to as soon as he had pushed shut the door. He didn't see much that looked to offer any help. There were trees outside but none he could get into; their roots were in the creek and it was too far to risk a drop.

Turk didn't like it. The narrow six-by-ten cell—which was all it really amounted to—gave him a feeling of being trapped, yet he knew if he tried to go somewhere else now the move would be regarded with suspicion. If he was to help Holly at all he would have to proceed with a great deal of caution, because he sure wasn't going to help anyone dead. And he could be dead damned quick if he was caught in this caper.

He pulled off the white shirt he'd been wearing since Silver Lake and, regretting there wasn't a washbowl or water in the room, got into the blue one, more than half minded to go out and hunt up a barber. He realized he was deliberately trying to put off thinking about Holly and, though he was all tangled up in his mind about her, he reckoned a real man would face it.

He didn't know what ailed him really. Everything seemed to be all mixed up and nothing appeared to be the way he'd always had it figured. His whole scale of values looked to be busted wide open and even Curly Bill, by God, that Turk would have sworn was unchangeable as rock, didn't seem like he had when Turk was drawing down his wages at Ruebusch's Roman 4.

He put his coat back on and his hat and went down the stairs.

Kelly, back of the bar, was still yawning on his glasses, and there was a couple of fellows with their elbows hooked over it and one of them was Thomas that he had met with John Ringo that morning outside Charlie Tarbell's Eagle Hotel at Charleston. He was so narrow between the ears Turk guessed he could look through a keyhole with both eyes at once.

"I'm goin' to scout up a barber," Turk said with a nod at the barkeep, "and see about gettin' myself a soak in his tub."

"Across the street," Kelly waved, "about ten doors down."

Turk had to wait his turn at the tub so he let the fellow shave him to help pass the time. After the barber had put powder on his face with a kid's-size feather duster, Turk guessed he might as well go ahead and roach his mane while he was at it. "Reckon you're kind of new around here," the barber said after he'd run through the most of his jokes. "You don't look like a miner. Guess you're figurin' to latch on with Curly Bill's bunch."

Turk let it ride. The barber frowned but kept snipping. He wet Turk's hair down with some fancy smelling stuff which he shook out of an opaque bottle. When he pulled off the striped sheet and Turk had paid him, he said, "You kin go along in there now if you want to."

Turk felt a heap better when he got out of the tub. The sun was heeling low in the west, putting an edging of color around the knobs of the Three Sisters and a few of those nearer peaks and deepening and darkening the shapes of some of the others. He was remembering the key Bill had tossed the barkeep and beginning to do some tall wondering about it.

Kelly, when he got back, was setting out some fresh sandwiches and Turk helped himself to a couple as he passed. The narrow-faced Thomas and his hard-eyed companion were still anchored to the foot rail nursing a pair of whiskies. Thomas said, "Red, I want you to know Charlie Snow."

And to Snow: "This is the jigger that put that winder in Fanshaw."

Turk didn't care for the tone of that last nor for the look he got from Snow's brightening glance but he gave them a Curly Bill nod and went on up the stairs. Night was closing down fast and there was something he wanted to do before Kelly got around to lighting the lamps.

He heard more guys coming in and pushed open his door, closing it again without entering the room, standing there listening to the mutter of voice sounds, concealed from the men down below by the overhang.

Very cautiously then he tried the next door and the door just beyond, trying to locate the one Bill had used that key on. The third door wouldn't give and Turk put an ear against it, twisting the knob again and hearing with quickened breathing the faint screak of springs beyond it.

Was this the one? Was this where they had her?

He caught the pad of bare feet moving around inside and his heart got to thumping and a mounting excitement almost choked off his breathing. He was totally unprepared for the door's sudden opening and lurched forward, off balance, almost impaling himself on the cold steel of the knife the girl held in front of her blanket-wrapped shape.

He stumbled back in alarm; and that was when he realized the scurvy deal he'd got from fate. With that window back of the girl he couldn't make out her features but even in this gloom he knew it wasn't Holly's hair.

TEN

THE ROOM LOOKED VERY MUCH like the one he'd changed his shirt in except there wasn't any blanket on the bed; it was around the girl. She clutched it to her with the hand that held the knife, pulling him away from the door with the other one, sending it shut with the push of a foot. Now the light from the window fell across her face and the look of her eyes, still surprised, revealed pleasure. And the edges of something else which eluded him.

"So you have followed me here, Turkey Red." She spoke softly, almost wonderingly, more as though the words were for herself than for him. "I am glad," she said simply; and moved back a little, away from him. "If you will step outside a moment I'll get into my—"

Turk's harsh growl cut her off. "I didn't come here to talk." Anger was beginning to work up through the shock of his disappointment and he glared at her, forgetful in his suspicion, of what this girl had done for him. What he had seized on in the confusion of his teeming thoughts was that she was turning up too often for coincidence.

A concerned look twisted her gamin features and she said quickly, "Your shoulder hurts?"

"Hell with my shoulder!" But he was remembering now those two nights and those days she'd spent nursing him through that delirium in Frank's loft, and it made him look an ungrateful cur; but he went on with it anyway, determined in his baffled rage to get this business of her settled anyhow. "I want to know why you been follerin' me around!"

"But I haven't," she said; and then her face changed its shape and she clutched her blanket tighter with scorn coming into the flash of her eyes. "Hoh!" she said, flinging back her black hair and staring him up and down with thinned lips. "What gives you this idea, eh? You got poco dinero—a lot of money, maybe? Many horses?"

"Never mind," Turk growled. "I don't want you follerin' me. I got troubles enough without you mixin' into them!"

She looked at him carefully. Gave a hard little laugh. She swapped her hold on the blanket and with no other warning came straight for him with the knife.

Turk had never heard of The Woman Scorned but he was certainly in the way of collecting a first-hand sample of some very stormy reactions. He got a glimpse of bare flesh as she let go of the blanket and after that he was much too taken up with trying to keep from getting skewered to have any time for sightseeing.

He tried to get hold of her wrist and very nearly got his throat slit. He backed away from her, panting. She followed, eyes watching for a chance to get at him. The flats of his shoulders hit the wood of the door.

It was the end of the line. He couldn't go any farther without pulling it open. He couldn't do that without twisting around and he dared not take his eyes off her that long. He said, "For Christ's sake, Rita!" and sweat dripped off his chin.

Her eyes were like live coals shining at him, the measured slap of her feet a voodoo beat from the jungle. He glimpsed the plunging glint of the knife and winced away from it, dragging his back down the scrape of the door as the gleaming steel sheathed its length in the upper panel.

Before she could yank it loose he had hold of her. She fought with the silent fury of a wildcat. To get under that blade he'd gone into a squat and now he had no chance to pull out of it. The advantage lay with her and she used it, angrily driving a knee into his chest. She grabbed a handful of hair and banged his head against the door. He got both arms around her legs and strove desperately to throw her. It wrenched her grip from the knife. She went down on her back and it shook the breath out of her.

This apparently enraged her. She grew wilder than ever. She slammed a knee into his face and the whole room went black and rocked in a shuddering blaze of bursting lights. When he dragged up his hands something hit him in the stomach. Half-crazy with pain he clouted her then and when he heard her cry out he clouted her again. She fell away from him, limp; and in that cessation of hostilities he heard boots on the stairs.

He was too sick to get up. Even desperate as he was with their approach he couldn't make it. He heard the boots split up as though they moved in two directions, and one portion of this sound was obviously coming nearer. Turk did what he could. "Get away from there —" he growled through the rasp of his breathing. "Can't a man have a gut ache without the whole camp gettin' in on it?"

He heard the boots mill to a standstill, caught the mutter of whispers. Someone laughed nastily. The boots reluctantly moved off down the stairs and, outside, a lift of wind whirled through the massed foliage, tossing a clack of branch ends against the back wall of the building.

When the tension finally went out of him, Turk felt weak as a dish rag. He would have killed anyone who came through that door then. It was a sobering thought and he considered it, trying to dig up the cause for such a feeling and wondering where this crazy streak was taking him. Then it was the girl's queer stillness that was troubling him and he stared to push himself up, shamed and regretful and halfway worried he might have hurt her.

He couldn't see why these things always happened to him; and in the confused tangle of his bitter thoughts the frustration that was in him cried out against the uncaring way fate was using him. He'd never asked for much of anything. Just the chance to be a part of what went on around him, to have a feeling of belonging—his own small share of that respect men gave to others.

He shoved up onto an elbow and in the graying gloom saw the girl's eyes flutter open. She knocked the arm off from under him. He came down onto her like a sack of dropped feed, his chin jarring into a firm but yielding surface. A whimpering cry rushed out of her, but instead of striking back at him she locked both arms around his neck; and abruptly their mouths had got someway tight together and he could feel the fierce way she was straining her shape against him. He felt the thump of her heart; and her lips, responsive now with passion, made him increasingly excited; and amazed to find himself liking this—and kind of half angered too— he pulled away from her, struggling to get onto his feet.

She whispered something he didn't catch, and said, "Is this how the gringos ..." letting the rest of it go, reaching up for him. "Turkey—now!" she cried in a stifled voice; and aghast, he whirled to his feet. Embarrassed, revolted, he stumbled blindly toward the door, hardly conscious of what he was doing, knowing only the need to get out and away from her. Ought to be horsewhipped, his seething mind told him, rolling around with this half-growed strumpet and Holly, a prisoner, not a rope's cast away!

Not a rope's cast away...

The words plunged through him like stones through a millrace, rooting him there, rigid stiff with eyes staring and the split-up sound of those boots noisily tramping across the whirl of his thoughts.

The blood pounded into his throat, almost choking him with the conviction of Holly's nearness. And then his shifting glance picked up the haft of that knife skewered into the door where the girl had driven it. He spun round to see her standing with the blanket clutched about her, winklessly watching him.

Hating himself he went back to her. Led her over to the bed and sat down with her. It turned him sick to see that expression of hope breaking through the confusion which had stopped her tongue's clatter, to feel that cold little hand closing round his own. But it was the only chance he could see. He had to do it. He couldn't get that key from the barkeep himself.

Her hand squeezed his. "Take me with you. I am strong. I can ride. I will cook for you and sometimes at night when the moon is low I will bring my gifts through the shadows of your blanket. Even though it pleases you to beat me...and I will not ask for the marriage."

In spite of everything it touched him. Her heightened color, the strange mingling of shyness with pride in the way the words came out of her, almost weakened his resolve until his mind threw back at him the coincidence of her turning up at Tombstone, Charleston and now here at Babcock's, and the things Arch had said at Silver Lake to Flack about her. He pulled his hand away impatiently.

She must have sensed what he was thinking. At least she told him she'd been hunting for her brother—a half-brother, really, the son of her father's first wife, it appeared; a bad lot who had caused the old man much worry. "But he cannot see it," she urged softly. "His poor heart is breaking because this nogood has gone away from him and taken up with others like himself who rob and cheat and kill defenseless people. So for a while I go with the *chalanes*—the Gypsy horse dealers who travel everywhere, and dance for my keep like any *gitana*—gypsy; and I find this one and follow him, but it is all of no use. He laughs at me when I speak of our father and calls me a bad name." She spread her hands helplessly. "There is no more I can do."

Crazy as they sounded her words carried conviction. But they didn't explain how she had known he was crouched on that porch back of Tombstone, or how she'd found him at Charleston and now happened to be here. He mentioned this, and even in the near dark of this tree-thickened gloom he could feel the surprise that looked out of her face.

"But I saw you in Tombstone—I saw you come onto the veranda to hide. And I did not know where you went when you left. I heard the guns, but you were gone—all of them were; and I had not yet talked with my brother. It was natural I should go to Charleston. The corral of 'Pancho Stealwell,' as my people call him, is a place where all the time these hunted ones go for fresh horses and information. I feel sure my brother will go there. And perhaps, I think, you may come there too, so I take your horse—"

"You took High Sailin?"

"How else would he get there?"

Turk was shaken but not convinced. Perhaps he did not wish to be—for hadn't Tex Willbrandt of the peppermint breath given the impression Curly Bill had sent High Sailin over there? Scowling, Turk said, "Your talk's sure improved; you wrangle our lingo a heap better than I do!"

She shrugged, not answering, when Turk got up and took a turn about the room. She pulled the blanket a little closer around her shoulders, her glance following him. "I can help you—" she began; and he came back, saying, "Maybe you can."

His expression looked worried and a little bit nervous. "There's a girl in this place...about your size and damn pretty, and they're holdin' her—Bill's bunch—figurin' to make her husband kick in with a pile of jack. He's a rancher over near Benson. I happen to know he won't pay them a cent. I've got to get her out of here—you want to help me with that?"

For a long breath she stared at Turk without moving. Then she pushed back her hair and got up off the bed. She went over by the window with the blanket pulled tight around the curves of her figure and stood looking into the deepening dusk. "Who is this woman, eh? What is she to you?"

"I just told you she was married—"

"And what has that to do with it!"

"It's her looks," Turk said, trying hard to explain it. "Hair that's the color of a field of ripe wheat—and that ain't all. You ought to be able to figure what'll happen if these brush jumpers don't git their hands on that money! The girl's a lady— Ruebusch's wife! The feller I used to ride for."

She showed a little more concern. "He is your friend, this one?"

"I ..." Turk frowned. "I wouldn't hardly say that— but it ain't him I'm worried about. It's just that ..." He let the rest go. He said, "I ain't blamin' Bill—" and stopped again, struck with the futility of attempting to put into words an impulse he didn't half understand himself. It wasn't that he imagined Holly might have been trying to find him, or that he still had any hope of ever persuading her to go off with him, but some way or other he just couldn't help feeling tied up with her troubles. In spite of all that had happened he still couldn't get Willow Springs out of his head.

She rasped a bare foot across the splintery boards and turned around to eye him unreadably. "What do you want me to do?"

"Barkeep's got a key to her room—that guy Kelly,"

Turk said, looking more hopeful. "You ought to be able to wean it away from him. You could tell him she's sick, that she wants you to come in there, that when you find out what's wrong you could maybe fix—"

"When I get this key, what are you going to do then?"

"I'll find some way to slip her out," Turk growled. "We'll put her on a horse and git her headed for Benson."

"She is prettier than me, this woman?"

"Hell, she's the most—" He stopped and looked at her more carefully. "What difference does that make?"

"Are you not afraid that someone else may run off with her?"

Turk rubbed a hand across his jaw and chewed his lip. This kid had a head on her shoulders. The possibility hadn't occurred to him, but he could see that she was right and he would have to keep his eyes peeled.

"Glad you thought of that," he grunted. "Guess I'll have to stick with her a ways. Have to scout up some clothes and she'll need a horse, too. We'll have to hide that hair. Reckon you could darken her face up a little?"

Rita said, "I will take care of her."

"Good girl," Turk nodded. "You go ahead and git that key."

She said, "I will have to put some clothes on," and Turk, with his cheeks turning hot as a stove lid, went over and glared out of the window while she got into them. He was still there, and still feeling about as comfortable as a .22 cartridge in a 12 gauge gun, when the door closed behind her and he was left alone with his problems.

ELEVEN

SHE TOOK LONGER than Turk had reckoned on and he was pretty near fit to be tied when she got back. The noise from downstairs had considerably increased and she had to get a candle lit before she would put the key in his hand. "Yeah," he said, "that looks like it, all right."

"It is the one," she assured him. "I found out where she was before I went down there after it. We exchanged a few words. I thought it might be wise to let her know what was planned; and it was well that I did because that Kelly did not take any chances. He went up and talked to her himself before he would give me the key."

Turk gave it back to her and she said, "We will have to move quickly. I think Kelly will send some men to find and tell Bill."

"Yeah." Turk scowled. He hadn't thought of this, either.

She pushed him toward the door. "There is a large tree behind this place that has its feet in the water. You bring the clothes and horses. She will wait for you there."

"How you going to git her out of here?"

"She will have to go through this window— they have nailed the one in her room. But she has two blankets she will tear in half and with mine this should be enough. You'd better hurry."

Nick's place was doing a pretty fair business when Turk started down the stairs. Kelly had a helper back of the bar and four of the gambling rigs were surrounded. Thomas and Snow—the former facing the stairs—were gabbing with three other hard looking customers. Turk saw the hatchet-faced Thomas nudge Snow and mutter something to him out of the corner of his mouth. Snow looked up and snickered. Two of the others looked around.

Turk could feel his ears begin to burn. He was remembering that these wallopers had probably helped to make that boot sound when he'd been having his hoedown with Rita. But they didn't try to get in his way when he passed them. "How's tricks?" Kelly called, and Turk jerked a hand at him and shoved on through the batwings.

It was full dark outside and the wind had got up again. Turk, lengthening his stride, cut straight for the place where he had left his horse. He wasn't going to bother with no goddamed clothes. The sooner he and Holly got to whacking leather the better. He still felt mean about Bill but Holly's health and mental comfort were things he couldn't well ignore; and there was Rita, too, to be thought about. But he'd have to take care of first things first; and that Rita, from all he had seen of her, was pretty well able to take care of herself.

The boss wrangler was gone when Turk reached the corral, but his handy man fetched out High Sailin. Turk threw his saddle on and hurriedly cinched up. He asked the fellow if he'd a nag he could borrow, something with bottom and a little burst of speed. "One of the boys just got in," Turk said, "and his mount's about done up."

The man shuffled off and came back with a brush-scarred buckskin. "This yere bayo coyote oughta make it," he said, and Turk looked him over. The horse was built like a jackrabbit but Turk had forked enough good ones to grunt quick approval. He was scared to ask the man for a saddle. He'd put Holly on High Sailin.

Turk swung up and the man passed him the buckskin's halter shank. "Bound for Skeleton, are you?"

Turk looked down into the man's homely face. "A loose tongue has took care of more damn fools than shovels."

The fellow showed a sour grin. "You must be a new broom." Then he said, leaning nearer, "There's jest one thing you got to watch in this camp and that's to make almighty certain you don't cross up Curly Bill."

* * *

TURK CIRCLED in the dark and fetched his horses down off the mesa. He found it hard to restrain his impatience when he thought of Holly holed-up beside that tree and probably scared half out of her senses. He wasn't feeling too good himself with this business and was considerably plagued by recollections of Rita. When Bill heard about that key he sure as hell wasn't going to like it. Turk got to thinking he had been pretty all-fired thoughtless roping the kid into setting this deal up, then riding off and leaving her to weather Bill's wrath. Made him look like a stinker. Made him feel like one, too. He was half of a mind to ride back up there and get her.

He sat scowling a moment before he put High Sailin up the bed of the creek, hauling the buckskin by the halter shank behind him. The girl had done a lot for him but, damn it, a man had to tackle first things first and his obligation was unquestionably to Holly. If he hadn't taken advantage of her that day at the Willow Springs linecamp...

It was blacker down here than the inside of a cat, and the few stars he could see through the slat and flap of the sycamores didn't help no more than pouring water on a drowned rat. He had to leave the footing entirely up to the horses. Once a branch slapped him so hard across the face he came within a hair of going right plumb out of the saddle.

After that he kept an arm held up in front of him. But he couldn't shore off his uncomfortable thoughts about Rita or take away one jot of his uneasiness about Bill.

They'd be bound to come after him.

It wasn't the prospect of violence which had Turk sweating. He didn't believe Bill would take a gun to him. It was what Bill would think, him doing this to Bill after he'd taken Turk in like he had and made a place for him. They'd been friends, the way Turk saw it— good friends; and that was the way Turk wanted to stay with Bill, knowing all the while that they could never go back to how things had been before Bill's bunch had grabbed Holly.

The creek's right-hand bank became the side of the mesa, and every clack of a hoof against stone ran Turk's hackles up. His nerves became pulled so tight the whole back of his neck ached; and abruptly, black and ugly atop the treacherous slope, he saw the back of Nick's place against the lesser black of sky. It had a secretive sinister look crouched up there with the shine of yellow light filtering down through the trees' swaying branches.

He pulled up High Sailin to take a quick squint around, not locating anything but not feeling right either. The shadows up under those wind-bent branches looked thicker than smoke and were piled deep enough to have hidden away Geronimo and half his damned Apaches.

Turk didn't like it and High Sailin didn't either, nor the buckskin that came up now and stopped by his shoulder. The buckskin blew through his nose and High Sailin' gingerly hunched himself as though quite ready to bolt if he got the least encouragement.

And suddenly both horses' ears pricked toward the blackness off to the left of Turk. After staring a moment Turk saw it too, a solid black in the wind-slapped shadows that couldn't be anything but a human shape. It was fright, not guts, that kept Turk from yanking the gun from his holster.

How long they stayed motionless staring at each other there was no way of telling, but abruptly Turk's pistol was in his grip, stiffly pointed. He had the hammer thumbed back but was afraid to let go of it lest the roar of the explosion bring the whole camp down on him.

When he got enough spit gathered to pull the

words from his throat, he gruffed, "You, over there—come out of that!"

For long moments nothing happened, then the blackness stirred again and the darker chunk moved up to where he could see its arms were up even with its head; but that was about all the could see. But now a shift in the wind put a silver of light through the tossed-about branches and sweat came out and lay cold on Turk's cheekbones. The light only cut that shape across the middle but it showed him the remembered color of Holly's dress and the tails of her scarf hanging down from covering her hair up. He got the shakes so bad he nearly forgot to pouch his pistol.

The impatient shake of High Sailin's head brought him back to the pressure of passing time. "Don't stand there!" he growled, and came out of the saddle, exasperated with her. "Here—" he said, holding the reins out, "climb onto this horse and let's git the hell out of here!"

As she came forward through the gloom to take the reins from his grip, something in the way she moved caught at him and he went cold all over. And it wasn't just the water from the creek sucking down his boot tops.

His arm shot out and jerked the scarf off her hair and got hold of the front of her, pulling her toward him through the sliver of light. One look at that mop of black hair was aplenty.

"So you reckoned I'd go with you, never knowin' the difference!" Choking with rage he snarled thickly: "Where is she?"

He saw the upsweep of her chin, her defiance; saw the curl of her lips. But when he started to yank the reins from her she cried, "Wait—I will tell you!" and grinned at him bleakly. "She is there where I found her—"

"And how did you git to be wearin' her things?"

"I said it was your wish—a part of the plan— that we should change. And because she is a fool she took them off and gave them to me. But I did not give her mine." She shook the hair back off her cheeks and laughed openly. "She waits in the room with no clothes for you to save her."

"You damn hellcat!" Turk swore, coming within an inch of striking her. "Give me the key!"

Her grin turned cruel, mocking him. "The key I have left in the door—on the outside," and she laughed again as he flung into the saddle. "It is too late for you to save her. Curly Bill was on the stairs when I came down from the window on the rope we made with her blankets."

TWELVE

TURK HAD no clear remembrance of how he got up that slope from the creek. Reaction was still churning violently through him when he sprang down from the saddle in front of Nick's batwings. He tried to tear from his mind its seething load of frustration and anger that he might, at least with some degree of clarity, assess the damage her prank had done; but his thoughts were too wild, his confusion too great for reasoning. He knew only that he must reach Holly at once.

He shoved Nick's slatted doors off his elbows and rushed in with a hand flying back for his gun. The fetid air with its reek of unwashed bodies, bad breath, smoke and whisky, almost gagged him; the glare of the lamps half blinded him and noise rolled against him in a solid wall of sound.

The place was packed.

The day shift from Galey's smelter crammed the gambling rigs and bar six deep. Horse-soldiers in blue tunics set off by yellow neck rags, whiskered desert rats and redshirted miners showed thinly sandwiched in with these, rubbing shoulders with big-hatted cowhands and dark-faced vaqueros from below the international line. Turk had no heed for any of this. His stare, cutting over the smoky sea of shifting headgear, was riveted on the spindle-railed balcony as he bitterly fought to get through the sweating crush.

"Watch where you're goin'—"

"Get out of my way!"

"Who the hell you shovin'!"

He was trapped in the solid middle of it, furious, when he saw Holly's door opening and her coming out of it and Bill right back of her, talking and laughing, with a hand on her shoulder. She had on a blue shirt like the one Turk was wearing and pants, just like a man, with their bottoms thrust into fancy-topped boots that must have set someone back more than a little.

It was the pants Turk's shocked stare clung to longest. And it wasn't just the way she filled them out that got him either, though it may have had something to do with the dark rush of blood that pounded into his cheeks. Decent women didn't wear pants!

With her thighs pressed against the balcony's rail she stood with Bill, staring over the packed room. She moved her hands and her mouth moved and Turk saw Bill chuckle, and her grinning back at him.

Turk couldn't understand it. But that was Holly, all right. No mistake about that part.

He saw Bill taking a squint at his timepiece, turning it around so that she could eye it, too. Turk saw her lips move again and Bill throwing back his head in a laugh. Bill patted her shoulder. They were turning away then and Bill, leaning closer, was handing her something which to Turk's incredulous eyes looked almighty like a key. While his tangled emotions were still reeling under this he saw her turn at the door, lifting a smiling face which Bill, pulling her against him, kissed with bold assurance.

Turk swung around, blindly making for the batwings. He ran squarely into a man and shoved him aside without even looking. "Better hev a drink," came Willbrandt's voice somewhere to the left of him, "you sure look like you could use one." Turk caught a whiff of the man's peppermint breath but brushed on past him without a word. He knocked somebody else out of his way and kept going.

He was less than ten feet from the half-leaf doors when they squeaked and swung inward and there was Rita in Holly's dress staring impudently at him. He didn't stop to think but caught her roughly by the arm. "Come on—let's git out of this goddamn camp!"

Thomas came through the doors with Charlie Snow on his heels and, seeing Turk and the girl, pulled up directly in their path. The wedge-faced Thomas, too drunk to grasp Turk's condition, gave Snow a nudge that promised some fun and had his mouth halfway open when Turk hit him in the stomach. As the man came jackknifing forward, eyes bulging, Turk hung one on his chin and Thomas went down and out in one motion.

Snow's hand started hipward. Something glimpsed in Turk's stare stopped the hand short of leather. A whisper of escaping breath leaked out of him and he backed carefully off till he was out of Turk's way.

"Hey Red—Turkey Red!" came Bill's bull-throated shout, and before Turk could move Bill was up with him, laughing and slapping Turk's shoulder.

And Turk stood there, tongue tied, with his face like pounded metal, listening to the boom of Bill's jovial voice and suddenly inexplicably, hating it. Hating the feel of Bill's hand on his shoulder and seeing a heap of things now which anyone, he reckoned, but a damnfool kid would have savvied from the start and had the sense to sheer away from.

"Time to be hittin' leather," Bill rumbled, stepping between Turk and Rita with that easy assurance Turk had recently so admired, and with his hand on Turk's shoulder slipping Turk on through the batwings. The blackness of the windy street came up and closed like fog around them and Bill, twisting his head, wanted to know where Jake and Ringo were, and Snow's reedy tones said they were over in back of Jack Dahl's place waiting with the Clantons and the horses.

Turk caught up High Sailin's reins and, twisting away from Bill's hand, swung into the saddle. Stilwell and Willbrandt got hold of their broncs and mounted too. And Turk, wanting out of this, knew he couldn't get out; that he was sucked up into this now with the rest of them, chained and shackled by knowledge that wouldn't ever let him go. He was part of Bill's border legion now and a man didn't quit Bill Graham and stay healthy.

* * *

SKELETON CANYON WAS a runway of smugglers that curled like a snake through the wildest regions of the Peloncillo Mountains, entering them from the Animas Valley and coming out near Douglas at the far southern end of the San Simon.

Noon's sun filled its trough with a blinding glare that had every inch of Turk crying for water. His eyes felt like baked marbles in the trapped heat crawling off the smoking rocks, and there was no talk now and, among the others, no smoking on Bill's orders. He had hidden them well, leaving Turk and himself wholly alone on the trail.

They were here to latch onto a mule train which, according to Old Man Clanton, had come up out of Mexico to pick up guns and bullets in Tucson where the fat little merchants were salting away a tidy profit from such strictly cash transactions. Even in the light of his own new and private views about Bill, Turk couldn't find much fault with laying a trap to stop and rob a gang of Mexican smugglers.

Still, he didn't like it. Nor did he care for Bill's reticence with regard to that business of the key and Holly's clothes. Nor the odd way Bill, every once in a while, would look at him. Since Bill wasn't one to hide his anger it seemed obvious Holly hadn't mentioned Turk's name. But the barkeep would certainly have told him about the key and Holly would have named Rita on account of the clothes and to explain her own lack of them. Was Bill then so pleased with the results he'd forgiven Rita? Or had she been dealt with after they'd left? Turk felt sick every time he considered this and was so worked up he didn't half know what he was doing.

A couple of carpenter birds began berating each other over in the willows that fringed the gurgling creek, and a road runner squawked and whacked his bill against the shale and kind of teetered on his legs as though about to collapse. Suddenly he went bounding straight up into the air and came down with a sparrow in his mouth and started running.

Turk wished he had a drink, and wasn't thinking of the kind he could have by going to the creek. He wished those Mexicans would hurry up and get here. The plan, as he'd heard Bill tell it, didn't call for any shooting. Bill and Turk were to handle the stopping, holding the dons in talk while Bill looked them over and gave the rest of his outfit time to get set for any last minute changes which might seem desirable. Once Bill was sure they'd got hold of the right party he was to whistle a snatch from *La Paloma,* after which he and Turk would move on up the canyon—this to block escape in case the dons attempted to bolt.

The place picked to get the jump on these smugglers was known as the Devil's Kitchen and, considering the heat, Turk thought it aptly named.

There was a kind of greasy shine to Bill's face as he lounged in the saddle, sleepy looking as his horse. He could have passed, like Jake Gauze, for a Mexican; it was, in fact, what he proposed to do.

A week ago Turk would have felt greatly complimented to have been teamed off with Bill in this fashion. Now, with more understanding, he sourly suspected he'd been chosen to work this part of the deal in the hope his looks would set at rest any feelings of disquiet their appearance might cause in the minds of the intended victims. He was more than half convinced here was the reason—and the only one—Bill had taken him on in the first place.

He felt a strong distaste for the entire venture. The way he looked at it, robbing Mexicans was in the same class with taking candy from a kid. No tricks needed.

Davy Crockett had told it all when he said one toothless old half-awake Texican could hold off thirty of the best the dons could manage with one paw tied and both legs broke. Turk was a heap more concerned with his uncomfortable thoughts of Rita when, faint through the sunlit silence, came the far-off up-canyon tinkle of a bell.

Bill came out of his slouch. He rasped the back of his hand across his jowls and yawned and stretched. Then he looked over at Turk. "I'll do the talkin'. If them dons happens to come up with any fancy notions, you roller my lead. Don't try anything on your own hook."

Not till Turk nodded did Bill remove his gaze. Then he took a look at his pistols and, putting them away, bent a keen inspecting frown across the skylined rocks and chaparral masking the top of the nearest rim. Evidently satisfied, he kneed his pony out into the trail.

By this time the bells were considerably closer. Dingle dangle, creaking of leather, plopping hoofs and a mumble of voice sounds made quite a commotion kicked around through the rocks and shored up with echoes. One of the bunch was even tickling a guitar, as though smuggling was no different than punching cows or any other job. Mexicans, Turk concluded, didn't have sense enough to pound sand down a rat hole.

And there they came, strung out all over, with a bighatted don on a prancing black stallion at the head of them—the *patron*, like enough, to judge by his trappings. There was another fellow riding just a couple of strides behind him; this, Turk reckoned, was probably the boss the don hired to pass orders to the rest of them. He had a corn husk cigarette stuck in his face. And, back of this pair, came the mules picking their feet up to the musical clink clank of bulging pack saddles—*aparejos*, the Mexes called them.

Turk could see the mules in a long weaving line curling around through the rocks and the dust they were raising. He counted eight additional riders, at least three of them looking to be younger than he was; it was the handsomest of these that was playing the guitar. He had tiny golden bells on his sombrero. The *patron* had, too.

He looked a bit taken aback at finding Turk and Bill in front of him and sent a gabble of Spanish flying over his shoulder that, when relayed by the second man, brought the whole train to a standstill. The pretty kid quit fooling with his guitar and the cigarette-smoking *segundo* put a hand to his gun stock. The whole bunch looked worried and Turk could see they weren't fighters.

Bill, stopping his horse, grinned and spoke politely, describing himself as a local rancher out with one of his cowboys trying to find some strayed cattle. He cussed the July heat and inquired about the old fellow's health in the don's own lingo, quite as though he considered Mexicans the salt of the earth.

He made quite an impression. The old don smiled and quit chewing his lip. He said he was Miguel Garcia of Hermosillo, and asked about Bill's health. Bill allowed he was still able to totter around, and after swapping a few more pleasantries Don Miguel described himself as a merchant of pots and pans bound for Tucson to trade for Navajo blankets. He said friends had told him these mountains were filled with robbers and, while he had no money, he had been forced to mortgage his store to secure this load of kitchenware and would be ruined if thieves should take it.

Bill said his cook might find use for a few pans if the price was right. The old don looked shocked. His poor stuff, he explained, was much too crude for so grand a *caballero;* as the Virgin well knew, the cheapest he could find, fit only for paupers and Indians. He said, crossing himself, he hoped he would not encounter any bandits.

"With pots and pans?" Bill laughed. "The only real outlaws around these parts are too busy stealing cows to bother with anything else." He said, still speaking Spanish, "Now if it was gold your packs were filled with, or a bunch of those silver dollars, you might have something to get in a sweat about."

Bill winked, whacking his high when he said this, as though making up something to laugh at. The old don's grin looked a bit on the parched side and the pockmarked *segundo,* spitting out his cigarette, dropped a hand to his gun again.

Bill made out not to notice. "Well, so long," he said, and picked up his reins. Don Miguel said, "Go with God," and waved a hand. The Mexicans with the mules got back in their saddles and prodded the train into movement. All the bells started tinkling, hoofs plopped, leather squeaked and the bulging *aparejos* clinked and clanked.

Turk saw Bill swivel a furtive glance at the rim. Turk followed him down the line, listening to Bill tossing quips at the mule men about the fun they would have with the girls at Tucson and how long it would take to count the skirts they had on them and which would be the first to cry hello at what these guarded.

Turk had heard the like more times than he could remember but he thought it a cruel jest with Bill figuring to grab all their silver.

When they reached the young fellow with the guitar, Bill said, "Can you play *La Paloma?*"

"But, of course, senor," he assured Bill, smiling.

"Go ahead," Bill said, "there's a buck in it for you," and the kid right away started plunking and chuckling while Bill joined his whistle to the lilt of its chorus. "Something else?" the kid asked when he'd finished. "No," Bill grinned, "that ought to do the first rate," and flipped him the promised cartwheel.

The dust was thick back here at the end of the train but Turk could see the pleased look on the kid's face as he caught it. *"Mil* gracias!" he cried, sweeping off his belled hat. "May the saints—"

That was far as he got. The rest was lost in a racket of rifles. Gouts of flame lividly lanced from the brush and rocks of the canyon wall. Anguished cries and frantic curses mingled thinly with the piercing screams of terrified horses and the frightened braying of the panicked mules. In that first unbelieving glance Turk saw three of the Mexicans reel out of their saddles while a fourth, with foot hung in stirrup, was dragged bouncing away through a curtain of dust.

"Git that old geezer with them bells on his bonnet!"

"Git 'em all!" Bill yelled—"every sonofabitch' one of 'em!"

Turk stared at the man with a crawling horror, remembering with bitter clarity how this same Curly Bill, not an hour gone by, had declared when Turk brought up the matter there would be no need for shooting.

Turk yelled at Bill, his face mottled with shame and fury as he drove High Sailin through a tangle of motion, trying to catch hold of Bill's arm. "Are you crazy, man? God damn it, you said—"

The guitar kid with the grin still froze to his face badly reeled in the saddle but clutched a grip in the mane of his horse and stayed on. Bill's swiveling guns tumbled a man from his mount so close to the boy the blood spattered on him and the kid, with a squawk, clapped heels to his horse and took off in wild flight with his yell sailing back like it was made out of goose quills.

"Git that kid!" Bill snarled, savagely triggering on empties.

With leaves and twigs raining down across its rump the kid's bronc tore through the screen of willows bordering the creek. Bill sheathed one smoking emptied gun and was fumbling fresh loads from his belt to the other, while attempting to drive his pitching horse after the kid, when the pockmarked *segundo* came tearing up out of the dust with a blazing rifle, driving straight at Bill.

Turk fired without thought and saw the smuggler's horse plow head first through the shale. Flung clear, the lanky Mexican scrambled to his feet and lunged at Bill with a lifted knife. There was no time for nice distinctions. Bill, Turk knew. The Mexican was a stranger. Turk shot the Mexican through the head.

Bill was down, too, but now he rolled to his knees. He came onto his feet and picked up his pistols, shaking the sand out, replacing spent cartridges with loads from his belt. He looked around and found his hat. He cuffed the worst of the dust out and clapped it on. He glared around at Turk then with that shock of black hair curling down across his forehead. The both of them knew Turk had ruined his aim but he didn't say anything. He swung around on his heel and went clanking his spurs toward where the rest of his bunch was coming down off the rim.

The jamboree was over. Two mules had been killed and lay with busted packs where the guns had dropped them. Dead Mexicans were everywhere and one of them, not so dead, tried to drag himself up with a whimpering groan. Jake Gauze, spying the man, emptied a pistol into him and then, stepping closer, crashed a boot into his face.

Reaction hit Turk then and he rode into the willows, retching. Ringo was cursing the vanished mules which had stampeded down canyon in the wake of what horses had got clear of the slaughter. Even through his misery Turk could hear the vicious swearing and the angry bickering of Billy Clanton and two of the others rolling the stiffs for rings and cash.

Turk hung over the saddle with both hands choking the apple till nothing more would come up. Spent and weak he got down then, shivering and sweating, and staggered over to the water. He flopped on his belly and closed both eyes, shuddering. He put his face in the murmurous creek but couldn't wash away the taste. Nor was he able to drown the screams or drive from recoiling memory the hideous sights he'd been forced to witness. He guessed these things must be a part of him forever and in an access of horror he wished that he could die.

But the worst of it finally passed and he got shakily to his feet. His mind shied away from thoughts of Bill.

He tried to twist himself a smoke but after tearing three papers he put the rest of the stuff in his pockets. And that was when he saw Gauze watching him.

The black browed squatty toad of a man stood grinning in the willows. Anger came into Turk's throat like bile and all the frustrated bitterness of these last weeks threatened to fling his hand to gun butt when Jake laughed at him with open jeering mockery. But this was what Gauze wanted, it was a baleful shine in his hooded stare, in the curl of the fist hanging spraddled above the man's cutaway holster.

And suddenly Turk was cool again, master of himself with a strange new certainty that never had flowed through his veins before. He saw a puzzled light creep through the gleam of Jake's stare and turned away from the man, stepping into his saddle.

Jake cursed him with all the foul oaths of the border and Turk's ears turned red but he didn't let it throw him. In the grip of his new assurance he could hear the man's foulness without letting it push him one inch from his decision.

"Rabbit," Jake growled with his lips curled back, scornful. "Not even a jack—jest a runty damn weavily cottontail!" He scrinched his mouth up and spat. "All right, Diapers. Come along. The boss has got somethin' he's cravin' to say to you."

He wheeled off through the brush and Turk let High Sailin follow. When they came out on the trail Bill was putting Ringo in charge of going after the mules which by now were probably scattered halfway to Douglas. He looked up and around with his eyes like hot iron when they came slamming into Turk's; then he took a second look and seemed to control himself with an effort.

He got onto his horse, which one of the others had fetched up, and sat awhile scowling before impatience swung his shoulders about to wave Ringo off with the most of the rest of them on their hunt for the mule packs. Only three men stayed with him—Willbrandt, Gauze and that whiskered Jim Hughes.

Bill brought his look back to Turk.

"Reckon you saved my hide," he said, trying to call up his grin and making pretty rough work of it, "so we'll fergit a few things that ain't been settin' too good with me." That was how he put it though his eyes didn't look like they were about to forget anything. Then he said with the growl getting into his voice again, "Just keep in mind hereafter that when I give an order every guy in this outfit jumps! You understand?"

"Nothin' wrong with my hearin'."

"You better remember it, too."

Turk didn't answer. It was Bill that turned away.

The others, with wooden faces, made a business of climbing into their saddles—all but Jake. Jake rubbed the flats of his pantlegs and hunched his bowed shoulders, looking from Bill to Turk and back again. At last, with a sneer, he got onto his horse.

"I'm headin' for town," Turk said; and Bill's roan cheeks came around with his eyes, bright and narrow, looking almost like glass.

"I'm goin' now," Turk added, and put High Sailin crossways of the trail.

A vicious anticipation leaped into Jake's stare. Jim Hughes' whiskered cheeks stayed neutral. Bill's eyes became pieces of jet in his dark face and the peppermint snapped between Willbrandt's teeth.

"Hell," Bill said with a queer strangled gruffness, "we're all goin' now—"

Turk didn't wait for them. He didn't crowd High Sailin but kept him out in front like he was mindful to ride by himself. Jake's hand slid to gun stock but Bill caught his wrist and let Turk get away with it.

"Not yet," he growled. "I still got use fer that fool."

THIRTEEN

IT WAS dark when they came by a short cut to Galeyville, dark and close to midnight—not that this made any great amount of difference. Curly Bill's new headquarters was an all-night camp and Turk caught the unholy din of it long before High Sailin's tired hoofs brought them up onto the mesa. Lamps in the saloons and honkytonks stippled the gray dust of the street in a patchwork of light and shadow and the wail of the fiddles cut above the locust sound of men's voices. Six Key Joe, at the piano in Nick's bar, was making the ivories talk.

Turk was passing Jack McConaghey's saloon when he stared back over his shoulder to gauge how much time he might have to find Rita. It was impossible to tell. He couldn't see Bill or the three who were with Bill, but it was a foregone conclusion they were not far behind—a quarter mile perhaps.

Turk knew he was in for trouble but he wasn't expecting the kind that came at him. He was turning High Sailin to make for Nick's tierack with the light from McConaghey's splashing full on him, when a shape shoved out of the mouth of an alley. "Hold up there!" this man called; and Turk—lips pulling tight across the shine of his teeth—recognized the voice of Buck Linderstrom.

He saw the lift of gun steel in the Roman 4 man's fist. And at the same time, off to the left of him, another crouched shape came out of the shadows. *"Where is she?"* Ruebusch's voice snarled.

"Now wait a minute—" Turk said, and dived from the saddle under the scream of lead as gunflame ripped the blackness to the right of him. He struck the dust rolling, letting the horse go, and came up breathing hard with his gun clearing leather. A shape darted across the light from McConaghey's and he put two shots into that bedlam of sound. He heard a man screech and saw Strehl going around in a staggering circle.

Something cuffed at Turk's waist and his straining eyes picked up Linderstrom as High Sailin veered off with head down and heels flying. The man was almost on top of him when Turk whipped his gun up, the two pistols roaring almost in unison. The range boss grabbed at his stomach and collapsed. The man on Turk's right started throwing lead at him.

Something hit him like a fist, smashing Turk half around; and he heard men yelling and, above this, the rushing pound of fast traveling hoofs. He got onto one knee in the strangling dust and saw Ruebusch, against the lights, running toward him, and he hollered at the man but Ruebusch kept coming.

Turk clawed himself upright and hoof sounds hammered the fronts of the buildings. He wanted to live. He knew he ought to cut Ruebusch down but he couldn't do it. He saw Bill's face and Jake's above the manes of their horses and he tried to warn Ruebusch, crazily holding his fire with the bullets slapping round him, pleading with the man and finally, furiously, cursing him. The sudden crash of Winchesters threw up a roaring wall of sound. The man's legs went out from under him, spilling him all spraddled out into the ballooning dust of the street.

Incredibly he got up again, stumbling toward Turk, still trying to kill him, the hammer of his gun over and over striking futilely against the heads of emptied shells. Once more Jake's rifle crashed. Turk saw Ruebusch's hat fall off. The man stopped moving and rose, straightening fully, on the toes of his boots. The gun fell out of his hand. He took one additional step and crumpled.

The wind had fallen. A brooding silence closed around Turk, broken only by the scamper of fingers across the keys of the piano in Babcock's bar.

Turk felt the weight of the pistol he was holding. The gun sagged to his side and his knees started shaking. It was reaction, he knew. The horror came and then, hard on top of it, Bill's call. .

In an access of revulsion Turk struck out for Nick's blindly. He didn't want to have to listen to Bill, didn't want even to have to look at him again. Bile came into the brassy taste of his throat. He heard the ring of spurred boots as someone behind him broke into a lumbering run. Turk didn't look. He didn't wait, either.

He pushed through Nick's batwings and the warmth of the place and its smell came at him through the wavering sway of that sea of white faces. He thought he was going to be sick.

He fought the nausea down and men opened up a

path for him the way, he suddenly remembered, they had always done for Bill. This too had been one of the things he had coveted; the right of fame, he thought, hating it.

He reached the stairs and started up them, hearing the batwings squeak behind him. He could feel the drag of men's stares reaching after him and his feet purely seemed like they were weighted with stove lids. He put a hand on the banister to steady himself. In this frozen hush his boots made an intolerable racket on the steps.

His head came level with the top of them. There was something going on beyond the red-yellow shine of Rita's shut door; he caught the wheeze of labored breathing, the sudden frantic rip of cloth.

If the goddam stairs would only stay where they'd been built! Still gripping the banister he got to the top of them just as the door of Rita's room was yanked open. He saw the scratched and sweat-filmed gleam of Thomas' face and lunged for him. But his legs were unwieldy and his feet wouldn't track right. Thomas, ducking, twisted away from him and spun onto the balcony, dragging at his gun.

Turk spun, too, reeling after him. The forgotten pistol in his fist laid open Thomas' white face from left temple to chin. The man staggered backward and with a screech went through the rail. Turk, off balance, would have gone through after him if Rita hadn't grabbed him.

He shook his head to clear his eyes and thought it was time Kelly got the lamps lit. Under his left ribs the shirt was sticking to him soddenly and Rita was crying something over and over and through the deepening gloom he saw Jake's face with Curly Bill's behind it; and he said, "I'm takin' her out of this!"

And Jake Gauze said, "You ain't goin' noplace—" and that was all Turk heard. The blackness was complete.

For a long and miserable while about the only thing Turk was conscious of was the feel of a cool comforting hand softly pushing the sweaty hair off his forehead. Later, other fancies came occasionally to wander through the jumbled impressions of his fevered delirium. This was generally in the mornings when he'd be staring up into those outside trees watching the way the wind shook their tops, wishing Holly's cool hands would come back to him; and, sometimes, in the darkness he would put out an arm and, finding her, pull her closer, hearing the troubled whisper of her voice but not understanding what it was she seemed trying to tell him. The best times, though, were when he'd find her lips with his and feel hers come back at him, desperately almost.

Those times he'd tell her things he wouldn't have told another soul, and he would feel the sobs shaking her and couldn't understand why she'd be crying now about it when she hadn't cried at Willow Springs. He guessed he never would savvy women. But as soon as he got things straightened with Bill they'd go off someplace by themselves, he'd tell her, and build a spread of their own where folks didn't know anything about her or him. And she would kiss him, queer like, and sometimes she'd cry, not making no sound but hanging hold of him like she would never let go. Once she said, "*Si*—yes, yes," like she was dying, "*si, querido*, love of my soul," and it would give him a laugh—a real belly laugh—to think of her talking like a dadburned Mex. "Sleep," she said. "Pretty soon you will be strong and perhaps get drunk, forgetting these beautiful plans we have made. Perhaps you will curse me and these nights you have spent here," and she'd got up and hurried out. Sometimes Turk couldn't figure her at all.

* * *

AND THEN HE was on the mend again. At first just sitting up in bed with pillows back of him, afterwards graduating to a chair. It was a red-letter day when he got onto the porch. He decided this shack was quite a ways from town. He didn't hear much of its racket except such times as he would wake up at night. There was a grove of live oak about this hideaway of his, and the different green of juniper. The only person he saw was the old Mexican woman who came each day to clean the house and take care of him. During this convalescence his thoughts only touched Holly once and then with a scorn mainly directed at himself. He didn't recall the hallucinations of his fever.

It was on the morning of the third day prior to sitting up that he first saw the old woman. She told him her name was Dolores. He was still pretty weak but his head was clear. He asked her how long he had been in the bed. "Ten days," she said, counting her fingers.

He guessed it had been touch and go for a while. He must have lost a lot of blood.

The first day he sat up he asked about his horses. The old woman said they were being cared for in town. "Why not here?" Turk wanted to know. He had his own guess at the answer but he didn't find out from Dolores.

Five days later she let him walk under the trees, but he soon tired and was glad to get back to his chair on the porch. He must have been a lot closer to not making it than he'd figured.

When she called him in to a kind of mulligan she made that was better than it looked, he asked her bluntly why Rita was so pointedly staying away from him. The old woman shrugged. "Has she gone?" Turk demanded—"has she left town?"

Rita, she said, was dancing at Babcock's.

He didn't know what had made him think old Dolores would know the girl. He was sure now it was Rita who employed her. "And does she never ask of me?"

"Every night," the woman chuckled. "She gives me the medicine to put on that place in your side."

Turk had reckoned as much, remembering how she had cared for him at Charleston. He kept his voice casual. "How long was she out here before you showed up?"

The old woman grinned and shook her head at him.

"Well," Turk said testily, "How'd she git me out here?"

"Curly Bill help her. And Pancho Stealwell. That Jake Gauze no like it. Say pretty soon kill you." She drew a finger across her throat. "Curly Bill laugh."

Turk got up and buckled his shell belt around him and spent the next hour cleaning and oiling his pistol. Then he dumped out the loads and replaced them with cartridges from the unopened box that was still in his coat pocket. It had been Bill, like enough, who had given out the order to keep his horses in town. Turk had seen too much to be allowed to pull out.

With his morose thoughts again on Rita, Turk's mind cast back through the hours he had lain in that bed watching the tops of wind-bent trees; and he unearthed a few hazy recollections that darkened and tightened the twist of his scowl. Of course. No wonder she was staying away from him now. In the blind alleys of his delirium he had probably called her "Holly." He seemed to remember that she had cried a lot...

When Dolores got ready to leave that evening he fished in his pocket and gave her a handful of coins and told her to bring him a razor.

She was back with one the following morning. It must have been used to shave hogs. He spent a couple of hours getting the blade in shape before he dared put it against his skin. Even then he looked like he'd been pulled through a knothole. When he finally got done he cornered Dolores in the midst of her cooking. "What's the latest gossip flyin' around?" he wanted to know.

She said Johnny Behan had got the sheriff's star. "Guess who he has made deputy—Pancho Stealwell!"

It did seem a little raw, Turk thought, to go pinning a badge on Frank Stilwell's shirt. All past favors appreciated, it still looked pretty brazen. It had been said, and with considerable justice, Frank had worked the roads so much in these parts all the stage teams stopped whenever they got within sound of his voice. The way it looked to Turk this country was getting so all-fired crooked a man couldn't half the time tell up from down.

"What about Bill?"

She said that, according to what she'd heard, Bill and some of the others had gone down into Sonora right after they'd got back from Skeleton Canyon and run off a big herd of steers to Clanton's ranch in the Las Animas. Clanton was to locate a market. While Bill and his gang were waiting for the Clantons to get another herd together, a bunch of Mexican cowboys, trailing over from Sonora, had caught the bunch napping and recovered their stock. Bill, Ringo, Gauze and some more of them had gone after and caught them in San Luis Pass. They'd been a whale of a fight. Fourteen Mexicans had been killed and Bill's crowd had headed back for Clanton's with the steers. On the way they had tortured like Apaches the eight wounded vaqueros they had rounded up after the battle.

Turk left the shack. He had seen enough during that mule train deal to realize this report was in keeping with the real character of Bill's outfit as he had now come to know it. These were not cowboys. They were renegades, wolves of the chaparral, vicious conscienceless killers no more burdened by scruples than a pack of mad dogs.

It had not been easy for him to arrive at this estimate; and the possibilities it turned loose in his mind were too infinite, to harassing for Turk to sit around with. He quit the shack knowing he had to face these things.

He'd no idea how long he prowled or where that distracted jaunt had taken him. But it was a man who came back, a man tired and peaked but one who had taken account of himself and found where he stood in relation to his fellows.

He had been pretty foolish.

* * *

ANOTHER WEEK CRAWLED PAST, seven days of dread and worry. On the eighth he cleaned his gun again and in the middle of the morning set out for town.

Harassed as he had been Turk had wasted no time in idleness. He'd devoted most of those hours to regaining his strength and making himself fit by many miles of tramping through the dappled sun and shadow underneath the live oaks. He had worn dusty paths through the sparse grass and prickly pear and had done much practicing beneath the trees with his pistol. Never, firing a shot, but whirling and twisting like a man with the twitches, yanking his gun from leather from every conceivable type of disadvantage. He wasn't satisfied yet but the pressure of time and of his hunger for Rita wouldn't let him put off longer coming to grips with this thing.

The first problem, of course, was to get hold of his horses. He went straight to the corral from which he'd borrowed the buckskin the night his plan to free Holly had fizzled. Neither animal was in sight.

Turk didn't waste any words. He told the old wrangler he was looking for his horses. The man looked at him without any particular expression. "Thought you was borryin' that dun fer someone else."

"I was. And still am."

"Well, you ain't borryin' him here."

"You know where he's at?"

"Don't know an' don't wanta know." The old man, tightening his jaws about his cud, turned away.

Turk caught hold of his arm. "This is important—"

The old fellow jerked loose. He scrinched his lips and spat. "You'll get nothin' outa me. You won't get outa this camp, neither."

Turk looked at him narrowly. "Why won't I git out?"

"Because Bill's done passed the orders."

"You mean he's having me watched?"

"I dunno about that. But you won't get no horse, an' you better not try to make off with any. I warned you not to go crossin' up Bill!"

Turk, turning away, went on up the street. This was going to be even less easy than he'd figured. But he could measure the problem now with a cool and uncomplicated interest. Bill had thrown down the gauntlet when he put Turk afoot. The past was canceled out. There was no strings on Turk now. He had no further need for guessing. From here on out it was going to be toe-to-toe slugging with hell's doors open and yawning.

Turk crossed over to Nick Babcock's. Curly Bill wasn't under the trees with his beer; his horse wasn't at the tie rail.

Turk was just as well pleased. He wasn't nursing any illusions about the outcome if he were forced to cross guns with Bill. He pushed through Nick's batwings, hanging fire by the wall until his eyes could make out who was in this gray gloom.

Three men were at the bar. There was nobody at the tables.

"Well," Kelly said, "you finally made it, did you?"

The three heads came around. Charlie Snow, Jim Hughes and Tex Willbrandt. The memory of something tugged the corners of Snow's mouth. Tex, cold sober and with the inevitable peppermint lozenge padding out one cheek, called, "H'are you, feller!" and beckoned him over.

Turk shook his head and lifted one of the chairs off the top of a table. Tex came over with his glass and his eyes didn't miss much. "Still feelin' pretty puny, eh?"

"I've felt better," Turk said grimly. "What's the chances of you roundin' up a couple of horses?"

"Damn poor." Lowering his voice with a covert look toward the bar, Tex said, "I tried to tell you once what this outfit was like. You're stuck with it now. William's laid the law down. No horses for you or it will be too bad for somebody."

"What's the idea?"

"Well," Willbrandt mumbled, kind of chewing it over, "it looks like there's somethin' getting ready to come up where nobody in the bunch but mebbe you kin get the job done." He said to the question in Turk's eyes. "I think the boss is figurin' on sackin' Matamoros."

Turk half got up and then dropped back in his chair. He said grinning, "Quit hoorahin' me."

"I wish to Gawd I was," Tex growled. "This ain't no bull. He's just brash enough to try it. Told Jim Hughes they got statues in a church down there made outen solid silver. He's had me scoutin' wagons—"

"Wagons!" Turk looked at him dumbfounded. "They've got a garrison at Matamoros and at least two forts with cannons. He must be off his rocker!"

"You don't have to convince me," Tex sighed lugubriously. "He's up to somethin', all right. Won't let a one of us off the mesa. Only thing that's been holdin' him up is waitin' fer you to get well, I reckon."

He sloshed the whisky in his glass, morosely watching Hughes and Snow push away from the bar. Turk listened to them dragging their spurs toward the doors. He saw Tex glaring after Snow. "That ugly bastard's had it in fer you ever since you knocked his pardner off the balcony that night."

"Kill him?"

"It might better of. He won't never be the same again."

"Where's Rita?"

Willbrandt gave him a sharp look. "And that's another one'd sooner see you buried than not— that good fer nothin' brother of hers. If it wasn't fer Bill he'd of fixed you already."

"I don't even know the guy—"

"Hell you don't. You know Jake Gauze, don'tcha? That's who I'm talkin' about. He's said flat out you're a spy Earp's planted on us and more'n a few of 'em believe it. Which is still another reason you better figure to stay put. Him and John Ringo swing a heap of weight in this outfit."

Turk scowled at his fist. He knew he had to try anyway, even if the whole camp came after him. Tex was watching him. Turk said, "There's no need for you to git mixed up in this. Just tell me where the horses are and—"

"Man, they'll blast you into doll rags!"

Turk said, "Where's Rita?"

"Up in her room, I guess. Sleepin'." The rusty-haired Willbrandt shook his head. "Hate to see you try it, kid. If you'd wait a spell..." He must have seen Turk's mind was made up. He swore irritably. "Your horse and that buckskin are over back of Jack Dahl's. Bill's keepin' a watch on 'em —Joe Hill and one of the Clanton's. I'll go—"

"You'll stay right here. If you've got to do somethin'

you can tell Rita and Holly I'll meet them back of McCon—"

"You damn idjit," Tex growled, "you won't get ten feet—"

"All right," Turk said, pushing up from the table, I'll go tell them myself." But Willbrandt caught his arm, pulling him down again.

"By Gawd, you're crazier'n Bill. At least don't drag that doll-faced one into it. She's—"

"Tex," Turk broke in. "I rode for Ruebusch's outfit. It's on account of me he got killed. The least I can do is try to git his wife out of this." It was a moral obligation the way Turk looked at it. Holly might be selfish and shallow, and maybe a few other things he didn't want to think about, but she was at heart a good woman living a life that was worse than death. He hadn't forgotten what he'd seen on the balcony, but the way he saw it now she'd been acting a part with Bill, cozening the man till she could get away from him. She couldn't possibly care for ...

"It'll be the first time," Tex grumbled, "I ever helped a man commit suicide, but if you're bound to do it I'll tell 'em. Back of McConaghey's. When do you want 'em there?"

"Give me half an hour," Turk said, discovering Kelly's stare fixed upon them. Kelly kind of jerked and swiped his rag along the bar with somewhat more vigor than looked to be called for. Turk watched him a moment, then got up and went out. He didn't reckon the barkeep could have heard enough to matter. He might, however, decide to tell Bill they'd been chinning.

Turk snorted the frown off his face and went on. Getting frittery as a nervous horse, he thought. Let the old fool tell Bill; by that time they'd be off this damned mesa. He hoped Tex wasn't going to get in trouble over this.

He sauntered all the way down to the far end of the street, trying to build up the notion he had nothing more important on his mind than his hat. He even shot the breeze a while with the barber, Ridge Cullum, who was squatting on his stoop mashing flies with a talcum box. Every time a new crop would bed down on this slaughter he would grind the box down again, smearing a few more into the bloody boards while he grumbled and cussed at the state of his business.

"Some days," he said, "there just ain't enough hours to take care of these sports, then I'll go for two weeks without splittin' a whisker. Times, by Gawd, is changin'! A lot of these bums is shavin' themselves and they'd sooner go dirty than wait for the tub. Used to be a feller'd get his hair cut every ten days, reg'lar as clock work. Now they wait till it's curlin' round their collars! Take a look at that shelf of tonics—that'll show you what this trade is a-comin' to. Ain't sold a drop for nigh onto six weeks!" He slammed the talcum box down on a few more unfortunates. "I'm goin' to get in some other line of work. Best job in this country," he growled testily, "is undertakin'."

Turk pushed on. When he got to the end of the street he started back, still dawdling. He saw Milt Hicks coming down the walk, saw him jawing with Cullum. Saw old Ridge wiping off his talcum box and Hicks, climbing the steps, follow Cullum inside.

Turk cut left behind the Mercantile. He stopped and stood listening for a couple of minutes among the discarded tins and broken crates. He didn't guess anyone was following him but he waited a bit longer just to play double safe. Then he went on toward the rear of Jack Dahl's, scanning the oaks that grew behind the place carefully.

When he got about four doors from them he began catching glimpses of the pole corral. He saw a flash of coffee color through the branches which he took to be High Sailin; and afterwards saw the buckskin, which was the bleached-out shade of coffee with a mess of cream in it. There were eight or ten other horses in the pen with them. He didn't see any guards hanging around.

He began to feel a little more hopeful. If they'd been watching the horses ever since he'd been in bed with that wound they must be pretty well fed up with it. Even taking their turns at it, and if only for the last few days, they'd by this time be looking on the whole deal as crackpot. Nobody but Jake had ever seemed to give a damn if he was with them or not; even downing two men in that street fight with Roman 4 wasn't going to make the bulk of Bill's outfit take him serious. Turk remembered that Tex had said there weren't any of them allowed to quit the mesa right now, but not even this could dampen his sudden rise in spirits. He had a hunch he was going to bring this off.

With this pen full of stock he'd have no trouble mounting Holly. Probably be plenty of saddles around; anyway he and Rita could do without hulls if they had to.

He was just a shade uneasy about how Rita might react to having Holly along, but he didn't see how he could just plain up and leave her. He reckoned he owed her at least the chance to get away.

Some remote part of his thinking suggested she might not be finding time so heavy on her hands here, but he brushed that notion aside with contempt. She was here because she couldn't help herself. Maybe she had kind of led Bill on, making the most of what chances she had. He didn't see how a man could honestly hold that against her, everything considered and Ruebusch being dead and all. There was a cold streak of practicality running through Holly, but she'd pile out of here quick enough once she saw the way.

His blood began to warm as his thoughts swung back to Rita. There, by God, was a girl a man could tie to, and he was glad at long last he'd gathered sense enough to know it. The thoughts of coming home to her would give a man plenty of peck to get on with. You couldn't judge the whole world by what you found around Tombstone. There were other, better places. Someplace he'd find a country both of them could fit into. He'd put his wages into cattle ...

The sight of Joe Hill jerked his mind away from his thinking. There was a rifle in the crook of Hill's arm. He seemed to be lounging against a tree half asleep but he was doing it where he could watch the corral and Turk knew he would have to take care of Hill first. He spent another three minutes trying to turn up a Clanton before, deciding there wasn't any Clantons around, he commenced injuning up to the tree Hill was propping.

He was reaching for his pistol, getting ready to jump, when Ike Clanton said from out of the branches, "Just unbuckle the belt, boy, an' let that thing drop."

FOURTEEN

IT WAS HARD—DAMNABLY hard, but Turk did it. He didn't have any choice, knowing Ike would be covering him and that a gunshot, even if it didn't out-and-stop him, would fetch the rest of them running before he could ever expect to loose the horses. His time would come, he thought. Better to play along for now and let these galoots think they had the upper hand on him.

They did have, too. Hill came away from the tree, chuckling; and back of Turk, as Turk's gun-weighted belt hit the ground, Jake Gauze laughed nastily. Then the others moved up and were suddenly all about him, sneering and snickering as Hill, waving Turk back, picked his belt up.

Bill said, "Boy, I'm surprised at you."

He didn't look surprised though. He looked like a cat with a mouthful of goldfish.

Turk, having nothing to say, kept his jaws shut.

Bill beckoned Charlie Snow up. Still considering Turk, he said, "Ain't no use in you latherin' about McConaghey's kid—nor about them two girls. They ain't over there. Holly come her ownself and told me what you was up to no sooner than Willbrandt got out of sight."

He grinned at the look of Turk. A couple others snickered.

Turk was lost in the chaos of conflicting thoughts, unable to believe it. The blood roared in his ears. His fists clenched so tight the nails bit into his palms and he was seized with an impulse to smash them into Bill's face. Snow, narrowly watching him, dug the barrel of his pistol into Turk's ribs. He said, "Gawd, what a sucker!" plainly hoping Turk would try something.

Turk had sense enough to know it. The pent-up needs in him turned him giddy. Bill wavered in his vision like something seen through red mist. It got worse when he thought of Rita, but he was helpless and knew it.

He shook his head to clear it and Bill's face came into focus. Bill's dimples were still showing and a reflection of the mocking grin still rode the stiff set of his heavy lips, but there was no mirth in his glance—nothing but the cold black shine of his anger.

"How far'd you figure I was goin' to let you go?"

"I wasn't thinkin' of you," Turk said; and Bill snorted.

"Git his horse," he told Gauze, "an' tie him into the saddle. Hicks—go help Ike and Hill git them grub sacks from Kelly. We're pullin' out right away. John," he growled at Ringo, "you go after Tex and git him roped onto a horse same's the kid here. Zwing, you go pass the word to the rest of the boys. I want every man packin' a—"

He never got to the end of that sentence. A shout

went up in the road out front. A racket of boots and cursing swept tumultuously nearer through the gut of the passage between Dahl's place and the next to the left of it. For these shreds of split seconds the gang's attention was divided.

Turk didn't wait for anything better. Slamming around in the midst of this uproar he clouted Snow's pistol away from his ribs, hearing a yell as flame burst from its muzzle. He twisted the weapon out of Snow's grasp and struck Snow across the face with the butt of it. As the man reeled back, taking two others with him, Turk crashed a boot at another man's shin and, coming full around, buried his gun-weighted fist in Jake's stomach.

The very fury of his attack held them stunned for a moment. Air left Gauze like the gust from a bellows and as he came doubling over Turk cracked him across the head with the pistol. Turk kneed another as Gauze went down.

Turk reversed the gun and slashed with its barrel. Clanton, trying to leap clear, got hung up in his spurs. Bill's bull-throated roar sailed above the shouts and cursing and Turk, alerted, saw Bill's gun coming up. He lost his advantage trying to duck away from it, crashing into a man whose arms locked about him like the jaws of a vice. He still had his gun free but he couldn't shoot Bill. He stamped sharp heels viciously onto the booted toes of the man who held him, hopes soaring again as the fellow's arms fell away; but the chance was gone. He saw Bill's face springing toward him, saw the gleam of Bill's upswung gun slashing down. He tried to twist away but hands caught him and held him and blackness enveloped him in a bright blaze of rockets.

He didn't see Rita tear out of the alley and crash full tilt into the arms of Zwing Hunt. He didn't know Jake Gauze kicked him twice in the face or that Charlie Snow, staggering over, would have killed him out of hand if Bill hadn't stopped him. He didn't know another thing till he came groggily back to full miserable consciousness nearly an hour later to see the ground reeling under him and realize he was roped face down across a horse.

The dust kicked up by other horses almost strangled him. Every jolting stride of the animal beneath him went like a slap of a hand through his head and he was sick, vomiting wretchedly.

He must have mercifully blanked out again. The next time he opened his eyes it was night and he was stretched on the ground with his wrists lashed behind him and both ankles tied together with rope. He didn't realize this until he tried unsuccessfully to roll over. Pain splintered through cramped arms and legs with the effort. His head and face commenced to throb and he could hardly breathe. His stomach muscles, bruised from contact with the saddle, sorely knotted but the convulsion did not bring anything up. He guessed there was nothing left to bring up.

His face felt as though a horse had lain down on it and his thickened tongue found gaps in his jaw teeth. He thought his head must surely burst and it took him a considerable while to understand the claret lacings of light permeating the blackness came not from the expanding and contraction of his skull but from the flicker and flames of an open fire. It was after this he realized the top half of him was soaking wet.

He heard the growl of Bill's voice tell someone to

"git the ropes off him," and felt boots approach and rough hands pulling him over. The pain set him crazy when the loosened ropes let the blood pound through his limbs again; and he groaned, trying to writhe away from it.

"You ain't hurt," Bill said. "You got off damn cheap. Sit up there now and put your mind on what I'm sayin'."

Turk's hands wouldn't hold the weight of him. He dropped back, helpless, on his face and chest and somebody, cursing, pulled him over and, catching him under the arms, dragged him back about ten feet and propped him up against a tree. Zwing Hunt said, "You want me to give him another drenchin'?"

Bill said, "Git away from him. He ain't goin' noplace in that shape."

Turk's head began to clear, but getting it off the ground did little to relieve the splitting ache and throbbing pound of it. He had to hold it still in order to keep his stomach quiet.

His eyes began to function again and he saw Curly Bill and Jake Gauze's squatty shape and, back of them, others of the gang hunkered down around the fire among the gear and blankets that lay scattered about. He couldn't make out Bill's expression with the flames behind him that way.

Jake, farther over, was turned enough that half of his face was lit up by the glow. The venom in his glowering stare leaped against Turk like the glint of a razor.

Bill said, coming nearer, "You got one chance to set yourself straight with this bunch. One chance. We're goin' down to Mexico. You'll be helpin' Jake crack a bank when we git there."

Turk couldn't laugh because his face hurt too bad. He managed a croaking sound though and Bill got the drift. He hunched burly shoulders and cracked his knuckles, saying thinly, "You'll go through with it, kid. Take a look to the left of you."

Turk wasn't minded to give them any satisfaction, but curiosity finally turned his head and the shock of what he saw all but paralyzed his thinking. Rita, heartlessly trussed as a calf for the branding, lay motionless huddled a few feet away from him. Holly's dress, ravaged but still around her, more resembled a dishrag than anything better. The bedraggled hem of its skirt was above her shapely knees and there was dirt ground into them; one sleeve was torn away from the shoulder and a dark bruise showed above the swell of her breast. He saw dried blood on her cheeks and though her eyes were open they were like glass doors in an empty house.

"She's all right," Bill said. "Been handled a little rough is all. How much more of it she gits will be strictly up to you."

Turk's rigid face was the color of a wagon sheet. Now that the first awful sickness had passed, the stunned incredulity that had held him silent was loosening its hold and a black rage was pounding through him, a towering monstrous fury the like of which he'd never known. He sat there shaking like a man with the ague but this was not the kid who had been duped at Willow Springs.

He got hold of himself. "I'm listenin'," he said finally.

Bill chuckled, throwing a look at Jake Gauze. "You can take them ropes off Willbrandt now." He brought his glance back to Turk.

"Here's the deal. I'm takin' the most of the boys down to Matamoros—everything's set. At Mier we split up. Jake will take ten men, includin' you and Willbrandt, to Monterrey. One of the banks there will be holding fifty thousand in U.S. dollars—payrolls fer gringo mines. You'll pull the stickup and keep the bank crowd under gunpoint while Hughes and Tex Willbrandt is sackin' up the dough. The rest of the boys, with Jake, will be holdin' the horses and keepin' things quiet outside. It's a pushover—Jake'll give you the details later. We'll wait fer you at Hyler's Pass. Rita stays with us."

He didn't make any remarks about what would happen to her if Turk or Willbrandt fouled up the bank job. He didn't have to.

* * *

THEY REACHED Guerrero ten days later. It was a grueling trip and they were all saddle gaunted and the horses needed a rest. Bill used nothing but the best but they were in hard shape. Bill decided to spend three days around the place, where he would pose as a Texas cow boss on his way to Villaldama. But Jake Gauze said to hell with the rest, his boys would take the trail to Monterrey come daybreak. Bill, grinning, struck off for the town with Ringo and Ike Clanton while the rest of the outfit offsaddled and those appointed to the task commenced preparations for supper.

Turk saw Rita being untied to help with this but he was sent by Hughes to hunt for wood or cow chips and did not get to speak with her. She'd been kept away from him during the rides and there had so far been little chance at their camps for him to do much more than speak a few brief words of reassurance to her. There were galled places and several running sores where her ankles had been roped each day to the fish-cord cinch underneath her horse's belly, and she looked gaunt and utterly hopeless. There was a volcano of resentment building up inside of Turk but there'd been nothing he could do about it. Nor had he been able to talk with Willbrandt. The three of them were under constant watch and Turk had done what he'd been told to do and kept his mouth tight buttoned lest things be made more difficult for her. But he was storing it up.

He made three trips to the fire with his towsack full of cow chips before he could get a word with her. Billy Grounds was peeling spuds but Hughes called him off for something before Turk got there. It left the girl briefly alone with him.

She plainly meant to ignore him but the second time he spoke her name it brought her head around. She stared, unwilling to look at him, off across to where Hughes stood talking with Grounds. Turk said, "I'll make this up to you, Rita."

"It doesn't matter."

"Of course it matters!"

"Nothing matters any more," she said listlessly. "I'll soon be dead."

The resigned indifference of her tone both shocked and angered him. "Don't talk like that!" he said sharply. "I've been pretty much of a fool, but soon's I git back from this Monterrey thing—"

"You won't be coming back," she said harshly. "When you've done what they want Jake will kill you."

"He may try but I'll be back. You can count on it."

Her eyes touched his face. There was life in them now. He was reminded of the look sometimes seen on a prodded bull. "Why do you keep talking about it? You don't have to pretend you are interested—I don't want your pity." She said with a look almost of hate on her features, "Go back to your ripe wheat woman if you get free— she has had more experience, she will know how to please you!"

Turk's ears were hot and the blood was pounding in his throat but he was going to have his say if he had to grab and hold her. He did reach out but she eluded his grasp. There was plenty of fire in her now. Her eyes blazed at him.

Turk's voice was bitter but it was stubborn, too. "You got a right to them thoughts, a heap more right than you know, I reckon, but when I git back I'm comin' for you. No matter where you are I'm going to find you. And we're going to find a priest and git the right words said, words that'll bind you and me together forever—"

"Forever," Hughes said, coming up with his gun out, "is the hole you're bein' dumped into if you don't pick up that sack and get back to your dung huntin' pronto."

FIFTEEN

IT WAS long after dark and they had two fires going and most of the bunch had eaten and were scattered around, some working over their gear, some cleaning their guns and some sleeping, when Curly Bill, Ringo and the rawboned Clanton got back from town. Bill's mouth was tight and his eyes looked ugly. "Put out them fires and saddle up," he shouted.

"What's the big idea?" Hughes said. "I thought—"

"We're gittin' out of here. On the double!" It developed that Guerrero had been packed to the gills with Mexican vaqueros holding some kind of a celebration. At first everything had gone smooth as silk. Bill had bought his supplies and a couple dozen extra saddle horses and the three had gone into a saloon for some refreshment. The local *patron*—a big rancher and his burly cow boss had been in there and these and John Ringo had got into a card game. Clanton and Bill had been at the bar drinking. When Bill left to find a man with a wagon to fetch out the grub he'd bought, Clanton had been making passes at a Mexican bar maid. The girl's husband had come in but Ike had tentatively smoothed things over when sharp words arose at the card table. The burly Mexican cow boss had accused Ringo of dealing off the bottom of the deck. Bill was coming in the door when Ringo jumped up and shot the man. Nothing after that seemed to Turk to be very coherent, but before the three had got out of there, there were four dead Mexicans sprawled on the floor, and one of them was the old don himself.

"Hell," Jake Gauze scoffed, "We can take care of a bunch of dumb cow hands—"

"We can't afford a fight now," Bill snarled, "we've got to git whackin'. That goddam cow boss has sent for the *Rurales*."

There was no more argument. The fires were doused and ten minutes later they were all in leather, riding. Nobody cared to invite gunplay with the Mexican mounted police who had a hard reputation and were recruited mostly from outlaws. Win, lose or draw, Bill's whole outfit knew that if they tangled with *Rurales* their bank and other plans were done for. They rode straight west on the trail to Paras. "We'll swing around it," Bill said, "and drop south to Agualeguas. We'll git into the hills and lose those bastards before we do anything else—we kin rest later."

The horses were staggering when they got into the hills, but they did get into them; and if they had not lost the vaqueros from Guerrero, at least they had seen no evidence of their proximity—nor did they now. Bill ordered the gang down for a two-hour rest.

In the rush of getting away from Guerrero there'd been no chance to pick up the supplies Bill had bought or the horses. Tempers were short. Bill and Ringo weren't speaking. In the milky half-light that was forerunner to dawn Bill was just making ready to call in the pickets when a sudden eruption of cursing broke out, terminated by the loud crash of gunshots.

Bill came through the gray gloom like the wrath of God. Zwing Hunt was down with a bullet through his groin and Milt Hicks stood over him with a pistol in his fist, daring Grounds to take a hand in it. Hunt, it seemed, had been discovered by Hicks sneaking grub from what was left of the outfit's scanty rations.

"You damn fools!" Bill snarled, sending Grounds reeling with a blow to the jaw. "Git into your saddles!" He waved his arms, including all of them. "Next sonofabitch pops a cap around here better put one into himself or by Gawd I'll do it for him!"

The pickets came in, drawn by the gunfire; and Charlie Snow, as the others moved off to catch up their horses, complained that Turk ought to be tied lest, during the day's run through these timbered hills, he try to get away from them. "Hell with that," Bill growled, still glaring at Hicks, "he ain't like to try nothin' long's we've got that damn girl." He shoved Snow aside and went tramping after his horse.

Turk hadn't even been thinking of flight but now looking up, he crossed glances with Willbrandt and saw the man's eyebrows lift. Turk threw the gear on High Sailin, remembering that Rita was riding the tough buckskin and that, in the confusion of quitting their last camp, Hughes had neglected to re-rope her ankles.

They moved south through the rolling hills at a dogtrot. The sun came up and fell hot and strong on Turk's left side and shoulder. But after a couple of hours it hazed over.

The terrain became more difficult. Their pace was slowed to a walk and Turk, still considering Willbrandt's show of raised eyebrows, reckoned thoughts of escape were exercising him too. They had little to look forward to, either of them—Rita was right about that. He'd seen enough of Bill's methods to know that once Bill's purpose was served and the gang had grabbed that bank dough, there would be no gnashing of teeth or wailing if Jake's crew came back with two empty saddles.

Jake had taken a dislike to Turk right from the start. And the guy was plumb crazy—mean and ornery was the way Rita had put it; completely no good, a renegade who had caused his family nothing but grief. A kill-crazy chaparral wolf. Look at the way he used his own sister—his half-sister really, but still blood of his blood. Never opening his mouth no matter how this bunch treated her.

An hour short of noon Bill called another halt to rest and graze the horses. They were in a cup-shaped valley ringed by open hills. The air was heavy, stifling. Bill sent three men up the slope to watch their back trail. Jerked beef was passed around, salty and thirst-inspiring. Fortunately there was water. Willbrandt sat with legs stretched out, his back against the hot slant of a boulder. Gauze motioned Turk over beside him and left Charlie Snow to stretch the saddle cramp out of their backs, but the most of the bunch simply sprawled in the grass, hats over their faces, catching what rest they were able.

Willbrandt said, "You better get that girl outa here. I don't cotton to the way that damn Grounds has been eyein' her."

Turk said, "Tonight?"

They'd been keeping it low, not even looking toward each other. Before Willbrandt could answer, Snow came catfooting over with a scowl and told them to shut their damned faces. He was spoiling for trouble, just looking for an excuse to work them over with his six-shooter.

Turk let the talk go, chewing down on his temper, but Willbrandt said, "You been noticing that sky?"

Snow swelled up like a poised pup, anger darkening the wrinkled skin above his collar. He stepped nearer to Willbrandt, yanking out his gun like he was minded to shut Tex's mouth himself. Just short of hitting him something stayed Snow's hand. "Get around the other side of that rock," he snarled. "You open your trap again to me and I'll give you something to sing about!"

Willbrandt got up with a shrug and moved around to the rock's other side, settling down again. He tipped the slant of his hat across his eyes. Something about the gesture infuriated Snow. Sucking air into his lungs he shouted for Billy Grounds and Joe Hill.

The two came running. "Grab that bastard and haul him up where I kin get at him!" Snow yelled hoarsely, snatching his belt off. Turk, watching the pair closing in on Tex, thrust a boot out and sent Grounds sprawling. Snow spun, cursing, as Turk jumped to his feet; he tried to catch Turk in the face with the buckle of that belt, but Turk put up his arm, diving under it, his other fist connecting solidly with Snow's jaw. Snow let go of the belt and let his head roll, afterwards leaping at Turk with a switch knife. Turk grabbed off his hat and threw it at the man. Before he could do anything else, or Snow could grab him, a big fist grabbed Turk and whirled him crashing into the boulder. There was a bone-bruising thud of flesh against flesh, a gasping whistle of breath, and Snow went by like the westbound express. Ringo, Jake Gauze and four or five others stood near enough to have grabbed him but no one put out a hand. He struck the trampled-down grass all spraddled out and got up, visibly shaking, with his face like putty.

"I ain't tellin' you fools again!" Bill roared. "That's dust back yonder! Pile into them saddles!"

The bunch took one look and ran for their horses. In the resultant confusion, Turk, pushing himself off the rock with skinned hands, caught a glint in the grass, reeled a few groggy steps and stumbled, falling across it. It was a gun, all right. He got it into his shirtfront and shoved to his feet. Tex, crossing in front of him, muttered, "Somethin' you oughta know. That bank—"

"Git whackin'!" Gauze shouted, whirling around and scowling back at them.

They pushed steadily into the hot winds from the south. Their sore-footed, dust raddled, dog-weary horses were still moving three hours later, but they were strung out now for half a mile and some of them weren't going to last much longer. The faces of the men were getting desperate, Turk saw, as they looked back across their shoulders. That dust Bill had spotted was drawing perceptibly nearer and was obviously whipped up by a large body of horsemen which no one doubted were *Rurales* reinforced by the dead don's vaqueros.

Bill pulled up, twisting around in his saddle, shoulders bulking sharp against the queer lemon look of the sky. "We're goin' to have to split up. Jake's boys will meet at Higueras—I'll look for my bunch outside

Aldamas. Mebbe we can lose those bastards in this storm. Five-six of you bust off into the east with Clanton. Some more of you go with Hughes—John, here, will take a few. Rest of you foller me. Let's go!"

The wind fell as dust whirled around them. Horses flattened their ears under the bite of spurs and flogging squirts as the gang streaked off in six directions. Some were bound to see gunsmoke but, equally certain, some of them, at least, would get clean away. It was the only chance they had with tired mounts. Turk tried to see which bunch Rita was wrapped up in but in that pounding bedlam of dust and confusion he could not find her. Charlie Snow came pelting astride his blue roan and struck High Sailin across the rump with his quirt and Milt Hicks came up behind him, hazing Turk after Jake. There was no chance of Turk getting out of it.

They ran down a ridge and quartered south again, belaboring their mounts through a rock littered gulch that, after two miles, opened into another pass between hills; and the wind struck them, cooler. There were six of them with Jake and Turk saw Willbrandt pounding along beside Gauze up in front.

They cut into another canyon and they were climbing through spruce and juniper. The country was getting rougher and darkness was closing in on them with the wind getting colder and colder. Coming out on ledgerock at the top of the grade Turk saw that the ones ahead of him had pulled up. Jake said, "There's two ways we kin go here," and pointed. "Down there, which is shorter and open, or off to the left up into them slopes where there's cover when we git to it."

Snow said, "You're bossin' this," and Jake twisted

his mouth at him. "We swing left then," he said, "an' be damn sure you remember it."

He led off, Willbrandt following; and then Turk saw Rita. She was trying to get back to him but Hicks turned in front of her, blocking the trail, grinning, forcing her on again. There was a lift of gladness in Turk, then flaring anger at Hicks overshadowed by a frustrating sense of futility. He still had the gun but he knew better than to reach for it. The watchful shine of these men's glances curled around him like a wall of knives, hemming him in with their distrust and with their readiness for violence. It was like the stench rolling off a swamp—that plain. Shivering, he glanced again at the sky; and back of him Grounds said, "Don't take root there!"

He kneed High Sailin after the others, following the rumps of their horses through the failing light, dogging them around the ribs of towering rocks and between the gray faces of balanced boulders that hugged the trail like crouching cats; and the raw wind beat against him, flapping the brim of his hat and his scarf ends.

Bill in his shrewdness had tied Turk's hands with his unvoiced threat against Rita, but that was past. Now they were both with Jake; and Turk, in Jake's scheme of things, was expendable. Jake would kill him out of hand on the thinnest pretense of an excuse. There was no need to ask where that would leave Rita. There was nothing Turk could do but play along.

They came onto a high plateau in the first full tide of a too early darkness with storm streaks flogging the tops of the grass roots and a hard wind roaring up out of the south. He had seen bad storms around Tombstone but never anything to compare with the look of the one building now. They crossed the spine of the bench with dust and flung grit pelting into their faces. Turk had to button his brush jacket to keep it from being ripped off him. Then, as they hit the far end of this open, the wind quit abruptly. It became so still he got to wondering if his ears were stopped up, but the others also were staring strangely about them. In this eerie light objects even at some distance appeared as sharply defined as though bathed in fluorescence. "Be a dinger," Willbrandt grunted, drawing black looks from those who rode nearest him.

Gauze turned his horse up the bleak slope ahead of them, still scowling into the south where, pale against the far horizon, there was what looked to be a considerable stretch of sand. Turk wondered what was gnawing him.

He found it hard to reconcile this dour killer with his relationship to Rita. He got to thinking inexplicably of what Willbrandt had been saying when Snow had broken their talk up. "That bank—" Tex had said, obviously attempting to get something across to him. Turk had a hunch it had been something important or Snow wouldn't have come tearing into them so rabidly. Turk was minded to try to come up with Tex now...

He waited out the climb till they came onto another grassy bench—this whole region was like that, tiny prairies locked between broken country and timber. They were high enough now to get a fairly wide view of it. Some of those stretches looked pretty ugly, not the kind of terrain a man would care to prowl come nightfall. But now, as his stare again touched that south horizon, he ceased to wonder at Jake's frowning looks. What he had taken for sand covered a greater area now. It was nearer, more like fog, a kind of lemonish dun in appearance, rough and wavery as though filled with movement and ragged along the high top edge like the mane of a horse with the wind streaming through it. *Dust!*

It was coming straight for them. It was still at a considerable distance but it was covering ground with an astonishing speed. Turk nudged High Sailin's ribs with a spur, putting the horse around Milt Hicks and easing him forward toward the girl's position.

Snow called after him but Turk ignored it. Shrugging out of his brush jacket he maneuvered the brown alongside the girl's buckskin. "Here...git into this," he said, holding it out to her.

She accepted it, smiling shyly; but her eyes as she buttoned it about her were solemn. Jake glanced back without speaking, hardly noticing, and almost at once his frowning stare returned to that towering onsweeping wall of dust. It was nearer, perceptibly nearer, Turk saw with a mounting excitement. If, as seemed likely, it should shortly envelop them...

He tried to catch Willbrandt's eye where he rode beyond the girl. But Rita, crowding the buckskin against High Sailin, leaned toward Turk, saying desperately, "We've simply got to do something. That bank—"

"Watch it!" Willbrandt growled.

Reflex put Turk's spur into the brown and the murderous sweep of Snow's swinging rifle butt, thus deprived of its goal, almost tore Snow out of the stirrups. Turk drove High Sailin hard at Snow's roan but Willbrandt's arm, catching Turk around the middle, dragged him bodily from the saddle. "Wait, you fool—wait for the dust!" Tex breathed.

Snow wasn't waiting for anything. He slammed his

horse into Willbrandt's mount pinning Turk, still caught in the circle of Tex's arm, between them. Twice Snow's sledging knuckles crashed into Turk's face before Turk, going limp, dropped into a maelstrom of churning hoofs. He heard Rita scream and was still enough conscious to cover his head with his arms, but he was struck three times before those hoofs cleared away from him.

It looked worse than it was because, in spite of the blood, in such close quarters the horses hadn't chance to put much heart behind their kicking.

A rough hand caught Turk's shoulder and hauled him upright. Milt Hicks this was, he noticed, and saw Rita running toward him. Snow's shape cut in between them and he saw Snow's fist coming at him again. He let his head roll with the blow but it was still bad enough. Snow's left hand got a hold on Turk's shirtfront and his right went back to full cock for another. More by instinct than anything Turk brought up a knee and Snow reeled away from him.

Hicks tightened his grip. "Grounds—" Jake yelled, "work him over with your pistol!"

Hicks had both of Turk's arms twisted back of him and things were happening so fast they hadn't yet had time to realize Turk was making his final stand. Snow was still doubled over, hugging himself, whimpering. Turk tried to ward off Grounds with an outthrust leg but Hicks kicked the other leg out from under him. Turk's whole sagged weight wasn't enough to buckle Hicks; but Rita was into it now, pounding Hicks and clawing at him.

If Willbrandt had sided with them they might have had a chance, but the rusty-haired pepper-mint-chewer remained wedded to his saddle with his gray cheeks strictly neutral.

As Grounds came leaping in Turk hauled up both knees and slammed booted heels down, hoping to connect with Hick's instep. Hicks was watching for it and shifted but Turk managed to put him off balance. He tried in the interim to get at Hick's holster and Hicks, trying to block that, tripped under Rita's pummeling.

They went down, Turk taking the brunt of it. But Hick's hold was loosened. Turk wrenched one arm free and dug in his heels, twisting with all the strength that was in him. It forced Hicks over, giving Turk a chance to pull some air into his lungs. Wind scoured his cheeks with grit and he heard the increasing fury of it howl across the bench. He scratched Hick's legs with his blunt-roweled spurs, writhing, struggling to break clear of the man. He flipped over, pounding his free fist into Hick's belly, and Hicks came back with shortarm jabs to the jaw. Turk, shifting again, saw Jake piling out of his saddle, face twisted with rage and impatience. "Get in there, Grounds, an' smash him!"

Grounds tried. Turk lashed out with a leg, the sharp toe of his boot catching Grounds in the knee. Grounds yelled, dropping back. Rita, with both hands clenched in Hick's hair, was beating Hicks' head against the shale littered earth. Willbrandt's jaded horse began pitching, getting into Jake's way as Jake snatched out his pistol.

Grounds was circling again. Snow, making sounds like a busted accordion, was on hands and knees trying to locate his six-shooter. Grounds, ready now, was coming in low with a lifted gun, plainly bent on cracking Turk's skull. Turk got loose of Hick's hold just as Grounds made his swing and that down-flailing gun barrel, barely missing Turk's head, buried its steel in Hick's throat with the sound of a cow coming out a bog hole.

Rita, letting go of Hicks' head, jumped up just as Turk gained his feet. He thrust her away from him. "Git your horse!" he gasped, flinging himself to the left as Grounds, recovering, fired. Another gun hammered back at Turk. He felt the slug break flesh along his right thigh and, wincing away from it, lost his balance. He went down, almost falling into the flame of Ground's gun, the powder blast half blinding him. He lurched erect, coughing, trying to get the picked-up pistol from the tatters of his shirt.

Strange, he thought, what pranks a man's mind played. Once he'd have given his right arm to ride with this bunch; now all he wanted was Rita and a chance to get out of this. He saw Grounds, through the drifting dust, desperately cramming his gun with fresh loads.

Turk had the pistol clear of his shirt now and lifted it. But that was immature, the Curly Bill way. While he stood hesitating, torn between a natural desire and the new hard-won knowledge of a man's responsibilities, dust came with a howling gust of wind, enveloping the bench, absorbing sound, blotting everything from sight.

He ran, filled with fright, calling Rita's name; and the wind took hold of him, buffeting and staggering him, suffocating as a blanket, fencing him in with his terror of losing her.

Like a ghost out of nowhere she appeared on High Sailin, kicked a foot from the stirrup and reached down a hand for him. Shaking with reaction he got a boot in the oxbow, was about to swing up, when a second mounted shape appeared through the murk. Barely discernible, it was bucking the teeth of the wind, pushing south at the very edge of visibility, perhaps thirty feet to the right of them.

Convinced it was Willbrandt, Turk cried out, shouting hoarsely. Catching hold of the brown's reins he was about to go plunging after the man when three coronas of light briefly blossomed through the dust. It was the tiny cork-stopper popping of gunfire that sent Turk up behind Rita and hammered his heels into High Sailin's flanks.

Twice within the hour Turk wanted to stop and rest the horse, but both times the girl's desperate voice kept them going. "Now," she said abruptly, "here there is a cave where we can take shelter for a little while."

"How come you know about it?"

"It is not far from Monterrey—all my life I have ridden these hills. Inside it will be dry and there'll be wood. We'll have a fire. A little one."

"But won't Jake...?"

"Hoh! He will never find this place; but we must not stay. We dare not chance that he shall reach the town before us. We must warn the garrison what he plans. My poor father's small life savings are in that bank. For him it would be ruin— You think this is perhaps too much I ask? To pay for our great happiness?"

His arm gripped her waist more tightly. Nothing would ever be too much for that. The soldiers might not catch Bill's bunch, but other soldiers, elsewhere, probably would before Bill was done with this. Turk wondered if Holly would be with him then. Probably not, for Bill was not the kind, Turk knew now, who could long be true to anyone. Or to anything but the wildness in him. But she'd make out; there would always be another man somewhere.

"No," Turk said, "we must let them know about Jake, of course. We'll push straight on. After we're married—"

"Ah, *querido*—heart of my heart..." Twisting around she pressed her cold cheek to his, and there was warmness between them. "We will do this thing then. And all I will care for after that—all I will care to be, I mean, is wife to a cowman. To you, Turkey Red!"

G STANDS FOR GUN

ONE

BEHIND THE COUNTER OF THE COME-AN'-GET-IT restaurant, the red-haired girl abruptly stemmed the crimson tide of her invective. Curiosity merged with the dark blue wrath in her stormy eyes as she swept an appraising glance across the lean figure of the man standing solidly just inside the swinging door.

Strangers, to Lisabet Corbin's experience, were common as rubble-rock in Tortilla Flat since the discovery of gold and copper deposits in the Superstitions two months back had boomed the town. But a *gentleman* was a thing uncommon rare.

Hoisting herself to a comfortable perch upon the back counter, Lisabet Corbin suspended her detailed libel of Stone Latham's ancestry, let the gum lay idle in her mouth while gravely she studied the sample Fate had sent her.

The unknown was broad of shoulder, wiry-waisted and lean of hip; a dusty, leather-faced man in worn range garb. Discovery of a stubborn chin, a hawk's beak nose and determined lips that just now were curved in a faint smile, rewarded her scrutiny. But it was his eyes that caught her instant interest. They were gray, like smoky sage, and serene and confident and quiet as they rested on Stone Latham's darkly scowling face.

Stone Latham's lips twisted in a' sneer and his lantern jaw swung belligerently forward. "What was that crack?" he said.

The four late customers ranging the stools along the plank counter stared at the stranger with an air of expectancy which told of their knowledge of Latham's prowess.

"I said," the stranger drawled, still faintly smiling, "that a man-sized gent had ought to be able to find better ways of amusin' himself than baitin' a defenseless girl."

Stone Latham, as the watchers caught their breaths in a united "Ah!" swept the stranger with a slow insolent glance that passed from head to feet.

"Are you aimin' to make somethin' out of it, pilgrim?"

The stranger's grin disclosed twin sets of hard white teeth. "Shucks," he said, "I was just makin' a observation, so to speak."

"Yeah? Well, observations is dangerous as hell in this man's town. I'd admire to hear y'u take that 'un back right pronto!"

The stranger made no reply. He stood there easily, his hands hanging at his sides, the lazy smile still on his lips. Then suddenly he laughed.

Lisabet Corbin tingled to a swift cold thrill as Stone Latham, his right hand dropping to his holstered gun, took three long steps toward the mocking stranger and flung back his left hand, palm open, to slap the stranger's face.

It was an old affair, this trick of Latham's. It was a thing Lisabet Corbin had seen Latham get away with time after time. For, timed to the sound of his slap, his naked right-hand gun had always either intimidated his victim or brought him to a speedy grave.

It was intended to do so now. With his right hand clamped about gun-butt, Stone Latham's left hand started toward the stranger's face.

But this time Latham's blow was not permitted to land. He checked it in mid-air. And for the most excellent of reasons—something cold and hard and rigid was pressed uncomfortably against his stomach.

The stranger's grin grew wider, but there was nothing humorous in the gray depths of his cold-eyed glance as he drawled:

"You're keepin' the lady waitin', hombre. She an' me is cravin' to hear you orate as how them disrespectful words of yourn was lies. An' you better orate quick."

An angry red washed into Stone Latham's scowling cheeks, then, swiftly fading, left them a sickly sallow gray. For the space of a hasty heartbeat he hesitated, then his hand came away from his gun and joined its mate above his head.

"I reckon," he growled thickly, "I was thinkin' about some oth—about someone else."

The something cold and hard and rigid dug deeper into the flabby muscles of Latham's stomach. "An' I expect you're allowin'," the stranger's drawl was inexorable, "that this lady's reputation is plumb unreproachable, that there was no occasion for either your remark or the insinuatin' sneer on your kisser, an' that in the future you'll see that it goes hard with any polecat that maligns her in your hearin'?"

Stone Latham licked burning lips while a vein throbbed wildly on his temple. His eyes were venomous with hate when he finally snarled:

"That—that's right."

The stranger stepped back with an easy smile, exposing the fact that he'd menaced Latham with nothing more dangerous than a rigid index finger.

But though the watchers saw, none snickered.

Stone Latham, when he could trust his voice, said wickedly, "I'll be rememb'rin' that. An' I'll be rememb'rin' *you!*"

The stranger's smoky eyes grew mocking.

"Shucks," he smiled, "I'd feel cheated if you didn't."

***

LATHAM SHOVED the swinging door wide and strode angrily forth into the dusty night, followed a moment later by two of the stool-warmers. The two remaining customers, as the stranger moved forward, withdrew to the counter's far end and opened a low-voiced, well-gestured conversation.

"Concernin' me," the stranger told himself. Aloud he said to the girl, "I'll have some ham' an' aiggs, ma'am, an' a cup of black java."

She leaned toward him across the counter and her eyes, twin pools of slumbering passion, were deep and dark and blue. "Y'u hadn't ought to have took up for me, stranger. Stone Latham's a bad man to cross. He's orn'ry enough to carry sheep dip an' he'll lay for y'u sure."

"I don't expect I'll be worryin' a heap about Mr.

Latham," the stranger shrugged. "I reckon his bark's a lot meaner'n his bite."

"Y'u don't know Stone Latham," the girl said earnestly. "I'm wantin' to thank y'u for what y'u done for me, an' I'm wantin' to give y'u a piece of good advice. Get on yore hoss an' get out of these mountains quick."

"Shucks, I couldn't do that noways, ma'am. I'm figurin' to bed down here an' stay a spell. I allow I'm goin' to like this town."

"This town," she said vehemently, "is a place where a sidewinder would be ashamed to see his mother!"

"Shucks," the stranger chuckled. "I reckon it ain't that bad. Why, you're here, ma'am."

Her red lips twisted. "I fit the town, Mister, as y'u'll learn quick if y'u insist on stayin' here till someone plants y'u. 'Cordin' to the lights of *decent* people, Stone Latham jest told Lize Corbin to her face what they've been sayin' behind her back for weeks."

Her blue eyes probed the smoky gray ones of the stranger as she defiantly added, "I'm Lisabet Corbin. Folks here call me Lize—when they ain't callin' me somethin' worse."

The stranger doffed his shabby hat and smiled infectiously. "Why, ma'am, I'm proud to know you. I'm S. G. Shane, though mostly I'm knowed as 'Sudden.' I reckon you an' me will get along first rate."

An instant longer her probing stare remained upon his face. Then abruptly she turned away. But not before he'd seen a telltale sign of moisture in her eyes. He shook his head a little grimly. Poor kid! Evidently she had lost what some people valued above all else—her reputation. Probably some man had made a fool of her, had somehow taken advantage of her, and this hairy-chested Tortilla Flat had rubbed salt in her wounds. Towns were like that, he mused; once a woman strayed from the straight and narrow they could not rest till they'd dragged her down and clogged her path with mire.

He studied her as she moved about the stove, stirring up a batch of tantalizing aromas as she worked preparing his meal. Her hair, so flaming red, was alive with glinty gleams of copper where the lamplight struck across it, and was openly rebellious as though never having known the curbing influence of comb or brush. Hers was a vital figure, alive with life and natural grace. She was like some wild thing held captive in a cage. Belted overalls and a blue flannel shirt such as riders wear detracted nothing from her primal loveliness; the faded jeans but emphasized the slender longness of her shapely legs, and her flannel shirt but accentuated the alluring contour of her breasts. He admired her clean-limbed stride and the pluck that would not let her run away, but held her here to face the slurs and slander of this gold camp.

She placed the meal before him. "Y'u came from Texas, didn't y'u?"

Her unexpected question drew a frown. But the frown swiftly faded beneath a grin. "I reckon you called the turn, ma'am. You didn't see my hoss by any chance?"

"Y'u got the look of a Texas man," she said, adding, "I'm from Texas, too—way back. My Dad was a West Texas cattle man. My mother died when I was a kid. Then Dad, he got the gold fever an' we been followin' the gold camps ever since."

"An' where's your Dad now, if I might ask?"

"If y'u was to ask folks back round Pecos, an' they'd heard the news, I reckon they'd opine he was in heaven," she said slowly, wistfully. "But if y'u was to put that question to the mavericks of Tortilla Flat they'd tell y'u Dry Camp Corbin—the ol' fool—was down in hell wheah he belonged. Y'u see, one of Jarson Lume's gunslicks downed him when a rumor got spreadin' round he'd struck it rich."

Shane sat up straighter on his stool. His face seemed whiter and his chin thrust forward grimly.

"Jarson Lume, eh?" His voice was cold with a crackly crispness that drew the attention of the two stool-warmers at the counter's farther end. "I've heard that name before, ma'am. He's some pumpkins round these diggin's, I reckon?"

"He's top screw," said a cold, grim voice from the doorway. "An' he's some partic'lar who tosses his name around."

Mr. Sudden Shane paid no attention to the interruption; he did not even turn his head to examine the speaker. His eyes remained on the girl's face, taking note of the sudden color that stained her cheeks and the look of mingled anger, loathing and resentment which, at the sound of the newcomer's voice, had flashed into her stormy eyes.

"You was sayin', ma'am?" Shane queried.

But Lisabet Corbin was not listening. Her blazing eyes were fixed above and beyond his shoulder; on the man at the door, he guessed. With one swift lunge her right hand dropped beneath the counter and came up with a sawed-off shotgun.

"Get outa here, y'u polecat!"

A harsh laugh a-drip with insolent mockery struck the ears of Sudden Shane. He turned, then, slowly, on his stool and let his calm, appraising glance play over the newcomer.

The man by the door had a cold, bloodless face, handsome despite the tight, thin-lipped mouth and foppish tiny black mustache. He was clad in the flat-brimmed hat, frock coat and black string tie of the professional gambler. He fingered his tiny mustache with a characteristic gesture and laughed again, slowly, softly, now.

"My dear, you are letting your nerves get the best of you. When I entered I believe I heard you and this, ah—gentleman—discussing me. Haven't you learned that it's bad form discussing a man behind his back? Tut, tut, my dear, tut, tut! Give you time and you'll learn a lot, I'm sure."

Deliberately ignoring both the girl and her shaking weapon, the man in gambler's clothes now turned to Shane. "I don't believe I have the pleasure of your acquaintance, sir."

"If you think it'll be a pleasure, you're mistaken," Shane drawled coldly. "I've got no use for woman-baitin' skunks."

No expression on the gambler's immobile countenance betrayed his feelings. No least twitching muscle gave any fraction of his thoughts away. His unwinking flinty eyes were baffling as he said,

"Neither have I. I'm Jarson Lume, stranger. I own the SQUARE DEAL, a gentleman's resort across the street. I don't believe I caught your name?"

"I don't expect you did."

"Hmm. I understand you had a little run-in with

Stone Latham a few minutes ago. I know Latham pretty well and I'd like to warn you that he's not a forgiving man."

"I'm powerful astonished to find we've somethin' in common," Shane commented, and turned back to his meal. The girl was no longer in evidence and he guessed she had retired to the back room to escape Lume's obviously unwelcome company.

Lume came up and took a stool beside Shane. He gave the two men at the other end of the counter a long silent scrutiny at which, dropping coins to pay for their grub, they got up and slunk away.

"Got 'em pretty well gentled, ain't you?" Shane commented.

"Look here, stranger; it strikes me you're adoptin' the wrong attitude here—" Lume began, when Shane cut in curtly.

"My attitude suits me right down to the ground."

"Well, it don't suit me, by Gawd, an' what I say in this town goes!" Lume growled. "There ain't no middle course in Tortilla Flat; folks that ain't for me are against me—an' fools who are against me have a habit of kickin' off sudden. Do I make myself clear?"

Shane grinned. "What you got in mind?"

For a moment Lume eyed him intently, then relaxed. "That's better. You're showin' good sense. From what I heard about your run-in with Latham, you've got guts. I've got plenty of jobs for men of your caliber," he added, and paused suggestively.

"I ain't exactly in need of work," Shane said slowly. "Got a bit of cash left over from my last...job. But I'm always willin' to lend a open ear to a good proposition. What you got in mind?"

A faint smile fleetingly crossed the gambler's thin lips, but he took care not to let Shane see it. "Well, I'll tell you," he said confidentially. "I need a man to take a shipment of gold out to Phoenix. 'Course the stage'll take it out, you understand. But I need a gent on the box that'll see my shipment goes through without a hitch. I don't dare keep too much money on hand in this camp; too many crooks willin' to risk their necks in a try for it. There's places gettin' stuck up here right and left. Had three robberies in town last night. A killing, too."

He looked at Shane keenly, scrutinizing his bronzed countenance as though weighing him, as though striving to determine his potential value. "Yes," he muttered at last, "I've got to get some of my dinero into a bank, an' the sooner the better for all concerned. Trouble is, the stage has been stuck up six times in the last month."

"Kinda wild country up here, I reckon," was Shane's comment. "I can see your angle, though. You want somebody to ride the stage an' see that your shipment ain't taken off."

Jarson Lume nodded. "That's it."

"Got any idea who's pullin' all these stick-ups?"

"I've got notions," Lume admitted, "but nothin' definite enough to act on. This town ain't got its growth an' she's tough as hell. A man has to be right careful what he says around here unless he's got a hankering for Boot Hill. The way I look at it, it's cheaper to hire a shotgun guard than it is to make accusations without the evidence to back them up.

"There's plenty in this town have got it in for me already. I don't know why, I'm sure. Take Lize Corbin, now." He shot a covert glance at Shane. "She's got some wild notion I had somethin' to do with her old man getting rubbed out. Nothing to it, of course, but there it is. I can't dissuade her of the notion an' she threatens to salivate me every time I set foot on this side of the street."

"Well," he concluded, "do you want the job?"

"Trip to Phoenix an' back, eh? An' after that?"

"More trips. In between times I'll find somethin' else to keep you busy," Lume said easily. "But that comes first. I'll pay you two hundred dollars for the trip —if you get the shipment through."

"Quite generous," Shane commented drily. "An' if I don't?"

"Not one damned cent."

"Fair enough. I reckon you've hired yourself a man. When you shippin'?"

"Stage pulls in from Globe tomorrow afternoon an' leaves for Phoenix tomorrow night at seven sharp. By the way, what am I supposed to call you?"

"Shane—S. G. Shane's the name."

"Glad I met up with you, Shane," Lume said, and held out a lean right hand which Shane somehow failed to grasp. Lume stared hard, endeavoring to make out whether the insult had been deliberate or whether Shane had not noticed his gesture. But he could make nothing of Shane's expression as Shane was looking the other way, toward the door to the rear room in which Lisabet Corbin was angrily pacing the floor. With a curt, "So long," Lume strode softly into the turbulent night.

Shane sat still, and there was an odd little smile on his lips.

TWO

"RECKON I misjudged y'u some considerable, Texas Man. I allow y'u are jest about as orn'ry as the rest of the fly-by-night owlhooters that have come driftin' into this here town ever since some damn fool went an' located gold an' copper in Fish Creek Canyon!"

Sudden Shane looked up into the scornful face and contemptuous dark blue eyes of Lisabet Corbin. He did not need a telescope to decipher the anger, the loathing, and the bitter disappointment that filled those flashing orbs. She had weighed him, found him wanting. The heat of a sudden flush warmed his cheeks beneath their bronze.

"Shucks, ma'am," he said, gravely considering her. "Now I reckon you have gone an' jumped to a bad conclusion."

"Damn bad, cowboy—an' I ain't doubtin' it's correct!"

Cold hostility bulged into her voice. "Don't tell me! I saw y'u grinnin' like a chessy cat after yo' palaver with that stinkin' tinhorn!"

"Why, ma'am, I expect you are right about my grinnin', though I hadn't figured I was doin' it that open-like."

"Y'u addlepated fool! D'y'u think y'u can p'rambulate around with skunks like Lume an' not get to smellin' jest like 'em? If yo' goin' to lay down with dawgs, y'u gotta expect to git up with fleas I'm a-tellin' y'u!"

"Now, ma'am, I was only—"

"I can't hang that buck in my smoke-house!" she cut him off. "Ain't y'u never heard that jestin' lies brings serious sorrers? I seen y'u an' that—that damn' Lume huddled up gassin'! Thick as cloves on a Christmas ham, y'u was! Shane, I'm rightdown disappointed in y'u!"

"Shucks, ma'am. Don't you reckon I had my reasons?"

"I sure do! Y'u seen which way the wind blowed strongest an' piled yo' hay accordin'. But y'u'll git burnt if y'u go to playin' with Jarson Lume! Him an' Latham an' Bronc Walders an' a bunch more snakes of the same stripe is all mixed up together. Them an' Marshal Wolf Brady—who is a dang coyote—jest about runs this town."

Shane's gray eyes lost their accustomed twinkle and he looked away uncomfortably. She sure was a heap positive in her notions, he reflected. "Shucks, ma'am," he said with a little grin. "You ain't figurin' to class me with them reptiles, are you?"

"Y'u got me fightin' my hat," she admitted angrily. "I jest can't make y'u out! First off, y'u make a monkey outa Latham. Then y'u git thicker'n splatter with Latham's boss! Y'u got a screw loose someplace? Why, y'u lunkhaid, them scorpions'll jest natcherly tie y'u up in knots! But go ahead—I reckon y'u been weaned some time. If y'u wanta hitch up with them varmints it's yo' business an' none of mine.

"But I'm a-tellin' y'u," her red lips hardened in a bitter line and her voice came thickly, as though choked with feeling, "if yo' goin' to run with them y'u can't eat here. That's final! Slap yo' dinero on the counter an' git goin'."

"But ma'am!" Shane expostulated. "This Lume jasper offered me a job. Ain't nothin' wrong in takin' a job— even with a tarantula—is there?"

"Job, hell. Don't y'u know that butcher-bird's jest fixin' to git y'u killed off nice an' safe? I bet he offered y'u a job ridin' shotgun to a shipment of dust an' nuggets! Didn't he?"

The cold contempt in her flashing eyes had not abated by a fraction. Shane stirred uneasily under her fixed regard. "Well," he admitted reluctantly, "he did offer—"

"I knew it!" she snapped vindictively. "Why, y'u dang lunkhaid! D'y'u think that slick coyote ain't got y'u figgered plumb center? Yo' the fifth fool he's hired fo' that job."

"The fifth? What's happened to the others?" Shane asked innocently.

"Three of 'em got killed tryin' to scare off stick-ups an' the other one—'cordin' to Jarson Lume's tellin'— tried to skip off with the shipment himself. The driver," she paused to glower at him scathingly, "blowed his brains out!"

Shane's glance searched her face intently. "Are you runnin' on me, ma'am?"

"Do I look like the runnin' kind?"

"Well, but that's terrible, ma'am."

"I allow that's what them four guards thought when they was cashin' in their chips! Y'u can't play 'round with Jarson Lume."

"But, ma'am, he wouldn't dare pull nothin' so raw as that—" Shane began, when her short laugh cut him off.

"Listen," she told him. "Jarson Lume would dare anythin' if he saw sufficient profit. I'm a-tellin' y'u. I know that polecat from hocks to horns!"

"But mebbe—"

"There ain't no buts to it, Texas Man. If y'u are Lume minded, y'u play yo' hand out as y'u see fit. Y'u sort of throwed in to do me a good turn tonight so I'm a-warnin' y'u. I don't aim to be beholdin' to no damn man. I've passed y'u the word; y'u can take it or leave it It's up to y'u. Now clear outa here; I'm figun' to close up pronto."

From open doors and windows great splotches of golden light seeped out across the hock-deep dust of Tortilla Flat's single crooked street, collecting in pools that but accentuated the sullen darkness of the moonless night.

Oil flares, placed at appropriate intervals, served to illuminate the misspelled legends scrawled across the high false fronts of the town's flimsy buildings, and painted on the garish signs hung out above the town's plank sidewalks.

There were saloons and gambling halls, a hotel, several blacksmith shops, two stores and three honkytonks. The largest honkytonk was Gar-Faced Nell's Place—a brothel of the lowest type. Everything went inside its tarpaper walls, and many a gent had its denizens seen rolled and chucked out in the dusty street to sleep off his knockout drops.

But the biggest resort of all, a combination dance hall, gambling hall and saloon, was the SQUARE DEAL—owned and operated by the poker-faced Jarson Lume.

Tortilla Flat's main stem was not a long one, but it fairly teemed with life. Cowpunchers rubbed elbows with hairy-faced and red-shirted miners; sleek, pale steerers walked cheek by jowl with mining engineers and cattle magnates; tinhorns, barkers, come-ons, homesteaders and pimps—all mingled freely in the flotsam-jetsam composing the boomtown's boisterous population. Many of the big, burly fellows one could see on every hand walked with the rolling gait of the dismounted horseman. More than an equal number were horny-handed from grubbing in the soil and cliffs and creeks of the surrounding mountains.

When Sudden Shane stepped out upon the planks before the Lone Star Grub Emporium there was a tiny smile on his genial lips. A twinkle came into his eyes as he recalled the girl's warning. Lize Corbin was a good sort, he reflected; undoubtedly tomboyish, yet every inch a man's woman from her flaming head to her booted feet. Grace was in her every movement; she was possessed of a pantherish vitality and had a tremendous store of nervous energy and pluck. Not many women, he told himself, would have the nerve to outface this hell-roaring camp and tell it in plain terms what she thought of it and the men who bossed it. There was, he felt, much about her for a discerning man to admire. In the parlance of the country she was a "square-shooter"—he would cheerfully have bet his last dollar on the fact had he been called upon to do so.

And someone in this coyote town, some two-legged varmint calling itself a man, had handed her a raw deal lately. He would have known it even had he not overheard Stone Latham's slurring remark. The fact was patent in the defiant tilt of her chin and in the resentful light of her stormy eyes. These bespoke, to Shane's mind, the decent woman putting up a plucky front to a sneering world. He was all for her; but he did not intend to let her influence his plans or sway him from the course of action he had determined to adopt.

With the thought his jaw swung forward stubbornly; nothing should prevent him from accomplishing his aim, or sidetrack him from the purpose which had brought him here.

Mounting his horse he urged the animal down the dusty road till he reached the Miner's Rest, and there tied his mount to the scarred hitching rail among a group of others. With saddle-bags across his shoulder he mounted the board steps and strode into the dingy office.

Several men were seated in its restricted space with chairs tilted comfortably back against the walls None of these displayed the least interest in Shane until he said:

"I'd be obliged for a room. Be wantin' it indefinitely. How much?"

A bald-headed man with beetling brows looked up at him, arching his shaggy brows inquiringly. "Stranger, ain't y'u?"

Shane looked thoughtful while the others eyed him curiously. He pushed his hat back to scratch his head; brushed the corn-colored shock of hair back off his forehead and suddenly grinned. "Well, yes," he finally admitted. "I reckon I could be fitted into that category. Ah—how about that room?"

The beetling-browed man stared at the others; they stared back. One of them, a tall man with heavy face and long, drooping mustache, nodded slightly.

The bald-headed man cleared his throat. "I can let you have a room, stranger. But she'll cost y'u right smart. My rooms rent for ten bucks a day."

Shane grinned. "I didn't aim to buy it," he said.

"Y'u couldn't buy it fer all the gold in this camp, stranger. Rooms is scarce in Tortilla. I've charged—"

"Listen, fella. If I had ten bucks I wouldn't be wantin' your room."

"Huh?"

"I wouldn't be wantin' it because I'd be afraid for my life in here with that much dinero on me."

"Are y'u tryin' to be funny, mister?" the bald-headed man demanded with a scowl. "Ten bucks a room is my price— an' it's payable in advance."

"Well," Shane said, turning toward the door, "I sure hope you'll be able to rent it."

"Hey—where y'u goin'?"

"I'm goin' to fix me up a deal with one of these resort owners," Shane said, and went on out.

He climbed into the saddle and rode back along the dusty road till he reached the Square Deal. There he dismounted and, tying his buckskin, entered the resort.

When his eyes had grown accustomed to the glare of the coal-oil lamps that were bracketed about the great barnlike room, he leveled a quick glance through the wavering haze of tobacco smoke. But he did not immediately see Jarson Lume.

Making his way to the long plank bar he joined the line of men bellying it and had a drink. It was while he was toying with his second, that he saw the coldly handsome face of the Square Deal's frock-coated owner.

Lume saw him at the same time and came toward him, stopping momentarily a number of times to return the greetings of acquaintances. When Lume came up he reached out a lean white hand. "Glad to see you here, Shane. Havin' a good time?"

Shane shook his hand with a show of cordiality. "I allow I'm gettin' around. Can you tell me where I can find a place to put up?"

"Well," said Lume, "there's the Miner's Rest down the street. They might take you or I could put you up here, if you don't mind doubling up with one of the boys."

"Mebbe I'd better put up here, where I can be handy in case you want me for anythin'."

"Good idea. Go up the stairs over there an' go along the balcony till you locate room number ten. If there's anyone in it'll be Bill Halleck. He runs one of the faro layouts here. He's off tonight. 'F he happens to be up there, just tell him I said you were to put up with him."

Shane nodded and started for the stairs. As he skirted the dance floor the music being furnished by the sagebrush orchestra came to a stop. Followed a stamping of feet and clink of spurs interspersed with the tapping of high-heeled slippers as couples started off the floor. A number of near-tight customers bumped into Shane who passed the encounters off with grins. He had almost reached the stairs when he came face to face with Stone Latham, a frowsy, scantily-clad blonde clinging to his arm.

Stone Latham came to a jolting stop, a bold intentness in his glance, a cynical curve to his lips. There were men who had hinted that Latham's folks on his mother's side had worn moccasins, that he would rather take his man in the back than elsewhere, and was partial to a knife, but Shane could tell by a look at his heavy eyes that such hints had not been made in Latham's presence. For though the man had swagger, there was something about him that told Shane he'd plenty of nerve to back his swagger up.

Latham said, "Still here an' on top the ground, eh?" and his dark, lean-carved face crinkled into a grin, a grin, however, that was not matched by the light in his eyes.

Out of the corner of his eye, Shane saw Jarson Lume coming toward them. He flashed his teeth at Latham and was about to pass on to the stairs, but Latham's left hand reached out and caught his arm.

"Just a minute, fella. I got some good advice for you. Pull your picket pin an' drift before a hunk of lead cuts sho't your rope."

"Is that a warnin'?"

"Just good advice; you better heed it." Relinquishing Shane's arm, Latham moved off with his blonde enchantress.

Shane grimaced and went up the stairs He quickly found the door with a crayoned #10 upon it, but stopped irresolute as his hand reached out for the knob. The sound of voices came from beyond the door; a girlish giggle, a half-hearted protest and a man's deep growl.

Shane's lips tightened. "I'm thinkin' Bill Halleck won't be wantin' to be disturbed just now," he told himself, and retraced his way down the stairs. Reaching the bottom he took out his watch and squinted an eye at its dial. Ten after twelve. Much too early to turn in, in an all-night town. "Mebbe I better go out a spell an' mosey around takin' in the sights," he mused, and made his way to the door.

He stepped outside, saw a man fumbling with his pony's reins.

"Get your hands off that hoss!" he snapped, and started forward.

As he cleared the porch something tugged at his open vest and a shot rang out, slamming against the buildings across the street. Shane stopped short and a second slug ripped through his hat. He caught the flash this time and his gun came out and up, bucked viciously against his palm as a livid flame belched outward from its muzzle. Came a blur of movement from the man beside his horse, but the fellow wasn't fast enough. Shane's shot struck him in the chest and smashed him backward out of sight.

He whirled in time to see the first man sprinting desperately toward a building corner, men ducking from his path as though from a plague. With a shake of the head Shane let him go. He was returning his gun to leather when a heavy hand fell on his shoulder and whirled him round. A tall man faced him and he felt the man's gun shoved into his stomach—hard.

The man's face was tautly parted over the yellowed teeth behind his drooping black mustache. His voice had a leaping rasp, "Hell's lookin' you in the eye, stranger—one move an' you're due for plantin'!"

THREE

SHANE READ murder in the tall man's heavy face, and for a long-drawn moment remained utterly motionless while silence spread a sound-proof blanket across the roaring camp. No faintest whisper disturbed the breathless hush.

Almost curiously, one might have said, he searched the tall man's face, noting the long, drooping mustache, the brown hair and the piercing black eyes beneath the shaggy, scowling brows. He remembered; this was the man he had seen in the Miner's Rest—the fellow toward whom the others had looked for orders.

Shane's seeking glance rested fleetingly upon the tense whiteness of this man's fingers where they gripped the prodding gun. A shiver, it almost seemed, would have caused that gun to roar.

Then a hard grin cut Shane's bronzed jowls angularly.

"Why, you look some peeved," he said.

An oath fell softly from the tall man's lips. "I'm waitin' to hear whyfor you cut down on Groll that way."

Shane looked to where the boots of the man he'd gunned showed grotesque and motionless in a cleared patch between the horse's hoofs. "I allow," he drawled, "you're referrin' to the fella that was figurin' to make off with my hoss. Where I come from, the little fittin' reward for a hoss thief is a hasty chunk of Mr. Colt's fodder. Are you hintin' it's a crime to kill a hoss thief?"

"We're partic'lar who does the killin' in this man's town. By Gawd, I've got a notion to git up a string party in yore honor!"

Shane's serene gray eyes met the other's calmly. "You represent the entertainment committee?"

"I represent the law, by Gawd!" the tall man's tawny eyes seemed sheathed in a scarlet fog, his twisted lips wreathed a malignant snarl. "Who do you think you are?"

"Me?" Shane seemed surprised. "I'm S. G. Shane."

"Yeah? Well, here's some damn good advice for you, Mister S. G. Shane! This here's a peaceful camp what ain't none partial to killers an' such like. 'F you figure to keep head an' body together, by Gawd, you better git outa this town 'fore daylight. It's the Law talkin' at you —Me, Marshal Wolf Brady!"

"That so?"

"You're damn well right it's so! All the signs is pointin'—"

"I never did believe a heap in signs," Shane's cool drawl cut in.

"You better believe in these signs, Mister; they're pointin' to a quick grave, an' the hole is jest yore size! Git out before daylight or you'll be planted here permanent!"

The collected crowd broke slowly up and disintegrated as, without another word, Marshal Brady wheeled and strode away.

Shane's low chuckle was rich with music. He did not appear greatly worried, and wasn't. "Shucks," he told himself, "it looks like I'm goin' to be right unpopular 'round Tortilla Flat."

Having extracted the spent shells from his gun and reloaded the emptied chambers, he sheathed it and strolled leisurely down the plank sidewalk, studying the heterogeneous mass of humanity which surged unendingly up and down the dusty street.

Here a three-card-monte man plied his doubtful trade upon a tiny three-legged table. There a shell-game artist operated. Over yonder a man barked loudly of the theoretical value of some pet mining stock. He discouraged a sallow-faced, shifty-eyed advertiser of a house of joy and sauntered on. It was an interesting town, he could see; a place of turbulence where life must hang upon the swiftness of a man's trigger-finger.

As he reached the intersection of an alley angling away between a pair of crazily-leaning buildings, a woman's scream stopped him. Thinly it knifed through the scraping fiddles and stamping feet, through the heavy murmurous drone that was the voice of this Tortilla Flat. Tensing, he peered squint-eyed into the drifting shadows between the buildings. Again that scream slid up a sobbing scale that chilled his blood.

Then he was hurtling forward, stumbling through the darkness, his gun gripped ready in his hand.

From out the murk came a strangling sob, the pant of labored breathing, a curse and the slap of struggling bodies. In a window of the building to the right a shade snapped up and flung a bar of yellow light across the alley gloom. A hot, unreasoning anger took Shane as his eyes made out the scene.

In the arms of a lithe, swarthy-faced man struggled a panting, sobbing girl. Even in that instant of snarling wrath Shane realized that her sobs were not born of fear or despair; they were unmistakable sounds of fury.

But he had not paused to analyze these thoughts. As that leaping shade flung its bar of light across the murk he sheathed his gun and sprang. The sound of his striking fist as it met the swarthy chin was like the smack of a board on water. Even as the Mexican's hands fell from about the girl and she pulled free, Shane's left took the man in the stomach and wrung a grunt of agony from his bleeding lips. The swarthy one doubled and Shane's right came up from his boot straps in an uppercut that lifted the would-be seducer clear of the ground and smashed him backward in a sprawling, motionless heap.

Shane's eyes swept to the girl and a startled oath escaped him. It was Lize Corbin and she met his widening stare defiantly as she strove to pull her torn shirt across her jutting breasts.

"Habit of yores, ain't it?"

"You mean rescuing ladies from distress? Why, ma'am, I'm powerful glad I got here when I did," Shane said, and his voice was coldly grim.

It seemed to bring some subtle thrill to the girl for she ceased her movements with the shirt and swayed forward slightly, toward him, some inexplicable light chasing a portion of the storminess from the intent glance that searched his face.

"Y'u ain't mean...y'u ain't meanin' that—"

"I'm meanin'," Shane drawled, "that if I'd got here a

minute later I'd prob'ly have killed that skunk. An' the Lord knows there's killin's enough chalked up against me now."

The soft light vanished from her eyes and left them bleakly blue. In them swam anger, resentment, a sullen devil-may-care defiance. Yes—and a wistful gleam of disappointment.

But Shane did not see; his eyes and mind were grimly fixed upon that outsprawled figure in the dust. His right hand dropped to gun butt and his eyes were cold and hard as he waited for the swarthy man to regain consciousness.

The girl touched his arm. "Y'u dished him out plenty, Mister. Leave him be. Tortilla Flat wouldn't call what he was fixin' to do no killin' crime." Her ripe red lips twisted bitterly. "He was only aimin' to spark Lize Corbin, an' the whole town knows she's the property of the first sport that can tame her!"

"I don't like to hear that kinda talk, ma'am. You go along home, now. What I cal'late to give this two-legged polecat won't be no sight for a woman's eyes to look at."

"Y'u crazy lunkhaid! Ain't y'u in bad enough now with the vinegaronse that run this town—"

Shane cut in, "What handle does this varmint go by?"

"That's Puerco; he's a pal of Marshal Brady. Y'u better leave him be less'n y'u got a hankerin' to be planted 'fore the sun climbs outa bed."

The gleam of Shane's white teeth flashed coldly behind his parted lips. "Shucks, ma'am. Plantin' is a game that two can play."

"Not in this town. The plantin' here is all done by Brady an' Lume an' Latham—'ceptin' for what they hire out to their friends." She seemed, he thought, to want to get him away from here. Probably afraid one of those she'd named might come along. He noticed with a wave of color that in her effort to convince him of her point, she seemed to have forgotten her torn and buttonless shirt. As she leaned forward in her earnestness he could see through a rent in it the rounded contour of a creamy breast. He turned away his eyes in agitation.

"—friends didn't take up where he left off," she was saying passionately, "they'd get theirs back on me after y'u cleared out."

"I don't reckon we need go into that, ma'am. I ain't figurin' to leave. Not yet, leastways. This town has got me interested. The cordial welcome these leadin' citizens been handin' me is rightdown fetchin'. I betcha I'm goin' to be a well-known man in Tor—"

"What yo' goin' to be, y'u crazy lunkhaid, is a well-salivated corpse—less'n y'u climb yo' hoss an' burn a trail outen here pronto!"

"Shucks, ma'am, I reckon you're some mistaken." His grin, meant to be assuring, appeared to infuriate her further. She stamped her foot and swore like an angry pirate. "All right, y'u fool!" Wheeling, she turned her back on him and started off. "Don't never say y'u wasn't warned!"

Shane let his glance play over the man he'd felled. A cold, malicious gleam entered his smoky eyes as with a groan the Mexican stirred. The swarthy face writhed painfully. Then the black eyes came blinking open. With a curse the fellow got an elbow under him. Then he saw Shane.

His lambent stare focused sharply, revealing a fiercely malignant blaze of hate as his right hand went streaking hipward toward where the walnut stock of a heavy pistol protruded from an open holster.

Shane drawled softly, "Don't do it, fella. You ain't nearly fast enough."

The swarthy man must have correctly gauged the grim earnestness of that soft drawl, for his reaching hand abruptly stilled. With a grunted oath he got to his feet. "Well?" he glared "Wat you fixin' to do now, eh'?"

"I'm fixin' to give you a piece of good advice. Folks have been givin' me advice ever since I struck this town. Must be catchin' 'cause now I'm givin' you some. Just this, hombre—don't never let me catch you in reachin' distance of Lize Corbin again. That's all. Now *git*."

The silver of the moonlight and the ochre of these barren mountains lent a softening languor to a country harsh and spiked by day. But Sudden Shane, as he was known in Texas, gave no attention to the appearance of this land. His glance was alert and keen as he retraced his steps toward the Square Deal, but the brightness of his gaze was not for beauty—it was for a possible hostile move on the part of some hard-case friend of one of these men he had antagonized. He did not mean to be caught napping.

When he reached Jarson Lume's establishment the place was still roaring wide and handsome, though dawn was hardly forty winks away. An all-night place in an all-night town, Shane thought. He grinned tightly for this place was in his blood. A man's town, this, where fortunes hung on the turn of a card or the flip of a knife. A hell-hole, yes— but where life rode swift and high.

He shoved through the Square Deal's swinging doors and got his back against a wall. He stayed there till his eyes grew accustomed to the glare of the coal-oil lamps Then, peering through the swirling haze of tobacco smoke, he made out the tall, gaunt form of Stone Latham moving toward him with Marshal Brady in his wake.

Shane stood loosely waiting, his arms hanging at his sides.

When the others brought up before him, Shane said, "Latham, you're cuttin' your string pretty short, ain't you?"

His dark and lean-carved face held mockery as Latham answered, "I don't need a long string to handle saddle tramps an' gun-slicks. Don't you reckon you'd better mosey? The Marshal here tells me he gave you till daylight to pull your freight. It's gettin' close to daylight now."

"Is it worryin' you?"

"Not me. You're the one that should be doin' the worryin', fella."

Shane laughed coldly. "Well, somehow I don't seem to be. An' I'm allowin' I'll be still in this town long after sunup, too."

Brady grunted, "That ain't no lie. I've got yore restin' place all picked out—got the coffin measured, too."

"Well, I hope you measured 'er long an', slim, Mister Two-Gun Toter," Shane drawled with a sardonic grin. "Most of the specimens I've seen in this town lean towards a railish figure, an' if anyone occupies your coffin, Brady, the corpse won't look like me."

Latham grinned at the Marshal. "Looks like he's callin' yore hand, Brady. You goin' to let him get away with it?"

Brady sneered. "When the time shoves up, I'll lay him out."

"Yeah?" Shane leaned slightly forward and the smoky gray of his eyes grew darker, dangerous. His tone was low, cold, even.

"This," he said ominously, "is as good a time as any, Brady. I ain't leavin'. What're you goin' to do?"

Brady's bloodshot eyes grew anxious as they studied the tranquil Texan. It was Shane's tranquility that seemed to bother him most. It was as though he feared Shane had somehow laid a trap for him and now was inviting him to step forward and get himself snared. His hands clenched and unclenched spasmodically while a dull red suffused his cheeks. The Adam's apple bulged in his throat, bounced grotesquely up and down; a barometric indication of the state of his nerves.

Shane's grin was taunting. There was wicked amusement in his eyes as he drawled ironically, "Latham, it looks like the cat run off with your friend's tongue. I'm wantin' to know what he's figurin' to do now that it's settled I'm goin' to remain in this town. Perhaps," his drawl grew softer, "you'd like to take up his burden?"

"Hell," Stone Latham sneered, "I'm not enforcin' the law in this man's town! He's the one that ordered you out. It's up to him to play his hand."

Brady gulped painfully and his eyes slid away from Shane's. "It—it ain't daylight yet," he muttered lamely, and turned away.

Shane looked after him sardonically, and grinned when he noted the redness of the lawman's ears. Then he swung his glance on Latham. "I seem to recall," he said amusedly, "that you, too, was advisin' me to drift last time we met."

Latham's lips curved a cynical smile. "The advice still holds good. But I ain't reckonin' you'll take it. Gun fighters are all alike, to my experience. Each one thinks he can't be beat—till another gent's blue whistler cuts him down."

"D'you think the lead that'll cut me down is in your gun?"

Stone Latham shrugged. *"Quien sabe"* he said, and walked away.

Shane snorted and climbed the stairs to the balcony. He moved unhurriedly toward the room whose door held a chalk-marked #10. He paused outside a moment. But hearing no sound of voices from within he grasped the knob.

The door was swung on its hinges in such a manner that it opened inward. As Shane turned the knob he gave the door a healthy shove and dropped upon the floor. And lucky that he did.

A jet of flame belched outward from the darkness of the room. Lead sang above his head as his gun was coming out and the smashing report filled the tiny room with reverberating thunder. A wicked smile creased Shane's grim lips as the hammer dropped beneath his thumb. The sound of a falling body reached his ears as booted feet stormed up the balcony stairs.

Swiftly Shane stepped into the room and struck a match. A crumpled figure lay on the floor, a smoking gun still clutched in one outflung hand. Shane studied the narrow face but could not place it as belonging to anyone he knew. "Reckon he's that Bill Halleck jasper I was s'posed to share this two-by-four with," he mused.

"Looks like the bossmen of this town are some anxious to get me out of the way. I expect this little trap was Jarson Lume's idea of bein' playful. I wonder how much he knows...?"

The slap of booted feet converging on the room drew him abruptly to his feet. He snuffed the match and dropped it. Sheathing his gun he stepped out onto the balcony and saw half a dozen men sprinting toward him, Brady and Stone Latham in the lead.

At his sudden appearance the running group stopped still.

"Who fired that shot?" Wolf Brady scowled.

"I did, Marshal," Shane drawled evenly. "With my little pistol I fired that shot." His eyes flung a challenge at the staring group. "What you figurin' to do about it?"

"Do! Do?" the marshal spluttered. "Why, dammit, you're under arrest!"

"Take it easy. You'll be gettin' apoplexy if you don't watch out."

With a snarl Wolf Brady's hands flashed hipward and came up in gleaming arcs. But the gun that spoke was Shane's, and it spoke but once. Marshal Brady coughed and sagged. With a sob he fell to his knees; pitched forward on his face.

Weaving left and right Shane's leveled pistol menaced the group. "Anyone here feel like makin' somethin' outa this?"

They stiffened to the drive in his voice. Motionless they watched him with wooden faces.

"Shucks," he said, "ain't Brady got no friends among you?" His gray eyes, so like the smoky sage, rested invitingly on Stone Latham's. "How about you?"

"Don't look at me," Stone Latham said. "I never did like Brady, nohow."

Shane said curtly, 'Two of you hombres lug Bill Halleck out of my room. I ain't never accustomed myself to sleepin' with a stiff. An' right now I'm aimin' to get some shuteye. It won't," he added ominously, "be healthy for any gent to go perambulatin' round my door. I'm a light sleeper an' I'd hate mighty much to be disturbed."

FOUR

BEHIND A DOOR LABELED "PRIVATE OFFICE," in a room partitioned off beneath the balcony stairs of his establishment and made as soundproof as his dexterity and the tools he had to work with would permit, Jarson Lume and those who owed him "Boss" sat in grim conference.

An atmosphere of tension hung over this gathering that was not the least bit lessened by the savage scowl on the countenance of Lume himself. Plainly the things which had happened since Shane's arrival in Tortilla Flat had upset his usual impassivity. He paced the floor with nervous stride, hands thrust deep in frock coat pockets.

Stone Latham, cold and cynical, sat at one end of the long plank table toying with a deck of greasy cards. Next to him sat the lithe and slender Puerco, his swarthy face framed by an Indian's mane of black coarse hair, a surly pout on his thick, repellent lips and a bold discoloration at the edge of his receding chin where Shane's hard fist had landed. At Latham's other hand sat Bronc Walders, his restless glance constantly roving about the room. A slouch hat with a chin strap gave him a hard-case appearance that was ominously borne out by the shiny grip of his double-action Colt and the scuffed condition of its holster against the unscratched black surface of his fancy batwing chaps.

Jarson Lume abruptly wheeled to face his lieutenants. Determination lay plain in the forward jut of his clean-shaved jaw.

"Gents," he said gruffly, "somethin's got to be done about this drifting gun-slick. He's too damned fast for my peace of mind. We've got to get rid of him and quick. Already he's snuffed Wolf Brady and Halleck. Gents, this Shane has got to go!"

A sneer contorted Stone Latham's cynical face. "Bravo!" he jeered, and grinned as Jarson Lume's cheeks grew dark. "How you figurin' to get rid of him?"

"I wasn't thinking of askin' *you* to gun him," Lume said coldly. Concentration wrinkled his brows as he took another turn about the room. He stopped with his back against the fireplace and hooked his elbows on its dusty mantel.

He said, "I've engaged him to ride shotgun guard to a shipment of gold."

A silence settled across the room and held for a number of moments. Then Latham said, "It won't work. This Shane's too slick to be taken in by that game. You'll have to figure somethin' else. The stakes are too important to run such risk right now."

"There's bound to be a strong element of risk in dealing with a man like Shane," Lume answered. "No way of getting around it. We'll load the strong-box with rock rubble an' start him off. Kettle Belly Dunn an' his boys will stop the stage at Keeler's Crossing—"

"They'll never cut it," Stone Latham growled. "Shane'll blast that bunch to hell! Mark my words, you've got to think up somethin' better'n that, Lume. This Shane ain't no ordinary leather-slapper. He's got brains an' knows how to use 'em. Ever notice his eyes?"

Jarson Lume's straight thin-lipped mouth grew tight. Through his teeth he said, "I'm figuring to have Wimper ride inside the stage."

Bronc Walders nodded, grinning. "That'll do it. While Shane's busy throwing lead at Dunn's bunch, Wimper can send a blue whistler through his gullet easy as rollin' himself a smoke. Hell, it'll be like takin' candy from a kid!"

But Stone Latham, apparently, was not convinced. He said no more, but the saturnine curve of his lips told plain as words what *he* thought about this plan.

"Well?" Lume snarled, "what's wrong with it?"

Latham made no reply but his shrug was eloquent.

A soft, peculiar knocking on the door at that moment interrupted the business before the meeting. Lume growled, "Come in!" and the door swung open abruptly and as quickly shut behind a short, squatty man with a squint in one eye and a weather-beaten face whose right cheek bulged to an oversized cud of tobacco.

"Well? What is it, Lefty?" Lume demanded.

"I got the dope on that payroll for the Copper King," Lefty Hines announced out of the corner of his mouth. "It's comin' through from Phoenix on the next up-country stage."

A feline sparkle lighted Lume's cold eyes. His companions straightened to attention.

"How many guards they sendin' with it?" Stone Latham asked.

"None!" the newcomer chuckled. "They figger it won't attract no notice if they don't guard it. Figger they'll get it through that way. Yuh know they've alius hired a bevy of shotgun guards on the other trips. When we lifted their last shipment, Obe Struthers said by Gawd he would have to close down if the next shipment didn't get through."

Lume smiled coldly. "How much gold they got stored up there? Stamp mill's been running pretty regular, seems like. They ought to have quite a pile ready to go out."

"They have. Looks to me like this would be a damn fine time to stage a raid."

"Against all them guns they've got scattered around that office?" Stone Latham sneered. "You must have water on the brain!"

"Hell! we could pull it easy," Hines pointed out "They swap shifts day an' night All their tough guns are on the night shift. Daytimes there's on'y three fellas guardin' that office. Three fellas an' ol' Obe, himself. Gripes, you couldn't ask for a better lay!"

"Hmmm." Jarson Lume breathed, and took a turn about the room. "We might be able to cut it at that."

"If we got away with that gold," Bronc Walders muttered, "an' stopped their payroll, too, I'm bettin' we could buy Obe Strainers' Copper King Mine for the price of a new hat!"

Hines nodded. Looking curiously at Lume, he said,

"I thought yuh gave us boys strict orders to lay off that dame what runs the Come-An'-Get-It?"

Lume's cold immobile face swung toward Hines swiftly. No least ripple of emotion crossed it. "I did." And after a brief pause during which his lambent gaze searched the squatty man's features, he added, "An' I meant it. Lize Corbin's to be left strictly alone, far as this gang's concerned. I made one mistake in that skirt, an' I don't want her riled one damn inch further. One of these days she's gonna be worm money in my pocket"

Hines grinned mirthlessly from a corner of his mouth as his squint-eyed glance passed from Lume to Latham, and from Latham to Puerco. It flicked back to Latham, then, and he said, "I reckon that order don't include Stone Latham, eh?"

Latham grinned as Lume said coldly, "No. Latham's workin' under orders."

"I guessed he musta been when I heard how that driftin' pilgrim handled—"

"That'll be enough outa you'" Stone Latham purred. There was a bold intentness in his glance as his hand dropped suggestively to gun butt.

"Shucks, Stone, I wa'n't meanin' nothin'," the squatty Hines said easily. "Jest tryin' to get things straight in my think-box, is all. I reckon," he tossed the jeer across the silence carelessly, "Puerco's been workin' under special orders, too?"

There came a fraction of absolute silence; then, through the shredding stillness, Puerco's breath came raspingly and he ran a shaking hand round the collar of his greasy shirt.

Stone Latham, his eyes thin slits, rose slowly from

his chair; moved softly backward from the table. The cold, bloodless face of Jarson Lume taut.

Fingering his tiny mustache, Lume drawled, "Just what is the meanin' of that crack?" And his words fell across the hush with the metallic clink of pebbles in a box.

Hines grinned malignantly. "Yuh know that alley between the Warwhoop an' the Jug O' Rum? Well, I happened to be saunterin' past it a while back an' I heard some right peculiar sounds. I stopped. An' right then a curtain in the Jug O' Rum flew up an' lit that alley like the sun was shinin'. I seen a certain gent here wrastlin' with that Corbin dame. He had her shirt half torn off."

"Yeah?"

"Yeah. Well, I didn't butt in, figgerin' 'twas none o' my never-mind. Wa'n't no need of me puttin' in my oar nohow 'cause that stranger what mixed it with Latham an' rubbed Wolf Brady out was headin' for the gal an' this gent like a fire hoss when the third alarm starts ringin'. He wasn't wastin' any words neither, by cripes! He jest waded in an' bounced a coupla haymakers off this gent's chin so quick 'twould make yore haid swim," and Hines looked saturninely at the shrinking Puerco.

"One gah-tham lie!" the Mexican shrilled, kicking back his chair. "I nevair touched thees—"

Bronc Walders' hoarse laugh, like the rest of the Mexican's words, was lost in two smashing reports that burst across the room like towering thunder, beating back against the walls in deafening waves of sound.

Stone Latham and Jarson Lume both stood with smoking guns in hand as Puerco's knees buckled and spilled him, retching blood, across the floor. A wicked snarl was on Latham's lips and Jarson Lume's cold, bloodless face was taut.

Lume said, "The next sport that makes a play at Lize Corbin can expect the same. By Gawd, I'm runnin' this camp, an' it's high time you birds was recognizin' that when I say a thing I *mean* it! Walders, throw that carrion out in the alley."

* * *

SUDDEN SHANE HAD no intention of going to sleep when he shut the door of #10. Nor did he. To be sure, he sat down on the bunk, took off his boots and dropped them heavily on the floor. But—then he quietly put them on again. After that he settled comfortably back against the wall and built himself a smoke.

There was a whimsical light in his sage-colored eyes as he leisurely puffed his quirly. No remorse for the men he had killed was bothering his cogitations. Those men, to his way of thinking, had received exactly what their actions merited. The first man had been loosening the reins of his horse—a trick to lure Shane into a line where the horse-thief's hidden helper could cut him down. That the scheme of this twain had not panned out was hardly any fault of theirs; they certainly had been serious enough. Yes, Shane mused, killing was no more than they deserved. He had been generous and lenient under the circumstances, having killed but one. The bullying Marshal Brady had come asking for what he got. So, too, had the bushwhacking Bill Halleck.

It was Shane's suspicion that the horse thieves had been hired by Lume to rub him out. Halleck, too. But the marshal— Well, Shane was willing to bet considerable that Brady had been sicced on him by Latham.

What, he wondered, was the connection—if any—between Stone Latham and Jarson Lume? Somehow he had a hunch there was a connection, that Lume and Latham were working hand in glove to part this camp from its gold and copper. And Shane, be it known, was a man who loved to give his hunches the free rein.

His thoughts swung to the man whose scribbled note had brought him to this camp. Obe Struthers, owner of the misnamed Copper King. Shane's lips quirked humorously as he thought of the mine owner's letter. It had been both brief and pointed; four words—"Business going to hell!"

Struthers had been pretty sure that would bring the man to whom it was sent, Shane reflected. He was probably in a stew right now because the addressee had not shown up.

With a frown Shane's kaleidoscopic thoughts shifted to Lume and Latham again. He had made an enemy of Latham; perhaps of Lume. At any rate, it was beginning to be apparent that the Square Deal's proprietor was not intending to take any chances. A strange gun-slick was better dead.

Shane chuckled softly as he smoked his cigarette. "There's many a slip 'twixt the cup an' the lip,'" he quoted. "An' the best laid plans have a uncommon bad habit of goin' haywire. Mister Jarson Lume'll find I'm a dang hard gent to kill. If I got anythin' to say about it."

And, sitting there with one foot drawn up on the edge of the bunk and his hands clasped about the knee, he looked very much as though he'd have a whole lot to say about it. He gave off an air of cold efficiency as he sat there musing. His eyes, so alike in color to the smoky sage, were serene and tranquil. Though his square-cut features were intensely aquiline, he had a genial mouth and laughing lips that were ever showing his strong white teeth in a way that was mighty attractive, yet did not detract a fraction from his hard look of capability.

He thought of Jarson Lume. The fellow's cold eyes and lips warned him that a man must be cautious in his dealings with him. He had heard, through that grapevine telegraph of western gossip, that few men had ever been on back-slapping terms with Lume. It had been rumored widely how on first arriving in this camp, Lume had gunned out two men's marks over some trivial disagreement. It seemed that Jarson Lume held small faith in the efficacy of Golden Rules. Rumor insisted that a number of the camp's former big men who had crossed Lume in public, had later been rubbed out in private where none had been on hand to prove their passing had been attended by fair play. All that had saved Lume's neck upon these occasions had been the care and secrecy with which the suspected murders had been carried out.

Lume, Shane reflected, was plenty slick.

His thoughts wandered to Lisabet Corbin. His hands clenched tightly as the image of Puerco crossed his mind. The skunk! He'd better keep his paws off Lize or Shane would see that he got an enlightening introduction to Colonel Colt!

Shane had no use for Mexicans, having been raised along the border.

A knock upon the door abruptly terminated his cogitations.

"Come in," he drawled and, rising, dropped his hand to gun butt.

A girl entered; the frowsy blonde he had seen earlier with Stone Latham.

"Close the door," he said, and crossed his arms, his glance upon her painted face enquiringly.

That she had something to say, was evident; her trouble seemed to be in arriving at a satisfactory opening. After several false starts, she blurted, "You better clear out of this camp right quick!"

He smiled in a way all his own. "Ah," he said, and blew a cloud of smoke ceilingward. "Nice of you to tell me."

"I'm dead serious. Stone Latham will kill you if you don't!"

Shane appeared calm and indifferent. "I wouldn't let that worry you none, ma'am. After all, I been weaned a week or two an' ought to be trusted to know what I'm doin'. I've been in camps like this before. An' Stone Latham ain't the first of his kind I've had a run-in with. I reckon I'll get along."

She came suddenly toward him where he stood beside the bunk and placed her hand upon his arm. "You're so young," she said. "So young and honest looking. I—I'd hate to see you killed."

Shane grinned at her, coldly. "What's the—" He broke off as a double concussion shook the floor beneath his feet.

The girl caught a hand to her carmined lips; her eyes stared wide and frightened.

"Just some of the boys celebratin', I reckon," Shane said. "Nothin' to get alarmed about, I expect. Does Latham know you're up here?"

Her hazel eyes reproached him. "Listen," she said, coming closer. "You don't know what you're up against here. Stone Latham—"

"What's the game, kid?" He reached up and caught her hands to ward them off.

She threw herself against him and began to struggle. Her lips parted in a scream that sent tingling chills across Shane's scalp. There was some trick about this business, was the thought that crossed his mind.

And while his hands still gripped her twisting wrists and her body was jammed close against his own, as though to prove his thought correct the door bulged open and across the girl's bare shoulder his eyes met the bold, sardonic stare of Stone Latham.

"Well," Latham breathed, and, "*Well!* You damned woman-thievin' polecat!"

Even as Latham's hand sped downward for his gun Shane, with what seemed a miracle of dexterity, flung loose of the cursing girl and slapped his hip.

A visible shudder ran through Stone Latham's rawboned body and his descending hand was arrested midway in its swooping arc. His widening eyes hung as though fascinated to the black orifice of the pistol which, like magic, had appeared in Shane's right hand.

A cold, mirthless grin framed Shane's white teeth.

"Almost, hombre—almost," he drawled. "But not exactly quite. One of these times I might get a little careless an' your friends'll be luggin' you out on a shutter."

FIVE

THE SUN, gilding in its passing the brazen upthrust crags of the Superstition Mountains, and gilding, endowed them for fleeting moments with cloaks of gold and lilac, was slinking off to bed when Sudden Shane opened his eyes and yawned. Throwing his denim-clad legs across the edge of this bunk that once had been Bill Halleck's, and tugging on his boots, Shane crossed to the open window and stood there looking out and breathing in great pungent drafts of the cooling, invigorating air.

His untroubled glance took in those towering escarpments brooding in slumbrous silence so far above the flimsy structures of this town. Then, drooping lower, his roving gaze took in the gathering shadows that filled this tiny level men called Tortilla Flat. He watched how the drifting gloom rolled in between the buildings, choking the dusty alleys with a thickening murk that even crept insidiously up the frowning cliffs that hemmed this wicked camp.

Night's coming would be swift, he mused. And swifter still would be Death's coming and the sinister slither of his sickle snuffing souls in this place of turbulence and greed, once the darkness fell.

Shane shrugged away the thought and moving from the window turned his attention to a careful inspection of his gun. It did not seem to have been tampered with while he slept, but he could afford to take no chances. Emptying the bullets from its chambers, he replaced them with fresh ones picked alternately from the loops of his wide black belt. Then, holstering the weapon, he pulled his hat low down across his eyes and, opening the door, went out upon the balcony overlooking the bar, gambling layouts and dancing floor beneath.

He stood for some time by the railing, letting his somber, wary glance play over the sights below. No one needed to tell him that, from now on, the guns of this camp's sporting element would leap from leather to snuff his light with the first opportunity permitted them. Cat-eyed watchfulness and speed incredible was the price of a gunman's life. One careless fraction of a second on his part now would return him to that dust already hiding so many forgotten men. Knowing this his face was grave as he stood there idly contemplating that shifting scene below.

The outsides of the Square Deal's windows now were blackened by the garish light of the fifty coal-oil lamps that were bracketed along its inner walls. Below Shane, streaky stratas of lazy-swirling tobacco smoke drifted above the hatted heads of the variegated throng patronizing the many pleasures offered by Jarson Lume's establishment.

Playing stud at a table almost directly below him,

Shane saw the blonde girl who, early this morning, had almost given Stone Latham the chance he was wanting. She was sheathed in some clinging material of pale blue that made alluring contrast to her yellow hair. In the latter, now, she wore a high-backed Spanish comb a-sparkle with imitation gems.

Three men were with her. One was a paunchy gent whose right hand seemed to love the handle of his gun; another had restless straw-colored eyes, sneering lips and a chin strap on his hat; while the last member of the male trio was a sawed-off man with close-set eyes in a pock-marked visage that was as evil as any Shane had ever seen.

This last-mentioned hombre caught Shane's glance upon them and muttered something under his breath. His companions suddenly looked up. Seeing Shane, the man with the chin strap scowled. Then all three returned their attention to their game. Shane continued to watch them for a while, but finally tired of it and descended the stairs.

He threaded a leisurely way among the gambling tables and thirsty customers headed for the bar. Even in a camp of this sort, he reflected, it seemed a bit unusual for a resort to be so heavily patronized at this early hour. For a time he speculated on the matter while he studied the boisterous throng, but finally gave it up and shoved through the Square Deal's swinging doors.

Night, he saw as he stood beneath Lume's wooden awning, had already veiled much of the sordid ugliness which stamped by day the physical dimensions of Tortilla Flat. But he found nothing beautiful in it even now. This place, he reflected, was a very paradise for outlaws and hunted men of all descriptions. Only one law could function here—the harshly sudden law of Colonel Colt. And listening to the nocturnal sounds about him, he opined that it was a law that functioned regularly.

He became aware that he was hungry and turned his steps through the hock-deep dust toward Lize Corbin's place.

He noted abstractedly how lights from open doors and windows threw bars and pools of gold across the blue shadows dappling the street, and how the stars high up above him looked like guttering candles in the purple bowl of heaven. But even so, his keen gray eyes were alert to the things around him. Had some pistol-yanker tried to catch him napping, he would have received a surprising jolt. For Texas Shane's reputation as a quick-draw artist had kept him always on his guard against the glory aspirations of lesser guns. And the habit clung.

He thought again of Struthers as he crossed the busy road. Obe Struthers' pointed note had not been sent to him, but to his brother, who today—had he lived —would have been just eight years older than Sudden Shane. But Jefferson Shane had been killed four years ago by dry-gulch lead. Evidently Struthers had not heard. Struthers and Jeff had once been pardners. So Sudden Shane had come to Tortilla Flat at Struthers' call in his brother's stead. The Shanes had always been noted for things like that; in Texas it was said that when a Shane once called you "friend," he'd fight for you till hell froze over—and then skate for you on the ice. Sudden Shane was a man who believed in keeping up traditions.

When he entered the Come-An'-Get-It he saw that

the place was filling up. A good dozen customers bestrode the stools along the oil-cloth covered counter. Taking one of the few still-vacant stools, Shane leaned forward on his elbows and grinned at the bustling girl.

When she got around to it, Lisabet came and stared at him inquiringly. "Well, speak up, stranger. Y'u ain't the only pebble on this beach!"

Shane chuckled. "I'll take some eggs fried sunny-side-up on a raft of ham. An' a cup of Java. An' some apple pie, ma'am. How's business? Flourishin'?"

An angry light flared in her stormy eyes. "Good as could be expected—considerin' yo' still hangin' round an' bumpin' off my best customers!" And with an expressive sniff, she went off about her work.

Shane thoughtfully rasped his chin with a lazy finger. "Pretty sassy," he reflected, "considerin' the scrape I got her put of las' night. Reckon that old saw 'bout whistlin' gals an' crowin' hens ain't far from wrong," he concluded enigmatically.

The man on the stool beside Shane gave him a grin. "Can't noways satisfy that dame," he observed through a champing mouthful. "Coldest critter on Gawd's footstool, bar none. Even Lume can't get no place with her —an' that's sayin' somethin'.'"

Shane nodded without comment. So Lume *had* been monkeyin' around! Was he the polecat who had put the sullen resentment in Lize Corbin's eyes?

He reached out and caught the plates and cup she sent slithering down the counter, loaded with his order. He dumped four spoonfuls of sugar m his coffee and began the serious business of "feeding his face."

One by one his companions finished their meals, grabbed toothpicks and sauntered out, leaving their money beneath their plates. He watched the girl clear the dirtied dishes from the counter, disappear with them into the kitchen. When she returned she stopped before him and leaned against the counter, eying him soberly.

"I didn't get a chance to thank y'u for what y'u done last night," she said. "I'm thankin' y'u now."

Shane flushed. "Shucks, ma'am, don't be mentionin' it. I'd have done the same for anybody." And his flush grew hotter as he saw the old resentment flare up in her eyes and realized he'd put his foot square into things again.

"Yes," she said with stormy glance, "I reckon you'd a done it for any—"

But there he cut her off. "Don't say it, ma'am. 'Twouldn't be noways fittin' an', besides, the hard cases round this town that had orn'ry notions have begun to opine as how they mebbe made a mistake in readin' your brand. They're beginnin' to figure mebbe they've had you all wrong plumb from the start. Ain't no sense runnin' yourself down when other folks is startin' to run you up."

"The only reason they're figurin' to run me up is account of y'u. I reckon y'u are some shucks with a gun, Shane. Looks like most of the salty hairpins in this camp is right anxious to keep outa yo' way since y'u downed Wolf Brady an' Wild Bill Halleck. But I ain't allowin' that's helpin' me none. They'll keep theah dirty tongues off'n me all right, when yo' around. But when y'u leave they'll come snarlin' round ag'in. Y'u oughta know a fella cain't make a silk purse outen a cow's hind end."

"You ought to smile when you say that, ma'am. 'F I heard a gent make a remark like that about you, I expect

I'd bend my gun on him quick. Shucks," Shane gravely added, "trouble is with you, ma'am, you're lettin' ancient hist'ry obscure the silver linin' of your cloud."

"Well, the trouble with *y'u* is y'u ain't got sense enough t' know when yo' reached the limit. This sportin' crowd here'll git set right sudden an' *psssst!* Theah'll be a *bammm*, some flame an' a puff of smoke an' y'u'll be plumb washed up an' in yo' coffin! I'm a-tellin' y'u! I've seen it happen befo'. Theah ain't no gent tough enough to buck this camp an' git away with it. Shane, yo' ridin' for a fall!"

Shane only chuckled amusedly. "I reckon not—"

"Jest like all the rest o' the men!" she flashed. "Confident as Billy-be-damned an' plumb stiff-necked as hell! If y'u had any sense, y'u'd git right outa this sink of iniquity an' settle down on some nice quiet ranch an' mind yo' own business."

Shane's eyes twinkled. He had a ranch of his own back in Texas right this minute. But he held his face sober as he looked Lize Corbin in the eye; there was no need of airing the fact, he thought.

"Why, ma'am," he gravely drawled, "I reckon I'm a box-head for not thinkin' of somethin' like that sooner. I'm plumb mortified a lady had to point it out to me."

She regarded him suspiciously, as though sensing laughter in his words. But his face was faintly flushed and showed no sign of mirth.

"Where do you reckon I could get me such a place," he asked, "in case I decide to do that little thing?"

"How do I know? Use yo' ears! Use yo' eyes I Theah oughta be plenty of spreads for sale. Lume an' his tough guns has raised so much deviltry in this country I allow y'u oughta be able to pick up a place right cheap 'Course the on'y way y'u could keep it stocked would be with a hard-case crew what didn't give a damn for gold-minin'. Everyone round thisaway has done got gold colic bad. Couldn't git 'em to work at no ordinary chore for all hell. I allow theah'll be one hellimonious passle of paupers in this country when this boom curls up."

"Well, ma'am," Shane said, bowing to her and slipping some money under his plate, "I reckon I'll go put my ear to the ground an' see what I can discover along them lines." He glanced at his timepiece. "Yep, I reckon I better be siftin' along."

"I expect yo' better be siftin' quick. Stone Latham is crossin' the street an' he's got company. If y'u an' him is figgerin' to have a ruckus, I'd admire for y'u to have it outside. These fixin's here cost me money."

But he could tell by her strained expression that it was not the fixings she was worried about, but him. She was anxious for him to get away without a meeting with the saturnine Latham. He wondered if she knew about the run in they'd had this morning in the Square Deal's Room Number Ten. He decided that she didn't, since it would be unlike his conception of Stone Latham for the man to air a thing so greatly to his discredit. This morning Latham had had all the breaks yet his gun had not come out of leather. Either Latham's nerve had snapped at the crucial moment, or native caution had bidden him stay his hand.

Shane looked at the girl. Concern lay plain in the pale rigidity of her cheeks. For some reason she evidently did not want him to engage Stone Latham in a gun battle. He couldn't see why she should be concerned—unless it was because of what he had done for her, and she feared Latham's friends might throw in too and down him. He dismissed the matter with a careless shrug.

"I can't run away, ma'am. What has to be has to be. This is one of them situations that has to be brazened out. I reckon I'll just wait an' see what they got on their minds."

"Y'u dang lunkhaid!" she flared. "I reckon yo' tryin' to get yo'self killed off!"

"Shucks," he drawled gently, "it's uncommon hard, ma'am, to dodge a shootout by hustlin' off. Them fellas'd figure I was aimin' to cut my stick an' they'd put a wrong interpretation on it. They'd—"

"Git killed, then, if it'll be any satisfaction to y'u," she snapped, and flounced back into the kitchen.

Shane grinned ruefully and rasped his jaw. "Sure is a spitfire," he marveled.

But his face grew quickly sober as boots clumped heavily across the board walk outside.

Stone Latham pushed through the door, followed by two other men who crowded on his heels. There were scowls on the faces of the latter, but Latham's features were wreathed in a saturnine smirk.

"Howdy, Shane," was his greeting. "Like to have you meet a coupla friends of mine; Birch Alder an' Shoshone Mell. Boys, this is S. G. Shane."

Shane nodded coolly, but did not offer to shake hands. "Howdy," he said, and waited, his hands hanging loosely at his sides.

"So y'u are Shane, are y'u?" Staring curiously, Alder drawled, "Y'u are makin' quite a rep."

"It ain't my fault if folks round here wants to

commit suicide," Shane said modestly. "I do my best to avoid these things but—"

Alder shot a stream of tobacco juice between his broken teeth. "Humph!" he sneered and, moving forward, climbed upon a stool.

Shane turned a little to keep all three men within his vision. He did not like that "Humph!" of Alder's, nor did he like the fellow's move. It seemed to him just a bit too deliberate, as though the thing had been according to some prearranged plan.

He looked Birch Alder over carefully. He was a solidly built man, muscular, and heavy of face. Years of the wrong kind of thought had drawn a corner of his mouth downward until his coarse features held a perpetual sort of leer. There was a sneaking droop to his big shoulders that spelled "Gunfighter"—an epithet backed by his two bone-handled Colts in tied-down holsters.

The other man, Shoshone Mell, was a lanky, thin-lipped hombre who moved with a slouching shuffle. A cropped black mustache adorned his upper lip which, when taken in conjunction with the tuft of black hair on his chin, gave him a cast of countenance extremely reminiscent of the face of Lucifer His dark and sunken eyes held smoldering fires in their gleaming depths. And Shane saw notches on the worn handle of his gun.

"Looks like you are travelin' in big time company," Shane said to Latham with a grin.

Latham grinned back felinely. "I always travel in big time company," he boasted. "Lume still got you on his payroll?"

"No, but he doesn't know it yet. I quit five minutes ago."

A shadow crossed Latham's features but vanished instantly. "A good thing," he approved "The sooner you get out of this town the longer you'll have to keep on eatin'."

"Ain't nothing the matter with my appetite," Shane said cheerfully.

"There will be if you ain't on your way right quick," was Latham's significant reply. "When you leavin'?"

Shane looked at Latham's two gun fighters an' drawled, "I'm figurin' to leave right now, if it's all the same to you"

"Glad to see you showin' sense," Latham said, and sneered "I allowed you'd see the light."

"What light?"

"The light my friends here make."

"Shucks," Shane drawled softly. "You wasn't allowin' as how they could *make* me leave, was you? 'Cause if you was, I reckon I'll stay on awhile."

"Aah," Birch Alder sneered, "he's just blowin', boss. Y'u wantin' me to lun him out?"

Shane said quickly, "I'd admire to see you try," and his gun gaped wickedly at Birch Alder's middle.

The gunman's mouth fell open in surprise and consternation. "Geez," he muttered "Where'd y'u hev that hid?"

Shane grinned and, like a wink, his gun was back in leather. The movement had been so swift no eye had followed it. Latham's men stared blankly. Latham sneered as Birch Alder asked, in a voice newly tinged with respect, "What'd y'u say yore name was, Mister?"

"Shane—S G Shane"

"What's the 'G' stand for?" Shoshone Mell chipped in.

"Gun."

Birch Aider heaved a sigh "I'll hev to take my hat off to yore speed," he said reluctantly. "Y'u sure are sudden."

"That," drawled Shane with a cold, tight grin, "is what the 'S' stands for."

SIX

IT WAS SAID that his mother, a dance hall girl from Deadwood, had died in a drunken stupor while his father was making bets in the Coffin Bar as to how much longer she would last. Certainly young Jarson Lume had been fed quantities of violence with his pap, whatever else may be said either for or against him. His character was the result of wild ancestry, mixed blood, and the turbulent environment of the gold camps and boom towns in which his sire, notorious for his owlhoot exploits, had dragged him up

No other age or country could have aroused in Lume the rugged force and individuality he had found so necessary to dominate the snarling pack of wolves who brought to him the greater portion of his wealth. In this rough land none but the strongest could survive. That Lume had made himself a leader here, bespoke the man's ruthless efficiency; bespoke, too, a deadly skill in the use of Colt's "persuaders" and an iron nerve that up till now had never faltered.

Yet in these last few days Jarson Lume had noticed

a change in himself. He had become aware of a latent sense of caution of which, hitherto, he had not known himself possessed. It was disturbing—very. And it dated, he felt bitterly, from the arrival of this hombre, Sudden Shane!

Jarson Lume's straight thin-lipped mouth twisted venomously as he grimly eyed the circle of men about him. He had summoned these lieutenants of his to find if anything had been learned of Shane's movements since he had abruptly left town two days ago The reports they had given him were lame and entirely inadequate. Stripped of subterfuge and alibi, such discoveries as these brainless fools had made were absolutely valueless. Not a single man of the bunch had any idea where Shane had gone. The fellow had veritably dropped from sight!

"Too bad you birds ain't got any eyes in your heads," Lume lashed them. "To hear you jaspers talk, a gent would think the damn earth had developed a mouth an' swallered him, boots, spurs an' pistol!"

Birch Alder snarled something under his breath and clenched his fists.

Lefty Hines swore softly.

"Mebbe you could do better," Stone Latham sneered. "If you got out an' tried, mebbe you'd work off some of that fat you been gatherin' lately!"

An abashed silence settled tensely down across the room. Through it the men's breathing sounded harsh and rasping while Jarson Lume slowly rose from his chair and faced Stone Latham.

Latham's cheeks went gray, but he stood his ground, the sneer still on his lips.

From behind the towering crags of the Superstition

Range the dying sun threw splotches of gold and saffron across the splintery floor, and stained the window glass with lilac. Jarson Lume noted these things subconsciously as he somberly eyed his lieutenant and strove to find the right phrase with which to nip in the bud, so to speak, the flare of mutinous defiance to be sensed in Latham's words, and even more in Latham's tone.

The silence grew so long-drawn as to be almost insupportable before at last Lume spoke. And when he did, his husky voice shoved his words across the hush with the grating rasp of a rusty hinge.

"Latham," he said, "I've killed men for less than that — squashed 'em like I would a scorpion. By rights, I ought to rub you out! An' I would if you wasn't the only man with guts in his belly of all this mongrel breed. Now you clamp a latigo on that tongue of yours, by Gawd, or I'll cut it out!"

Again cold silence crept across the room, and only the mournful soughing of the wind through the cottonwoods outside disturbed it. Hot color flooded Latham's cheeks and a red fog was across his eyes. But he held his tongue.

And then Bronc Walders' voice ran hurriedly across the stillness:

"Yuh know, I've been thinkin', Chief. This Shane pelican won quite a bit of money before he pulled his stake. Won it at one of the poker tables here. I was playin'. Like I said, I've been doin' a heap of thinkin' since then an' I figger there was a reason why Shane kep' pilin' up the chips."

Lume regarded him steadily. "Spill it."

"Wal," Walders hesitated, glanced uneasily at

Stone Latham and abruptly blurted, "Latham's woman was settin' in on that game!"

Lume turned the information over slowly, scanning it from various angles. Suddenly in the dim far reaches of his mind a subtle thought clicked into place. The lambent eyes in the cold, bloodless mask that was his face glowed with a new suspicion as they probed Stone Latham's. "Go on, Bronc. You interest me strangely."

"Wal, as I recall it, Shane won every time that damn blonde hellcat dealt."

Latham took a half step forward, menace in every line of his angular rawboned body, his right hand spread clawlike above his holstered pistol. His bold eyes swam with wrath as they fixed themselves on Walders' grinning face. He opened his mouth in a ripped-out curse:

"You lyin' bastard!"

Lume, watching them, saw the gloating look fade swiftly from Bronc Walders' countenance. A sinister leer took its place as his hand, too, slid hipward. Jarson Lume swore through locked teeth. "Git your hands away from them damn guns!" he snarled. His snaky eyes glowed with a wicked fury. "The first fool to put his paw to iron'll die!"

Bronc Walders spared him a lightning glance and relaxed, grinning. He had seen the black snout of Lume's derringer leveled with stiff malignance from the gambler's hip and knew that for the present he was safe. Stone Latham was never the man to sign his own death-warrant.

"I'm countin' three, Latham," Lume purred ominously.

With a snarl Latham removed his hand from the

proximity of his thigh and the look he snapped at Lume was bitter. "Can't you see what this lousy saddle tramp's up to?" he jeered. "He's tryin' to split us up, to turn one man ag'in the other. Look at the way he got us to wipe out Puerco!"

Lume shifted his flinty gaze to Walders' face. "Hmm. Just what you mean by that?"

"We don't know," growled Latham, "that what he said about Puerco was true any more'n these lies he's passin' 'bout Gracie. I know damn well Gracie wouldn't double-cross us like he's puttin' on!"

"You never can tell what a woman'll do," Lume observed coldly. "Mebbe she didn't pass him the cards to take them pots an' mebbe she did. But one thing's certain—Shane nicked me for eight thousand bucks. Somethin's screwy somewhere!"

"What objective could she have to pull a stunt like that?" Latham demanded hotly.

Lume looked at Walders.

Bronc Walders said, "I figger she thought mebbe Shane was figgerin' to gun Latham an' wanted some way to get him outa town quick. I allow she reckoned that if Shane won a pile of jack he'd fan dust pronto." He added pointedly, "He sure fanned dust."

"Why, you orn'ry hound!" Latham snarled. "There ain't no damn two-legged jackass can beat—"

"*Sit down!*" venom oozed from the husky voice with which Jarson Lume shoved his words across Stone Latham's brag. "Sit down an' git a latigo on that jaw of yours before I bust it plumb off!"

Latham sank sullenly into a chair and glowered at Walders between slitted eyes. The muscles along his jaw stood out like strands of rope. A vein throbbed heavily on his left temple.

When not in the grip of rage or excitement, Jarson Lume took pride in his enunciation and always tried to use words that would do him credit and give him the front of a good education—a thing he had never had. The present occasion was an instance of this vanity.

"Now," he said precisely, looking at Stone Latham, "it was not Walders who gave us that line on Puerco. It was Hines, here, as you'd have remembered had you paused for a moment's reflection. You have an annoying habit of going off half-cocked, friend. Now this skirt angle is a thing I mean to go into carefully. There's something uncommon odd about this business—particularly the way in which this fellow, Shane, disappeared. One minute he's here and the next he's gone. Smacks too much of magic. Like his draw."

"Alder," he lifted his voice an octave, but its huskiness remained. "You go tell Gracie I want to see her right away. You'll likely find her in her room upstairs if she's not on duty."

After Birch Alder's muscular body had vanished through the door the stillness, like a wayward schoolgirl, came halfheartedly creeping back, as though fearful of what it would find. Surprised at lack of violence in this abode of sudden death, it curled around the room and settled down among the shadows, adding to the general air of gloom an atmosphere of waiting; a brooding, hushed expectancy that brought cold chills to more than one back as man watched man in narrow-eyed alertness, and Jarson Lume watched all.

It was nearly dark outside. In the room the thickening murk was interspersed at intervals by the glowing points of cigarettes as first one man and then another warmed his lungs with the mellow fragrance of good Bull Durham.

Clumping boots presently approached the door and it was flung open, letting in a long lean bar of light from the lamplit bar beyond. A girl entered with a swish of silken skirt and was swiftly followed by Birch Alder who closed the door behind them.

"Let's have a light here," Lume said curtly.

A pair of matches burst red across the gloom as two men reached for lamps. When they were lit and their yellow radiance had driven back the shadows, Lume fixed his lambent glance upon the girl.

"Well, Gracie, what have you got to say for yourself?"

"What do you mean?" Her cheeks were pale and there were deep circles beneath her mascaraed eyes.

"Bronc Walders here suggests that you manipulated the cards the other night so that Shane was able to walk out of here with eight grand of my dinero."

The girl looked at Lume with a haunting fear in her eyes. All color had washed from her face, causing her carmined lips to stand out like a smear of blood.

"That's not so," she whispered, backing away. "I tried every trick I know to break his luck. But he was too slick—he was wise to all my stunts an' a few others besides. When he cashed in—"

Lume purred wickedly, "Are you tryin' to tell me, Gracie, you let a drifting gun-slick outdeal you at your own game?"

"As God's my witness," she cried desperately, "I did my best!" She flashed a glance at Latham, at Walders and whirled wildly upon the gambler. "What's that damned renegade tryin' to do? Turn you against Stone Latham?"

Bronc Walders laughed.

Jarson Lume eyed her coldly. "I don't know what he's tryin' to do," he said, "but I've a notion some sucker in this outfit is tryin' to double-cross me. An' if I catch 'em at it, it's going to be almighty unhealthy for 'em!"

"If you're talkin' to me," Stone Latham sneered, "you can save your breath. If you don't like my style I know plenty other gents that'd jump at the chance to have me with 'em. An' gents who ain't in the habit of pinchin' nickels till the buffalo howls."

Jarson Lume got slowly to his feel and his eyes were ugly. "Are you meanin' to insinuate I'm a cheap spore?"

Stone Latham's lantern jaw thrust forward "It goes like it lays," he gritted. "I've worked with you a long while here an' there, Jarson Lume. I've done things you couldn't hue another gent to do. I've pulled plenty chestnuts outa your fire. But I've never yet tun with an outfit what was so uncommon quick to put another gent in the wrong. This mangy pack of coyotes have been snarin' round my heels long enough. Either you're callin' 'em off or I'm cuttin' my stick! I ain't used to havin' guys put watchdogs on my trail. 'F you don't cotton to my style no more, put Bronc Walders in my job—he seems to have a right gusty hankerin' for it. I allow 'twould be interestin' to see if he could fill it."

A tense cold stillness shut down and hemmed the tableau in. It was like a scene from a wax museum. Bronc Walders with his restless, glittering eyes and ugly scowl; Latham standing gaunt and moveless with his right hand spread above his gun butt, full lips crooked in a cynical, defiant curve; Kettle Belly Dunn with his pale hard eyes and wooden features; short, squatty Lefty Hines with his weather-beaten face bulged about an oversized chew of Brown's Mule; Birch Alder, sneering, ready to back Latham's play; Shoshone Mell, his dark, deep-sunken glance a smolder of kindling malignance as he slouched beside the door, and Jarson Lume with no more expression on his bloodless, darkly handsome face than might have been read in a sandstone crag.

The blonde Gracie stood with clenched hands, her pleading glance on Latham's face, terrified lest he draw and be snuffed out by Lume's hired killers. And beside her the pockmarked Wimper with his hand about the haft of a knife.

In this situation but a spark was needed to set off the dynamite of flaring passions. And a spark was swiftly furnished; a spark that affected the threatened break and massacre as sandbags do a leaking dike, a spark that fused these mounting enmities and jealousies into a strong united front against the outlander.

The door banged violently open.

The eyes of every person in that room fixed amazedly upon the dusty, panting man who stood framed against the barroom light.

He was a big, huge mountain of a man, with bushy-browed black eyes in a swarthy copper face. He was garbed in the picturesque regalia of the California dons; silk lavender shirt, embroidered waistcoat, red sash, wine velvet-and-silver slash-bottomed trousers. A fine sombrero was pushed far back on his head and secured beneath his pugnacious chin by a buckskin thong looped through a perforated adobe dollar. As he stared around at the motionless figures he wiped the sweat from his forehead with the back of a hand, and grinned.

"Buenos noches, amigos."

Lume's husky voice shoved through the silence, "What are you doing here, Tularosa?"

The Mexican doffed his sombrero in a rakish bow to the girl, then stood twirling it by its chin thong as his eyes held those of Jarson Lume. "I tell you, senor, sometheeng 'as 'appen' that makes me of the heart sad —yes, ver-ry. I am come for tell you of eet."

"Well, get on with the tellin'," muttered Bronc Walders, and got an enigmatic look from Latham' and a scowl from Tularosa.

Lume said, "Yes. We're busy here."

"Beezee, eh? Wal, you weel be more beezee w'en I tell you some damn fool have bought our ranch at Keeler's Crossing—"

"*What!*" cold fury was concentrated in that single word Lume drove at the grinning Mexican.

"Si, some Tehanno 'as bought the place for the back taxes. Seguro si. It ees the trut'."

Latham asked, "The Keeler's Crossin' spread we use for lettin' the brands heal on our rustled stock?"

The Mexican bobbed his head, still grinning.

Bronc Walders' eyes got smoky and threatening. "An' you let 'im move in, I reckon. What's so damned funny?"

"Fonny?" Tularosa shrugged with Latin grace and spread his hands. "I'm theenk you weel call it the one damn good joke w'en I tell you that thees hombre who bought the rancho, she's fella called Shane. An' I'm theenk you weel laugh som' more w'en I say that thees

Shane tell me Senor Lume ees-w'at-you-call setteeng heem up in beeznez."

Gracie swore in a most unladylike manner. "He told me when he cashed his chips that night he was aimin' to buy himself a ranch!"

An oath formed on Stone Latham's compressed lips. "Sure," he stared at Lume. "I told you that pelican was smart! You see what he's done? He's beat this place out of a grubstake an' for back taxes, that *you* insisted we shouldn't pay, he's bought the key ranch in our relay string and at one move thrown a spoke in our wheel that'll put us plumb outa business as far as cattle are concerned until we pry him loose!"

Jarson Lume took one long step that brought his face within inches of Stone Latham's. He snarled, "Shut your mouth, you loose-jawed fool! You tryin' to tell the whole damn Flat? I'm runnin' this show an' I don't need no advice outa you!"

He whirled on Tularosa as Latham's cheeks went pale with anger. "You," Lume jabbed the Mexican's chest with a rigid finger, "take Wimper an' burn the wind gettin' back to Keeler's Crossin'." His cold eyes flashed about the group and finally settled on Kettle Belly Dunn.

"Dunn," he snapped, "you corral your boys an' follow Tularosa. I want that meddlin' slat-sided Shane rubbed out. I don't want to see any of you birds round the Flat again till you can bring me back his scalp!"

SEVEN

SUDDEN SHANE HAD BOUGHT his ranch in haste and now was finding ample time on his hands for repentance. This spread at Keeler's Crossing, he had found after buying it sight unseen, was in need of considerable repair. There was work enough in sight to take care of a full crew of cowboys. And he was finding now what Lize Corbin had pointed out to him when suggesting he buy a ranch—that punchers in this country at this time were scarcer than crow's teeth on the Painted Desert.

He had managed to pick up one man on a hurried trip to Globe. But the fellow had such a hang-dog cast of countenance that he looked more like a surly stage-robber than he did an honest hand. He gave his name as Alibi Smith and said he'd answer to it. Looking him over, Shane had opined Smith had corralled the habit of excusin' himself soon's he'd stepped out of the cradle.

"But dang it, I hev to!" Smith had expostulated. "Folks take one good look at me an' start sprinklin' salt on every word I say. Hell, if I could sue my pan for libel I'd be one of the richest men in the country! I can't hold no job down, nohow. An' I'm a A-1 worker, too! Every time somethin's missin' round a place folks jest natcherly paw my duffle over to see did I hook it!"

Shane chuckled at the recollection. He and Smith were seated beneath the strip of wooden awning which served the adobe shack ranch house as a porch. It was nearing noon of a hot day. Smith had just knocked off working on the corral which, like everything else about the place, was in need of attention.

"I reckon," Shane observed, looking interestedly at his new hand, "that your life, Smith, must have had a lot of ups an' downs, eh?"

"Wal," Smith scratched his head, then pulled his hat down low above his eyes and wrinkled his long nose. "I dunno about the ups, but I allow I've had a heap more downs than usually falls to the lot of mortal man. Mr. Shane, I've shore had a powerful lot of downs."

"Durin' some of the down periods of your life," Shane commented slyly, "I s'pose you have met up with a number of hard-case characters."

"Wal," Smith rubbed his nose reminiscently, "a few that was tolerable hard," he admitted cautiously.

"I've got to get more men," Shane confided. "I've got a notion they'll have to be pretty tough to do me any good. I'm expectin' a young war round here most anytime. I— Who's that comin' over there?"

Smith looked the way Shane pointed and saw a horseman splashing across the creek. The stranger seemed in no apparent hurry, yet he was moving right along and appeared to be heading directly toward them. "It ain't no hairpin I ever seen before," Smith denied.

As the stranger neared them Shane looked him over from head to foot. He looked thin as the brand on the

Fence Rail cattle, and he was angular and blessed with protruding front teeth that seemed constantly trying to pry his lips apart. He had an Adam's apple so prominent that Smith felt moved to confide in Shane:

"Looks like a dang baseball had got stuck in his craw!"

The stranger pulled in his horse a few paces off and sat looking down at them curiously. Then abruptly his glance swung to Smith and glowed with the venom of an adder.

"That there bump yer a-lookin' at, Mister, is all there is left of the larst bloke wot made a narsty remark abaht my afflickshun. I'm some'at tender on the subjeck as yer'll bloody well find out if I 'ear any more aspershuns flung in my dirreckshun!"

Shane looked from the newcomer to the gaping Smith and was hard put to repress a chuckle. He did not know which of the two seemed the more villainous looking, Smith or the funny-talking stranger. Smith's jaw abruptly shut with a clack of teeth and he returned the horseman's glowering stare with interest.

"Aw, go roll yore hoop," he sneered. "A fella thin as you are couldn't scare my shadder—let alone me."

On the heels of this defiance there came the crack of a pistol and dust jumped from the adobe wall between Smith's fingers. He jerked his hand away with a startled oath and his eyes grew big and round as he saw the pistol in the horseman's hand and the tiny wisp of smoke curling lazily from its muzzle. The fierce look was still on the stranger's homely countenance as he swung his glance to Shane.

Shane said, "Nice shootin', pardner. What's your trade when you ain't vacationin'?"

The stranger twirled his gun by the trigger guard as he let his eyes play over Shane. "Hit ain't none of yer bloody business," he said insolently, "but I don't mind tellin' yer I'm a trigger-slammer on which yer can smell the brimstone from hell's backlog! An' 'oo might yer be to be arskin' all the questions?"

Shane laughed and said, "Shucks, I'm S. G. Shane—"

"The bloke that feller Lume's got 'is knife out for?"

"Well," admitted Shane, rasping his chin, "I don't know as Lume's whettin' up his knife for me but somebody surely is."

"Yer said it!" applauded the scrawny stranger. "'E's 'ad some flyers hoisted fer yer—I seen 'em. 'E's got 'em plarstered orl over Tortilla Flat! 'One thousan' dollars reward fer the capture, dead er alive, of S. G. Shane, wanted fer the killun' of Marshal Brady!'"

Shane was perturbed at this unwelcome news, but did not let it show upon his face. Fast work, he was thinking grimly. But aloud he said, "Shucks, it looks like Jarson Lume is gettin' rightdown reckless with his money. Was you aimin' to collect it, stranger?"

The stranger spat significantly. "Bless me, no! A fine mug I'd be to 'elp 'im out, wot? 'Im that 'ad me pinched an' fined fer runnin' a bit of a crap game out in front of 'is blarsted Square Deal! Blimey! I tell yer straight, Mister, if that bloody marshal 'adn't took me rod away I'd 'ave punctured 'is mortal tintype, s'elp me!"

It came to Shane as he studied this curious fellow thoughtfully, that here was a brand for the burning. Always providing of course that Lume had not discovered his whereabouts and was seeking to install this queer fire-eater among Shane's outfit as a spy. But that, to Shane, seemed hardly likely for he felt that had Lume located him he would have dispatched some gunslicks swiftly with orders to put an end to him. And, since Shane had not seen this fellow during his stay in town, it seemed reasonable to suppose the man was-, like himself, a stranger among the Philistines.,

He said, "But you've got a gun now."

"I sure 'ave!" admitted the horseman most emphatically. "An' I won't be back'ard abaht usin' it. Not 'arf."

"Care to take on a job?"

The stranger looked suspicious. "That sounds a bit like work, Mister," he opined. "Work's like soap—fer them as likes it. Still..." he appeared to hestitate, then finally added, "If wot yer got in mind could be described as a contemplated meanness ter that Lume jarsper, I'm all fer it," and he grinned in a peculiar twisted manner.

"I allow Lume an' me is apt to have a run-in sooner or later," Shane agreed. "Someone is certain sure tryin' to lift my hair, an' I wouldn't be none surprised to learn it was Brother Jarson or Friend Latham. You ride with me an' you'll go places, fella—fast."

"Yus," the stranger nodded. "But there's places where a bloke mightn't give a damn ter go. I don't aim ter git where I'll be shovin' up the daisies."

"Well, of course, there's that possibility," Shane admitted. "But I think I can promise you plenty of fun before your harp gets handed down. What do they call you, friend?"

"Bless Jones."

"Well, I'm glad to know you," Shane said gravely, shaking hands with the scrawny horseman.

Smith squinted up at him. "Bless? That's a helluva name!"

"Yer wantin' ter make so'thin' out of it?" Jones demanded, glowering.

Smith backed water quickly. "I was jest expressin' a opinion—nothin' pers'nal."

"Better not be!" Jones revealed his buck teeth in a scowl. "'Orace, me ol' man christened me. Hit's a 'andle I ain't never overworked. Wot's *yer* name, pal?"

Smith flushed and looked uncomfortable. He swallowed with apparent difficulty and licked at his lips as though they scorched. He was plainly mortified as he reluctantly admitted faintly, "Albert Percival, but it ain't my fault."

Shane chuckled. Horace and Albert Percival! More ludicrous names for such a pair of hard-case characters he would have been hard put to imagine.

Smith muttered under his breath and his cheeks flamed darkly.

Jones looked positively murderous as, dropping a hand to gun-butt, he snarled:

"Wot the bloody 'ell yer laffin' at?"

Shane's laugh deepened. Then, sobering to a wide grin, he remarked, "Parents sure ain't got no sense of decency when it comes to wishin' names on their kids. The kind we got forces a gent to become a leather-slappin' hell-bender in order to keep from gettin' trampled on. I was awarded Shelley Garrimonde Shane!—but don't never tell nobody!"

The others guffawed loudly and the ice was broken. Shane got out a bottle and friendship was cemented. Jones announced abruptly, "Comp'ny comin'. Bit of dust cuttin' this way fast. Over by that red butte. Yer'll see it in 'arf a sec."

Shane, peering beneath a shading hand, said, " "Light down an' rest your saddle, Jones. I'm offerin' you the foreman's bunk. Smith here answers to the call of 'Alibi.'"

Presently Shane saw the dust cloud Jones had mentioned. It was speeding nearer fast. "Fella's crazy to be crowdin' a hoss like that in this heat."

"Some blokes ain't got no sense," Jones remarked. "Not 'arf."

"Right," Smith growled, looking covertly at Jones. "Some is born dumb an' others works hard to get that way."

Jones, not catching the look, sniffed. He was holding his glance on the speeding rider ripping up the yellow dust. "That bloke is makin' real lather," he grunted, biting off a ragged chew from a chunk of Star Plug.

Smith eyed the plug and a wistful look crept into his gaze. But Jones put the remainder in his pocket without further ceremony. "Yus—makin' real lather, 'e is. Wonder wot 'e wants?"

"Stick around a spell an' mebbe you'll learn—if yore hoss don't cave in beneath yore rugged weight in the meantime." Smith's tone had an edge of sarcasm but Jones only sniffed and kept his saddle.

"Some blokes' tongues is alius waggin'," he observed, "but they don't never say nothin' fer a grown man ter listen at."

"Why, it's a kid!" Shane muttered, still eying the oncoming rider. "Mebbe someone's chasin' him."

"Naw—we'd 'a' seen their dust if there was."

"Blimey! It's a greaser kid!" Jones muttered after a moment.

A short time later the Mexican youth pulled his horse up on its haunches three feet from the men before the ranch house, showering them with dust and pebbles. His dark eyes sped from one to another of the three, perturbed.

"Senor Shane?"

"Right here," drawled Shane stepping forward.

The youth fumbled in a pocket of his ragged chaps and brought forth a scrap of dirty paper which he extended.

"For Senor Shane," he said and, whirling his horse, was off before a protest could be voiced.

"Yer think I better storp 'im?"

"No, let him go," Shane said, unfolding the paper the youth had given him. "He's just a messenger..." His voice trailed off as he took in the single line of scrawled writing that crossed the paper's center. With frowning brows he read it aloud:

"Lume is sendin' some hell-benders after yore scalp."

There was neither salutation nor signature.

* * *

JARSON LUME CHUCKLED DEEP DOWN in his white throat as he looked at Stone Latham in his office under the balcony stairs in the Square Deal. The usually inscrutable Jarson was feeling well pleased with himself for he felt that he had done a neat stroke of business in tacking up those rewards for Shane, on the heels of sending Tularosa. and Kettle-Belly Dunn after the outlander's scalp.

"Why don't you grin, dammit?" he asked. "We've got that salty Shane fellow sewed up so tight now it would take dynamite to break him loose."

"Well," Latham said sourly, "he's dynamite, all right. Don't never doubt it."

"Why all the pessimism?" Lume scowled at his chief lieutenant. "If Tularosa, Dunn, Wimper an' the rest of that bunch ain't able to stretch that pelican's hide, we can rest secure in the knowledge that one of these reward-hungry townsmen will pot him sure."

"Yeah? Mebbe!" Latham gave a silent laugh, like an Indian. "You are slick, Jarson. I'm allowin' that. But you're not up to standard this last week or two. You're gettin' rattled. Neither Tularosa or Dunn or their men will ever bring you Shane's scalp. Neither will these fool townsmen. Shane will outsmart you again. You wait an' see. You got to get up hell's fire early to get ahead of that hombre."

Lume's scowl grew dark. "You got somethin' better to suggest?"

"No—an' that's the hell of it. I admit he's got me stumped. Thought I had him sure the other night; I had things all fixed an' he walked right into the trap an' out again, cool as you please. He's got guts, Shane has. You got to hand it to him. An' he's hellimoniously fast with that smoke-pole he packs."

"A curly wolf!" Lume sneered.

"A curly wolf!" Stone Latham spoke very solemnly.

"Cripes," Lume growled. "The fella's human, ain't he? Bullet'll cut him down as quick as the next, won't it? Then what's so damned tough about gettin' him?"

"Who's goin' to stand up to him an' fire the bullet?"

"What's the matter with bushwhackin' him if he's so damned fast?"

"Nothin'—but I wouldn't want that job."

"You are getting uncommon particular, Stone Latham."

"I'm gettin' sense," Latham grinned. "Bushwhackin's gettin' damned unpopular round this town. We'll be gettin' the troops in here, or the rangers, if we don't watch our step. Where the hell would we be then? I tell you, we've got to take this business slow an' figure every inch of the way. There's a rumor round now that some of these damned miners an' prospectors are goin' to form a vigilance organization. You know what that'll mean!"

"Listen," Lume said huskily. "Listen, Latham! We've got to get rid of this Shane quick. We can't afford to wait! How do we know he ain't a ranger himself, pokin' round to get the goods on us? He's here for some damn reason; he ain't no common drifter."

"You are right about that." Latham studied the wet rings left on the table by bottles and glasses. "I'll see what I can do."

* * *

"WE BETTER GET the hell outa here," Alibi Smith muttered nervously. "If we wait for them hairpins to git here, we might be given jobs pushin' up the daisies!"

"Blimey, yer a odd bloke!" sneered Jones unpleasantly. "Bless me if I don't believe yer wear, yer rubbers w'en it rains!"

"I got a sense of proportion, that's all," Smith said

defiantly. "What the devil good'll it do anyone for us to stay here an' get murdered?"

"Aah! Did yer ever storp ter think yer might do a bit 'ave murderin' yerself ?"

Smith looked uneasy. "I wouldn't want to have to kill a man," he muttered.

Shane looked at him and grinned. "Well, that's a good Christian sentiment," he opined. "But when fellas like this Tortilla Flat crowd won't play accordin' to the rules, an' insist on s'tackin' the deck—why, then it's time to raise your foot an' scatter their teeth on the sidewalk."

"Wot yer goin' ter do?" Jones asked.

Shane's smile was whimsical. "Why, boys, I'm figurin' to set right here an' greet 'em with the hand of friendship when they come."

"An' if they spit in yer 'and," Jones questioned slyly, "will yer turn the other cheek?"

"Now I'll tell you, Bless. My calculations ain't got that far as yet. But—if these fellas get *too* obnoxious, I reckon it might be a good idea if we took 'em down a peg."

EIGHT

AS HE RODE through the blue silver of the waning night, bent upon the mission Lume had given him, the burly Tularosa's chin sagged forward on his chest and his eyes became mere squinting slits behind the smoke spiraling from the cornhusk cigarro hanging straight from his thick red lips. Tularosa was communing with himself and his thoughts were far from pleasant.

It was a miserable thing, he was telling himself, that a dog of a gringo like Jarson Lume could snap his fingers and watch men jump to obey his wishes. It was extremely distasteful to think that he himself was one of those who jumped. More, it was damnable—surely all the devils in hell were laughing!

What had this Jarson Lume that he himself did not have? Brains? *Pah!* He had brains enough to fill two such skulls as the head of the grasping Lume. Guns? *Christo,* he had as many guns as Lume, and men who were as quick to use them.

He scowled at the black mass of horsemen riding about him. It was very quiet; only the jingling of spurs and the creaking of saddle leather and the muffled beat of the ponies' hoofs disturbing the eternal stillness that is ever associated with Arizona nights. In the far distance a coyote's howl rang thinly.

Tularosa asked himself why he should be risking his life against a man like Shane because Lume had issued certain orders? What was Lume to him? Nothing—less than nothing! A damned dog of a slave driver who squeezed the last drop of profit from all transactions before throwing his men the empty pulp, as a man might toss a bone to a pack of mongrel dogs!

Over his shoulder he sent a glance at the double line of steeple-hatted horsemen riding behind him with the moonlight glistening on their rifle barrels and their crossed belts of gleaming shells. His countrymen, all but two. He shifted his gaze to one of the latter, the paunchy dealer in wet cattle who was riding beside him, Kettle Belly Dunn.

To himself Tularosa sneered. This Dunn was a witless fool, a plodding clod content to carry out Lume's orders all his life instead of using what brains he had been endowed with to advance his position in life.

Carramba! He—Manuel Tularosa—was a man of vision, a man who could see a vaster profit in this enterprise with himself as the directing genius. He asked himself why he should not take the bit between his teeth and permanently take over the command of this rabble riding in his wake? *Madre de Dios,* it was certainly an idea.

But this dog of a Dunn—what of him? Would he lend his support to Tularosa's plan? He touched Dunn's arm, spoke soft, suave words close to the gringo's ear:

"For many nights we haff worked for the Senor

Lume, my frand. What do we haff to show for thees so-dangerous labor, eh? Theenk of the larger profit we could make if we were working for ourselves. *Carramba!* There would be no limit to our power!"

Dunn vouchsafed him a sour glance and spat from the far corner of his mouth. "Yeah? An' what would Jarson Lume be doin'? D'ye think he'd be sittin' round twiddlin' his fingers?" He sneered derisively. "Don't be a fool!"

"*Sangre de Dios!*" Tularosa snapped his fingers contemptuously. "The Senor Lume does not own Manuel Tularosa! Who ees thees grasping gringo that we should jomp through the hoop for heem? Thees Shane ees dangerous hombre. I haff talked weeth heem. Would you weesh for die, senor?"

"Hell, death's the common lot," sneered Dunn. "When my time comes shovin' round the bend, I expect I'll go out like I've lived—with my boots on an' a gun in my paw."

"Si, thees Shane weel keel you sure! Thees Shane ees—"

"Hell, he ain't so much," Dunn sneered. "Quit frettin' about him. We got plenty of men to wipe him out. What's eatin' on yuh?"

"Plenty- I do not like thees dog of a Jarson Lume. I do not like the way he combs hees hair; I do not like hees black mustache, nor hees flinty eye. In short, my frand, I do not like heem a-tall! I am not the peon to be driven like the plough-horse! I, Manuel Tularosa, am a man of vision, a man of brain, a—"

"What a hombre," chuckled Dunn derisively.

"You are right," said Tularosa felinely. "I am a man of guts. I say we should thumb the nose at Jarson—"

"An' I say," began Dunn belligerently, and stopped with a choking sob as Tularosa's right hand swung forward like a striking adder and sank a knife to the hilt in his left breast.

"What you say don' matter, frand," grunted the Mexican, withdrawing his blade and wiping it on Dunn's vest.

A moment later Dunn reeled and toppled headlong from the saddle. Tularosa held up his hand for a halt and the double line of bandits stopped their horses. The nearer men stared at Tularosa curiously. They had no love for the fat gringo he had stabbed, but were unable to comprehend the killing and were filled with a vague uneasiness.

Tularosa's white teeth flashed in his copper face as he threw the reins of Dunn's pony to a steeple-hatted rider.

"My frands," Tularosa said, "we are no longer fools to be led by the nose. Lume thees, Lume that—all the time Lume, Lume, Lume! From here out we work independently, robbing whom we please an' dividing the entire spoils among ourselves. I, Manuel Tularosa, shall lead you to amazing riches, to wealth uncountable. To hell weeth the gringo peeg!"

"*Viva* Tularosa! *Viva* Tularosa!" rang the shouts, and he who shouted loudest was the renegade gringo, Wimper, and the jet eyes glowed in his pock-marked face. Kettle Belly Dunn had been his closest friend.

* * *

IN THE SCANTILY-FURNISHED office of the Copper King Mine, old Obe Struthers peered grimly at the weather-beaten features of Lefty Hines over the rims of his tortoise-shell glasses. His wrinkled face showed lines of worry; the knuckles of the hand that gripped his desk gleamed whitely in the feeble glow of the flickering candle.

"So Lume is planning to stop the payroll I've got comin' through on tomorrow's stage, is he? The dirty skunk!"

"He'll stop it, too," Hines told him curtly, and spat an amber stream at the brass cuspidor in the corner. "He's out to break you, Obe, jest like he broke Milt Badger an' Ross Clark. He's had his eye on the Copper King ever since we drove that shaft on the sixty-foot level. He knows what we've got down there an' he means to have it. Somebody slipped him a chunk of that ore!"

"But they couldn't! I've had the men searched ev'ry time they went off duty! They haven't—"

"You didn't yank their tongues out, did you? Well, men'll talk, an' someone talked to Lume. I can't tell you how he got that chunk of ore, but I can tell you this—it came from the Copper King, an' it came from that shaft on the sixty-foot level!"

Struthers' face seemed to take on ten years of age. His shoulders drooped, his chin sagged forward on his chest and he stared unseeingly across his littered desk. He roused suddenly with a desperate snarl.

"The damned two-legged polecat! Ain't there nothin' that'll stop him?"

A faint sardonic grin tugged at the corners of Hines' tight mouth and a light of mockery swam in his lidded glance. But he took care that old Obe Struthers did not note these signs of his wolfish amusement. "It's hell, I reckon," he said unemotionally, "but we got to face the facts. Jarson Lume is runnin' this camp an' what he wants he gets. Seems like it would be better to give in an' sell out at the price he's offerin'—"

"Never!" Obe Struthers gritted, half rising from his chair.

"That's a long time," Hines remarked. "You better reconsider, don't you reckon?"

Obe Struthers did not reply to that but hunched deeper in his chair. His tired old gaze passed over the littered papers on the desk and sought the gun belt and holstered weapon depending from a peg above it, cobwebbed and covered with dust. For a fleeting instant there was a brightening flicker in his eyes. Then it spluttered out leaving them dull and inexpressibly weary.

These things did not escape the wary Hines and contempt lay open on his cheeks. A mirthless humor lighted his stare as the harsh crunch of booted feet on the graveled earth outside galvanized the old man to a tense rigidity.

"What's that?" He cocked his shaggy head to one side in an attitude of listening. "Somebody comin'?"

A faint smile crossed the gun fighter's mocking lips. "Sounds like it."

Struthers, rising from his chair, was reaching for his gun when the door opened quietly and Jarson Lume's black-frocked figure entered. He closed the door behind him casually and nodded to the mine owner.

"How's tricks?"

"You know damn well they're rotten," Struthers grunted, sinking back in his seat without touching the holstered gun. "An' you know why they're rotten, too! Lume, you're a polecat!"

Lume chuckled. "No secret about that," he said, taking a cigar from his pocket and lighting it. "I've come over here to make you a final offer. Ten thousand dollars for the Copper King. You can take it or you can leave it, Struthers—but I'm advisin' you to take it. You ain't got long to live an' you might's well enjoy what time is left."

Struthers seemed about to let himself go in a violent rage; seemed about to give vent to the terrible hate he held toward this man. He half started from his chair again but sat down heavily when Lume's left arm swept out and brushed the weighted gun belt from its peg. The thud it made as it struck the floor somehow drew Struthers' eyes to Hines. The gun fighter's red-rimmed eyes had shrunk to slits and he stood in a crouch with right hand poised like a talon above his pistol. His head seemed sunk between his squatty shoulders; his lips were twisted in a wanton smile and his left cheek was white from pressure where his oversized chew bulged against it Obe Struthers winced as he looked from Hines to the coldly-grinning Lume.

"So Hines is in it, too," he sighed.

"Hines," Jarson Lume remarked, "is a man who knows which side his bread is buttered on. You'll do better runnin' with the wolves, Obe." He fingered his tiny mustache. "Virtue may be its own reward, like they say in the copy-books, but it takes hard cash to buy good whisky. How about it? My time's valu'ble. You goin' to sell or ain't you?"

Obe Struthers knew when he was licked.

* * *

"IT'LL NEVER WORK!" declared Alibi Smith, rubbing his long nose energetically.

"Blimey, but 'e's cheerful as a 'angman's grin!" Jones hooted. "A reg'lar ray of sunshine!"

Shane looked at them and chuckled. "Oh, it might. I allow it's sure worth tryin' anyway." He eyed the nose that Smith was rubbing. It was the fellow's most outstanding feature; long and slender with a bony hump in its middle and an upward twist to its end. "You want to be right careful of that proboscis, Smith. It's the only one like it in seventeen counties."

Jones guffawed. But Smith scowled gloomily; he was touchy about his features. "There yuh go," he growled. "Runnin' down my anatomy instead of concentratin' on the details of that crazy scheme you're set to pull. What kinda flowers yuh want in case they're decent enough to bury yuh?"

"Listen at 'im!" Jones exclaimed. "Hell, we'll live ter tell whoppers ter yer gran'children!"

"Not if I know Jarson Lume, yuh won't," Smith sighed lugubriously. "When it comes to butchers he's the real McCoy an' he can hate worse an' longer than sixty-five Injuns. No kiddin'—you fellas better lay off that fast one."

Jones snorted. "Runnin' a sandy on that blighter will be sweeter'n kissin' the Queen of Sheba! I can just see 'is jaw boggin' down an' 'is eyes a-gogglin' when 'e finds out 'ow we've rooked 'im!"

"An' I can jest see yore mootilated corpses after his gunnies gits after yuh!" mourned Albert Percival Smith with a flip at his long skinny nose.

Six days had passed since the Mexican lad had practically foundered a horse to bring Shane that anonymous warning note. Six days during which no faintest sign of danger had distorted the routine life on the ranch at Keeler's Crossing. Growing restive with the dry monotony of bucolic existence, Sudden Shane had hatched up a plan by which he and Bless Jones aimed to deduct a bit of profit from the heretofore smoothly running business of the infamous Jarson Lume.

Alibi Smith shook a mournful head and Shane and Jones saddled their ponies.

"Cheer up, ol' undertaker," grunted Jones. "We ain't never been planted yet."

Smith rubbed his long proboscis. "There's alius a first time for everythin'," he sardonically pointed out. He directed a solemn stare at Shane. "Don't yuh reckon it'd be wise to deed this place to me in writin'—case yuh never git back alive?"

But Shane only chuckled, and presently he and Jones rode off.

* * *

"Y'U GIT OUTEN HERE, y'u dang chicken hawk!" Lize Corbin gritted, reaching down one hand for the sawed-off shotgun which she kept beneath the counter.

"You can leave that scatter gun where it is," sneered Jarson Lume. "I'm not going to bite you. Just drifted over to ask if you'd heard the news."

"What new—*Never mind!* I ain't interested in no news *y'u* could bring me. Git outen here now 'fore I lose my temper an' blow yo' middle plumb to glory!"

"Cussed if I don't believe you'd do it, too," Lume murmured in admiration.

"Yo' dang right I'd do it—an' I sure will if y'u don't haul yo' freight!"

"Well," the gambler boss of Tortilla Flat said, making as though to leave, "if you ain't interested in that driftin' gun-slick hellion what took up for you against Stone Latham—"

"What?"

"Oh, interested now, eh? I thought Shane's name'd fetch you. Well, you can figure the next time you set eyes on him he'll be where he won't be doin' no more meddlin' with things that don't concern him."

He eyed her over insolently. "I got a tip Shane's been seen over round Youngsburg. I passed the news on to the boys. They saddled up pronto an' hit the trail allowin' they'd be packin' Shane's hide back here before tomorrow mornin' or bust a gut. Ain't nobody left round town but Pedro Abrilla—that is, nobody else but some drunken miners an' a handful of barflies. Nobody's around that'll have any special interest in *you*."

"What y'u gettin' at?" Lize Corbin lifted her scatter gun and placed it handy on the counter. "Yo' wolf-pack'll never git Sudden Shane—he's a heap too smart for the likes of y'u! Y'u roll yo' hoop outen here now or I'll smoke y'u up sure as Gawd makes little apples!"

"That ain't no way to talk to your—" Lume grinned mockingly, "to the fellow who's goin' to be your husband inside the next hour."

"Husband, hell!" Lize Corbin snapped with unladylike emphasis. "I wouldn't marry y'u, Jarson Lume, if y'u was the las' white man on earth! I'd sooner be married to a sheep-dipped herder than to hitch up with a two-legged skunk like y'u. Why, yo' so dang low a snake's belly would pass clear over the top of yo' haid!"

A queer smile curled the lips of Jarson Lume. "Still feelin' proddy about that little affair of ours, eh? Well, I've seen my mistake, Lize, an' I'm plumb anxious to marry you now. I'm—"

"Yeah! Y'u are plumb anxious to marry the gold mine y'u think my ol' man found before y'u bumped him off!" she jeered, her stormy eyes flashing over him contemptuously. "Y'u better clear outen here now before Shane finds out what yo' up to. He'd knock y'u so far it would take a bloodhoun' a week to find y'u!"

Lume chuckled silently. "Shane ain't goin' to be in no condition to knock anything once the boys get their sights lined on him. He's all washed up. An' so will you be—unless you're willin' to listen to reason. Hell, girl, it ain't every skirt I'd ask to marry me! Get hep to yourself, Lize. Any bit of fluff in town'd jump at the chance to get a man like me—"

"Well, here is one bit that ain't figurin' to do no jumpin'!"

Lume's handsome, bloodless face abruptly darkened with rage. "No?" he snarled. "Well right there's where you're mistaken, girl. Grab 'er, Pete!"

Whirling, like some frightened animal, Lize Corbin saw behind her the swarthy grinning face of Pedro Abrilla. Cat-like, he had entered through a window in the kitchen and softly stalked upon her while she stood listening to the husky-toned voice of Lume. As Abrilla sprang she reached for the shotgun, but her fingers closed on empty air. Jarson Lume had snatched the weapon even as she reached.

"Call off yo' wolf," she panted, struggling in Abrilla's bear-like arms.

"You agreein' to marry me?" drawled Lume with a mocking grin.

"No I ain't!"

"Better treat her a little rougher, Pete," Lume advised. "She'll take a lot of gentlin'."

"Y'u damned coward!" the girl cried bitterly. "Y'u wait'll Shane—"

Lume sneered, "Shane won't be botherin' anyone any more. You better give in. One way or another I'll have you anyway. Whether you like it or not you're goin' to marry me this afternoon—"

"Y'u won't get no preacher to marry me against my wishes" Lize panted, kicking at the Mexican's shins.

"Don't count too heavy on that. There's lots of ways of makin' a man do somethin' he don't have no natural inclination for. There's a sky-pilot in the jug right now that I've been holdin' since yesterday for just this purpose. Coupla the boys roped him on the trail to Mormon Flat an' I had Latham arrest him for disturbin' the public peace. 'Fore I get through with him he'll be glad to do worse things than marry you for the sake of gettin' free."

He grinned as he saw that Abrilla had by now got the girl in hand. She was no longer struggling; she couldn't, for the Mexican held her in a vise-like grip that would have spelled a broken limb for her had she fought him longer.

Lume let his insolent glance dwell lecherously upon her. "Pretty as a little red wagon," he complimented. "Even with your hair all mussed an' your shirt half torn from your back you're the best-lookin' hellcat Texas ever spawned!"

She eyed him in sullen defiance, a light in her

glance that would have withered a lesser man than Lume. But Jarson Lume was used to women's tantrums and was not easily moved. There was no shame in him and his grinning lips were moist like a hungry wolf's.

"A foretaste of marital—" Lume broke off abruptly as the swinging doors banged inward. A breathless man burst into the place and stood there gulping while his round excited eyes took in the scene. Lume eyed him ominously, and his right hand slid inside his coat.

The man shrank back. "Don't shoot!" he panted. "I—ain't buttin' in! Shane's here!"

Lume tensed. "What's that?"

"Some fella—just brung 'im—in! He's claimin' the reward! Says he wants his money quick or he'll turn Shane loose!"

"Where is he?"

"They're both over to the Marshal's Office. Shane's tied onto his hoss."

"Hang onto the girl," Lume growled and, shoving the messenger out of his way, strode purposefully toward the door.

NINE

AS JARSON LUME stepped out into the hot smash of the afternoon sun his right hand went to his black mustache in a caress that was the epitome of triumph. His cold eyes glowed with a savage satisfaction. Somehow, he reasoned, Sudden Shane had eluded the hurrying posse. But the result remained as pleasing for someone else had caught him. In Jarson Lume this drifter, Shane, had met his match!

Yes, the fruits of victory tasted sweet indeed to Jarson Lume as he strode along through the hock-deep dust on a tangent that would swiftly bring him to the Marshal's Office. He could see Shane slumped in his saddle, hands tied behind him, ankles lashed beneath his horse's belly, his shoulders sagging with the weariness of resignation. The mouth of Jarson Lume quirked maliciously as his glance took in the sight.

Even now Jarson Lume had commenced to gloat. Within his warped, malignant mind were visions of strange and cruel tortures which he proposed to swiftly administer to this man who had defied him, who had mocked him and with the bitter iron of fear made raw his soul. In ecstatic fancy he could hear Shane's sobbing cries and pleas for mercy. What had Shane against him to have treated him thus? Who was this drifting gunslick? His agile mind swung down his past and found a number of disturbing possibilities. His lust for Shane's blood mounted.

The Marshal's Office at Tortilla Flat was an adobe addition to the peeled log building of the stage company. On a day like this it was an oven which even the flies shied away from. Just inside the door, astraddle of a chair, sat a slim wiry man whose abruptly grinning lips revealed a double row of bulging buck teeth.

Lume had made the acquaintance of this hombre at an earlier date and most emphatically did not like him. Sight of him now acted as a cold douche upon the rosy pictures in Lume's mind; they rocked, shivered and blacked out before a sudden premonition. What was this fellow doing here?

Passing the fettered Shane with hardly a glance Lume strode into the Marshal's Office and confronted the skinny outlander grimly. "Wasn't you told to get outa Tortilla Flat an' stay out?" he demanded.

"I sh'd say so," Bless Jones grinned. "But yer see I 'adn't any money an' figgered I'd ort ter get a stake tergether before I left. I seen one of yer reward posters describin' this hard-case hombre, Shane. Says I ter me, 'Jones, 'ere's yer charnce ter git a stake without much work, an' yer bloody well know it!' So I went out an' took 'im an' 'ere 'e is. W'ere's my money?"

Jarson Lume scowled at the angular speaker suspiciously. To his mind there was something altogether too glib about this fellow's tale. Yet he could not put his finger to anything especial.

"A pretty slick customer," he sneered.

"Blimey, yer said it—slick as they come!"

Lume fingered his tiny mustache thoughtfully. The man must be exceptionally handy with his pistol to effect the single-handed capture of this wildcat, Shane!

"Where'd you find Shane?"

"At 'is ranch. Does that make any diff'rence?"

"Well, no—but—"

"Never mind the buts. Wot I want is my money an' yer bloody well know it! Pay up or shut up!"

Lume's hand slid inside his coat as a dark wave of angry color flooded his cheeks. He was not accustomed to being spoken to in such a manner and resented it. This hard-case drifter was entirely too free with his chin music.

But he did not draw the gun his fingers sought. His reaching hand had hardly touched its handle when he found himself staring into the gaping orifice of a pistol conjured by Jones from the very air, apparently.

"Take it easy, Mister, unless yer yearnin' fer a harp an' halo!"

"I was getting you the money—" Jarson Lume began when Jones' strident laugh cut him off.

"Yus, I'll bet yer was!" Jones said, and prodded him in the stomach with his pistol. "Get it now, an' don't get nothin' else less'n yer wantin' me ter knock a few stars in yer crown."

Lume produced his wallet and, under the watchful eye of his villainous-looking visitor, proceeded to count out a thousand dollars which Jones stowed carefully in the patched pocket of his shirt, while his right hand continued to prod Lume suggestively with the gun.

"Much obliged," he grinned. "I can see yer a real gent which knows the ol' saw about the laborer bein' worthy of 'is 'ire." Still keeping his gun on Lume, he backed away toward the door. But stopped short and tensed when a shot rang out from somewhere down the street, dry and diminutive in the vast immensity of the stifling afternoon.

"Wot's that?"

Lume, too, was scowling. "I don't know." His eyes mirrored a distinctly worried light which did not escape the wary orbs of Jones. "Untie Shane's feet and bring him in here. We'll put him in a cell."

Jones said, "Mebbe yer'd better put that gun yer totin' on the desk over there were it won't be temptin' yer. An' be careful, Jarson, 'cause yer bloody well know I'd as life shoot yer as look at yer."

After the gambler had deposited his weapon as bidden on the desk, he stared impatiently at Jones. "Well, get on about untyin' him. What are you waitin' for?"

Jones grinned slyly. "If there's any untyin' ter be done, yer the one that's goin' ter to do it." And he motioned with his gun significantly.

Lume's cold face was immobile as he' strode past Jones and out the door. But he could not keep the angry flame of vexation from his cheeks.

"Careful, now," Jones admonished with widening grin. "'E might kick yer in the chin. 'E's a vengeful hombre an' uncommon vicious in 'is 'abits."

Lume snorted and, bending, untied the buckskin thongs that lashed the prisoner's ankles beneath his horse's belly. But hardly had he done so when Shane's spurred heels smacked hard against the animal's ribs.

Lume jumped backward hurriedly in startled alarm as the horse rose to its hind legs snorting. The next instant its fore-hoofs came down smashingly and it was off in a cloud of dust that enveloped like a fog Jarson Lume's black-coated form.

The gambler's blazing eyes swung swiftly to Jones. That versatile individual was gaping after Shane's diminishing dust-screened figure with open mouth and bulging eyes.

Lume swore roundly. As though released from a spell by the gambler's abuse, Jones' drooping gun came up in a bursting arc of livid flame. The roaring reverberations smashed against the houses fringing the street on either side, but strangely Shane rode on with unabated speed—and that, despite the fact that his hands were lashed behind him!

"Blimey," ejaculated Jones, registering chagrin, " 'e's got away!"

Lume, fists clenched, moved toward him ominously, his usually inscrutable face a mask of fury, his dark eyes gleaming balefully.

But, as though not noticing the gambler's advance, Jones sprang hurriedly to his saddle. With swinging quirt and driving spurs Jones pounded after the vanishing Shane while Lume scorched the fetid air with mighty oaths.

* * *

A SHORT DISTANCE OUT of town, screened from sight by a bend in the upward-climbing trail, Shane lounged in the saddle and waited for the pursuing Jones. When Jones reined his horse in beside him, Shane chuckled. "I'm allowin' that worked just like a charm."

Jones' lips curled derisively. "Blimey, it was like takin' candy from a kid! Lume swelled up like a poisoned pup w'en 'e seen yer dustin' outa town. Lume 'e's mad as a drunk squaw!"

"An' just as dangerous, I reckon," Shane said thoughtfully. Then he laughed. "Our little exploit ain't goin' to boost his stock a heap, I expect. He'll have to get us now to save his face."

"Won't 'e though?" Jones chuckled delightedly. "I wonder if 'e's 'eard the old one 'bout them as sups with the devil needin' long spoons?" Then, sobering, he added, "But just the same, between you, me, an' the gatepost, all that saved our bloody bacon was that stunt of yers, sendin' in that kid with that tale about yer bein' seen at Youngsburg. If that 'adn't pulled all 'is butcher-birds outa town, we'd be buzzard bait this minute!"

Shane nodded. "We better be rockin' along. You got that money?"

"Ave I?" Jones displayed a toothy grin. "An' 'ow!"

* * *

BACK IN TORTILLA FLAT Jarson Lume was raging. Outwardly he was coldly saturnine, but deep inside his frozen-faced exterior he was an erupting volcano of destructive fury. He needed something to act as a safety valve to his turbulent emotions, and he had not long to seek to find the very thing he needed in the person of

Pedro Abrilla, he who had been left to guard Lize Corbin.

When the boss of Tortilla Flat came striding savagely inside the Come-An'-Get-It he was all primed to force its owner to go through a marriage ceremony with him. He would show this bedeviling baggage who was boss in short order, he had told himself He'd had enough of her tantrums and was all fed up She would marry him before the sun went down or he would break her damned neck!

But when he got inside Lize Corbin's place his eyes sprang wide. He saw no sign of the girl but Pedro Abrilla was supporting himself against the counter with a shaking left hand, while his equally shaking right was clamped against his thigh as though to stop the bright red blood that was seeping steadily between his fingers. There was no gun in the holster on his belt; there was no weapon on the floor, either, other than Lize Corbin's discarded scatter-gun.

"Well, what's happened here?" asked Lume quietly, a grim note in his husky voice. "Where's the girl? How did you get shot? Why," he growled, with a touch of impatience that revealed a hint of the lashing bitterness and hatred that was gnawing away his habitual complacency, "don't you say something? Speak, by Gawd, or I'll shut you up for keeps!"

The Mexican lifted a grayish face that was filled with pain. What he read in Lume's blazing eyes drove him back against the counter, a look of dog-like pleading in his fearful glance.

"Senor! As the good God ees my weetness, I could not help eet! Thees hellcat snatch my peestol an' queek like a flash she fire! *Madre de Dios*, she ees one devil!"

Three swift steps brought Jarson Lume to a scowling stop before his wounded Myrmidon. In a brutal arc his right clenched hand slashed forward and stopped with a sodden thud against Abrilla's jaw. The luckless Mexican was flung off his feet as though struck by a flying beam. He lay where he fell, sprawled limply on his side with glazing eyes.

Jarson Lume dusted his knuckles and, with a final scowling glance about the place, shoved through the swinging doors and out into the dusty street.

Six hours later, with his back to the fireplace in his private office, he faced his men. They were a dusty, sullen-faced lot after their fruitless trip to distant Youngsburg chasing an elusive quarry who had never been there. He met their glowering looks with a stare that was hard as flint.

His voice was strongly alkaline, "I'm telling you for the last time that this damned leather-slappin' hellion has got to be rubbed out. I don't care how it's done, but I want it done quick. Each time I've sent a bunch against him he's outwitted 'em. What has happened to Kettle Belly Dunn and Tularosa and the men who went with them, I don't know. I can't get a line on them. But I do know this; there hasn't a one of them turned up in this camp since!

"Something has got to be done sudden. I'll pay any two men of you fifteen hundred dollars apiece if this Shane disappears permanent inside the next twenty-four hours." His cold glance surveyed them grimly. "I'm askin' for volunteers."

No one spoke, none stepped forward or moved at all, in fact. The silence became a concrete thing through which men's breathing rasped uncomfortably.

It grew long-drawn to the point of strangulation. Then Stone Latham's voice cut across it insolently:

"Why don't you take on the chore yourself an' save yore damned dinero?"

The air seemed to tighten up and chill. Yet no expression relieved the pale immobility of Jarson Lume's bloodless countenance. Neither by sniff nor scowl did he betray even a taint of thought or feeling. His instincts were locked behind the angles of his high-boned cheeks, behind the opaque hardness of his eyes and the straight-lipped line of his mouth.

He kept his glance on Latham fixedly, immovably, until Latham shifted his weight and sneered. And even then he held it there until the silence threatened once more to become insupportable. Then he said harshly:

"Since no one's volunteerin' for this chore I'm givin' it to Stone Latham and Lefty Hines. Twenty-four hours, I said. Remember, if the job ain't done inside that time you'll not get one damned penny. But you'll do the job just the same— or you'll answer to me."

No brag or bluster marked his tone, but the ominous threat his words contained was felt by all. Jarson Lume was out for blood!

* * *

SUDDEN SHANE, jogging along the winding trail that would take them to Keeler's Crossing, paid no further attention to his strange companion for some time. His thoughts persisted in dwelling upon the incomprehensible Lize Corbin. Not alone her clothes but her very personality was different from that of other women he had known. She was no wan, pale flower misplaced by mocking circumstances in this roaring mountain camp; she belonged here, yet there was something visibly wholesome about her that set her off from the others of her sex. Tomboyish, a creature of strong reactions, there was none the less something about her unutterably feminine and magnetic.

She contemplated life with eyes that,, though rebellious, were unafraid. That something extremely odious was constantly threatening to leap from her past and overwhelm her was obvious. Yet she carried her head erect, her chin thrust bravely forward, defiant and unashamed.

Shane lashed himself with opprobrium; he savagely resented her ability to dominate his thoughts. In moments of weakness he felt that he should have stopped by to see her while in Tortilla Flat; somehow he felt that she expected him to. But he hated himself for these moments of weakness; this girl was nothing to him —could never be anything to him. He had no wish for a more intimate relationship with her. He cursed the weak-kneed instance when first he had come to her defense, involving himself with Stone Latham and then with Lume, burdening himself with this succession of gunfights and dodgings that had followed in its wake.

He had come here for a purpose, and that purpose had nothing whatever to do with Lize Corbin. But instead of accomplishing his original design, all his time thus far had been occupied with turbulence occasioned by his stand with regard to this red-headed tomboy!

Hour after hour they rode northeast in silence. The dying sun sank lower, gilding the wilderness of towering crags and bastions about them with a veritable riot of shifting, glowing color. They seemed to be crawling toward the gates of heaven, such altitude they had attained. The air was crystal clear and filled with a piney tang, the dust and stifling heat left far below in that maze of canyons that now were filled with encroaching darkness.

Boulders, seemingly fashioned and dropped by mighty hands, strewed the bare escarpments that rose like bald-headed men about them, casting grotesque purple shadows that dappled the sunlit patches of greenish rock.

Higher and ever higher they climbed until at last they could look down upon the vast tumbled expanse of chaos that on maps is marked "Superstition Mountains." Great jagged divides, spiny hogbacks, desolate plateaus and mesas, long serpentine ridges—some sinister with dark masses of towering timber, others harsh and bleak in their ugly nakedness—lay spread about them like the toys of some weary giant. They could see Haystack Butte and Dutch Woman Butte, Methodist Mountain and Aztec Peak, their western most reaches aglow like molten gold. Behind them Tortilla Mountain, Weaver's Needle and portions of the Apache Trail lay black and stark against the sun's last smile. To the southward Iron Mountain, Black Point and lesser crests rose in shimmering blues and lavenders, while ahead Granite Mountain, Nonesuch Rocks, Klondyke Mountain and the Apache Peaks seemed to frown upon their advance in sullen hate.

And now they were dipping down into the rising blackness of the night that hid all things in a swirling gloom. More slowly now than ever they went, each forward step a peril, a chance of falling untold feet to crash and rot on the unseen rocks below. It finally became so dark they dared not trust their ponies longer on this treacherous trail they followed, and they camped until the coming of the dawn.

In the first fierce light of the rising sun they resumed their way again, its dancing shafts throwing their elongated shadows before them and warming the frozen air.

They got their first view of Keeler's Crossing around seven-thirty, while still some distance off, and the sight dropped Jones' jaw.

"Albut's gorn!" he croaked.

Shane's lips pressed tight and grim. Alibi Albert Percival Smith was indeed gone, he saw. And gone was more, besides. Gone were the buildings of his ranch, reduced to a few charred posts and smoldering ashes.

TEN

THROUGH THE STILLNESS as Jarson Lume's voice trailed off, came the clattering thump of bootheels drumming out an approach. Lume's opaque eyes wheeled as the sounds came to a stop outside the door. Hard knuckles, beating roughly on its panels, awoke the echoes.

Jarson Lume growled softly, "Come in," and his hand slid inside his coat.

The door opened hesitantly and a little man came sidling in with a crab-like motion and stood blinking his close-set beady eyes in the yellow glow of the lamps. He ducked his head ingratiatingly the while his wary glance regarded the scowling men.

"Well, gents," he whined, "here I am."

Bronc Walders guffawed. "As if anybody give a damn!"

Lefty Hines heaved a grunt and bit another chew from his plug of tobacco.

Stone Latham said nothing, nor did he move in any way.

He kept his eyes on Lume and his Indian cheeks were dark with resentment.

Lume said curtly, "Shut that door." And when the door was shut, "*Now,* we'll have your story—an' it better be good. Why ain't you with Kettle Belly an' Tularosa?"

"Kettle Belly's dead," whined Wimper, uneasily. "Tularosa killed 'im."

"What's that?" Lume snapped. "If you're lyin', Wimper, I'll—"

"I ain't lyin', boss. You know I wouldn't lie to you. What I said is Gawd's truth, so help me—"

"What the hell do you know about Gawd?" Bronc Walders jeered.

Wimper paled and shrank back against the door as though wishing it were open. "It's truth, I'm tellin' you," he muttered desperately, well knowing the temper of these men. "Gawd's truth, so help me! Tularosa got big ideas—figured he'd break with you an' lead them paisanos in raids on his own an' hang onto what loot he took. Kettle Belly mustn't of agreed with 'im, 'cause all of a sudden Tularosa pulled his knife an' let poor Kettle hev it to the hilt!"

"When'd this happen?" Lume scowled viciously.

"Same night we left here."

"Then where the hell you been ever since?" Bronc Walders snarled.

"I been with Tularosa. I couldn't git away. We been raidin' over round Globe. Yesterday mornin' he got the big idea there might be loot at the ol' ranch on Keeler's Crossin'. Figgered mebbe this Shane had that money—"

"I thought he'd spent that dinero he won here buyin' up the ranch," Lume interjected suspiciously.

"I dunno nothin' 'bout that," Wimper muttered. "I

on'y know what he told the men. We rushed the place las' night. There was only one cuss there, a ugly lookin' jasper which Tularosa tortured in hopes he'd tell where Shane kep' his money. We left him down the pass a ways after we'd burned the buildins."

"You mean to say that double-crossin' greaser burned that spread?" Stone Latham growled, roused at last from his silence by this angering news. "That's the place we hold the cattle while we're lettin' the brands heal over!"

"Sure, I know. Tularosa said that bein' we wasn't with Lume's crowd anymore it wasn't doin' us no good an' we better burn it so's to call a halt to your brand-switchin' ac—"

Lume cut him short with a ripped-out oath. "He *what*!"

"He said we better burn the ranch at Keeler's Crossin' 'cause it was the most important one you had, an' that if we gutted it right it would stop your boys from handlin' any more cattle till the buildins an' c'rrals could be built up ag'in. Meantime, he proposed to grab that Bottle-A herd bein' held on Sunrise Mesa an' glut yore market. He figgers he can break you—"

Jarson Lume swore luridly through clenched teeth. There was a bloated look to his taut cheeks that was poisonous as he described in ghastly detail what he proposed to do with Tularosa when next their trails should cross.

When he stopped for lack of breath, Wimper said with a horrible smirk. "That won't be noways necessary, boss. I stopped his clock last night. Shoved my Bowie between his ribs, I did, an' cut my stick before them damn paisanos found out what was up!"

* * *

THE SUN STRUCK down on Keeler's Crossing like a brassy hammer, blistering the sand and dry-curled grass, heating the gritty wind until its breath was like the draft from a furnace. The sky shimmered like a sheet of tin.

Bless Jones, with one leg crooked about the saddle horn, regarded Shane gloomily. "Ain't this 'ell?" he sympathized. "Wot yer goin' ter do?" His glance played somberly across the charred remnants of the buildings they had spent two weeks repairing. "Skunks wot done this ort to be 'amstrung, by cripes!"

Shane grinned ruefully. "I been expectin' somethin' like this," he said. "I reckon it was too much to hope Lume wouldn't be payin' me back for buyin' this spread with money I took out of his Square Deal. He hasn't got no sense of humor."

"Yer bloody well know 'e ain't! Wot yer reckon they done with Albut?"

Shane's gray eyes clouded. He rasped his chin thoughtfully. "I wish I knew. I'm afraid—"

"Look!" Jones pointed excitedly up the trail leading down from the bluffs. "We're goin' ter 'ave comp'ny."

True enough; down the rocky trail a rider was coming slowly, carefully, lest a misstep spell disaster. The rider's clothes were worn and dusty and heavily-seamed with wrinkles; the shirt many-hued with patches. The rider was lithe and willowy, sure and graceful in the canted saddle, face concealed—save for a rounded chin—by the down-turned brim of a shabby hat.

Shane's eyes, as he watched this rider's progress,

were narrowed thoughtfully. There was something familiar about them.

His thoughts were broken at this point by Bless Jones' startled:

"Bless me! Hit's a gal!"

Shane swore beneath his breath as he recognized Lize Corbin, for she it was. And from Shane's viewpoint she could not have come at a more inopportune time. Right now a trip to Tortilla Flat was in order; a visit to even the score with Lume for the burning of these buildings. It was a thing he did not care to put off, for he was anxious to get m touch with Struthers and find out in what manner he could be of service to his dead brother's former pardner.

So it was he eyed the approaching girl with grumpy disfavor, though deep within him a voice cried out that he was glad to have her here But he stifled its cry with savagery; he could not be burdened with a girl—he *would* not.

"Shane, y'u dang lunkhaid, h'are y'u?" She flashed him an eager smile, just as though her parting from Tortilla Flat had not been filled with turbulence and fraught with dire possibilities of shame.

She drew up nearby, sat lounging in her saddle while she regarded him expectantly. "Well," she managed, as the silence lengthened, "even if y'u ain't glad to see me, y'u might pretend y'u are. Y'u look like I might hev poison ivy on me, or somethin'."

"Shucks, ma'am," Shane drawled, removing his hat —a gesture which was imitated by the watchful Jones. "I reckon I'm plumb glad to see you, but..."

Her eyes flashed round, taking in the scattered heaps of ashes and the smoking, blackened posts. 'This the spread y'u bought?" And at his nod, "Jarson's one fast worker, ain't he?"

Her glance swung back and searched his face. "But what?" her eyes were on his squarely.

"But—" Shane shifted uncomfortably, finding his saddle unusually hard. "But...Well, you see, ma'am, right now I got a heap to do an'—" he floundered hopelessly beneath her level regard, his sun-darkened cheeks showing his embarrassment. "I—I—"

Her head went up, like that of a spirited pony. Scorn flashed from the stormy eyes that stabbed his conscience. Her mouth became a white and twisted line.

"Why lie? I reckon y'u have heard them things that's bein' said about me. Oh, I know what that lousy town is sayin'! I guess y'u are scared y'u'll get *contaminated!* Well, y'u needn't to worry—I'll keep away!" And, with a choked little sob, she whirled her horse and roweled across the muddy creek and into the trail to Globe.

"Here—wait!" Shane called, but without avail.

"Blimey!" Jones said. "Yer done it now!"

* * *

WHEN LIZE CORBIN raced away from Keeler's Crossing, she was shaking with a fury she had never known before; the hatred and resentment she had felt for the man who had betrayed her and then ignominiously cast her aside for a newer flame was as nothing to the storm aroused in her by Shane.

She drove her horse with quirt and spur, caring not where she went so long as it was away. She rode with a red fog before her eyes and a terrible ringing in her ears. Her heart beat against her breast with a tumult that seemed certain to loosen it from her body, and her breathing came in panting sobs.

Miles sped beneath the pony's hoofs like paces, yet still she urged him on. The drive of the whistling wind, the fierce clattering pound of hoofs and headlong careening movement went well with the storm within her and in some small measure seemed to ease her tortured spirit.

That Shane, of all men, should have treated her thus! Had he driven a knife in her heart and twisted, he could not have hurt her more. What a horrible thing to find oneself madly in love with a man who valued one's regard so lightly! With a man who cared no whit whether one were near or miles away! With a man who appeared to *prefer* one somewhere else!

It was hateful, contemptible, *unbearable!*

But it was true!

She lashed her spirit raw with bitter, endless thoughts of Shane until at last exhausted, her passion consumed in its own white flame, she brought her lathered pony to a halt.

She cast a heedful glance about. Rimrock seemed to hem her in from all directions save ahead. Ahead the trail rose twisting through a veritable maze of boulders; boulders small, toadlike and ugly; boulders towering tall and mighty; reddish boulders squatted precariously and sinister in the sand and clacking rattle-weed.

This looked like the trail to Globe, she thought, and shuddered to think she'd ridden its tortuous path in such abandon. Her red lips quivered and tears fell unchecked upon her cheeks.

But presently her sobbing ceased. "Bawlin' like a spoiled brat!" she upbraided herself, and added, "Lize Corbin, yo' a gosh-blamed fool!"

She smiled a little at that, a wan pathetic smiling of the lips. "Sure is lucky none of them lunkhaids back at the Flat is watchin', me now. I reckon they'd git a big kick outa seein' Dry-Camp Corbin's tomboy snifflin'." She shook her head disgustedly. "I must be gittin' soft!"

She peered beneath a shading hand at the trail ahead. After all, it did not greatly matter where she went as long as never again her eyes should fall on Shane, or Lume, or Latham. She would never return to Tortilla Flat where Lume could have his will with her; she must hide herself some place beyond his reach!

With the thought she straightened bravely in the saddle; with her knees she urged her tired pony on. Perhaps she dare not linger in Globe, but Globe would do for now—it must.

She rode with shoulders drooped dejectedly. What was the use of running away? Lume would run her down and bring her back; she knew it. There was no escaping him. She recalled that others had tried before. And, anyway, what did it matter? Nothing seemed to matter now...

The stopping of her pony roused her from the gloomy, forlorn mutations of her thoughts. She looked up to find the trail a narrow ribbon between two towering walls of greenish, frowning rock. A horseman blocked her path, sat lounging comfortably with one knee crooked about his silvered saddle horn. A cigarro depended limply from his gloating lips, its upward-spiraling smoke diffusing against the braided brim of his huge, chin-strapped sombrero. There was a light in his squinting eyes she did not like.

He was a big, huge mountain of a man, she saw. Sleek and swarthy, with black bushy brows overhanging piercing dark eyes that held just now a feline glitter as he found her glance upon him. His shirt was silk and lavender, there were flowers embroidered on his waistcoat that partly covered it, and about his middle was tied a bright red sash. His wine-colored velvet trousers had slashed bottoms, the seams alive with gleaming silver. White teeth abruptly flashed in the burnished copper of his face.

"*Buenas dias, senorita,*" he offered languidly, and doffed his huge sombrero with a calculated flourish.

"What do y'u want?"

"Ah, but did I say that I weeshed anytheeng?"

"Then turn yo' hoss an' let me pass," there was no compromise in Lize Corbin's level tone. She was badly scared by the things to be read in his gloating eyes, but she would not let him know it.

"The day ees too warm for such hurry, *senorita*. Your *caballo*, he needs the rest. I myself, Manuel Tularosa, shall find eet plaisant to beguile your tedious hours."

"Move pronto, hombre, or I'll let y'u hev it!" Lize Corbin's whip rose threateningly. She knew that name and quailed within for tales of Tularosa, and his way with women, had traveled far. "Move, I say!"

Tularosa's grin was mocking. "My," he said, and, "My!"

She swung her quirt and he took it on his arm and before she could pull it back, with a swift jerk he snatched it from her, wrenching her wrist painfully in the act. "Tularosa shall pull your fangs, leetle hellcat," and he threw the whip behind him.

She shrank from his leering face and made to whirl her horse. But he was too swift for her. Like a snake his arm shot out and grasped her pony's reins.

"Not so fas', my dove," he taunted, slipping from his saddle sinuously.

The next she knew she was in his arms, struggling desperately but ineffectually. There was a great roaring in her ears, a blackness before her eyes. But she could feel...

She could feel his heavy breathing on her face, and she could feel his supple muscles contracting as he crushed her to him with one great arm. She could feel the clumsy pawing of his hand...

How long this horror continued she could not tell, but suddenly she almost swooned for joy when a cold, familiar drawl said:

"*Hist 'em, polecat!*"

Tularosa's crushing arm fell loose and she staggered back to see Shane sitting his horse six feet away, his features stiff as some mask chopped out of wood.

Tularosa crouched like some great puma, glaring at the sudden apparition through bloodshot, narrowed eyes. His mouth was twisted in an ugly sneer and a muscle jerked spasmodically in his left cheek.

Shane swung lithely from the saddle. Lize watched him with cheeks that were" deathly white, her former anger forgotten in the thralling interest of the moment. Her personality reached strongly across the stillness, pulling at her heartstrings.

She watched him swing forward a pace or two, his catlike step hinting at a smooth coordination of mind and muscle that very shortly might prove deadly. She had a three-quarters view of his countenance. It was hard and colorless and taut; only his eyes seemed alive. They were heated with a smoldering, wanton flame.

She did not see his lips move but the cold, soft drawl of his words brought her a thrill of involuntary admiration:

"Mister, I reckon you thought this was your opportunity. I allow you was figurin' to make a little hay while the sun was shinin', so to speak. I'm sort of wonderin' if you are still inclined thataway?"

Tularosa sneered, white teeth flashing wolf-like in his copper face. His right arm stiffened perceptibly, bent above his holstered gun, his fingers spread in a claw-like droop. Lize could see the malignant hate and menace that glowered from his dark, deep-socketed eyes.

"Mister, I'm allowin' I'm goin' to kill you," Shane said harshly. And now *to* Lize the full intensity of his awful rage became apparent. There was an inexorable compression to his straight thin-lipped mouth that told of deadly purpose; his blazing eyes held smoking fury.

"Draw, you polecat—*draw!*"

For an instant there was entire silence in the canyon. Then thunderous echoes split it wide as Tularosa's hand swooped down and up. She could hear the whine of his hurried lead. Then Shane shot coldly from the hip—just once. Dust jumped from Tularosa's vest. She saw a cold grin cross Shane's face as the Mexican clutched at his chest and, staggering, crumpled backward in the dust.

ELEVEN

SHANE LOOKED at Lize and tried to say something but no words would come. He wanted to put his arms round her and apologize for his lack of enthusiasm when she had come to him at Keeler's Crossing. Instead, he sheathed his gun and built a smoke with slightly trembling hands. When he had it going and could no longer find an excuse in the business of its manufacture, he said gravely, "I reckon we better be ridin', ma'am."

Then he looked at her again. "Good Lord, Lize!" he blurted, and was beside her in an instant, and she was clinging to him, her wet face hid against his chest while relieving sobs shook her slender body.

Even after they had mounted, and he had settled in his saddle, Shane's blood still throbbed to her kisses. Hungrily his shining eyes fed on the soft pale oval of her face, on her fiery hair and scarlet lips, and on the new, shy wonder in her eyes. He was amazed that he could not control the tremble of his body as he covertly studied her while they turned their horses back toward

Keeler's Crossing. What mattered the cost, what mattered his mission, if he could secure this sweet rare loveliness for his own?

Passion he had not known that he possessed was in his blood; excitement, like a potent wine, pulsed through his veins. They rod in silence for a time while Shane strove mightily to bring some sort of coherent order out of the wild, ecstatic turmoil in his mind.

At last succeeding, he fell to meditating upon the predicament into which his new-found emotion for this girl was placing him. Obe Struthers had written his brother Jeff for help. Shane had taken up the burden out of reverence *to* Jeff's memory. But, so far, he had not managed to even talk with Struthers, though already he had been in Struthers' neighborhood for several weeks. *Now,* his new relationship to Lize was going to make this more difficult than ever. For how was he to go running risks for Struthers without a place to leave the girl? And he had no place. Even the doubtful security of the Keeler's Crossing ranch was no longer available!

He frowned a little in his intentness to find a solution.

Lize, with flushed cheeks and a touch of pride in her lifted chin, chose that moment to look at him. A little of the fire went out of her eyes at sight of his frown and she watched him anxiously.

But Shane, all unaware, continued wrestling with his problems, and his frown grew deeper, darker.

He could leave her, he was thinking, with Bless Jones. But where could he leave Bless Jones? The only answer seemed to be for the three of them to seek Obe Struthers out and if there was work for Shane to do, then let Struthers himself provide a safe retreat for Lize until Shane's work was finished.

That settled with himself, Shane relaxed a little and gave his thoughts to this ranch that he had purchased with money wrung from Lume's Square Deal. Who had burned his buildings? Lume? Or some of Lume's cohorts? But if so, why? And why had they thought fit to take Alibi Smith with them, unless they planned to use him for a hostage? And then, a hostage for what? Ransom? It seemed unlikely, at best.

His revolving thoughts turned to the burly Mexican he had bested. He felt no regret for killing that brute. Indeed, he felt a kind of savage satisfaction. Who had the fellow been? With slight curiosity he asked, more for the sake of making conversation than for any other reason.

"That...that *hombre*; who was he? Would you be knowin', ma'am?"

A look of loathing crossed the girl's flushed face. "Tularosa," she answered with repugnance. "A leader of hoss thieves, cattle rustlers, and cutthroats. I think he was connected with Jarson Lume." She regarded him curiously as he frowned. "Why?"

"I'm sort of tryin' to connect him up with things. Any of that tough bunch in town been botherin' you again?"

She hesitated and the flush deepened perceptibly in her cheeks. She caught the narrowing of his eyes and said, "Jarson was figurin' to marry me, yesterday. He—"

She broke off with a subtly pleasant, tingling as she saw his face grow dark.

Shane growled, "The orn'ry pup! I reckon he needs

a talkin' to... An' I'm allowin' he's due to get one. Wanted to marry you, did he? When was this?"

"Yesterday afternoon. He thinks Dry Camp Corbin passed me on the location of his mine. Seems like he'd given up his schemes fo' gettin' me to talk. I reckon he figured he'd marry me so's if the mine ever turned up he'd be in a position to grab it."

"Did—?" Shane began. But Lize cut him short with a scornful laugh.

"No, I sloped. He was all set an' sendin' fo' the preacher when some fella came bulgin' in a-yowlin' that some other gent had ridden in with y'u a pris'ner an' was shoutin' fo' his money. Lume must be right anxious to collect yo' scalp, I reckon, 'cause he went bangin' out the doah like the devil beatin' tan bark! I sure was scared fo' a minute, but I knowed y'u'd make the riffle so I cut my stick an' here I am,"

"I reckon Jarson Lume," Shane growled, "would eat off the same plate with a snake."

Her blue eyes twinkled fleetingly. "He's a pow'ful orn'ry man." Resentment obscured the twinkle the next moment and she added huskily, "There's others jest as bad."

"I reckon you're thinkin' of Stone Latham, ma'am. An' I'm allowin' he's in need of gentlin', too. I'm figurin'—" he broke off, struck by the peculiar expression in her eyes. "Why, what's the matter, Lize?" His voice was anxious.

"Nothing!" She managed a shaky laugh; said lamely, "I was jest thinkin'." But she did not confide what her thoughts had been about. Instead she changed the subject. "Who was that puncher I seen y'u with at Keeler's Crossin'?"

"Name's Bless Jones. Horace, his father called him, but he allows he ain't right partial to that handle." His lips quirked as at some humorous memory. "Tells me he come from England. He's folks over there, I reckon. Said his father was the earl of somethin'-or-other—Dickhouse, I believe he said. Anyhow, he's some fast on the trigger. I hired him an' another gent to work my spread. I reckon since last night what I need most is carpenters," he grinned ruefully.

* * *

PROLONGED inactivity was awakening spluttering fires of impatience and discontent among the rank and file of Lume's renegade supporters. They wanted gold to spend in gambling and more gold to throw away on the wenches of the camp. To get this so-necessary gold they must stage another robbery or stick up another stage or move their waiting cattle. Lume did not want any more robberies just now; things were shaping up, he said. To stick up a stage right now would be fruitless and even dangerous, for Lume had taken over the last large independent mine and such gold as was being shipped belonged to him. As for moving the cattle—impossible. Tularosa had burned the big corrals at Keeler's Crossing where of old it had been customary to hold the critters while altered brands scabbed over and still other brands were made through a wet blanket, and the next ranch in their owlhoot string was a long hard drive that must, in part, be pushed under the very noses of outraged authority.

But inactivity was bad, as Bronc Walders pointed out to Lume a short time after Hines and Latham had left on their lethal mission to Shane. Like the insidious growth of some unseen cancer it was undermining Lume's influence and dominance. Bronc Walders said as much.

"Look," he pointed out. "You better be givin' these wolves of yores somethin' to occupy their hands. When scum like them gets to usin' their hat racks, all hell is due to come apart!"

Lume grinned like a sleek black cat. "They're goin' to have their han's full pronto. Wimper," he faced the pockmarked whiner with an abruptness that shrank the little man back against the wall, "when this meetin' breaks up you corral all the loose saddle bums that's loafin' round here an' start shovin' them cattle we got at Horse Mesa on towards our Iron Mountain spread—"

"You can't do that!" Shoshone Mell jerked out. "No men can shove that bunch of wall-eyed brutes over that kinda country in a jump as long as—"

"I want them cattle started for Iron Mountain before mornin'!" Lume's voice contained no compromise. "An' by Gawd, Wimper, that scum of yours better get 'em there." There was something in Lume's eyes as he said the last that set the pock-faced man a-shiver. Lume's glance then whipped to Mell.

"I'm wanting that Corbin dame, Mell. You an' Alder bring her in."

Mell rasped his unshaven jaw. "I ain't keen," he muttered hesitantly, "on monkeyin' with no damn skirt. Better pick someone else—"

"I'm pickin' *you*, Mell; you an' Birch Alder," Lume's voice was dangerously soft. "But I ain't askin' you to run such risk for nothing. There's two grand apiece in it for you if you can cut it. An'," he added ominously, "you better cut it."

Mell shrugged philosophically and took up some slack in his belt.

"Uh-huh," he said.

Brond Walders, watching, grinned behind his lips.

Lume looked at Alder curiously, calculation in his glance. "Got any notion where to look?"

Alder nodded. He said bruskly, "I'm allowin' we have. Mebbe you ain't noticed it but that dame's a heap sweet on this Shane hairpin. Looks like aces to kings she'll be headin' for Keeler's Crossin'. I figger we'll amble over thataway a piece."

Bronc Walders' lips drew down; his eyes clouded up.

When Alder and his crony got up to leave several moments later, Bronc Walders too arose. He was following them to the door when Lume said,

"Wait a minute, Bronc. I got a little somethin' I'd like to be talkin' over with you."

Walders turned and his eyes slid over Wimper who grinned ingratiatingly.

Walders said, "You ain't figurin' to habla 'bout anythin' private with that scissors-bill hangin' round, are you?"

Lume looked at Wimper. "Clear out, Wimper. I'll see you in the mornin'."

"Heck, I—" Wimper broke off short and scuttled for the door as Lume's cold glance started storming up. Lume sneered when the door slammed shut behind him. "Minds just like a dog."

"I wouldn't have a squirt like him around," Walders

growled. "That little shrimp would sell his gran'mother down the river if he figured she'd bring a profit!"

Lume grinned. "You're gettin' jittery. Hell, I got Wimper right under my thumb. He's almost scared to breathe aroun' me."

Walders grunted. "Even a rat will bite." He looked at Lume inquiringly. "What was you wantin' to see me about?"

"I got some..." Letting his voice trail off, Lume reached inside his coat.

Something in his eyes must have given his intention away for Walders' hand dove hipward frantically—too late!

Flame lanced wickedly from Lume's reappearing hand. Rocking, roaring reverberations filled the room and set the lamplight flaring. Hot blood streamed down Bronc Walders' forehead and into his glazing eyes. He staggered blindly, lips parting grotesquely as he swayed and dropped. His hat fell off and rolled across the floor and Jarson Lume laughed mockingly as he stood above him, his smoking pistol still in hand.

Someone was pounding on the door but Lume paid no heed.

"So Wimper'll doublecross me, eh?" he sneered, derision in his glance. "Well, you blasted ranger spy, I'm damned sure *you* won't write Shane no more notes!"

* * *

"WHEN STONE LATHAM finds out what Lume is up to there'll be hell a-poppin' sure!" Birch Alder said to Mell as they left the Square Deal and stood beside the hitch rack untying their horses' reins. "D'you reckon Lume knows what he's doin'?"

"If he don't, it's sure enough high time he was findin' out," Mell grinned. "He may be cock-o'-the-walk in this man's camp, but Stone Latham is no safe man to fool with. You reckon that lousy Wimper really shoved a knife in Tularosa? Sounds mighty thin to me."

"Me, too," Alder concurred, swinging into the saddle. "Yuh know, Shoshone, I ain't real keen on this chore Lume has dished us out. I'd like it a heap better, I'm allowin', ef Latham wasn't mixed up in it. He'll be after somebody's scalp damn sure!"

"Yeah, I reckon. But two grand is two grand, no matter where you spend it. I ain't seen that much money in a coon's age."

"We ain't seen it *yet,* neither," Birch Alder reminded grimly. "I wouldn't put it past Lume to have us grab the dame an' then hightail it without payin' off."

"He better not look like it," growled Shoshone Mell. "Let's git goin'."

"What we goin' to do if the dame's with Shane?"

"Hang round outa sight till Shane has business elsewhere. Hell, he can't wet-nurse her like a yearlin' calf! He's gotta leave 'er sometime. When he does is when we act. Dig spurs an' let's git started. I wanta git my fingers on that dinero."

* * *

STONE LATHAM and Lefty Hines were half way to Keeler's Crossing when Latham abruptly pulled in his horse. "You better camp here till mornin'," he told his companion. "Too damn dark to tackle the rest of the way tonight. Don't build no fire or—"

"What the hell?" growled Hines. "Ain't you goin' to be here?"

"Not sure yet. I got a little matter to attend over round Weaver's Needle. If I can make it in time I'll join you."

"You don't think I'm figgerin' to tackle Shane by myself, do you?"

Latham sneered. "Hell, you can lay back of some boulder an' pot him off, can't you?"

"Not by myself, I can't! I got too much respect for my hide," Hines answered resentfully. "By cripes, I'm allowin' I'll wait right here till you git back."

"Don't be a fool. You—"

"I'd be a fool all right if I was to go solo after that damn leather-slapper!"

Latham regarded his companion thoughtfully in the starlight. He cleared his throat once or twice. Finally he remarked, "There ain't really any reason why we should jump this Shane, you know."

Hines started. After a moment's silence, "I guess you're right," he said. "What you got in mind?"

"It might not be a bad idea if we pulled out. Lume's headin' for the rocks. I got a feelin' the minute I clapped eyes on Shane that Jarson's number was damn-well up. I'm gettin' plumb fed up on his domineerin' ways, anyhow. What say we cut our stick? Lume's figurin' to ship out some dust tomorrow night. We might stop the stage an' make a haul." He looked at Hines craftily.

Hines shrugged. "Well, that suits me," he said. "But what about yore woman?"

A scowl crossed Latham's features and his high-boned cheeks grew dark. "What was that remark?"

Hines read a warning in that soft-toned purr. "I said," he muttered hastily, "that I'd be plumb proud to help you stop the stage."

Stone Latham grunted and relaxed. "A loose jaw," he spoke reminiscently, "has helped many a gent into a quiet bunk under Boot Hill's weeds." He began pulling the saddle from his horse. "The fella that's learned to hobble his tongue is the gent who's goin' to live long enough to be tellin' boogery tales to his gran'children. Let's rest these nags a spell."

* * *

"TOMORROW," Shane said to Jones, after Lize Corbin had turned in between her blankets and he and Jones sat smoking beside the campfire, "we're headin' for Tortilla Flat. I got to find a fella named Struthers who owns a mine."

When Shane had returned to Keeler's Crossing a couple of hours before, Jones had exhibited no surprise at seeing the girl accompanying him. Now he ventured, hesitantly, "What you figgerin' ter do with the calico?" and he jerked his thumb toward where Lize lay. "Goin' ter take 'er along?"

"Have to," Shane admitted. "No place here to leave her. I'm goin' to put it up to Struthers to find a place for her till I get through with a few chores I got mapped out."

"If them chores 'as got anything ter do with that bloke, Lume, I'd admire ter 'ave a part in 'em," he growled. "I owe that bloke a couple."

Shane grinned. "I'm allowin' that Jarson Lume will figure in them some prominent. I expect he's been takin' all the profit out of Struthers' mine an' Struthers is aimin' to have me see what can be done. We'll have to keep our eyes skinned when we get to town. Some of Lume's hired polecats'll prob'ly have their guns oiled up for us."

"Don't yer know it!" Bless Jones grinned.

"I wish," Shane said soberly, "I knew who sent us that warnin' the other day. I'd hate mighty much to find I'd perforated him by mistake, along with Lume an' the rest of them renegades."

He sighed. "Well, let's turn in so's we can get an early start."

TWELVE

MORNING HAS a way of coming swiftly on the desert; a burst of orange flame sears the rim of the world and night is changed to day. But in the mountains it is different.

A pale wan light comes crawling insidiously across the earth, and the darkness slowly scatters on the heights while the stars and moon grow dim. The chill of daybreak snaps into the air and the far flung canyons' depths loom gray and desolate among the tumbled chaos of upthrust crag and bastion. Slowly the eastern skyline seems to crack and great red jagged streaks leak through its misty veil. Then the veil itself dissolves before this warming influence and the heavens become a brilliant, flawless blue through which the sun's fiery ball slowly rises, cloaking each towering spire and rocky escarpment in robes of shimmering gold.

And so it was on this morning as Shane and Jones and Lize Corbin rode in leisurely silence toward distant Tortilla Flat Shane had intended going to the Flat three days ago, as he had confided to Jones that night beside the campfire. But one thing and another had cropped up to change his mind and cause him to postpone the trip. One of these things was the presence of Lize Corbin.

Each passing hour he felt more strongly drawn to the girl. Why? He could not have told. He found something strangely alluring in the poise of her flaming head and in certain of her mannerisms. He loved the expressive Latin way in which she shrugged her shapely shoulders. He counted the time well spent when he watched the sunlight glinting through the copper of her hair and he took a personal pleasure in observing the varying shades of blue that flashed from her level eyes.

Sometimes he detected surprise in the glance she threw him when he did little things he knew would please her, and there were occasions when there were gleams of jealousy in her gaze though he had been unable to figure exactly why.

That she was a creature of impulse, he understood. But a flame of loyalty, he had discovered, burned strong and high within her. And he recognized, as in himself, that in her there was a stubborn streak that would ever refuse to consider the chance of defeat for anything she set out to do. It must have come as an inheritance from her dad, old Dry Camp Corbin.

When walking, she had a clean-limbed stride that fascinated, and she could ride as well as any man. She made a mighty attractive picture as she rode along ahead of him with the sunlight striking down across her hair. He reflected that soon she would have to put on her wide-brimmed hat, for the morning was rapidly growing hot. He sighed, and squinted out across the country spread about them.

The surface of this land was slashed and broken by the deep purple gashes of ravines and gullies and canyons which seemed to alternate in some crazy, incomprehensible manner with timbered ridges, long shaley hogbacks and flat-topped buttes and mesas that already lay shimmering in distorting stratas of heat. This writhing haze traced distant mountains in' dim blue etchings across the buckling skylines and even made a few more-favored ones appear deceptively near.

As the morning advanced the hot smash of the brassy sun beat down upon the thirsty earth with increased venom. The overheated air grew stifling; filled with tiny dust particles that irritated dry throats and nostrils as a red rag does a bull and reddened the rims of smarting eyes.

Then suddenly Bless Jones pulled rein where he rode in the lead. He sat motionless in the saddle scanning dead ahead from beneath a shading hand. When Shane and the girl had joined him, he growled, "Wot yer make of that? Looks like dust ter me—mebbe cattle, or mebbe 'orses."

Shane, following the direction indexed by Jones' outthrust pointing hand, saw a boulder-rimmed ugly gash leading into a valley some seven or eight miles off. Above the gash drifted a lazy ephemeral cloud which he knew for dust.

"You're right, Bless," he admitted. "That is dust. Somebody's shovin' cattle into that valley, looks like. Now I'm wonderin' why they'd be wantin' to do that? I'd say that valley wouldn't graze more'n three scrawny critters for half a day."

"Yer bloody well knows it," Jones affirmed.

"Rustlers!" Lize Corbin said with curling lips.

"Some of Jarson Lume's long-loopers. I'm bettin' y'u bedded down on one of Jarson's relay spreads!"

"Relay spreads?" Shane looked puzzled. "What you mean, ma'am? I didn't know Lume was in the cattle business."

"Well, he handles critters off an' on. Mostly other folks' critters, I reckon. They steal 'em one place, so the rumor goes, an' drift them a few at a time down a chain of small spreads until they emerge in some other state under a diff'rent brand—a brand that's good as gold."

"I still don't see—"

"Look!" the girl exclaimed. "If y'u happened to buy a ranch that was in the middle of his string, for instance, he'd be stuck with the cattle he had at the other end, wouldn't he? Well, then, he'd have to get y'u out; one way'd be burnin'. Somebody burned yo' place, didn't they?"

"Yer damn well shoutin'!" growled Jones, and spat. "Wot's more, they done poor Albut in!"

Lize looked questioningly at Jones. Shane said, "He means Alibi Smith, a fella I hired who's disappeared."

"Oh!" her face whitened. She laid a hand on Shane's arm. "I'm so sorry," she said impulsively. "Won't anyone ever stop him? Him and the men under him have practically made the boneyard at Tortilla Flat—"

"They may be decoratin' it themselves before this thing is finished," Shane cut in grimly. "Do you know an ol' codger called Obe Struthers—"

"The mining man?"

Shane nodded.

"I've heard of him. He used to own the Copper King—"

"*Used* to own?" Shane's eyebrows raised. "Don't he own it no more?"

Lize Corbin's eyes darkened swiftly; her mouth was tight and white when she answered.

"No—he sold out to Jarson Lume."

The muscles tightened along Shane's clenched jaw. "I thought," he said slowly, "that the Copper King was a pretty good thing."

"It was dang good, I reckon," Lize told him. "Jarson Lume don't never bother acquirin' mines what ain't no account."

Shane's cheeks paled with anger. To him it seemed plain that pressure—considerable pressure—must have been brought to bear on Struthers to effect this sudden sale.

"Where's Struthers now?"

"I heard he was hangin' out at the Miner's Rest. Someone said he was figgerin' to locate another bonanza. He'll be a fool if he does, 'cause Lume'll gobble it jest like he done the Copper King an' a whole passel of other mines in these here mountains."

"It's just possible, I'm allowin'," Shane drawled heavily, "that Lume'll be coughin' up these mines again. A fella can't never tell. Stranger things has happened." His eyes swept over the distant valley. "Cattle, all right," he said. "Some consid'rable. They're milhn'— see? Them punchers is figurin' to rest 'em."

He looked appraisingly at Jones. "I'm wonderin' if you'd like to pay 'em a visit, Bless?"

Jones grinned felinely. "Yer sure said somethin' that time."

"Got plenty cartridges?"

Lize looked from Shane to Jones. Then she grabbed

Shane's arm. "Don't do it, Sudden!" Her cheeks were paling in swift alarm. "Look—y'u couldn't cut it! There's six riders with them cow-critters. Six to two! Y'u wouldn't stand a chance!"

Shane smiled mirthlessly. "We wouldn't figure on stackin' up against them fellas. There's other ways a couple of smart hairpins could keep them steers from leavin' this country. How about it, Bless?"

"Yer on!" Jones said, and winked. "Might give 'em a bit of their own, wot?"

* * *

THE WESTERN SKY glowed like molten copper as the sun slid down behind the purple mountain crests and flung their elongated shadows obliquely out across the valley. There was more grass here than Shane had thought, but there was none too much and Wimper, as he sat his saddle gazing out across the restless cattle, was feeling boogery. It might be wiser, he opined, to shove them on a bit and risk the chance of scanter forage than to remain in this rimrocked hole where the cattle were plainly uneasy.

Yet it was getting late in the afternoon and he did not relish the thought of pushing these lowing brutes across this treacherous terrain once night fell. The valley's lack of water was the factor which finally decided him. He beckoned a circling rider.

When the fellow rode up, Wimper said, "Shove 'em on.

We'll try for a better place. This hole's too blasted dry an' hot. Come night, these critters'll be in a mood to bolt if a cricket creaks. Get 'em rollin', Ed."

The puncher scowled. "We might have to bed 'em down in a worser place," he objected.

Wimper went ugly and his hand dropped suggestively to his hip. "Who's roddin' this drive?" His voice held no sign of its usual whine. His pock-marked face flamed darkly. "You go pass the word along that we're movin'—now!"

The rider muttered, but cantered off.

Soon the moving cattle were rolling up a stifling cloud of dust as they streamed eastward from the valley, swinging down a wide stone-carpeted draw. This soon widened to such an extent that Wimper felt justified in hoping it might broaden into another valley. A bigger one perhaps, with grass.

An hour later his hope came true. The forward-dancing shadows of the bawling herd reached out across an undulating plain. Waving grasses that reached knee-high attested to the presence of water. "Springs, most likely," Wimper growled to one of his companions. "Start 'em millin', Joe."

Joe and the others did their work well and two hours later, having detailed three men to circle riding, Wimper returned to the tiny campfire the cook had been sweating over and had supper with the rest. At nine-thirty he wrapped himself up in his blanket and lay down with his booted feet to the fire.

* * *

SOMETIME IN THE night Wimper sat bolt upright, staring into the dark. The fire was reduced to a heap of glowing embers. There was no moon and only a few faint stars were visible in the leaden vault of heaven.

Miles away a lightning flash threw a pale illumination and was gone. An unknown fear held Wimper motionless.

A breath of cooler air brushed his taunted cheeks. In the darkness around him he could hear the swishing of the long grasses in the gathering wind. Scattered drops of rain struck down. Ashes swirled about the embers of the campfire. Wimper shivered.

A pulse of nervous excitement beat against his throat Yards away his attention was caught and held; his eyes dilated. Something was stirring soundlessly in that yonder gloom. Its movements held the stealth of a stalking cat—a mountain cat, A fear, swift and searing, brought him to his feet with a muttered oath,

His bulging eyes clung fascinated to that dim-seen, swift-flitting shadow in the lesser darkness of the midnight gloom. There came a sound like the crunch of booted feet on gravel. The deep bronze of Wimper's cheeks gave place to a sickly pallor. Throat parched with fear he yanked his gun.

But he did not fire. Thunder rumbled hollowly in the distance on the heels of another lightning flash. Wimper held his lean-muscled little body moveless; only the close-set restless eyes stabbing here, there, and all about gave hint of the tension under which he labored. Then suddenly—

"Christ!" he cried.

Off there in the night, northeastward, a point of light was flickering, growing, red against the murk. And even as Wimper stared another tiny flame licked up from farther to the north and gathered headway rapidly, fanned by the wind sweeping through the swishing grasses.

With twitching body and the desperation of a trapped rat Wimper scuttled for his horse, colliding with another form which—springing from its blankets—seemed motivated by the same idea.

Wimper cursed with lurid fury as fear spurred him to his feet. Both men reached their horses simultaneously; jerked the saddle cinches tight and flung themselves aboard.

Wimper flung one hurried look backward across his shoulder. "Roll yore tail, boy! That fire'll be a ragin' fury inside the next two minutes!"

The puncher, too, looked rearward. The flames were gaining headway fast; great fiery tongues were showing above a dense black rolling cloud of smoke that was pouring toward the bedded herd.

"What about the cattle?"

"To hell with the blasted cattle!" Wimper shouted, and used his spurs with desperation, for well he knew that once those cattle tore loose all the cowboys in the world could never stop their headlong rush within a distance of several miles—and that fire would drive them the very way that he, too, was forced to head.

It was not a thought one cared to linger on, and Wimper was doing no lingering.

His big roan ran for all it was worth, but now above its pounding hoofs Wimper could hear the frightened bawling of the cattle as they came lumbering to their feet. Somewhere not far behind him a frenzied steer let out a defiant challenge that set the herd in motion.

Again Wimper flashed a look behind. Three of his men were strung out there on pounding ponies and behind them like the fantastic background of some melodramatic painting plunged the bawling herd, tails up, a churning indistinct bellowing mass of frenzied beef.

Wimper shuddered and drove his lathering horse with quirt and spur. Where were the rest of his men? Cut off between the herd and fire? Or gone down beneath that sea of slashing hoofs? Wimper dared not think, but feared the worst.

With heartbreaking effort, nose and tail outthrust in one straight forward-hurtling line above its pistoning legs, Wimper's horse held its own against that thundering horde behind.

When next he looked only one man rode behind him and the horns of the leading steers were scant inches from the rump of this white-faced fellow's mount.

Wimper strained the aching muscles that were driving his spurs and quirt. But his horse was giving its utmost now; not another fraction of speed could the gallant animal produce.

The minutes clicked by with drumming beat. Cold sweat broke out on Wimper's back and neck and face as a sobbing cry went up behind and was instantly blotted in the noise of that wild stampede. Smoke, hurled by the rising wind across the backs of the snorting, bellowing herd, swirled about his head and brought tears streaming from his smarting eyes.

Some minutes passed and he dared another glance behind. He could see the lightning playing across that sea of tossing horns. The herd was gaining, gaining, gaining, and—

"*Gawd!*"

He rode alone!

* * *

CHILL RAIN CAME DOWN in torrents, lashed stinging across his ashen face. He knew that he was in the pass now even though he could not see a thing on either side or even ahead, for the clatter of hoofs rose hard from off its rocky floor. Even the flickering glow of the fire-licked grasses was left behind by the canyon's twistings and only his horse's instinct served as guide through this pouring murk.

The jarring thunder of pounding hoofs rang loud in his ears, hurled forward by the gusty wind that plastered his sodden shirt against his back. His heart was in his throat; he was shaking as with ague.

Then suddenly his horse had lost its stride, was skidding on the slimy gumbo under foot and was going down. His equine scream was tangled with Wimper's sobbing cry. Then both were lost beneath the hoofs of the lumbering steers.

THIRTEEN

"THAT STORM IS COMIN' bloody fast," Jones shouted in Shane's ear as, the fire started, they headed for their horses on the run. "Be doin' dam' well if we make that cave where we left the girl before she strikes!"

Shane wasted no time in words but sprinted faster.

They reached the horses. Shane's blue roan was moving at a hard run when he settled his lean frame in the saddle and his other foot found the swinging stirrup. Then he spoke, the wind tearing words from his mouth.

"All hell's goin'...come apart...cattle sees that fire!"

A malicious grin curled Bless Jones' lips. "'Ere's one night I'm bloody well glad I ain't no blarsted rustler!"

They rode in silence then, their upper bodies bent forward over their ponies' necks. This onrushing storm was going to play hell with the mountain trails, and they knew it and had no desire for it to overtake them out of shelter.

"Reckon this'll teach that blarsted Lume ter mind 'is P's an' Q's!"

"I allow it'll mebbe save the bulk of some rancher's cattle," Shane roared back. "Between the fire an' the storm them steers are goin' to cover some rearward territory, or my name ain't Sudden Shane."

He felt no more regret for the possible loss of life their move might spell than he had felt for the deaths of other men his .45 had heralded. The men who were with those cattle were rustlers, thieves who were constantly preying on the small-spread ranchers who strove so valiantly to keep body and soul together in the bleak and desolate wilderness of this mountain country. Should proper authorities have captured Lume's long-loop riders, and an honest and unprejudiced trial gone through, they would have hanged. His move in stampeding the stolen herd had saved not only the ranchers but the state a deal of money. He felt no modicum of regret for what he'd done, but only a coldly grim satisfaction.

They arrived at last within sight of the cave, yet still a good half mile away. Then rain lashed down across their shoulders and stung their faces and though they managed to get on their slickers without halting, their clothes were sopping wet before they could get them on.

They rode in shivering silence, listening to the wild beat of the windflung rain, and the squashy *plopping* of their ponies' hoofs. Shane huddled forward in his saddle, squinted eyes peering through the murky, watery gloom ahead in vain endeavor to catch a glimpse of the campfire they'd built inside the cave for Lize.

It seemed an eternity to Shane before they sloshed to a halt before the hole-pierced cliff that once had been the home of forgotten cave-dwellers. Shane's eyes abruptly widened. He could catch the reflected play of the firelight now where it struck tangently from the entrance, and in its glow he could see that Lize Corbin's horse was gone from where he'd left it hobbled!

He left the saddle with a ripped-out curse, struck the shaley ground on skidding bootheels and vanished inside the cave to reappear a moment later with a face gone ghastly white.

"She's gone!" he blurted crazily. "Gone—*Gone!* Some polecat bastard's been here an' carried her off! Oh, Jones, I'll cut his *heart* out when I get him!" His voice was filled with a merciless hate.

Bless Jones returned his stare in stunned surprise. His expression seemed to say that such a thing was impossible. "Gone?" he echoed. "Then it's Lume or some'v 'is 'ellions 'as got 'er!"

Shane's face, in the reddish glow of the firelight, was twisted by his emotions. Hot rage was gleaming from his smoky eyes that were alive with the portent of imminent volcanic action. There came a drive to his voice that made Jones stiffen in his saddle:

"We're headin' for Tortilla Flat; if we don't find Lize Corbin, or if a hair of her head's been harmed, by Gawd we'll take that camp apart an' hang Jarson Lume from the awning of his own damned joint!"

* * *

THE SHORTEST WAY TO Tortilla Flat from where they were was by way of the old stage road from Phoenix, which passed through Mesa, Apache Junction, Youngsburg and Mormon Flat. Shane intended to strike tie road somewhere between Youngsburg and Mormon Flat. It was almost morning now; they could not possibly reach their destination before the darkness that now was thinning to a watery gray gloom closed again about this desolate land. But, determined to make the best time possible, Shane—followed by the faithful ex-Cockney—started at once.

There was no trail where Shane was leading, not even the veriest ghost of a trail. He picked his way by instinct and traversed canyons apparently choked with rock rubble from ancient slides; he crossed barriers that would have stopped another man before he started. Up and down he led and round and about great bluffs and mesas. The storm passed on or they left it behind and the sun shone down upon their backs with unrelenting fury while they pushed doggedly on with neither food nor water. Only Shane's iron will kept them going when they came to the bleak and shimmering alkaline expanse of some ancient lake bed. Heat waves crinkled and folded above its forgotten floor and the white, clinging alkaline dust rose about them in clouds that brought tears from their reddened, stinging eyes and made breathing, even through the screening folds of their neckerchiefs, an almost unbearable ordeal.

Jones asked once if Shane thought they were lost. Shane growled back some sardonic reply which Jones did not catch. But after that Jones kept still.

Their lips grew parched and cracked as the long hot hours dragged achingly past. Their nostrils burned as though scorched by the flames of hell itself, and their tongues became immovable cottony lumps whose swelling threatened to stop their breathing entirely. Dust-devils, whipped up by a furnace wind, whirled across their path and one came apart above them, literally showering them with its cargo of superheated grit. Long since their eyes had closed to merest squinting slits, their eyeballs seared by the burning glare. Talk was impossible and neither man attempted it.

Noon finally came. The torture of the lake bed lay behind. Ahead lay the scarcely lesser torture of the blistering dun expanse of cactus-dotted desert. Above them a buzzard serenely circled the brassy sky on outspread wings while the flaying sun beat down without respite.

They did not stop. They knew their horses could not last much longer, but a glance at Shane's face told Jones that to remonstrate—even if he succeeded in making himself understood—would be useless. Shane's eyes held but a single purpose and it was as unswervable as adamant. He meant to reach Tortilla Flat and Lume in the shortest possible time, and the grim-clenched line of his stubborn jaw forecast that all hell was not going to stop him.

The hot rays of the burning sun beat down upon this arid land like brassy hammers. Shane led doggedly on, grim as some ancient mariner. Their ponies gave out before the desert was spanned and they abandoned them, staggering on afoot.

Late afternoon found them studying the tracks of three horses leading across a lone, pine-shaded plateau. There were puffs of earth before and behind each print, showing the animals had been moving at a smart gallop.

Shane stared at Jones from red-rimmed bloodshot eyes. "That's them," he croaked, and went lurching on. Somehow, somewhere, Jones found the guts to follow, though his face was puffed and black beneath its crust of alkali dust.

Ten minutes later they came to a spring among sohie rocks.

Shane drank cautiously, barely wetting his long-numb. lips. He jerked Jones back with guttural noises when the man would have sated his fearful thirst; fought with him, forced him to do as he himself was doing.

An hour passed while they rested and washed the sticky white grime from face and neck and brows. They had no energy to spare in cuffing the grit from their clothing, but lay stretched out in intolerable weariness on the needle-carpeted ground beneath the pines.

When the hour had worn itself out Shane got to his feet.

"C'mon," he croaked. "We're movin'," and started off, his hat shoved back from his forehead to let the evening breeze lap coolly across its sweaty surface.

As long shadows from the distant mountains reached down across the country they sighted a tiny ranch tucked away in a hollow. When they got near Shane gruffed a greeting. A man stepped from the cabin door, a rifle held loosely in the crook of his arm. He eyed them scowling, not offering to speak

"We wanta buy coupla hosses," Shane got out with effort.

"Ain't got no broncs fer sale."

Shane's eyes swept across a pole corral inside which half a dozen horses eyed them curiously.

"How 'bout them?"

"Not fer sale," the surly ranchman said without compromise.

Shane did not compromise either. "Yo're a liar!"

Up came the rancher's rifle. His jaw swung forward

menacingly. "*Git!*" There were pale fires in his cat-like yellow gaze.

Shane half turned as though to go. His right hand slapped leather. Livid flame reached out from the explosion at his hip. The rifleman crashed back against the cabin wall with a bullet through his chest. The rifle clattered on the steps.

But the fellow was game. One hand clawed desperately for the belt gun in the tied-down holster on his leg. The flat sharp crack of Shane's pistol made a faint flutter of sound in the immense silence of the gathering dusk. The boss of this hidden ranch sagged back against the wall, slid down it to a sitting posture, then toppled forward to sprawl inertly across the dusty steps.

Shane pushed fresh cartridges in his gun, lips framed in a snarl "Go hunt us up some saddles, Bless. We'll want two of these broncs apiece."

Fifteen minutes later they rode out at a fast canter, each leading an extra horse. Night's thickening shadows swiftly hemmed them.

In the east a lop-sided yellow moon climbed into the purple sky. The stars paled before its argent glory.

* * *

FROM A SHELF of rimrock Shane and Jones stared down upon a winding, pale white ribbon of road that led up out of a dim-seen valley. They had changed horses several times in getting here and they had made good time. They were looking down upon the stage road to Phoenix, about two miles west of Tortilla Flat. Two unknown riders had just swung onto the trail below them. Shane's interest in them seemed strangely acute to Jones.

"Think yer know 'em?" he asked softly.

Shane said in a tiny whisper, "I'm bettin' one of 'em's Stone Latham; just his build an' sits the saddle similar."

"What yer reckon they're up ter?"

"Quien sabe?" Shane said, and shrugged. "However —we'll soon find out. Listen!"

Through the cold crisp moonlit air came the sound of wagon wheels, the jingling of chains and the clopping of pulling horses. The sounds came from the direction of Tortilla Flat A moment later they saw the stage lurch round a bend and come careening toward them. They could hear above the wagon-squeaks and the plopping pound of hoofs the singing snap of the driver's whip. They could see the shotgun guard upon the box.

"Look," Shane whispered, and following his pointing hand Jones saw that the two men in the road had vanished.

"Stick-up" he muttered hoarsely.

"Shhh! Looks like a double-cross, to me."

The stage came steadily on, the horses pulling against their harness on the steadily-rising grade. Shane and Jones could hear the driver's profane talk; could make snatches of it out above the rattle of the wheels. The coach lurched violently once as a wheel dropped into a chuckhole, careened toward the abyss that bounded the road's outer edge and seemed for an instant in danger of going off. But with lurid oaths and skillful handling of the lines the driver kept his four-horse team moving and the coach still on the road.

Jones took a deep breath. "Whew!"

Shane did not take his eyes from the scene below. "Close," came the driver's voice, and he spat over the wheel nonchalantly. "But I've had closer," he confided to the guard. "Dang lucky they ain't no passengers aboard. Reckon 'twould have scairt the liver outen 'em. Git-up, there!"

Two mounted shadows stepped into the road ahead of the lumbering stage There was a glint of metal and a lance of flame. Another. Two reports rocked against the rimrock where Shane and Jones crouched watching. One of the lead horses was down. The shotgun guard bent double and toppled from the box. An oath left the driver's lips and he hurriedly raised his hands as the stage lurched to a violent stop against the heap of kicking horses.

Three more shots rang out and the horses' struggles ceased.

"Anybody in that stage?" came Latham's voice.

"No." The driver's tone was quavery as though he knew how close he sat to death.

The faces of the hold-up men were masked, but anyone would have recognized Latham's voice, had they ever heard it. "Must be figurin' to quit the country," Shane thought grimly.

"All right," snapped Latham's voice, "come down outa it!"

"Comin'," the driver gulped meekly and, wrapping his lines about the brake, stepped gingerly down over the wheel and stood with his hands stretched as far above his head as Nature would permit.

The man with Latham dismounted and started toward the stage, very likely with the intention of relieving it of some of its more valuable cargo. But it will never be known for sure. Shane had seen enough.

"Drop that bird," he muttered close to Jones's ear. "I'll take care of Latham."

In the moon's soft glow that washed the road with blue radiance, Jones took aim and fired. The sound of the shot tore a hole through the night. Latham's companion in thievery doubled up and crumpled forward in the dust. Latham's horse reared with snorting fright just as Shane fired and took Shane's bullet from end to end. Down it went in a thrashing heap. But even as it fell Stone Latham left its back and, amid a very hail of lead, dashed to his companion's mount, vaulted into the saddle and was gone just as a mass of fleecy cloud passed below the moon and snuffed its light.

"Which way'd 'e go?" snarled Jones, peering wildly over the rimrock's edge. "Wot did yer want ter let 'im git away fer?"

Shane snorted. "I didn't do it a-purpose, an' you can stick a pin in that!"

Just then, with the same suddenness with which it had passed from sight, the moon surged free of its entangling cloud and again illumined the ribbon of road. It showed Stone Latham spurring madly along the trail to camp.

"There 'e goes, the blarsted gopher!" Jones growled. "Let me at my 'oss!"

"Hold on," Shane said, and grabbed him by the shirt. "Take it easy. Latham don't know who blew his game up Bitter Crick. Wait—we'll stand a better chance in town. We'll get him in Tortilla. Let's go down an' habla with that driver."

But when Jones had got cooled down sufficiently to listen, the stage driver was no longer to be seen. Evidently be had had all the shooting he was wanting for one night and had taken his chance and ducked.

"Wot abaht the gold?"

"If there's any on the stage, it prob'ly belongs to Lume. T'hell with it! C'mon, we're headin' for town."

FOURTEEN

GREED, *greed, greed!* Shane thought disgustedly as he rode through the soft, enfolding moonlight toward a reckoning with Lume. He would be glad to shake forever from his boots the dust of this turbulent Tortilla Flat! Greed, greed, greed! People round this country had gold colic so bad it was all they thought or talked about!

The mood of a moment ago was gone and the driving anger of that time when he had found Lize Corbin no longer in the cave was on him. The reckoning with Lume, he told himself, could not come too soon. Lume had done his best to get him killed off; Lume had stolen for a pittance old Obe Struthers' mine, and had robbed many another of his rightful property. And now Lume had overstepped the safety mark. He had had Lize Corbin kidnapped! The day of retribution was about to dawn!

And Shane, in this dark mood of reprisal, certainly looked like some destroying angel. Seen in the moonlight his face was cold and taut; his gleaming eyes were slightly squinted, the bold curve of his hawk's beak nose was more pronounced than ever, and his lips were a tight lean gash.

He could see Lize Corbin's vision ever before him on the road. Beautiful and fragrant as a rose, it was, the stormy blue of her eyes now a-shine with impassioned tenderness as when he'd held her in his arms after the killing of Tularosa. And always, across her shoulder, mocked the cold, sardonic face of Jarson Lume!

He was like a blight on all this land, Shane thought bitterly. The man's power for evil was a terrible thing. This country had been slumbering with the peace of centuries before Lume's coming; Tortilla Flat had been nothing but a trading post, a watering spot for cowboys and miners passing through the mountains to stop a while and exchange range gossip while the former cooled their saddles and the latter rested their homely jacks and burros.

And now look at it! ran his somber thoughts. A first class hell-hole if he'd ever seen one! Honkytonks, gambling establishments, saloons, brothels! Killings were so commonplace they no longer attracted attention—leastways, not from anyone but tenderfeet. And a stage-robber wore the marshal's badge!

"Wot yer figgerin' ter do when we get ter town?" Jones presently asked.

"I'm goin' to hunt up Jarson Lume, find out what they've done with Lize, then give Lume what he's been askin' for ever since he got here!"

"Kinder tall order, wot? 'Adn't yer better take 'em one at a time?"

"You keep out of this, Jones," Shane scowled grimly. "This is my fight, an' I don't want no help nor need any.

I'll show those damned scorpions a thing or two they'll be a right smart while forgettin'!"

Jones looked at him sideways and began to hum, "Oh, the king of France, he put on his pants—"

Shane's grim lips relaxed in a sudden smile. "Well, mebbe I did sound kinda boastful," he admitted, "but I'm allowin' I'm big enough to handle this situation without no help. An' there ain't no sense nohow in you gettin' mixed up in this fracas. You was hired to build a coupla buildin's on that spread I bought an' to help repair some more an' the corrals an' such like. You wasn't hired for your gun, Bless."

"Well, wot the bloody 'ell do yer think I'm a-carryin' this 'ere smoke-pole fer?" Jones asked indignantly. "Ter scare mosquitoes off? Not 'arf! A fine bloke I'd be ter stand around meek as Moses w'lle them curly wolves got yer ready for the undertaker, wot? Look 'ere, yer glory-'oggin' idjit! When the bullets starts ter flyin', the Earl o' Cockney's li'l son 'Orace aims ter be right w'ere 'e can 'ear their blinkin' w'istlesi An' yer can kiss the Stone on that!"

* * *

THOUGH IT WAS ALMOST midnight when they reached the town it was plain to Shane and Jones that no citizen was in his bed unless he were held there by a malady or gunshot wound The camp's night life was at full blast and a noisy blare of raucous sound destroyed the quiet serenity of the nocturne breeze.

Overhead, far up in the purple heavens, the stars peered down with awe. The dusty road ahead of Shane was splashed with crisscross bars of yellow light that poured from open doors and windows, for though the night was cool the activities of the larger part of Tortilla Flat's inhabitants were badly in need of the soothing influence of pure, clean air

Dismounting at the hitch rack fronting the Square Deal, Shane and Jones flipped their reins about the rail and strode within. Shane's firm, unhurried stride carried him to where a blank wall was at his back, and Jones took up a position there beside him. Both men manufactured cigarettes while accustoming their eyes to the glare of fifty lamps.

The atmosphere was heavy with the odors of leather, stale liquor, sweat, smoke and dust. The cigarette smoke swirled in heavy stratas a foot beneath the balcony ceiling, and the air above that level was blue with it. There were oaths and raucous laughter, flashing smiles and gleaming, hateful eyes; and occasionally the angry cry of some dance hall girl rose indignantly through the babelous din, while over all resounded the banged-out notes of an old off-key piano.

Here and there along the line of men bellying the ornate bar, space was left for a drunken companion who no longer had the use of his legs but sat sprawled limply upon the foot-rail of gleaming brass.

Above the gaming tables were hunched great darkfaced cowmen; big, bronzed, serious men whose cheeks were networks of intent wrinkles and whose gnarled hands were never far from the butts of ready weapons. The stakes were high. One false move on an opponent's part would have brought his death in an avenging blast of gunfire.

Shane and Jones leaned their backs against a wall

and watched the room through squinted eyes while they languidly puffed their smokes.

A big breed went slouching past, his swarthy face writhed in a scowl, one arm in a dirty sling. The minute remainder of a corn-husk cigarro showed between his thick lips and a burning resentment was in his glance.

Olive-skinned women, slender creatures of sensuous rhythm glided by, their red lips parted in flashing smiles, their luring eyes twin pools of slumberous dusk neath sweeping lashes.

Through the wavering smoke Shane saw a pair of men leave Lume's private room beneath the balcony stairs. They did not observe him and Jones smoking placidly against the wall across the room, but headed toward them, making for the swinging doors.

Jones said from a corner of his mouth, "H'in a bloody 'urry, if yer arskin' me!"

The first man was a solidly-built gent, muscular and heavy of face. Bad thought through turbulent years had drawn down a corner of his mouth and creased it in a perpetual sneer and there was a sneaking droop to his big shoulders. As he came hurrying forward his hands swung close to the .45s he wore on either hip. It was Birch Alder Shane was staring at, though he had no means of knowing this; nor, had he known, would it have made any difference.

For Shane's glance went swiftly past Alder and came to rest in narrowing intensity on the man behind. He was tall, rawboned and gaunt. He had a lantern jaw and heavy eyes beneath the rakish tilt of a down-pulled hat-brim. He moved with a saddlebound swagger that just now seemed filled with wrath. His dark and lean-carved face showed anger, too. His lips were set in a vicious snarl.

Shane shoved abruptly free of the wall against which he had been leaning, hands hanging loosely at his sides. Alder did not notice. But the other did. Shane saw the bold eyes swinging toward him, focus upon his face and harden, narrow. The snarl slid off the fellow's lips as he swung to a sudden halt, and his right hand brushed the polished walnut of his gun-butt.

Then, leisurely, the man came on, lips curving in a cynical grin. He came urbanely on until he stood facing Shane with right thumb hooked in gunbelt across a three-foot interval.

"Howdy, catawampus. Thirsty weather, ain't it?"

"I know a place that's thirstier," Shane drawled coldly. "Latham, where's Lize Corbin at?" His glance beat hard as flint against Stone Latham's high-boned cheeks.

Latham met his scrutiny amusedly, antagonistic mockery in his gleaming eyes.

"Why ask me?" he sneered. "'F I was to toiler all the peregrinations of a hustlin' skirt like Li—"

His voice broke off in a startled grunt as Shane's right fist rocked hard against his jaw. All the pent-up hate and bitter fury was in that blow, and it smashed Stone Latham backward to his knees. Before he could recover, Shane's left came up beneath his chin and sprawled him moveless on his back with glazing eyes.

A stunned sort of stillness gripped the hall for a space of seconds. Then, Alder, who had caught the last of the scene from the tail of his eyes, let a hand streak hipward for his gun. Other hands sped holsterward for vengeance.

"Kill the damned outlander!"

"Rub 'im out!"

"Get him, boys!" snarled Alder, and jerked his weapon free.

Shane's hand slapped leather as gun thunder shook the room, awaking monstrous echoes that jarred the swirling smoke and drove bystanders headlong in search of nearest shelter.

Black holes appeared like magic in the wall above and about Shane's crouching back. With slitted eyes he crouched there in the garish light of fifty lamps. The swift tattoo of his belching gun drove men frantically for doors and windows. Birch Alder, clutching at his stomach in sobbing agony, had hardly struck the floor before the place was cleared; deserted, save for himself and the grinning Jones and the three still forms that sprawled grotesquely near.

Bless Jones abruptly swore. "'E's gorn!" he snarled excitedly.

"What—"

"*Latham!* 'E's flitted like a bloody bird!"

True enough; Latham, indeed, was gone—vanished in those few tumultuous seconds!

* * *

"THE BACK ROOM!" Shane snapped, and headed for it stuffing fresh cartridges in the emptied chambers of his pistol, bootheels thumping hollowly.

Jones beat him to it, flung back the door and cursed.

"Empty! The bloody sparrow's 'opped!"

"Quick" Shane cried, sprinting for the swinging doors. "Don't let 'em get away!"

But they were too late. Dimming with receding distance they could hear the muffled pound of fleeing hoofs as they stood by the hitch rack fronting Lume's Square Deal.

The crowd came surging back. Shane grabbed a man and hissed:

"Where's Jarson Lume? Talk quick, fella, 'cause I'm in a sod-pawin' mood an' I'd as life horn you as not!"

With chattering teeth the fellow shook his head "Good cripes," he gasped, "don't take it out on me! I ain't seen Lume for fifteen minutes."

"Where is he?" Shane glared wildly at the crowd who shrank back before the things to be read in his blazing eyes. "*Where is he?* Speak up quick, by Gawd, or I'll tear this camp apart!"

"What's wrong, pardner?" growled a bearded, booted fellow in a red flannel shirt. "You look some riled up. Someone stole yore lollypop?"

"Some of Lume's stinkin' hellions've kidnapped Lize Corbin!"

Low growls of anger rose. But a man near Shane sneered knowingly. "I reckon," he said, "she won't be mindin' such a heap. Lize, she's used to sleepin' ou—"

Shane's right fist spun the man headlong in the dusty road Shane's cold voice lashed the crowd like icy water:

"If there's any more white-livered sneaks in this stinkin' camp aimin' to insult a decent woman behind her back, now's the time to do it."

A frozen silence held the group. One or two shifted their feet uneasily. Several surreptitiously departed.

Shane's cold drawl was contemptuous. "Then get the hell out of here."

"Wot next?" Jones asked with a tickled grin.

"Look over these nags that's tied up here an' pick us out a couple good ones that's long on endurance an' look like they might have a fairish amount of speed. I'm allowin' I've got a hankerin' to cast my eyes round Lume's establishment once more afore we roll our tails. Be with you in three shakes. Get some canteens an' see that they're filled with, water. Rustle a coupla saddlebags of food, too, while you're at it. The trail we're takin' mightn't have no stops."

Wheeling then, Shane went back inside the deserted Square Deal. A bartender stood staring idiotically at the dead men on the floor. A sawbones was bending anxiously above Birch Alder's prostrate form. Shane paid them no attention, but took the balcony stairs three at a time. One by one he went through the rooms that faced its railing. Three were empty. Four held terrified, huddling girls who shrank away from his burning glance. Then he came to number ten—the room he was to have shared with the late Bill Halleck.

It, too, was empty. Shane was about to turn away when his eyes caught sight of a crumpled bit of paper slightly protruding from beneath the pillow on the bunk.

Bending, he picked it up and smoothed it out upon a knee. Three scrawled words leapt to his glance like tongues of flame:

Lume——help——Lize

He thrust the paper mechanically in his pocket. The muscles of his jaws stood out in tense rigidity. So Lume *had* got her, had he? Shane's lips tightened grimly; cold glints of fury entered his smoky eyes as he swung to the door and out upon the balcony and down the stairs. His boots thumped hollowly in the unaccustomed silence and the tinkling of his big-roweled spurs was like the sound of clashing sabers as he crossed the deserted floor.

The doctor looked up from Birch Alder's motionless body. "I guess he's finished," he said conversationally.

"There'll be a lot more polecats finished before I get through," Shane growled, and pushed through the swinging doors into a burst of exploding light. How he escaped that murderous salvo Shane never knew. But something—buck fever, possibly—might have unsettled Mell's aim. For Mell it was; Shane saw him crouching at the porch-edge with a shotgun in his hands.

Mell had no chance to use the gun again. Like magic Shane's gun seemed to leap to his hand and bark. Mell went over backwards off the porch with a bullet between his eyes.

From across the street Jones came running awkwardly, a pair of saddlebags flapping from each shoulder; skin water bags filled his hands. "Wot's up? Wot's up 'ere, eh? Wot's orl this shootin' abaht?" he panted.

Shane took a pair of saddlebags and one of the canteens. "Where's the broncs?"

"Right 'ere," Jones said, and led the way to where a pair of wall-eyed, long-legged broncos stamped restlessly beside the rail.

"Them suit?"

"Yeah. Let's get goin'," said Shane, stepping into the

saddle atop a blue roan. "Lume an' whoever's with him prob'ly took the same direction as Latham."

"That's right, fella," a scrawny youth said, nodding. "I seen 'em haff a hour ago, it was. They was headin' off to'ards Globe. There's a short cut—"

But Shane was waiting for no more. The blue roan lunged forward beneath his prodding spurs. With a wink at the gaping boy, Jones, too, put spurs to his mount and went pelting in Shane's wake.

FIFTEEN

THE LOFTY SPIRES of the Superstition Range were etched ruggedly black against the starry skyline. For what seemed like centuries Shane and Bless Jones rode in silence, the vast quiet of the open spaces hemming them like a shroud, and the only sounds to lend accompaniment to the clatter of hoofs were the creak of saddle leather and the occasional jingling of spur chains.

Slowly the moon grew dimmer. One by one the stars faded and vanished from the brightening heavens. In the cold, pale light of dawn they stepped stiffly from their saddles. Jones walked the horses up and down to prevent their cooling too swiftly while Shane cast round for sign.

A bleak wind rattled eerily through the chaparral as Shane examined the trail. Tired and weary as he was, the smoky eyes beneath his puckered brows were keenly alert. He well knew the possibilities they ran of being ambushed. A thing like that would find appeal in Latham's Indian blood.

Striding out upon a bare escarpment overlooking a

tiny valley far below, Shane pondered the fact that only one set of fresh tracks showed in this trail. Where had Lume gone with the girl? Did Latham know and was he short-cutting in an effort to head them off? But why should he? What, Shane wondered, was the connection between Latham and Lume? Surely there was something more to it than the mere relationship of outlaw chieftain and right-bower henchman; no mere lieutenant, no matter how privileged, would dare such familiarity and insolence toward Lume as Latham had more than once exhibited, Shane felt. Therefore, he reasoned, there must be some deeper, stronger tie between these men. But what?

Still eying the valley through a rift in the morning mist, Shane shrugged. The roaring surge of anger that had taken him so recklessly into Lume's camp and dive a few short hours ago with the desire to rend and maim had cooled. The desire still pulsed through his veins, but it was a yearn now purged of impulse—a controlled anger, a deep abiding hate-that would brook no obstacle to its deadly path.

He rejoined Jones where he walked their horses up and down a narrow stretch of trail.

"Find anythin'?"

"Latham's ridin' a cold trail. Either he's not figurin' to join up with Lume's party, or else he's takin' some kinda short cut to where he thinks they're headin' for. Anyhow, we're stickin' to Latham; I've a hunch he knows what he's doin'. Let's go."

The sun climbed into a cloudless sky, its rays burning brighter with each passing moment, warming the air rarified and chilled by mountain night. Half an hour passed and only the occasional click of a horse's shoe against a rock or pebble betrayed their presence on the needle-carpeted trail along the timbered ridges. They climbed steadily higher into the mountains. The horses' hearts thumped softly against their knees.

Shane's blue roan set the pace, a swift running walk that often broke into a trot where the going was easier— a pace that would put long miles behind a rider between sun-up and dark, yet leave his mount with plenty of steam.

It was nearing noon when Shane, riding in the lead, suddenly drew in his horse and pointed silently. A group of tracks sheared into their trail from the northwest Three separate sets of tracks, Shane pointed out, Jones nodded.

Shane said, "Latham guessed right. I'm allowin' he's saved us a heap of time, Bless. I'm allowin' them prints belongs to Lume an' his party. One would be Lume's hoss, another Lize's. That means he's only got one man with him. He sure must have left town hellity-larrup to be travellin' so light. Somethin' must have give him a scare."

Jones nodded. "Yer reckon it was Latham?"

"Can't say. It's a cinch Latham wasn't in town when Lume pulled out with the girl."

"Mebbe they've split," Jones suggested hopefully. "I ain't never put no great store in this talk abaht honor amongst thieves "

"Well, Latham's on their trail, anyhow. An' that's the main thing We better be shovin' on."

"Where d'yer reckon they're goin'?" Jones asked after fifteen minutes of silent riding. "That feller back in Tortilla said Globe, didn't "e?"

"He wouldn't know nothin' about Lume's plans He

said they'd hit out on the Globe trail But these tracks now are pointin' dead on for Silver King. I'm thinkin' we'll be findin' 'em there."

"Well, 'ere's 'opin'," Jones said. "My backbone's a-rubbin' up ag'in' m' barkin' stomach an' if we 'ave ter ride much further I'm goin' ter fall plumb asleep right 'ere in m' bloody saddle."

Half an hour later as they were rounding a bend of a rock-choked canyon, a scant two miles from Silver King, the sultry afternoon quiet was shattered by a shot Something tugged at Shane's neckerchief. I—it was that close— as the report bear back against the towering walls m dimming echoes.

The abruptness of Jones' stopping sent up tiny bursts of dust. "Look out!" he yelled

But already Shane had marked the tiny puff of smoke ballooning above the glistening barrel of a rifle in a clump of rocks three hundred yards ahead

The pony lunged beneath him with hip-jolting violence to his sudden drive of spurs. Jones' voice died out in the pound of the big roan's hoofs as Shane hurled his bronc toward the ambusher's cover with whitened cheeks, teeth bared in a savage grin.

His racing palm smacked gun-butt as the dry-gulcher broke from cover. The hammer rolled beneath his thumb. The loud reports churned up like thunder between the canyon walls. The ambusher had dropped to a knee and was sighting down his rifle. Pale flame stabbed from its muzzle. Lead splashing off his saddle horn jerked a grunt from Shane. Abruptly the blue roan came apart beneath him. Shane hurled himself from the saddle as the bronc went down in a crashing fall.

Shane lit rolling, gun still clenched in hand. He was

up on his feet in an instant, hardly a hundred yards separating himself from the dry-gulcher who now was firing with desperate haste, fearful of being caught in his own trap.

Lead ripped through Shane's vest, tugged at his hat, jarred his balance as a heel ripped loose from his left boot. Then he was sprinting forward awkwardly in the wake of the fleeing killer who was making for a horse that stood at a little distance on spraddled legs, its sides a smear of blood from the slash of cruel spurs.

As the man threw himself into the saddle Shane fired again, carefully, deliberate—grim malice in his heart.

The man's rising leg missed going over the saddle by inches Shane could see the shudder that shook his slender frame Then he was crumpling groundward, one foot still hooked in the stirrup The horse was too spent to buck. It stood listless with down-hung head as though anchored by its motionless master. It did not even turn its eyes as Shane, followed by Jones, approached.

Shane released the fellow's foot from the stirrup. Jones came up cursing soulfully, while he lamented his luck in not having had a hand in the fracas.

"Mex, eh?"

Shane nodded wearily. Reaction was on him now as it always was after a killing. He felt a little sick at his stomach and strove to hide the fact behind a scowl. "Know him?"

Jones bent down for a closer look. Nothing squeamish about *his* stomach "I've seen 'im. Name's Pedro Abrilla— one of Jarson's "gun-packers. Mean customer with a knife.

I seen 'im carve a gent plumb scandalous the night before they run me out of their blarsted camp."

"Lume an' Lize..." Shane muttered thoughtfully. "This must be the fella that was ridin' the third horse. An' if this here's the bronc, they sure must have been spreadin' scenery right blurry-like. Looks plumb tuckered out."

"How you figgerin' ter git places now that bloke did in yer 'oss?"

"We're pretty close to Silver King," Shane said, squinting down the canyon. "Guess we better ride double a spell. I'll pick up a horse soon's we get there. An' I reckon we better be gettin'—pronto. The trail is warmin' up."

* * *

IN THE RED Hoss Saloon at Silver King Jarson Lume was talking with its proprietor in a back room. Lize was with them, watching them sullenly while they talked.

"Aimin' to put her in the business, Jars?" Red Fogle asked, his lewd glance passing over the girl's figure. "She's a likely baggage an' oughta attract plenty trade."

Jarson Lume's voice, though well-modulated, was icy. "No. This lady is my wife, Red."

"S'cuse *me!*" Fogle was rising hastily and clawing at his cast-iron hat when Lize Corbin's voice lashed vibrantly:

"Yo' a damn liar, Jarson Lume!"

Fogle stared uncertainly from the girl's flushed cheeks to the sardonic smile on Lume's thin, bloodless lips. "Well," he said dubiously, "anything you folks say is all right with me. I ain't knowin' nothin' about it one way or the other. An', beggin' yore pardon, ma'am, I ain't givin' a damn one way or the other."

Lume chuckled silently. "You always was handy with the right answer, Red. Fix us up some grub. We're half-starved. After that find us a place upstairs where we can sleep. We've had a damn long ride. I left Pete Abrilla on the back trail a ways. Keep your eyes peeled for him. 'F anybody else comes round askin' for me, keep yore lip buttoned tight. An' let me know."

Fogle winked. "I get yuh, boss. How's tricks up Tortilla way?"

"I'm through with that camp," Lume said shortly, and changed the subject. "Any of the boys in town?"

"Three or four, I reckon. Rest went out on a little shindig las' night an' ain't got back yet. You wantin' to see 'em?"

"Not now—later, mebbe. Rattle your hocks now an' fetch that grub before I fall apart."

With a final admiring glance at Lize, Fogle went out and closed the door.

The minute he was out of sight Lize flared. "If y'u think y'u are goin' to get me into one of them upstairs rooms with y'u yo' plumb crazy as hell!"

Lume grinned wolfishly. "Shucks, you'll be lookin' forward to a little privacy like that inside a month," he sneered. "You better make up your mind to marry me an' do it quick if you're so damned virtuous. 'Cause, one way or another, I'm aimin' to have you. An' when Jarson Lume makes up his mind to have a thing, he has it! Think it over, Lize."

Scorn and loathing were intermingled in Lize Corbin's stormy glance. "Y'u'll never get *me*—I'd kill myself first!"

"You ain't goin' to get no chance," Lume chuckled. "I ain't lettin' you out of my sight till the knot's been tied."

"Y'u—y'u *beast!*"

"Better save them endearin' terms till after we get hitched up," he smirked.

* * *

AFTER THEY HAD EATEN and Lume had seen Lize locked securely in an upstairs room from which he had assured himself there could be no escape, he came downstairs again and drew Red Fogle to one side, where it would be impossible for other customers to overhear.

"Red," he studied Fogle's face intently, "d'you know a man called 'Whisk' Lipari?"

"Short, stocky, black-faced hombre?"

Lume nodded.

"I know him well enough," Fogle admitted cautiously. "What about him?"

"Know if he's in town?"

Fogle considered. "I reckon he is," he finally said, pursing his heavy lips.

"Where can I find him?"

Fogle's eyebrows arched a trifle, then drew down in a beetling scowl. "What kind of a deal you got in mind?"

"There are times," Lume pointed out significantly, "when ignorance is sure the height of bliss, Red. This here is one of those times."

Lights glinted dully in the resort-keeper's glance. He drummed upon the bar with nervous fingers, took a deep breath and let it slowly out.

"Well," he said, as though washing his hands of the business, "I reckon you know what yo' doin', Jars. If you was to wander over to the Gold Gun yo' curiosity might get satisfied." With the words he turned his broad back and strolled huffily away.

Jarson Lume grinned sardonically, pulled his hat rakishly down across one eye and left the place.

Outside the afternoon sun sent its brassy rays down slanch-ways across the town, sending the elongated, distorted shadows of its flimsy buildings flat and black across the dust-choked road. Heat waves lay in stifling stratas above the blistering boards of its plank walks, above the sand-scoured and sun grayed wooden awnings. Long shadows bathed the distant mountainsides in a mantle of somber purple.

Jarson Lume stood before the Red Hoss and let his veiled glance rove the deserted street. It came to a final rest on an establishment obliquely across the way. His lips curled as he looked down at the bottle-like sheen with which he had, but a few short minutes ago, managed to imbue his boots. With a shrug, then, he strode out across the squalid dust.

When he stepped inside the Gold Gun's swinging doors he swiftly got his back against a dirty wall and, from between slitted lids, sent a searching glance stabbing through the smoky half-light.

There had been laughter in the place but it had quieted at his entrance. Jarson Lume was tempted to press the white 'kerchief, peeping from the breast pocket of his black frock coat, to his nose as he let his glance play over the motley group of sweating humanity that was ranged along the bar. But he repressed the impulse.

A man in a pinto vest and frazzled corduroy trousers tucked into cowhide boots detached himself from his unsavory companions and, with a significant jerk of expressive eyes, moved toward a rear door. Lume followed.

He found himself in a bare back room whose only furnishings were a rough table, two chairs, and great quantities of dust. The man in the pinto vest flashed Lume an intent, appraising glance,, then his yellow eyes slid away. He jerked a nod of greeting. "Long time no see."

"How you doin', Lipari? Wallowin' in dinero?"

Lipari grinned—a twisted grimace which did nothing to enhance his ugly looks. "What's on yore mind?"

"I got a chore for you. There's two grand in it."

The yellow eyes did not even blink, but regarded Lume craftily. "Who you got it in for, now?"

"I'm askin' the questions," Lume said, curtly. "Do you figure you can use the dinero—?"

"Did you ever know me when I couldn't?" Lipari countered with a grin.

"Not the point. D'you want it, or shall I pack it someplace else?"

"I'd have to know what mark you was figgerin' to remove. I ain't the man to buy any gent's pig in a poke"

Lume nodded. "I'll spread my cards on the table. Me an' the wife is takin' a little pasear across the country. Someone's on my back-trail. I want 'em stopped right here. An' permanent."

"Who?"

"You're gettin' damn partic'lar in your ol' age," Lume snapped coldly.

"I'm findin' that it pays to," was Lipan's blunt comeback. "Who's trailin' you an' the skirt? Come clean, Jars, or I'm passin' up the pot."

"Well, it's no one you know. Fella called Sudden Shane, an' some two-bit gunslick he's picked up."

"Shows you don't know ever'thing, Jars. I reckon you're talkin' about a gent called S. G. Shane. Right?"

Lume was surprised at the other's knowledge, but he kept the fact to himself. With expressionless countenance he grunted, "I've heard he gives that name."

"Well, this little chore will cost you real money, Mister. That guy's hell on wheels, an' I've got no hankerin' to be committin' suicide. This chore, Jars, will cost you a cool five grand or the deal's off "

"It's off, then, far as I'm concerned," Lume said, and started for the door.

SIXTEEN

BUT HE DID NOT LEAVE IMMEDIATELY. He halted with his hand on the knob and looked back across his shoulder. Whisk Lipari had not changed his position by an inch. He sat sprawled loosely across one of the chairs, thumbs hooked in his suspenders, a wolfish grin on his twisted lips.

"Oh yeah?" he said, and laughed. It curdled the silence wickedly and snapped a dark flush into Jarson Lume's white cheeks.

Lume's husky tones grew ugly. "Have a care, Lipari. You ain't so *damned'* valu'ble to me, you know. There's been other guys that *thought* they were."

"Meanin' where are they now, eh?" Lipari sneered. "I reckon I'll get along—with or without your help."

"I wasn't talkin' about help, my friend."

"Oh." Lights shifted in Lipari's yellow orbs. He drew the left down in an exaggerated wink. "Well, I can get along with or without your damned enmity, too! I ain't been no hired gun all my life, Mister. I've been a lot of things you'll never be; not even if you corner all the gold an' copper mines in this country! Go laff that off."

Lume's scowl ironed out. "All right. Five grand it is, then. I'll pay you when the job is done."

"Like hell!" sneered Lipari. "You'll pay me now, or get yourself some other sucker. This Shane pilgrim ain't what I'd call a tame gorilla. The guy that downs him is gonna earn what he gets. An' if I'm the guy, I'll do my collectin' in advance. You wouldn't be the first sidewinder that tried to pull a sandy."

Lume's bloodless face grew pinched and venomous. "Are you tryin' to—"

"Stow it," Lipari growled. "Pay up or shut up!"

Hate glowed in Lume's cold eyes. "Lipari," he wrenched out explosively, "you're a dirty damned blood-suckin' leech!"

Lipari's chuckle shrank to a satanic grin. "Blow off all the steam you've a mind to," his drawling voice was contemptuous, "but if you ain't figgerin' to pay, you might as well pull your picket pin now an' drift. Five grand's my price; no more nor less. You gonna pay or ain't you?"

Lume's face was bloated poisonously; his cheeks trembled, so vicious was his wrath. His hand half reached inside his coat so that, for a moment, it seemed he meditated violence. With a sullen oath he drew back the hand, thrusting it instead inside the side pocket of his coat and brought it immediately forth with a thick roll of bills.

"You know," said Lipari sardonically, "a fast draw will beat four aces all of a twitter." And, "You've been packin' that hideout gun so long you're beginnin' to stand slanchways."

"You must be doin' real well, Jars," he added a moment later, eying the currency. "That roll's big as a wagon hub. You act damn tight for a fella that's fair wallowin' in velvet."

Lume paid no attention but went on counting out the bills. When the pile on the table before Lipari represented five thousand dollars he put the rest—which had not been noticeably diminished—back in his pocket. "See that you do this job right, or I'll be back for an accountin'," he gruffed, and once more started for the door.

As he reached it Lipari's voice came mockingly:

"When you get outside, tell Nogales to come in—I got a job for him."

The door slammed behind Lume viciously.

* * *

WHEN JARSON LUME stepped into the street, the sun had dropped from sight behind the towering peaks and long shadows dyed the mountains' flanks with dusk while the summits stood out like crags of liquid gold. But Lume had no eyes for beauty in that form. He crossed the dusty road with determined strides, his face thrust grimly forward, and entered the lamplit interior of the Red Hoss Saloon.

Red Fogle followed him to the rear room where they had sat less than two hours before with Lize.

Lume came at once to the point. "Fogle, you got a man in your string, or a couple of men, who are handy with their smoke-poles and would be glad to earn a bit of cash?"

Fogle's beetling brows went up. "I thought you was figurin' on dealin' with Lipari?"

"You ain't bein' paid to think," Lume said icily. "Have you got the men or not?"

"Yeah, I got a coupla boys that ain't no slouches when it comes to throwin' lead," he admitted, interestedly. "What's up?"

"There's a couple of would-be gunslicks trailin' me," Lume confided, "that I want rubbed out as soon's they show. I aim to be gone before then, but whether I am or not has nothing to do with this deal. Now listen," he added, and proceeded to describe Shane and his companion. How he knew that Jones was with Shane remains a mystery, but he had many ways of finding out the things he took an interest in.

"This job," he concluded gruffly, "pays well—a thousan' bucks apiece. I'm leavin' the cash with you." He counted it out and put it in the other's hand. "Now clear out; I want to do some thinkin'."

But when Fogle had closed the door behind him, Lume's words were certainly belied by his subsequent actions. He removed the gun from the shoulder holster beneath his coat, took the cartridges from its cylinder and replaced them with others taken from his pocket Then he spun the cylinder critically. Placing the snub-nosed 38 inside his coat pocket he blew out the lamp and left by the rear door, moving with cat-like, noiseless steps.

His way took him down a string of gloomy alleys whose tin-can-littered ground gave off no sign of human presence as he advanced, angling always closer to the street. He at last emerged upon it, but only after carefully scrutinizing the surrounding shadows to be sure that he was not the object of some loiterer's attention.

Like a shadow he flitted across the dusty road, gained the far side without encounter and slunk softly into the gloom-choked space between two buildings. One of these was the Gold Gun He rounded it, pausing a moment at its rear to make certain he was not observed. Slowly, then, every sinuous nerve strung taut, he advanced on the single window.

At first he thought the room must be deserted, but suddenly realized as he neared it that the window was draped with a heavy blanket. It had not been half an hour before when in that room he had propositioned Whisk Lipari. If Lipari was in there now...

With his right hand tensely gripping the snub-nosed .38 inside his pocket, Lume's left hand found the door unlocked and thrust it open. He could see, almost instantly, the broad squat form of Lipari seated at the table. The money Lume had given him was still piled there before him and it came to Lume that Lipari had been gloating over it.

A flush of rage flamed Lume's cold cheeks; devil's temper lit his eyes."

"*Lipari*," he whispered hoarsely. And as Lipari whirled, flame bit from the pocket of Lume's black coat. A malicious laugh escaped him as Lipari, eyes bulging, hands clutching at his chest, sagged forward across the table's top. With one swift motion Lume scooped the currency from the table and, stepping back across the threshold, softly closed the door.

* * *

TWENTY MINUTES later Jarson Lume stepped once again inside the swinging doors of Fogle's Red Hoss Saloon. He stepped inside and stopped abruptly, gaze widening then narrowing to regard the half crouched man across the room with gleaming eyes that were hard as flint.

"Well," he purred smoothly into the vibrant silence, "I hadn't expected you so soon—" and was checked by the other's malignant sneer.

"No, you bet you wasn't, you double-crossin', back-bitin', woman-stealin' whelp!" Stone Latham's voice, like the man himself, was coiled like trigger steel. *"Where's my wife?"*

"Your *wife?*" there was genuine amazement in Lume's startled tones. "What the hell are you talkin' about?"

"Lize Corbin, damn yore soul to hell! *Where is she?* Speak, you white-faced bastard, before I lead yore guts!"

"She asked me to take her out of the country," Lume said calmly, only the tiny fires in his lambent eyes betraying the lashing anger that tore at him, an anger born of hatred of the man before him and jealousy that that man should have had his way with Lize where he himself had failed.

"She didn't say why she wanted to leave," he went on, "except that she found the people hateful, slanderous an' vile—I guess she was thinkin' of *you* when she said the last. But she sure didn't say she'd ever hitched up with you. From the way she talked, I'd judge marryin' you would be the last thing she'd ever think of." There was a cold, calculating mockery in the grin he turned on Latham.

Latham scowled red-eyed and a spot of white appeared in either cheek. His tall, gaunt form slowly straightened. There was a bold truculence in his glance, and his lips held a cynical curve.

"You're a slick hombre, Jars, taken by an' large. Slick as a sidewinder's belly," he said. "But you're not foolin' me one damn minute longer. *Where's my wife?* I'm not figurin' to ask again."

"She may be your wife," Lume's husky voice with its taunting timbre worked on Latham as a red rag appears to work upon a bull. "She may be your wife." he repeated slowly, nastily, "but she's my woman now—an' I ain't tired of her, yet!"

With a strangled sob Stone Latham, the ever-cautious, clawed wildly for his gun.

From the burned right-hand pocket of Lume's black coat, a streak of flame lanced lividly. Stone Latham's limbs abruptly suspended all lethal motion and a great amazement, not unmixed with fear, distorted his paling face He took one forward step and staggered Then the hinges of his knees let go and dropped him in a grotesque heap.

Jarson Lume's cold glance flashed round from face to face. Men quailed back before the message in his blazing eyes. Lume's lips twisted m a contemptuous sneer. "Well, any of you pelicans aimin' to take up where he left off?"

The silence in the Red Hoss bar remained unbroken.

SEVENTEEN

"WOULDN'T IT P'R'APS BE BETTER," Jones asked hesitantly, "if we waited till after dark to go into this bloody Silver King? 'Oo knows wot we mig'it be bargin' inter if we goes rompsin' in there now? Blimey, it fair throws me ter the goose-pimples jest ter be thinkin' of it."

Shane regarded him suspiciously; abruptly chuckled "Yeah, I'm allowin' you look scared as hell," he said "But I reckon you are right, at that. We'd be askin' for it if we was to go sashayin' into Silver in broad daylight. Reckon I'm gettin' plumb careless." He squinted out across the yellow earth. "Reckon we better wait till night; wee hours are figgered best for takin' a enemy unawares."

He stepped down from the blown horse's saddle. Jones, too, swung down.,

Jones said, "Any'ow, yer wouldn't 'a' got far on that bonerack till 'e 'ad a spot o' rest. That Mex musta pushed 'im cruel 'ard."

Shane nodded. "I reckon." He looked at the dead man's horse with a critical eye. It had shown neither curiosity nor interest at Shane's dismounting. It showed none now, but stood there on spraddled legs, head down, breathing heavily. Sweat trickled from its belly.

Jones squinted to where the sun was sinking from the darkening sky. Its descent was washing the towering canyon walls with gold and in their crevices creating cobalt shadows. "I got a yearnin' void wot's pinin' ter be filled," he said, drawing up the slack in his belt. "Any of that grub left?"

"Nope—nary a crumb," Shane answered, grim of voice. He seemed to have relapsed into his customary urbanity again. His face expressed once more the placid patience of one to whom time holds no import. And yet there was that air, that arresting air of confident efficiency about him, an atmosphere of unhurried capability. There was a cool serenity about his smoky eyes that told of a man at peace with his conscience. If he was worried longer about the fate of Lize Corbin, one would never have guessed it from his features.

Jones watched him roll a cigarette with one deft twirl of his fingers—no hesitancy there, no tremble. Jones marveled at his composure, but said nothing, content to leave his thoughts unaired.

Shane unsaddled the Mexican's horse and put him on a rope. Stretching his own long frame Jones proceeded to do likewise. Then, like Shane, he sat down on his bootheels and devoted his time to gravely smoking while the thickening shadows of dusk gathered softly in the canyon.

* * *

IT WAS NEARING two on the following morning when they approached Silver King, and was so dark—there being no moon—that Shane and his mount were but a shadowy blur three lengths ahead. Jones' lips quirked humorously. A few minutes now and they would know what they would know, he told himself.

The labored breathing of the horses reached out before their nostrils, disturbing the misty murk. Jones had been startled more than once by the eerie shadows of tall saguaros and yellow-stalked sotol shoving up at them out of the gloom, and upon one occasion had even been chagrined to find his gun in hand. He had put it covertly away while watching Shane's broad back with a guise of shame that he had been so callow. In his actions, that is to say. For, personally, he was far from callow, though about his character there did lurk a certain naive charm of which he was totally unconscious. He would very likely have shot any man so reckless as to tell him.

Jones marveled much at Shane's display of horsemanship. He had observed how the slightest flexure of Shane's fingers on the reins held the instant power to stop the dead Mexican's caballo. He recalled how half an hour ago when riding through the desolate waste of sand a coyote's howl had almost spooked his own mount, and how a mere touch of Shane's bare hand had sufficed to quiet him.

The silence of this vast land seemed absolute. In his soul Jones felt the stillness of this desolate Arizona to be a sinister thing; a thing of menace, dangerous and creeping, a thing that mocked and followed one about with saturnine leer. Only Shane seemed unaffected. Only the creak of saddle leather, the occasional jingle of spurs and the muffled plopping of the horses' hoofs disturbed the monstrous hush.

All this country appeared to be waiting, Jones thought bodingly. Mystery crouched upon its mountain crags; stark threat scowled hotly from its deserts. Even the vegetation was equipped with stinging spikes and there was a grim formidability about its animal life. It was a land whose paramount law was survival of the fittest—a hell where weaklings shriveled and died.

Though the hour was late they did not find Silver King completely dark. Three dives were open, throwing hurdles of yellow light across the dusty road. They filled the night around with confusion, noise and raucous laughter. As he listened to the brassy notes of a decrepit piano and a dance hall girl's high treble wail Jones thought more kindly of the desert's silence and would have welcomed it for a space.

Shane led the way to the largest establishment where they swung down and tethered their mounts to a spot Shane chose near the end of the hitching rail. Then, loosening his gun in its holster, Shane said quietly, "Let's go," and led the way through the swinging doors.

The place was far from crowded. Neither was it deserted.

Several men bellied the crude plank bar that marked off its farther end. There were several gambling layouts being desultorily patronized and a tiny bit of cleared floor about the tinpanny piano where gentlemen might sling a wicked hoof with the percentage girls who draped their slinky forms about the room.

Jones, having noted the misspelled sign as they were

entering, knew this dive for the Red Hoss Saloon of one R. Fogle, prop.

He kept his glance divided between Fogle's customers and Shane, alert and wary for his cue.-Shane seemed perfectly at ease as he stood there squinting complacently through the smoke of his cigarette, thumbs hooked in his cartridge belt, his form in a hip-shot slouch.

No one seemed to be paying them any great attention, he thought, but watched suspiciously—none the less—three hombres who were standing with heads together whispering, halfway down the bar. One, a square-bodied, square-faced tow-head with popping blue eyes and a crack-like mouth amid a maze of whiskers, seemed to be talking most of the time and he waved his hands emphatically to illustrate his argument

Jones' lids closed down till only slits of his eyes were visible as he stared more closely at the trio. There was something wrong with that picture, he told himself. What it was he could not so easily define, but there was something...

He looked at Shane. Shane appeared to pay the men no notice, yet as one of them abruptly, left his companions and swung his steps in their direction, Jones saw Shane wheel slightly with a deep drag on his cigarette.

It was the square-faced towhead who approached. He stopped a few feet off and said to Shane, "Ain't yore name Shane?"

Jones saw a red-haired man with heavy lips edging toward them from behind the gambling tables and unostentatiously dropped his right hand to let it rest upon his gun as Shane said, "Do I know you, friend? Your face don't seem uncommon familiar. Perhaps you've made a mistake," he added softly.

"Yo're Shane, ain't yuh?" the towhead persisted.

"What gives you that idea?"

"Why, yuh matches the desc—" He bit his words off short, cheeks darkening, popping eyes sinking dangerously inward.

"Ne'ermind. All I wanta know is are yuh the gent called S. G. Shane?"

The man's companions, and the red-head still edging closer, appeared to be listening with strained attention, as though something vital might hang upon Shane's acceptance of the name. Jones felt a cold chill of warning along his spine. His hand closed more firmly about the butt of his holstered gun as he waited for Shane's reply.

Shane's slow glance swept keenly over those others, and over the onlookers who had stopped all other business to watch the towhead and his companions as though fascinated. A chill seemed to have descended on the Red Hoss Saloon that was very different to its wonted atmosphere. Shane must have detected this for Jones observed the smoky hue of his eyes grow darker, dangerous. Tiny fires coalesced within their depths.

Shane seemed to maintain an attitude of aloof and suspended judgment.

"Are you Shane, or ain't yuh?" the towhead rasped with an oath.

The calm tranquility of Sudden's glance was maddening; even Jones could feel the tightening tension which had almost reached the snapping point. The towhead's cheeks flamed red.

Shane said with leisured drawl, "Why, yes, my

name is Shane, pardner. Were you aimin' to give me a reception— you and these other gents with the nervous feet?"

The towhead watched Shane with saturnine grin. "Reception's right!" he jeered. "An' I'm figurin' to run it. I'm figurin' to run you outa town on a rail, with a nice coat of tar an' feathers, Mister Gunman Shane!"

"Really?" Shane chuckled.

"Yo're damn' right—really!"

"What for?" Shane asked, and, "How did you get elected for the job?"

"I'm Marshal here," the towhead snarled, hand spreading claw-like above his holstered pistol. "You git outa this town pronto or you'll git put out plenty rough."

Shane's white teeth gleamed behind his parted lips. "I reckon I ain't never been put out of no place yet. An' I'm allowin' I don't expect I ever will. So you can get on with your tar-an'-featherin' an' your rail-ridin' any time you've a mind to. Go ahead, fella."

The towhead seemed a trifle taken aback by this unexpected situation. Jones saw his eyes flash hurriedly to where the red-head stood and turned his own glance in that direction just in time to catch the red-head's nod.

Shane's voice lashed out with a truculent snap, "Go on, hombre! Ain't no one settin' on your shirt-tail! Let loose your howlin' wolf!" And with the words, Jones saw Shane's gun snap out and stop tensely with its muzzle in the folds of the towhead's quivering stomach. The towhead's hands shot ceilingward with comical alacrity.

Shane grinned. "That's better," he drawled. "So you

scorpions were figurin' to cold-deck Sudden Shane. My, my! Your audacity astounds me. Tell your friends, Whitey, to back up against the bar. They better have their paws up where I can look 'em over without strainin' my eyes, too. I've got a itchy trigger-finger an' when my eyes start hurtin' I'm right apt to have a convulsion in that finger. That," his voice grew jeering, "would be awful bad for you."

Jones grinned as the towhead's friends began reluctantly retreating toward the bar. Shane certainly had a way with him, he felt. But Shane had ought to make those hombres part with their guns, he thought. First thing a—

"Lookout, boss!" he yelled frantically. *"This is it!"*

From the tail of his eyes Jones had seen the redhead's hand flash downward. Now it was coming up, gun-weighted, and there was a glint of triumphant satisfaction in the fellow's red-rimmed eyes.

Jones palmed his gun in a lightning motion even as Shane dropped below the other's shot. Came the rasp of steel on leather as Shane's long gun came out, while Shane with a roaring oath threw his body backward even as its muzzle cleared the holster; spat.

Belatedly the towhead's hand dived hipward. But it never reached his gun. Shane's shot took him in the shoulder, hurled him backward, smashed him against the bar.

Jones noted this subconsciously even as he slammed a shot at Fogle; missed, and fired again. Fogle staggered back beneath the bullet's shock but held his feet, striving valiantly to bring his gun to bear again. But in vain. Jones fired again and saw the red-head topple.

Then Shane's voice, overriding the tumult of reverberating echoes that churned the narrow space:

"The door—*quick!*"

Even with the words Shane began backing toward it, the gun in his hand weaving from left to right, holding the snarling crowd momentarily in check. One man dared dart a hand to waist. Shane slammed in a shot from the hip that knocked him sprawling across a poker table, carrying it, cards, chips, white money and a bottle of rotgut to the floor in a splintering crash.

The hands of the white-faced, cowed but sullen crowd reached upward with renewed zest.

Jones had reached the door. "Out quick!" came Shane's command. "I'll follow."

Jones backed out, his gun too held level at the hip; backed out and turned to see if the way was clear.

All he saw was a livid burst of flame that split before his eyes. The smashing rip of lead hurled him back against the doors where with outspread arms he hung poised for a fleeting instant. Then the muscles of his body loosened, spilled him backward across the floor at the feet of Shane. He was dead before he struck.

Shane's lips parted in a savage snarl that was like the cry of some wounded animal. That was all; he did not curse. But a spinning leap took him through the doors with flaming gun. He grinned with ghastly mirthlessness as his bullets drove Jones' killer to his knees in the dusty road. He laughed at the bloody sob in the man's clogged voice. Then he caught the pound of charging boots behind him.

With a slanchwise leap he scooped from the dust the killer's fallen gun and whirled, sliding his own emptied weapon back in leather, as the swinging doors bulged open to the headlong impact of the towhead's charging friends.

His lips curled back in a vicious snarl as he straightened to a crouch; eyes slitted, fiercely blazing. "So it's fight you want?" he lashed. "Well, *come an' get it!*"

With a cold fury almost unbelievable Shane drove his shots deliberately into that huddle of charging, cursing men. Gun thunder rose in huge crescendo, slamming heavily against the dark shadows of buildings across the street. The smashing rip of lead dropped the milling horde like quail.

Shouts, screams, curses intermingled in a tangled bedlam with the raucous bark of Colts. Through the red confusion some of the outlaws pistoled wildly. But their aim was mad, their trigger-fingers shaking. Shane's deadly aim demoralized their purpose. And suddenly, knowing their cause a lost one, those who could turned tail.

The thing was over as swiftly as it started. Against the yellow bar of lamplight streaming out beneath the doors, forms sprawled in crumpled limpness made grotesque, huddled blotches.

White-cheeked and sick from the terrible debacle Shane lurched blindly down the steps toward saddled horses, groaning as his clumsy fingers jammed fresh cartridges in his empty weapons.

Only vaguely was he aware of the disturbed antheap Silver King had now become. He hardly noticed the lights that were suddenly flaring in darkened windows, the half-clad men emerging hurriedly from false-fronted dwellings. His mind was filled with the image of Bless Jones—the lanky Britisher who never again would ride and laugh and curse and follow his lead on tortuous trails in dead of night. Jones, who had gone down fighting to the last

EIGHTEEN

TO THE GIRL who rode with wrists tied behind her back and legs lashed by their ankles beneath her horse's belly alongside Jarson Lume through the brightening light of dawn, it seemed that Fate was a cruel and bitter flung; that life was hard and the world an empty laugh of cold indifference.

Nothing but a series of griefs and hardships, of struggles and forlorn hopes marked the backtrail through her short span of years; ahead loomed a seared and blistered desert of shattered dreams. For the first time in months her shoulders sagged. What was the use of going on living? What had life to offer her? she wondered.

She somberly studied Lume's broad back where he rode a few paces in the lead. Every line and curve of that black frock coat was hateful. Even the slant of his wide-brimmed, flat-crowned hat seemed to mock and jeer at her, seemed to sneer with cold complacency at her fate. He did not even look around; he knew that she would follow, that she dared not turn her horse aside. Worse—she was forced to admit that he was right.

To leave this trail they followed, tied like a steer for slaughter, must surely spell disaster for this was a wild and desolate country through which they traveled. A country of few and scattered ranches; a land where one might ride for hours without sighting a single moving creature.

No, she dared not try to elude him, not here. To do so here meant death of thirst, of exposure; a death so tortured she dared not contemplate it even. But surely, she reasoned listlessly, death of contact with the desert was better by far than the thing Lume held in store for her!

Lume had gloatingly told her not half an hour ago that Shane was on their trail. He had told her, grinning wickedly, that he had aroused a reception committee to greet Shane at Silver King—a committee whose business it was to see that he got no further. He had pointed out that since she now could hold no hope of getting away, she might as well behave.

She had heaped abuse upon him with scorn and loathing, vowing she'd have nothing to do with him were he the last man, even, on earth. But Lume had only grinned his taunting grin.

Sunrise came to light the world, to gild this desolate wilderness through which they rode with the rainbow colors of hope and promise. But Lize Corbin's lips twisted bitterly as she watched through haggard eyes. Life held no longer any promise worth redeeming, and as for hope—well, hope was dead.

"When we get to Globe," Lume's voice came chuckling back, "you'll have your final chance to get hitched up. You better make up your mind before we get there, too, 'cause I ain't figurin' to linger none. Not that there's any hurry now," he added quickly. "But I'm some anxious to get on to Bylas—I got a deal on there."

Lize Corbin held a scornful silence. Why give the beast the satisfaction of an answer?

"Lucky the Indians are feelin' fat an' peaceful now," Lume continued. "It was along this trail the other side of Globe that that bunch of sneakin' redskins chopped the soldiers all to hell a short while back." He laughed with reminiscent glee. "I sold 'em some of the firewater that got 'em started. Figured it was a good way of keepin' attention away from Tortilla Flat."

Lize shuddered.

They rode a spell in silence. Then Lize thought she saw a way of getting under his skin as he was so constantly getting under hers. This talk of Indians was his idea of pleasantry. She believed she knew a way of taking that sneering grin from his mouth—for a time, at least.

"Y'u know," she said, as though thoughtfully, "y'u have been leavin' Stone Latham out of yo' figgerin'. He ain't goin' to like this business at all."

"What business?"

"This runnin' away with me. Stone Latham's a man to nurse a grudge an'—"

Lume's hateful laugh came floating back to interrupt her. "I reckon you're figurin' to tell me you an' him's been married," he jeered. "Don't waste your breath; I know all about it. No need for you to get all lathered up pinnin' any hopes on *him*."

"What do y'u mean?" Lize asked, a cold chill of premonition chasing the color from her cheeks. She had nothing but hate and loathing for Latham; but of the two she feared Jarson Lume the most. Jarson Lume who always got his way. "What do y'u mean about pinnin' any hopes on him?"

"He ain't in no position to be takin' up my trail right now." Lume's husky chuckle was sinister. "Him an' me has had a understandin'."

"Understandin'?"

"Yeah. He ain't got no objections to you hitchin' up with me. Said he didn't give a damn who you hitched up with next. Now," his voice grew suave and soothing, "you ought to be right glad to marry a man as big as me. I'm one of the biggest men in this country. I'm goin' to be bigger, too. I'm figurin' to settle down an' quit my hell-bendin' ways. I want a home, a wife, an' kids. I want you—"

"What y'u want, y'u lyin' polecat, is the information yo' figgerin' Dry Camp Corbin passed on to me after some of yo' bushwhackers give him a dose of lead poisonin'!"

"Now see here," Lume growled, stopping his horse and hers, too, with a hand upon the check-strap. "I've had enough of your tantrums. An' I've had all I want of your damned insinuations. You better make up your mind to side with me; I'm figurin' on goin' places. Hell, nothin's too big for me to get, gal! I got property—rich property—all over this damn state. Look," he dropped his voice confidentially, "I got my eye on the governor's seat right now."

"I don't give a durn if yo' got yo' eye on the President's seat; y'u ain't goin' to get me! Why," Lize cried with unutterable scorn, "I'd kill myself first!"

Lume chuckled. "Yeah? Well, I'll see that you don't

get no chance, then. What you figurin' to save yourself for, gal? Not Latham, sure? An' Shane is goin' to get himself rubbed out real quick—may be rubbed out now, I shouldn't wonder. Don't be a fool. I can give you anything you want; all the things you never had—good clothes, jewelry, position. Cripes, you stick with me, Lize, an' I'll take you places."

"Yeah, I bet y'u will." Her voice was drily sarcastic. "Jail, prob'ly, or the owlhoot trail!"

Lume snorted. "There ain't no man in the country big enough to shove Jarson Lume in a jail. Act your age, gal. I got this country sewed up. I can control the courts, I'm bossin' the minin' camps where most of the dinero is; I own some of the biggest ranches an' I've got a interest in them I don't own outright. What the hell more could you ask?"

"All that is so, I reckon," Lize said wearily. "But I'm not wantin' y'u, an' yo' not gettin me. So make up yo' mind to it."

"I ain't, eh?" Lume's husky tones turned ugly. "We'll see about that!"

With a swift cruel yank he jerked her toward him; one sinewy arm about her shoulders effectually preventing her from getting free of him. Bound as she was at wrist and ankles her struggles were so futile as to draw a mocking grin to Lume's bloodless, clean-shaven face. "Spirit," he purred, "is what I like in my string."

Lize's cheeks were alabaster white; her lips colorless lines of loathing as Lume, with a sudden oath, bent her back across his left forearm Then his face thrust close to hers. "There's no time like the present," he snarled, "for learnin' you who's the boss!"

He cupped a hand about her left breast and burned

her face with his kisses. He left her white and breathless and with pounding heart. Her eyes held the flame of murder.

He laughed as he let her go and his handsome, bloodless face held satisfaction. "By Gawd, but you're a beauty, gal!" His lewd glance played across the litheness of her body. "You've got what it takes!"

The lure of her seemed to rock him. He half leaned forward again as though to learn if her charms would improve upon acquaintance. But somehow she maneuvered her horse aside and saw him straighten with a chuckle.

"No more just now, eh? Well, you've earned your way, for the moment. But you're mine, an' don't forget it! I've put my brand on you, gal! You belong to Jarson Lume!"

* * *

TWO HOURS HAD PASSED since Sudden Shane had left the noisy turbulence of Silver King behind. It was light now, and although he had closely scanned his backtrail many times since dawn he had seen no sign of pursuit. He looked again, half turning in his saddle. But the rugged terrain behind loomed empty and desolate as ever. With a breath of relief he swung his eyes to the front, to the hoofprints of the pair of horses he had followed since the vanishing of darkness had permitted him to scan the trail.

One, he could see by the sign, was a paddler, and faster than its companion. The other was a "coon-footed" bronc of low pasterns. Neither was hurrying now, and Shane guessed that Lume had slowed the pace to conserve their endurance.

"Must be figurin' to cover a heap of territory," Shane opined. "I shouldn't wonder but what Jarson's aimin' to cut his stick."

His lips pressed tightly together at the thought, and the muscles bunched along his jaw. "Figurin' to take Lize Corbin clear out of the country."

The horse on which Shane had departed from Silver King was a good one. And lucky that it was, he reflected grimly, for there were not apt to be many places on the trail Lume was traveling where re-mounts could be secured. Lume was deliberately avoiding all common lanes of travel, sticking to the rough country, the desert wastes and rock-choked canyons where he would not be apt to encounter other riders who might get curious about the girl.

Shane's horse was a short-coupled blue roan, probably weighing a good eleven hundred pounds; an animal promising a deal more endurance than speed, but one that, properly handled, could cover ground for days. And Shane was of the opinion that the chase might well last that long unless some unforeseen circumstance intervened.

This horse of his, he reasoned, had likely belonged to one of those gun fighters he and Jones had encountered in the saloon of the Red Hoss. The saddle was ornately carved and heavily embossed with silver; a kak of the rim-fire type. A rifle scabbard was slung at an approximately horizontal position on the near side of the horse, passing between the two leaves of the stirrup-leather. A good repeater lay inside it, butt forward. He had examined it and found it fully loaded, and had discovered that there were more shells for it in one of the leathern pouches slung from the saddle horn.

He was well armed, having besides the rifle, that extra pistol he had snatched from the dust where Jones' killer had fallen. The loops of his belt had provided, however, barely sufficient cartridges to fill them. Should he shoot these out he would have to discard the belt guns and take to the rifle, a more awkward weapon in the event of close-range work.

The mutations of Shane's wandering thoughts turned his mind again to Lize. Where was she? he wondered, and was she safe? Reason and logic told him that she must be safe so far, at any rate, for Lume's headlong flight could spare the man scant time for dalliance. But should Lume hole up...

Shane dared not contemplate the possibilities of such an event.

In the chaparral stretches, in the blistering sand, in the glassy white of the midday sky he could see Lisabet's vision clearly—as clear and graphic, almost, as though she were there before him. He was startled, nevertheless, when looking toward the shimmering horizon he saw, in the near distance, a patch of rocky trail with two riders astride of motionless horses upon it. One rider was a woman—he could tell by the tawny hair that hung below her hat. He could tell it by her face which abruptly was turned in his direction; the face of Lize! Her wrists were lashed together behind her back and her ankles tied beneath her horse's belly. The other rider was the man in a flat-crowned hat and a black frock coat whom Shane had no difficulty in recognizing as Lume.

Shane was so startled he involuntarily checked the

blue roan's forward progress and sat there motionless, intent upon the drama being unreeled on the rocky trail. He saw Lume sway toward Lize and pull her toward him with a savage arm about her shoulders; saw Lume bend her back across that arm and cover her upturned face with kisses.

Shane's eyes were narrowed, blazing slits when Lume released the girl and sat regarding her with gloating grin. Shane's lips were white as his cheeks and a vein throbbed wildly on his forehead; his big fists were tensely bunched.

With a sense of nausea he saw Lume urge his horse in close to the girl's once more as though to renew his assaults while she struggled futilely against her bonds. Shane swore bitterly and raked the roan's flanks with reddening spurs. Yet as the horse lunged forward the riders, the rocky trail and all shivered, cracked and dissolved and naught remained where these things had been but sandy waste a-shimmer with waves of heat.

A mirage!

But realization of the fact did not cause Shane to slow his mount's pace appreciably. Somewhere the scene he had just been witness to was happening! Shane dared not linger here nor longer conserve the blue roan's strength. Lize Corbin's reputation was at stake—her life, perhaps!

That her reputation already brought sneers to the faces of righteous persons made no difference to Shane. *He* believed in Lize; believed her to be pure and sweet and good. His faith in her was above the evil tongue of scandal; whatever she had done, he thought, there must in her mind have been the best of reasons for her acts.

So it was that he drove the blue roan forward now,

one eye alert upon the trail, the other keen for possible ambush. He had no means of knowing how far away the tableau he'd watched might be. But he meant to get there just as soon as this horse, by the grace of God and his own sharp flashing spurs, could cover the distance.

Forward, ever forward, they went plunging into the rush and slap of the searing wind that was like a draught from Hell's furnace. A half hour slid by with only the whistling wind, the creak of leather and pounding hoofs to tell that they were not within a vacuum. Shane might have thought they rode a treadmill but for the dizzy blur of chaparral, rocks, stunted oak and pig-locust reeling constantly by.

Then abruptly Shane regained control of his emotions and checked the ruinous pace of the gallant horse between his knees. This animal's strength must be preserved. One final burst of speed, or the hardy ground-eating endurance for which this horse was gaited, might finally spell the difference between shame and virtue, or between life and death, to the girl he loved.

They rode at times across timbered ridges where the wind-whipped tracery of clacking branches provided a screening lattice against the burning rays of the brassy sky.

At other times they rode through flat bottoms where the vegetation was rank and stringy, and the sun beat down with unleashed venom that blistered all it touched.

Occasionally Shane would halt the blue roan's progress long enough to get down and closely study the tracks left by the horse of Lume and Lize. He stopped now for that purpose and, as he squatted there on his bootheels beside the shaley trail, a slow sardonic grin pulled at his lips. He was getting close; these tracks showed sudden hurry, proving that somehow Lume had sighted him and knew his Nemesis was drawing near.

Shane climbed back into the saddle with renewed confidence and hope. He now most definitely had Jarson Lume on the run; the man's actions, as shown by the hoofprints, proved it!

"He'd better slope!" Shane muttered grimly. "'Cause I'm allowin' when I catch up with him, the reckonin' he's been pilin' up these last weeks since I been in this country is goin' to be settled plumb permanent."

But if Jarson Lume had seen him and was, indeed, attempting flight through fear and desperation, he was putting his knowledge of the country to good use. The long afternoon wore slowly by and yet, when evening came, Shane still had failed to sight him. His only consolation was the reflection that Lume would not dare tarry to further his designs on Lize until a more propitious time. And this so-galling postponement of Shane's desire for vengeance but whetted his already feverish lust for blood.

NINETEEN

IT WAS dusk when Sudden Shane, tight of lip and grim of eye, rode into the copper town of Globe. Lights were beginning to come on in its houses, flinging slender lances, broad bars and glowing pools of golden radiance across the shadowed dirt of its broad main street.

Shane, after his long ride and weary hours in the saddle, was feeling pretty ganted as he swung stiffly from the blue roan before the hitch rack fronting the Copper City Grub Emporium and, tying the roan loosely to the rail, went inside cuffing the alkali grit from his clothing.

The restaurant was practically deserted at this hour. Shane saw no one at the counter but a whiskered old miner who lolled on his elbows above his emptied plate. The light in his faded eyes showed Shane his mind was far away; perhaps with the folks who, when setting out to make his fortune years agone, he'd left behind.

Shane took a stool at the counter's other end, from which position he could watch the door and any passers along the walk outside, who would be illuminated by the light streaming from the Emporium.

While his supper was being cooked in a back room Shane sat moody with his restless thoughts. Though he realized he must be pressing close to Lume, he felt anxious none the less about Lize Corbin. He could imagine well the nightmare this experience must be proving to her. Conjecture along these unpleasant lines brought out cold sweat upon his forehead.

When his food was placed before him he ate hurriedly, washing it down with cups of scalding coffee. He paid no attention to the plump and handsome waitress who was palpably willing to flirt. Indeed, he seemed not to even sense her presence.

His thoughts were still with Lize and his eyes, for the most part, remained focused on the door. He did not anticipate sighting any acquaintance here, but the turmoil of his border years had taught him caution, the value of being ever on his guard against surprise. Scarce wonder then that the waitress' many attentions went for naught.

As he ate he listened to the occasional snatches of conversation which drifted in from the night outside. The plank sidewalk rumbled hollowly to the oft uneven tread of booted feet as the citizens of Globe, their suppers eaten and their after-supper chores completed, set out to spend their loose change in such resorts as catered to their tastes. Lucky, carefree hombres.

***

AND THEN SUDDENLY SHANE'S LEAN wiry form went tense.

His cheeks went gray beneath their bronze as his eyes narrowed intently on the broad, black-frocked back of a tall man passing the door.

In an instant he was off his stool. Slipping a handful of change on the counter, he cat-footed swiftly to the door, passed through and onto the busy walk outside.

By the lights of stores and other business places he could see the tall man threading his way through the townsmen up ahead. He followed grimly, his narrowed eyes never leaving that black-frocked back.

So intent was he upon that man ahead that he jostled a red-shirted miner unintentionally off the walk. The fellow swore and Shane, never taking his glance from his quarry, apologized—but kept on moving.

A heavy hand caught him by the shoulder, whirled him round with a lurid oath. "Push me into that dust, will ye? By Gawd, I'll teach ye ter watch where ye're goin'!"

"No offense, pardner." Shane grinned, and would have started on. But the miner would not have it so; too much drink had made him ugly. He swung a haymaker at Shane's jaw which only missed by inches.

Shane swore and brought an angry right fist up from his bootstraps. It took the Cousin Jack glancingly upon his Adam's apple and thudded to a jarring stop beneath his stubbled chin. Without a sound of remonstrance the miner went over backwards, struck heavily on the walk. A flashing glance of Shane's keen eyes showed him other miners crowding up.

Shane squared off impatiently. "Listen, hombres; that gent got bumped off this walk by mistake. I was lookin' at someone else an' didn't see him. I apologized but he got tough."

"Aah, y'u damn' punchers think y'u own the world!" sneered another red-shirted fellow. "C'mon, boys, let's show this hard case what we do to leather-whackers in Globe! One of y'u git a rail! We'll fix 'im!"

Seeing that these men were not only ugly but determined to start a fracas, Shane knew from experience that he must take the offensive instantly. A man of action, no sooner had the thought flashed through his mind than he was wading in, caring not one whit what his lashing fists contacted so long as they struck home. He sent men reeling right and left before his furious onslaught. But he did not get clear. Others sprang to combat and he found himself hemmed in.

Striking, slugging, kicking, pounding, Shane swayed the sweating miners back and forth, bruising, maiming, cursing. This delay was making him frantic, for the man he'd been following was Lume!

The miners felt the turbulence of his emotions; his strength and endurance were those of a madman and the speed of his smashing fists incredible. One by one he bowled them down, or sent them staggering back into the gloomy shadows beyond reach of the lights where they gladly deserted the battle which had proved to be much hotter than they'd bargained for!

At last Shane found himself alone; alone, that is, save for a number of groaning ex-combatants scattered prostrate or on hands and knees about him on the plank walk and in the dust of the street.

But Lume, if Lume it had been, had vanished.

With a bitter oath Shane struck off down the walk with angry strides, glancing hurriedly into each place of business as he passed. With each progressive yard his anger grew until a raging passion was visible in his usually complacent gaze, and his mouth was a tight straight line.

Then, just as he was about to think that once again Lume had made good his escape, Lume came out of a cafe with several packages under one arm and without a glance to right or left continued down the street.

Cautiously, striding along behind a pair of conversing punchers, Shane followed, determined this time to trace the slippery Jarson to his lair.

Being careful that the punchers unconsciously screened him from Lume's vision, should Lume chance to glance around, each time he reached a lighted area, Shane followed his quarry to the Copper House, a dingy hotel on a side-street where shadows were more than plentiful.

Waiting until Lume had passed within, Shane moved casually to the porch where a group of hard-faced loafers sat smoking in chairs tilted back against the wall. As casually, then, he strolled inside as Lume's boots disappeared up a staircase at the rear of the littered lobby.

Shane thoughtfully regarded the sallow-faced clerk behind the desk in a railed-off portion near the stairs while he rolled himself a smoke. The man's eyes slid about uneasily under Shane's steady regard.

A preacher clad in rusty black came in and stopped beside the desk. Shane caught the words distinctly as the sky-pilot asked:

"Can you tell me, brother, if Mr. Judson is in his room?"

The clerk regarded the sky-pilot suspiciously. But at last said, "Yeah—room ten."

The preacher thanked him and started up the stairs.

Shane followed. The preacher paused before Number 10 and knocked. In a few moments Shane heard Lume's voice call:

"Who's there?"

The preacher said, "The Reverend Wilkes."

Shane flattened himself against the wall as the door swung open long enough to admit Mr. Wilkes and then swung sharply shut behind him.

Shane waited, devil's temper stirring behind the smoky gray of his eyes.

Abruptly he heard the rise of angry voices from beyond the door. In three long strides he was outside it, crouching, one hand grasping the knob. Softly he turned it and, as he had suspected, found the door locked.

Then he heard Lize scream, *"I won't! Y'u'll never make me!"* And the preacher's quavery voice raised in protest.

Shane waited for no more but hurled himself against the door, fury rioting in his veins, but one coherent thought thrusting through the red madness in his brain. It was much more than a thought; it was a gripping white-hot desire—he must reach and destroy Lume instantly!

The door gave way with a rending, splintered crash and the momentum of his blow sent Shane lurching on within, his blazing eyes taking in the scene in one swift stabbing glance.

Lume was on the aggressive; his face was hideous and awful in its savage passion as he grabbed for Lize—and missed. Both whirled as the door crashed down. The preacher's face was deathly white...

Jarson Lume cursed viciously, terribly as he glared.

Shane's lips were parted tautly over his hard white gleaming teeth; his rage was more awful than Lume's in the chill quiet of its intensity. His gray eyes, like smoking sage, alive with the cold warning of imminent violent action rode heavily across Lume's snarling features.

Lize Corbin's cheeks were deathly white, her lips entirely devoid of color.

The preacher like a statue stood, face gray, alarmed and fearful, his diminutive body taut. The room's temperature seemed to have dropped to zero, yet his forehead was steeped in sweat.

Shane's voice crossed the silence in a cold, wicked drawl:

"Lume, you've reached the end of your rope."

The atmosphere was aching while for two seconds there was silence. Lume broke it with a ripped-out curse and sent his right hand streaking inside his coat.

His gun glinted in the light, spat flame. But terror, or perhaps the passion that rocked him, shook his aim. The angry whine of his lead hemmed Shane; he could hear the bullets splintering the wall behind him Then his gun was out. It barked shortly from his hip—just once. A grin parted his lips vindictively when Jarson Lume clutched his chest and crumpled backward across a table that went down beneath his weight.

Shane sheathed his gun and, leaping forward, caught Lize as she would have fallen in her reaction from the strain. Her arms closed round his neck convulsively and she hid a tear-wet face against his breast while great sobs shook her body. The parson came out of his palsied trance and started for the door. But—

"Wait," Shane said, and stopped him with a foot

still tautly raised in air. Shane laughed at his embarrassment and the look of ludicrous panic on his face. "I'm allowin'," Shane added, "we're goin' to have a use for you directly. It'll oblige me mighty much if you'd just stick around a spell."

Pulling free of his protecting arm Lize brushed the tears from her starry eyes. "I—I— We can't!" she muttered dully. "It wouldn't be right. Stone Latham knew Dad passed me on the secret of his discovery. The location of his strike, I mean. He made love to me—I thought it was love. I—I— We're married," she finished miserably. "No one knew it...that's how the talk got started. He—he was seen leavin' my place before daylight one mornin'. But we were married proper!" she added defiantly, looking at the parson.

"No one could doubt it, Lize," Shane told her gravely.

"You are too fine, ma'am, for anythin' else. But you're not married to him anymore. Stone Latham's dead—Lume pistoled him in Silver King. An' it don't make a shuck's worth of diff'rence to me whether Dry Camp Corbin found gold or not—"

"But he *did!*" Lize interrupted excitedly. "He—"

"Makes no diff'rence. I got plenty dinero for both of us, an' a durn good ranch in Texas besides. Lize, there's nothin' more to hold me in this country but you. Obe Struthers, now Lume is finished, will get his mine back an' everythin' will be ironed out smooth as a whistle.

"Lize," Shane's voice grew soft with longing, "tomorrow's a new day. An' it's almost here." He flashed a significant look at the staring parson. "What say we start it right?"

A LOOK AT: THE SEVEN SIX-GUNNERS AND MULE MAN
A WESTERN DOUBLE

From Nelson C. Nye, Western Writers of America co-founder and Spur Award-winning author, two classic action and adventure novels of the American West.

In *The Seven Six-Gunners*, veterans of the Chisum-Murphy feud were bound to find themselves with enemies, and Flick Farson was certainly no exception. He'd been looking for a place to lay low for a spell, but Tombstone sure as shootin' wasn't that place. See, Flick knew about a payday to be had, hidden somewhere in the harsh and forbidding Arizona mountains. Would his wits match the speed of his gun, scoring him enough cold, hard cash to live the rest of his life on, or would fate have different plans...

In *Mule Man*, Brice Corrigan earned his nickname 'Mule Man' partly for the animal he rode, and partly for his foul disposition. The man and his mule were both stubborn as could be, and while that might have seemed like a bad thing, for Corrigan it was just a way of life. He'd signed on with this godforsaken crew of ten men just to be contrary to the lady who'd hired him, and he just had to prove her wrong. Now, they were headed out into Arizona's Chaco Canyon country with Jeff Larrimore, an anthropologist keen to have the crew digging for Anasazi cliff-dweller relics from thousands of years ago. The going wouldn't be easy, but Corrigan would stick it out come hell or high water...

Nelson Nye's award-winning westerns: "Start at top speed and keep going hell bent-for-leather

through to the smashing finish." – *Tucson Daily Citizen*

AVAILABLE NOW

ABOUT THE AUTHOR

Nelson C. Nye (1907–1997) was an American author, editor, and reviewer of Western fiction, and wrote non-fiction books on quarter horses. He also wrote fiction using the pseudonyms Clem Colt and Drake C. Denver. Nye wrote over 125 books, won two Spur Awards: one for best Western reviewer and critic, and one for his novel *Long Run*, and in 1968 won the Saddleman Award for "'Outstanding Contributions to the American West."

Nelson Nye was born in Chicago, Illinois. Before becoming a ranch hand in 1935, he wrote publicity releases and book reviews for the Cincinnati Times-Star and the Buffalo Evening News. He published his first novel in 1936 and continued writing for 60 years. He served with the U.S. Army field artillery during World War II. He worked as the horse editor for Texas Livestock Journal from 1949–1952.

In 1953 Nye co-founded the Western Writers of America and served as its first president during 1953–1954. He was also the first editor of *ROUNDUP*, the WWA periodical that is still published today.

CPSIA information can be obtained
at www.ICGtesting.com
Printed in the USA
BVHW071442100622
639488BV00016B/512